## PRAISE FOR *THE CONFESSION ARTIST*

"In this masterfully crafted psychological thriller set against the stunning backdrop of northwest Montana, Carbo weaves vivid prose and atmospheric suspense into a gripping tale that will leave readers breathless. A must-read for fans of thought-provoking crime fiction."

—Laura McHugh, award-winning author of *What's Done in Darkness*

"In *The Confession Artist*, Christine Carbo has written a terrific mystery full of intricate plots and intriguing twists that capture the reader and hold on to them to the end. She has created, in Crosbie Mitchell, a flawed but inspiring protagonist with the tenacity to resolve the mystery while putting others first. *The Confession Artist* is a tense and wild ride that lives up to its promise, a page-turner that will grip you from beginning to end, and a must-read to be added to your TBR pile.

—Allen Eskens, bestselling author of *The Life We Bury* and *The Quiet Librarian*

## PRAISE FOR THE GLACIER MYSTERIES

"Carbo doesn't do superficial. She gives her characters weight. And like her debut, *Mortal Fall* provides a story with dual tracks—the investigation into murder and the rugged journey of the soul."

—*New York Journal of Books*

"Carbo paints a moving picture of complex, flawed people fighting to make their way in a wilderness where little is black or white, except the smoky chiaroscuro of the sweeping Montana sky."

—*Publishers Weekly*

"[Carbo] writes with a sense of simple realism that comes from being a local. The grandeur and beauty of Glacier isn't overwritten, nor ignored . . . *Mortal Fall* is a well-written case of murder, set in a beautiful place."

—*Missoulian*

"*Mortal Fall* [is] a study of flawed, compelling characters and the ghosts that haunt them. It's also a fascinating look at the relationship of humans with the too-rapidly changing landscape of Glacier Park. And finally, it's the tragic story of the forces that can shatter a family. This novel works on so many levels, all of them masterfully crafted."

—William Kent Krueger, *New York Times* bestselling author of *Windigo Island*

"Grizzly bears, murder, mauling, and mayhem mix in [*The Wild Inside*]. Ted Systead's past and present intersect in an unexpected—and chilling—manner against the incongruously gorgeous backdrop of Glacier National Park."

—*Kirkus Reviews*

"Sharp, introspective Systead is a strong series lead, and Carbo rolls out solid procedural details, pitting him against Department of the Interior bureaucrats. The grittiness of the poverty-racked area surrounding Glacier plays against the park's dangerous beauty."

—*Booklist*

"[*The Wild Inside*] stays in your mind long after you've put the book down. Prepare to run the gamut of emotions with this fine treat of a story."

—Steve Berry, *New York Times* bestselling author of the Cotton Malone series

"*Mortal Fall* is a terrific read. With a masterful hand, Christine Carbo guides her readers through an intriguing mystery full of complex relationships and smartly developed characters. Her rich descriptions immerse you in the grandeur of Glacier National Forest as this riveting story unfolds."

—Allen Eskens, author of *The Guise of Another*

"An intense and thoroughly enjoyable thrill ride. Christine Carbo's literary voice echoes with her love of nature, her knowledge of its brutality, and the wild and beautiful locale of Montana. *The Wild Inside* is a tour de force of suspense that will leave you breathlessly turning the pages late into the night."

—Linda Castillo, *New York Times* bestselling author of *The Dead Will Tell*

# THE CONFESSION ARTIST

# OTHER TITLES BY CHRISTINE CARBO

## Glacier Mysteries

*The Wild Inside*

*Mortal Fall*

*The Weight of Night*

*A Sharp Solitude*

# THE CONFESSION ARTIST

*A Thriller*

CHRISTINE CARBO

This is a work of fiction. Names, characters, organizations, places, events, and incidents are either products of the author's imagination or are used fictitiously. Otherwise, any resemblance to actual persons, living or dead, is purely coincidental.



Published by Thomas & Mercer, Seattle

www.apub.com



EU product safety contact:
Amazon Media EU S. à r.l.
38, avenue John F. Kennedy, L-1855 Luxembourg
amazonpublishing-gpsr@amazon.com

ISBN-13: 9781662538209 (paperback)
ISBN-13: 9781662538193 (digital)

Cover design by David Drummond
Cover images: © amgun / Shutterstock; © Eivind Hansen / Getty
Interior images: © Paul Martini

Printed in the United States of America

Secrets, silent, stony sit in the dark palaces of both our hearts: secrets weary of their tyranny: tyrants willing to be dethroned.

—James Joyce, *Ulysses*

# Chapter 1

## Tim

Tim Mooney's stomach felt queasy. He couldn't wait to sweat out the alcohol from the night before as he walked from his hotel in Missoula to the path that paralleled the Clark Fork River. The playfully swirling water helped lift his hangover.

So, he hoped, would a jog.

He started out slow, his feet heavy, his head aching. His stomach flipped a little. He considered turning around and going back to the hotel to take a hot shower, but he wasn't a quitter.

He'd gotten this colossal headache from the champagne and vodka he'd consumed at Piquero's, a site he'd chosen for the big event because it was one of the highest-end restaurants in town. He'd had the duck confit, and it was to die for. He'd known the ambience of the place, with its rich, wood-fired smells filling the room, would put everyone in a festive mood.

That was the plan: Throw a good party for their quote-unquote Speaker Program. Get them used to la dolce vita. Make them think they can't live without the extra riches flowing their way.

As he ran closer to the university and started encountering college students, he picked up his pace despite the nausea. His breath flowed, maybe a little too raspy. He tried to settle it down. He didn't need to be wheezing like a middle-aged man when he passed young, fit women. He hoped they thought he wasn't so many years out of college himself.

His mind drifted to the previous night. He'd thought about canceling the "Speaker Program," given the sketch business that had cropped up out of nowhere. A drawing of a person had appeared on the internet with a warning that whoever was depicted had exactly six days to confess something or else they'd die. The drawing strongly resembled him, but emphasis on *resembled.* It wasn't him. And here it was, the sixth day, and all was fine. He wasn't worried.

Besides, he had thrown out on Facebook a mildly self-deprecating line to be on the safe side, joking about sometimes feeling like a glorified drug peddler. He was keeping his fingers crossed there'd be no blowback from his company on it. So far, he didn't think they'd even noticed.

It all felt like nonsense, though, and for the life of him, he couldn't figure out how—among all the people in the world—he could possibly be targeted. It would be different if he were a CEO or board member, someone with beaucoup bucks and power. Tim was far from that.

Plus, it seemed like a stretch to him that the cops or the public would make the connection to the two other people who were killed after the first two sketches came out. How many people are murdered on any given day in the US? Were they comparing, nationwide, all the victims to these random sketches? He'd read that the guy in Snohomish had been singled out because a local headline-seeking reporter who'd spotted the similarity hopped on the story and sensationalized it. But what about the woman in Santa Monica? How were they even sure it was her?

Maybe the first two did look exactly like the sketches, as so many on the internet claimed. But he figured there was still no solid proof that it was either of them.

Besides, only his wife, Mary, their teenage daughter, a few friends, and one of his coworkers had pointed out the resemblance between himself and this latest sketch. But still, he wondered if he should confess more seriously and sincerely than what he had posted so far.

What more would he divulge? The sordid details of his job that he wasn't super proud of, his rationale for sticking with it? Maybe the fooling around?

Nonsense. He had no desire to confess to anything more on any front. Besides, at the party the previous night, no one had even brought it up. And hot damn, even though he was looking over his shoulder a bit, he'd still had fun. He was certain the new physiatrist from Missoula he'd lured in was showing all the right signs of interest.

The speaker programs were, in theory, designed to gather health care professionals who could prescribe the drug and educate them about it. But all Tim had to do was get a bunch of friends and coworkers together, regardless of whether they had the ability to prescribe. Then pay his old standby, his main doc, Dr. Winnipeg, a large sum to attend, all from his company spending allotment. With all the scrutiny and lawsuits over the past decade, it wasn't like the good ol' days of mega parties, but the wining and dining at this level still paid off.

He'd been bummed a few more health care professionals hadn't shown, but at least Dr. Winnipeg and his crew made it, despite having to drive an hour from the reservation to get to Missoula.

It was a good deal for everyone. They all got to invite friends and he got to have some of his buddies from Missoula and Arlee. All Winnipeg and his PA had to do for their kickbacks was prescribe the fentanyl inhalant over similar medications. And why not? It was a highly effective product. That he knew. The FDA had approved it for cancer patients. So there was nothing to feel guilty about. It was designed to relieve breakthrough pain, and who would argue that alleviating such god-awful pain caused by cancer wasn't a decent thing, even if it was used for other ailments it wasn't approved for? So what if some of the docs he induced to prescribe sometimes also wrote scripts for non-cancer patients?

He could claim they went rogue, got greedy. Not his fault, even if the company *did* encourage him to suggest it on the sly. He couldn't be held responsible if they did it. If he told them to jump off a bridge, would they?

A few suggestions about titration didn't hurt. In other words, all they needed to do was up the dose here and there on each patient, just a hair. Maybe, if they felt like it—he often suggested—they should search their patient records for others who might benefit from the drug, even if they weren't cancer patients. Pain is pain. Does it matter which disease causes it?

And for Dr. Winnipeg, Lord knew that folks on the reservation were riddled with every ailment under the sun. What were they calling it these days? DNA hangover? Okay, maybe not that, but intergenerational trauma or something along those lines?

His superiors made it clear: Escalating doses fetched higher prices, which translated to higher commissions for the sales reps. And he needed more commission money. Mary was always nagging him about their credit card debt. They needed a loan to get a condo on the lake in Coeur d'Alene, but their debt-to-income ratio was too high. She insisted they change that. But Jesus, interest alone on those cards made it impossible to get ahead.

But damn, yeah, he had to admit, a part of him thought about the titration part more and more these days. Yes, yes, he thought as the trail led him away from the river into a forest, he would admit it: It pulled a twinge of guilt out of him. But again, the executives all said it was safe. It wasn't his job to question it.

Nope, no regrets. But he couldn't stop wondering if all these dealings had something to do with this sketch business. But if they did, why him? Why not his superiors? Again, it made no sense.

*Focus on your run,* he thought. *Enough about this nasty confession stuff.* He huffed and puffed and sent sweat rolling down his chest so he didn't need to regret the $120-a-glass aged Rémy Martin he'd splurged on, either. He couldn't even recall the full name of it now. He was sure it had had *Louis* in the title, but he didn't remember the roman number. The sixth, or maybe the eighth? He'd have to google it, for bragging rights.

His buddy Charlie, a brandy aficionado, would be impressed. He'd say, "Wow, Mooney, you must be rollin' in it these days. How can I become a rep, too?"

So yeah, Tim might have woken up with his conscience niggling him a little, but knowing he now was sweating out all the damage done, he was beginning to feel better. Plus, he couldn't believe what had happened at the very end of the night, when he and Doc Winnipeg's RN, Brin, stumbled out to her car. How he stood in the dark with her under the huge dome of the big sky and pointed out the Milky Way and the Little Dipper. How when they both lowered their heads from peering up, they almost tipped over. They'd both giggled.

When he'd leaned in, she pressed even closer, so he could feel her breasts. That was a bonus. He wasn't even sure if he found her pretty, but he'd enjoyed it, all right, the fullness of her lips and the smell of her hair. Something musky and calming. He brought her back to his hotel room. After all, he considered through his drunken haze, it wasn't wise to be alone when there was a bizarre threat with a face that looked at least a little like his on it making the rounds on the big wide web.

Brin left before the sun came up. He couldn't remember if they'd traded numbers or not, but he did recall that she knew he was married. It didn't seem to bother her. He needed to be careful if she ended up texting him.

He planned to be more cautious about his phone in general. Mary was getting a little more suspicious when he was on the road. The other day when he'd come in after going to the mailbox outside and had left his cell in the kitchen, she'd hastily dropped it when he'd entered.

He slowed his jog and stopped to do a quick stretch before returning. His trainer back home said his hip flexors were too tight. *Too much driving for your job*, she'd suggested. *And when you run*, she reminded him, *make sure you stretch.* He crossed one leg in front of the other and reached for the sky to open one of his hips.

He wondered if Mary could have something to do with this sketch thing. Would his own wife do *this* to him? Could she be Machiavellian enough to hop on the bandwagon of this insane national phenomenon to taunt him somehow, to get back at him?

*No.* He shook his head and looked around at the dense forest. He was just being paranoid. He was certain she didn't know about the others he sometimes slept with while on the road.

The trees surrounded and towered above. It felt as if the silent pines were all looking down at Tim, judging him. And that frightened him, too. He wasn't the type to notice *trees*. It meant, despite his hangover, that his senses were triggered. Again, he thought, paranoia. Stupid thoughts.

He peered up and away from the coarse bark to the late-morning summer sky. It was bursting with color, so full of promise. Life was chock-full of opportunity. You had to be willing to seize it. That's all. That's all he'd been doing for Carssen, the drug company he worked for. Hawking the stuff wasn't wrong. It was just his job.

Just because the sketch resembled him didn't mean it *was* him. And judging by how many people were already confessing their sins to the world, a *lot* of people out there thought they were the ones in the drawing. What were the chances it was actually him?

*You have six days to confess or die.* What kind of bullshit was that anyway?

He was about to start running again, to head back the way he'd come, when he heard the shuffle of leaves behind him. He whipped around but saw nothing. A deer maybe? Or perhaps someone else out jogging or walking?

He stood dead still, scanning the trees beside the path. Then he heard it again, a shuffle. A snap of a twig. Behind one of the tree trunks, he saw a flash of dark, like a navy sweatshirt or jacket, and something metal, like the barrel of a gun.

*What the hell?* His heart banged against his ribs. He was too frightened to call out to whoever it was. Electricity coursed through him, propelling him into a full-throttle run, his legs pumping faster than they ever had before.

With his running shoes slapping the gravel path, his own breath sharp in his ears, he made up his mind. His one-liner was not sufficient. As soon as he got back to his hotel room, before checkout, he'd confess more thoroughly, more sincerely.

It was still the sixth day. It wasn't too late.

# A CONFESSION

X: @Logan_Reed #SketchConfession—I didn't know he had stopped breathing when we left him there drunk in the game room at our house on Euclid Ave. in Syracuse in 2015. We thought he'd sleep it off. I was an immature SU college kid. I've thought so much about the past 9 years and have come so close to killing myself. Please, please let me know if this isn't enough. I know I have work to do to repair all the damage I caused to his family, but I didn't really want to kill myself then, and I certainly don't want to die now!

# Chapter 2

***Before***

At the forty-eighth latitude, I drive through the Continental Divide skirting the outside of Glacier National Park. Paxton Rhoads, the guy who hired me, calls it the "Backbone of the World," and it's hard to argue with that image.

Saw blades of mountains rear up on each side of me. The Middle Fork of the Flathead River snakes its way through small valleys tucked in between the river and the foothills. Old homesteads and roadside cafés cling to the old ways in the middle of nowhere, far from the transformation taking place where I live in the Flathead Valley, where wealthy out-of-staters buy up every inch of available real estate.

This countryside—brimming with all its beauty—always perks me up. Even quells the simmering rage inside me. But this isn't the time to think about my sister—and the upcoming anniversary of her hooking up with the wrong guy—or to wonder if the curtains will close around her and stay weighted in place. And whatever internet craziness is going on with the sketch-to-murder trend that is gripping the nation, the nuttiness with that crap seems even less likely to be a "thing" out here. My investigative work involves a lot less hype and a lot more stuff closer to reality.

When I reach Browning, past the Great Divide, vast, tawny prairies open before me. A strong wind hits my car and almost pushes it into the oncoming lane. I grip the wheel and stubbornly force the vehicle back between the lines. I'm on a mission for Paxton.

And for Clarissa.

And definitely for myself. New career. New opportunity—the first big one I've gotten since I switched to PI work nine months ago. And new chance to leave the past behind, like a snake shedding its skin.

Paxton's from the Blackfeet Nation, and he's hired me to investigate the death of his half sister, Clarissa. She was a journalist looking into the shady practices of a local oil and natural gas company owned by a wealthy businessman named Robbie Ridgeway. Her body was located downstream from rapids in the Teton River not far from his ranch.

My sister, Jess, is the one who referred Paxton to me. She works for a company called Rotical NanoLabs, a genetic research firm I use myself. Years earlier, Paxton and Clarissa had hired Rotical to find out if they were blood relatives, as their foster parents claimed. They had different surnames, but their foster parents said they came from the same mother.

Jess told Paxton I was getting established and likely to give him a deal. That was true. But I think he liked the idea that I used to be a cop. Key phrase: *used to be*. Dealing with a non-tribal PI meant he wasn't breaking social norms by hiring someone in the system.

Clarissa was a natural athlete, a star basketball player in high school who made it on scholarship to the University of Montana, graduated with a degree in environmental science, and was later drawn to journalism. Growing up on the reservation on the edge of the Divide, she was an experienced outdoorswoman. She would never have "slipped off some rocks" as the initial investigation suggested.

Paxton says Clarissa was undermining Robbie Ridgeway's plans to sell his oil and natural gas company to a bigger firm. Ridgeway's firm is the not-so-cleverly-named Ridgefield. The buyer was Volanex, based in Louisiana. Clarissa was in the process of exposing how Ridgefield's extractions were polluting a spring-fed peatland or fen that was nutrient and species rich and contained diverse flora that needed protection. Paxton maintained that

Clarissa was close to making the pollution public and that the resulting stain would've scuttled the deal.

And then Clarissa drowned. The police concluded *accident.* But I agree with Paxton. It all sounds too convenient.

After the reservation, I turn south toward Ridgeway's ranch north of Choteau. My plan is to drive around the town, ask some questions, get the community flavor for the guy.

I hit several gas stations first. Everyone needs gas. And Ridgeway definitely drives fuel-powered vehicles.

The gas station clerks don't have much to offer other than a little gossip about Ridgeway loving the *young ones.* And it's easy to come by other talk, too, at two of the bars, at a café, at a bakery, at the hardware store. Small towns are known to protect their own and don't love nosy strangers, but there are enough people in town who don't like Ridgeway that not all my questions go unanswered. Rumors and mention of sex trafficking, money laundering, and other shady operations all fuel my suspicions that he murdered Clarissa. And, if I can help it, I am not going to let another man get away with harming another woman.

After leaving the hardware store, I hit pay dirt.

A shiny black F-150 with a license matching Ridgeway's sits out front of the café I already visited.

I park on the opposite side of the street in some shade, kill my engine, roll my window down for a clear view for snapping photos, and sit. Being a PI involves a lot of waiting. But so did being a cop on patrol, which I did for four years before I resigned.

I quit for several reasons: First and foremost, to be there for Jess since the assault. And second, because my coworkers all saw me as toxic for reporting sexual harassment. But the third is the real reason, something I can barely even think about without feeling like I've suddenly grown a thick, slimy coat of skin.

Fortunately, I don't have to because I see a man matching the Ridgeway I've googled walk out of the café with another guy. Ridgeway's tall and imposing—probably six three—with dark, wavy hair and a broad forehead, but he has a weak jawline, making the lower part of his face look lifeless. He's wearing jeans, tennis shoes, and a lotus-pink, perfectly pressed button-up. The clothes look less like a rancher's and more like they belong on someone straight out of Los Angeles.

But I know he's from eastern Montana. I'm not sure what's worse: wealthy cowboy going for the city look or rich city guy going for the cowboy vibe.

The other guy wears jeans and has dark hair also, but it's curlier. He's in a black T-shirt. They're in a heated discussion about something. I pull out my telephoto and start snapping photos.

There's a lot of gesturing going on, and when the arguing intensifies and Ridgeway's voice rises, I catch words: "You shouldn't . . . Never . . . What if someone . . . On straight."

Finally, Ridgeway strides off, shaking his head, and hops in his truck.

I give him a moment to disappear down the road. I get out and go back into the café and find the same gal I cozied up to earlier. I pull out my camera, flick through some of the shots for her, and ask her if she knows the guy Ridgeway was chatting with.

"Oh yeah," she says. "Aaron Lasserio. He used to be one of Ridgeway's ranch hands."

"Used to be?"

"He was one of the rowdiest of the crew. But he's moved."

"You know where?"

"Actually, to your neck of the woods. Last I heard, he'd gotten a job at the local timber mill in Columbia Falls. Heard he got injured on the job, though, so I'm not sure what he's doing now."

Bingo.

Before I drive out of Choteau toward Ridgeway's ranch, I call Linda Holbrook at Graham Insurance, the company I know handles the timber mill's comp cases.

Since I became a PI, I've been surviving on no bennies and getting paid small amounts following a spouse around to document their cheating, tracking a teenager when the parents suspect them of doing drugs, or locating a deadbeat parent. But occasionally, an insurance company, like Graham, hires me and pays a decent wage to follow one of their claimants around to see if their assertions are legit.

Linda says she'll ask her boss and lets it slip that Lasserio's asserting that he fell on the job and hurt his back and was having a problem lifting heavier objects. I strongly suggest to her that they might want to hire me to check on the legitimacy of Lasserio's claim.

I hang up, hoping Lasserio's case will be a double gift: that I can deepen my partnership with Graham Insurance and dig more into one of Ridgeway's goons. And get paid.

But in the meantime, I want to talk to Ridgeway. Why is he still communicating with a ranch hand who is no longer cashing his paychecks?

The turnoff to Ridgeway's place is gated. I hit a buzzer and wait for a voice that comes through a speaker. Within a minute, someone asks, "What can I do for ya?"

"My name is Crosbie Mitchell," I say. "I'm a PI from the Flathead. I'd like to speak to Mr. Ridgeway. I need to ask him some questions about a former employee of his."

He tells me to hold on. I wait a few minutes more until finally the voice tells me to come on up and the electronic gate swings open.

Ridgeway's place stands below the eastern front. Yes, I say *stands* even though usually everything below the imposing ridges of the Rockies appears to *squat*. The house holds its own against the commanding backdrop. It's huge. Impressive, with towering prowl windows and massive beams. It looks like it comes right out of a glossy high-end real estate catalog.

I park behind the shiny black F-150 I saw in town. For whatever reason, Ridgeway didn't bother to park it in his six-car garage, where I imagine the Porsche and Jeep Wrangler I also know he owns must be safely stored.

The wind pushing my car on the highway has settled. It's over eighty degrees. A tractor drones in the distance. Crickets hop randomly out of the dry grass in the field beside the drive. The pungent, sweet scent of dry hay envelops me as I head up the long stone walkway to the front entrance with sprawling slabs of dark slate leading to a massive wood door.

I ring the doorbell, trying to squelch every nerve. When you're a cop, you're one of many. As a first-year PI, I feel alone. Exposed—naked—without my uniform and my gun, which I've gotten into the habit of not carrying since I don't really need it to follow around cheating spouses and unruly teenagers. But now, I feel very unprotected and foolish that I'm not following Patrolman 101 basic rules.

I'm still waiting for someone when I hear a scuffle of a shoe. I turn to see Ridgeway come around the corner.

I take a big step back.

He's carrying a rifle.

It's not pointed at me, but still, it gives me a jolt. There's something very creepy and incongruent about the whole look of an LA rich dude in a pink button-up sporting a rifle outside his multimillion-dollar abode on the eastern front.

"Hello." I force a grin. "Is that necessary?" I gesture to the gun. My nerves tingle all over. All I've got is a Leatherman in my pocket. "I'm a PI," I say. "And *I* don't even carry."

"Not sure where you're from, but out here, never know what's necessary and what's not. Never know if you're in need of self-protection. We have grizzlies around here, and you know we have a saying out here, right?"

"What's that?"

"SSS."

"SSS?"

"Shoot, shovel, and shut up."

I nod. Lick my lips, which are suddenly very dry.

"Why are you here?" he asks.

"My name is Crosbie Mitchell," I say. "And—"

"You a reporter?"

"No. Like I told your security guy, I'm a PI from the Flathead. I'd like to speak to you. I need to ask about a former employee of yours."

He eyes me suspiciously.

"Graham Insurance hires me occasionally to check on certain claims, that's all."

Finally, he walks over to me.

I step back, way back, but all he does is open the front door. Motions for me to enter. As he holds it ajar, he eyes me up and down.

My pulse pounds in my neck.

He waits, the heat of the August afternoon prickling between us, even in the shade of his massive covered entryway. I pause, sweat sliding down my back. I'm not sure I want to go in.

But I've come this far, so I step inside, every muscle in my body on notice. I don't plan on turning my back to this man, so I scoot over and make sure he goes in farther than me. I stay in the foyer as he enters the main room and, thank goodness, sets his rifle on a credenza by the wall.

The interior is immense. No surprise. Giant great room and a large kitchen. Open floor plan. Humongous appliances. Blond cabinets. A long rectangular gas fireplace sits in a slate wall. Space-age lighting fixtures hover. A wide curving staircase climbs to the next floor. The lack of a railing makes me unsteady on my feet, thinking how I'd feel with nowhere to put my hands.

The place is filled with art, mostly abstracts. But next to me on the wall is a whole lot of realism, a sketch of a naked woman standing with her arms above her head and her chest stuck out in case you're unsure that she's proud of her assets.

"I did that," he says when he sees me eyeing it. "You like?"

His question is more than a little creepy. "Nice," I say. The woman's precisely drawn nipples stare me down. She lacks mystery and complexity. There's another on the opposite wall of a young woman sitting with her legs splayed open, one hand on her breast, the other between her thighs and below her crotch like she's posing for a soft-porn site.

"That one, too," he says.

A maddening tangle of images fills my head about what he might have done to, or given, these young women so they'd pose for him. My fingers curl into tight fists and I have to tell myself to relax. "So," I say as professionally as I can muster. "Aaron Lasserio's been working for the timber company in Columbia Falls. He's filed a claim, and the insurance company has hired me to check on his history."

It's a hot lie, but I'm hoping it will become truth by the end of the week. Even as I feel the rush of excitement over being my own boss, my confidence goes to quicksand as I wonder if pulling a stunt like this is really the best choice for my first serious case as a PI. "Says he's hurt his spine," I add. "You know anything about that?"

"Why would I?"

"He used to work for you, no?"

"Yeah, but he didn't get hurt while working for me."

"But you still see him."

Ridgeway looks down at me the way a shark might eye a smaller fish. Cold, detached. Thankfully, the lustful appraisal has vanished, but this stare—with his lips thinning in irritation—isn't a good one, either. "I hardly know him," he says. "And why the hell would you come all the way over here to ask about some guy getting hurt on the job?"

"Just for his history. His capabilities in the past compared to now. How many hay bales could he lift? Simple questions." I rattle off a few more. Did he handle the horses? Did he stoop over fences all day, repairing them?

He holds up a hand. "I'm not the guy to talk to about what kind of a worker he was. If you want, you can talk to our head guy."

"But you're close to him, aren't you?"

"Close?" He pulls his head back. "Hell no."

"Oh." I fake surprise. "I happened to see you at the café. Seemed like you two know one another pretty well."

Ridgeway stares at me with disgust, like I just stole a puppy from a kid. "You stalking me?"

"Absolutely not. Small town. Only so many cafés. Very coincidental."

"So you're stalking Lasserio?"

"Well, that *is* what I'm paid to do." I'm getting better at believing the lie myself. My words sound confident, but his gaze is now drenched in skepticism, as it should be. My relationship with the truth is a tenuous thing. Let's say *situational.*

"You need to leave. I don't have time for this." Ridgeway starts toward me. I back up, but I'm in the foyer, so his coming toward me is his aim for the front door.

"There's another thing I need to know." I step forward again, toward him.

"Time's up."

"Clarissa Haynes." I know better than to blurt her name out like this, but I may not get another chance to confront him. And when I say her name, I make sure I'm looking right at him to gauge his reaction.

He stops dead in his tracks. Something uncertain flutters across his face, just for a fraction of a second, before he shakes his head. "Who?"

"Surely you remember her. From Browning? She pressed you about the fragile habitat on your property."

He goes back and grabs his rifle. My breath hitches at the not-so-subtle warning. He marches past me and opens the front door without saying a word.

I check my notebook. "On June 27?"

"News to me," he says. "But clearly, this is all bullshit about Aaron's so-called injuries." He motions with his head for me to leave and moves from cradling his rifle in both hands to laying the fore-end of the stock into the crook of his elbow without the muzzle pointing down as it should. Like he's about ready to lift it and aim. At me. "Get the fuck out of here."

Rage pumps through me. Who the hell does he think he is? Trying to frighten me like this? Packing a rifle around in his oversize house just to instill the fear of God into me? "It's a sad story," I say, calling his bluff.

"Shortly after she came here, she drowned. She was a big deal on the rez. Her brother claims she chatted with you the week before she died."

"She might be a big deal on the rez," he says. "But not anywhere else."

"*Was* a big deal."

"Indians die every day from overdoses, car crashes, drunk driving. She was probably blotto, like the rest of 'em."

My nostrils flare. My teeth grit. "Native American," I say as calmly as I can, trying not to show the rage coiling inside me, wanting to strike. "And no alcohol in her system."

"Maybe you shouldn't buy into gossip, especially when you're not even from around here."

"I have more than one source that says Clarissa came here and spoke—"

"I don't care about your sources." His jaw goes hard as a rock. He grips his rifle tighter. His ice-blue eyes go dead with a clear message: *Don't fuck with me*. "Look, Miss PI. I'm wealthy. And successful. That makes me a target. Got it? It's the way of the world."

"I understand that, but—"

"No." He shakes his head in a way that makes me feel like a child. "We're done."

I stifle the urge to blurt out, *You don't get to call the shots, asshole.* But of course he does. I'm on his property. And he's holding a gun. I walk outside. I turn and flash a chipper smile. I know all I need to know.

Right before he shuts the door, I hear him mumble, "Fucking bitch."

I resist firing something nasty back, but I got what I came for. He's lying about not knowing Clarissa.

On the way back to my car, I'm snared in anger. Rage fills my head like the thrum of electrical wires, drowning out the tractor motor in the distance and the boisterously chirping crickets. Each footstep takes on more fury, like I might punch right through the ground.

*SSS?* What a jerk.

When I pass his truck, I pull out my Leatherman and squat next to his tire.

I try to calm myself, try to listen to the voice inside me saying, *Do not do this. You can't afford to do anything wrong anymore.*

The air crackles with the dry heat from the ground. The sharp scent of cured rubber from Ridgeway's new tires pierces my nose. I'm gripping my Leatherman so tightly, the knobs of my knuckles are white.

I know I'll feel terrible later, but right now, I don't care.

I slide the blade in, right between the treads.

It's crude and minimal justice, but it's more than most people get.

# Chapter 3

***Six Days***

The thunderheads scale the peaks, billowing and rising above them like great white fuming beasts. Now they've spread over the valley, their undersides turning shades of deep gray and purple.

From my kitchen window, I watch the tree branches whip this way and that like they're possessed dancers. Lightning flashes. Thunder explodes.

Within seconds, Jess calls. She's frantic because the power has been knocked out on the east side, where she and Sam live.

I've been dreading this day for two weeks, since I returned from Choteau. I've already spoken to her several times this morning and planned on going over to check on her and Sam later this evening anyway. But now I rush over earlier, braving the storm.

It's walloping the rest of the valley with a good dose of howling wind, rain, and hail as I race south, past window, flooring, and furniture businesses servicing the construction boon in the valley. The wind splatters pea-size hail and quarter-size raindrops against my windshield. My wipers beat feverishly against the stabbing drops to swipe it all away, watery streaks smearing across the glass and silvery pearls clustering below the blades.

I turn the radio up, way up, to drown out the vicious onslaught.

"A new sketch from the killer, now known as the Confession Artist, has come out after six and a half weeks of no new sketches," announces the male newscaster with a honey-smooth voice against the roaring ferocity. ". . . same demand, to confess in six days or die. The search for the person behind the killings continues to intensify . . ."

*A new sketch?* Awful. And somewhere in the mess of this ugly thing that's captured the nation's interest, the killer has earned a moniker. *The Confession Artist?*

As if there's some Leonardo da Vinci act of genius going on. I roll my eyes.

The newscaster is now interviewing someone who says, "Everyone has been anticipating—practically demanding—a murder since the third sketch came out, like some high-octane reality TV episode. Only it's not TV. It's real life. But when no one turned up dead after the six days with the third, we all wondered if maybe it had all stopped. But now we have a fourth."

I turn the radio off. I don't need news or hype right now. Not this day—the one-year anniversary of that dreadful night. Other than the Ridgeway case and the fact that Graham Insurance did come through and I've spent the past week and a half surveilling Lasserio, there's only one other thing on my mind.

Jess.

Always Jess. And Sam. It's not that she's not a capable woman and mother. She is. Very. She's even benefited greatly from the true crime craze because of her work in genetic research at Rotical.

For several years now, she's hosted a popular podcast called *The Search*, which covers the recent rise of genetic genealogy and outlines many of the cold cases solved by it when relatives of the killer or rapist have added their genetic information to genealogy databases now mined by law enforcement. She's not only discovered her life's passion but turned her skills into a gold mine.

There was even talk at one point of transforming her podcast into a TV show on one of the streaming platforms, a true crime investigative series that would delineate how she's helped detectives solve cold cases—cases shelved because no matches were found in the criminal databases set up at the time. It used to be that DNA could solve a case only if it matched the genetic profile of someone in a criminal database or an existing suspect on record. Now a skilled genetic genealogist like Jess can often take an unknown DNA profile that has no hits in traditional searches and connect a name to it.

But that was well over a year ago, before Jess went to the Silvertip, before she hooked up with Coleman. Now she hasn't recorded a new show in months.

But there is a bright spot. She's due to give a talk at a conference in Dallas, CrimeCon, tomorrow. She agreed to the speaking engagement just one month after the rape, when she was starting some baby steps to get back on track—agreeing to see a counselor, trying to get her routine back, doing more fun things with Sam again.

Before, that is, I screwed things up for her and she got even more depressed, refused to make an appointment with a counselor, quit smiling and laughing. When we'd take Sam to the park to play, she'd sit there and watch us like a zombie, like she was only going through the motions. She's become jumpy, and she's not sleeping well, either, and when she does, it's at odd hours of the day that are not great for Sam.

All these months, I've been holding my breath that the conference is the one thing she won't cancel, and so far, so good. It's one small step in her getting her life a little more back on track.

She has Patrick, Sam's dad, lined up to take Sam while she's away even though Patrick's usually about as dependable as calling a cat to you when you need it. He disappoints Sam a lot. Says he's going to show up but cancels on him at the last minute. When he does show, he's usually forty-five minutes late. It breaks my heart watching Sam wait by the window.

But sometimes Patrick comes through when he hasn't seen his boy in a while, and so far, he's still planning on grabbing him later this evening. I already called him earlier and warned him not to be late.

But now, the storm. Normally, Jess wouldn't be bothered by her electricity going out, but these days, she's overwhelmed with the smallest of things. The power going out is like the universe reminding her that things go all wrong in the blink of an eye.

My tires fight deep puddles collecting on the uneven surfaces of the highway. *Please, please don't let it affect flights out in the morning.* I think of Sam and hope he isn't picking up on his mother's unraveling.

When I pull up to her house, it's six. To my relief, the rain has stopped, and a perky blue reclaims the sky above our valley like some grand master has flipped a switch. Bruised clouds cluster above the mountains to the east. This far north in Montana, even in late August, the sun doesn't go down until around eight thirty, so even with the power out, Jess and Sam won't be in the dark.

I enter straight into the main room to find Sam playing on the floor, where he's resurrected his bin of colorful plastic dinosaur figurines from his younger years. He's making soft growling and gnashing sounds. Relief washes over me that he's not running over to me stressed out and anxious like he sometimes gets when he's soaking up my sister's moods. I take my raincoat off and hang it on the coatrack.

He's so deep in concentration, he doesn't even look up when I say, "Hey, kiddo."

I walk over and give him a kiss on the head, his silky blond hair tickling my chin. He barely notices me. Hating to break his focus, I slide quietly into the kitchen.

Jess has taken out several pans, but she's not cooking. She's pacing. The pans sit untouched on the counter beside a bundle of broccoli, fresh garlic, a package of rice, and chicken still wrapped in its package.

"Hey," I say.

"What am I supposed to do with this raw chicken with no electricity?"

Her voice is too high, like she's on the brink of crying.

I hit the light switch to double-check that the electricity is still out, then grab the package of chicken off the counter. "It's fine," I say.

"It's *not* fine. Sam needs to eat."

"We'll get him something else, but I'm sure the power will be on in no time. I'm going to put this back in the fridge. It'll stay cold for a while if we keep it shut."

She shakes her head, a frantic twitch, like she doesn't believe anything will ever work right again. I think of how that one night has created a deep chasm between her and everyone else. The pit in my stomach grows. I hate seeing her this way.

"Why don't you go hang with Sam and I'll figure out something for dinner that doesn't need the stove." I put the package in the fridge.

"But I want to cook for him," she says. "He had pizza last night. We're supposed to have something healthy tonight. We're supposed to have chicken, rice, and—"

Right as she's about to add broccoli, the hum of the fridge begins and the light on the stove pops back on.

"Excellent," I say. I'm also about to say, *See, things will be okay*, but I don't want to set her off by sounding patronizing. I step up to the counter to start cooking.

"No," she protests. "I've got it." She puts the pan on the stove and grabs the olive oil. "Just go hang with Sam."

Her blond hair is pulled loosely into a messy ponytail. Dark smudges lie under her eyes, and the flesh of her cheeks is hollowed out, her cheekbones chiseled sharp. For months now, I've been able to feel her thrumming with her own agony—a deep, tormented vibration that permeates the whole house. And usually, I'm overcome with a strong urge to whisk Sam away, to bring him home with me just to get him away from it all for the night, but then I wonder if my own cantankerousness would be an improvement in setting the mood for a child.

"What?" she says. "Crosbie, it's fine. Just go hang with Sam."

"You sure?"

"Yes," she says. "I want to cook."

"But don't you need to pack?"

"I'm not sure I'm even going."

And here it is. What I've been expecting for months now. But I let the comment slide. It's the stress of the moment. She's not serious. She wouldn't cancel *this* last minute.

"Cros," she says. "Just please check on Sam."

When I go back into the living room, he's still deep in his imaginary world. I slide over to the couch.

Finally, Sam looks up at me, smiles, and comes barreling onto the couch next to me, a stegosaurus in one hand, a bigger *T. rex* in the other.

"Hey, bud." I give him a big squeeze. "I see you've got your old dinos out."

"Yep." He folds his knees before him, then returns to his play, gnashing the *T. rex* and the stegosaurus together like chips of flint.

I sit and watch. Wishing I could escape into an imaginary world like that, flee from the tornado of guilt constantly snatching away my most peaceful moments like they're unsecured mobile homes. Or to simply wake up each day and not feel a cloak of shame pressing down on me.

I fidget. I have a bad nervous habit of using my forefinger to pick at the skin around the thumb on the same hand. I'm doing that now. To stop myself, I grab a clothing catalog off the coffee table and mindlessly page through it. I pause on one of the models, who's wearing an earth-toned poncho over some effortlessly worn jeans, to admire her look. She has a natural air, her face free of worry.

Sam stops his playing and points his stegosaurus at her. "Aunt Crosbie." Except he says *Cwasbie* since he's still having a little trouble with his *r*'s. "You?"

*"Me?"* I tilt my head and study her. Like me, she's got dark hair, hazel eyes, and she seems tall, but does she really look like me? I hadn't thought so. I was admiring her whole vibe, just like I was admiring Sam's play. "No, honey. It's not. *You* think she looks like me?"

He nods enthusiastically before hopping down, returning to his other dinos on the floor. He resumes smashing them together, roaring and snarling louder now, like violence—and I might add, dino porn—is the most natural thing on earth.

In this moment, I have no idea this tiny interaction is an omen of sorts. That it's preparing me for a terrifying absurdity about to come down the pike, and that realistically, I'm not a great judge of who resembles me and who doesn't.

# Chapter 4

I toss the magazine on the coffee table. Sam keeps playing, and I'm about to go in the kitchen and see if Jess needs some help when my phone vibrates in my back pocket. I pull it out and see a text from one of my friends, Fiona.

OMG. The resemblance! Call me.

I text her back.

???

I wonder what she's on about, but the message sets my nerves tingling. Was there some video on TikTok of a woman resembling me doing something embarrassing at a bar or a party? That's all I need now.

Then from the kitchen, something shatters. Concern immediately snaps Sam out of his play. He rockets to standing, his brown eyes wide, a dino dangling in one hand.

"Don't worry, hon," I say. "Your mom just dropped something. You stay and play. I'll check." But my heart races. I resist the urge to dash into the kitchen in front of him. The last thing I want is to drum up more drama in his life.

When I enter, Jess is standing still beside a broken glass shattered across the counter and the floor. She's looking down at her phone.

"Cros." She looks up. Her face is white. "Have you seen this?"

Jess holds out her phone, steps my way.

"Stop, Jess," I say. Fortunately, it doesn't look like she'd filled the glass with anything yet when she dropped it because I see no liquid. "What?" I step over the mess and take her phone. "What is it?"

I look down at Jess's screen and see . . .

Me.

For a long moment, I freeze, staring down at me, with me looking back at me.

Below the sketch, a message stands in yellow: SAME DRILL. SIX DAYS. Cocky now, like the guy is self-satisfied he's grabbed the attention of the entire nation. Most of the world, too, thanks to social media.

"It's you," she says, breathy and dramatic, like she's starring in a horror flick. She puts a hand to her mouth.

For one tiny second, I agree. My heart hammers ridiculously in my chest.

The woman in the sketch has medium-length, dark, wavy hair tucked behind her ears, a thin nose, slightly upward-slanting eyes, and small brackets that frame her mouth even when not smiling. Like mine.

But no, I tell myself, reaching for some common sense. Okay, the sketch does look like me, but she could just as easily be the woman from the catalog Sam *just* pointed out seconds ago. "No," I say, still studying the screen. "It's not."

Jess's eyes are quarters, gawking at me like I'm an apparition.

"Jess, come on. No."

"Yes. Look at her. It looks just like you."

I do not need this right now. At all. Not on the anniversary of her rape. As surreal as this moment feels, calming my sister down is all I can think about. A high-pitched static plays in my head. *Make this better, Crosbie. Fix this. Make this better right now.*

"I mean," I say, "it's just a sketch. Sketches are vague. You draw. You should know."

She comes over, her shoe crunching on glass. She grabs her phone back to study it again.

"Where's the broom?"

She absently points to the kitchen door that goes to the garage while she continues to stare at her screen, now nervously swiping through articles to see what else is being reported.

On my way into the garage, I pull my own phone back out to open the news piece when a call comes in.

It's Wallace, my ex-boyfriend and the brother of my college roommate. Wallace and I have remained friends even after the breakup.

"Crosbie." He's a little breathless. "Where are you?"

"At Jess's." I grab the broom and walk back in.

"Have you seen it?" he asks.

"Yes. Was just about to read the article. Rest assured. It's not me."

"Rest assured?"

"I was just telling Jess," I say loudly so she can hear every word as I reenter the kitchen.

Her head pops up from her phone.

"These traits are so common," I tell Wallace. "Ask any detective looking for a suspect using only a composite. This is too generic. This could be *a lot* of women."

"It's . . . well . . ." he says. "It's the earrings."

*The earrings?*

"Hold on," I tell him. I no longer want Jess to hear any of this. "I forgot the dustpan," I say to my sister. I hand her the broom and go back into the garage, tap on the photo, and pinch to enlarge it to see one of the earrings. It's in the shape of a feather with a round stone in the center of the feather, halfway down.

What the *hell*?

A jagged tip of a small iceberg juts above cold waters in the center of my belly.

They were a gift from Wallace when we were dating. He thought it would be nice to give me a little something when I hung out my shingle a few months after I quit the force, like I deserved a reward for refusing to stay in a job where I felt like a venomous snake that all my coworkers gave a wide berth to in the hallways. What he didn't understand was that quitting was never going to make me stop feeling poisonous, but at least it helped seem like I was repenting on some level.

But here they are, dangling from the lobes of a woman in a sketch that looks very much like me, and it's been put out there by some sicko who's been terrorizing the nation. A fine sheen of heat prickles the back of my neck.

The earrings aren't entirely uncommon, though.

"Wall," I say, summoning levelheadedness. "A lot of people could have earrings like that." It's more of a question than a statement. I want reassurance so I can march back in there and tell Jess she can totally forget this whole ridiculous notion. "Where'd you get them again?"

"I told you when I gave them to you." He sounds miffed.

"No, I know. I'm sorry." God, I do know. He bought them from a friend from college, a guy who sells jewelry at farmers' markets, art walks, and festivals. He even sells them in gift shops, too, especially around Glacier and Yellowstone. They have a Native American, Western flair.

It was a nice gesture on Wallace's part, and I don't know why I asked. My quizzing him about where he bought them was about as callous and insensitive as when I abruptly parachuted out of the relationship. No notice and, I realized later, no care or concern for his feelings. I acted like we were teenagers instead of in our late twenties. Back then, I chalked it up to all the baggage surrounding his sister, Sophie.

Now? Well, I chalk it up to the strangeness of the conversation, of me trying to ignore the cold pit pooling in my stomach and the vertiginous sensation that things have suddenly tilted off-kilter.

And Jess. I need to get back into the kitchen.

"I got them from Kerry," he says. "They're not from a department store. They're not mass-produced."

"But they're sold in gift shops near the national parks, where millions of tourists come through?"

"True."

"And I'm guessing no one has a patent on feather-shaped jewelry."

"I guess." He sighs loudly.

"Plus, this sketch, it's black and white. You can't tell if those circles in the center are beads or gems or—"

"Yeah, but Crosbie, it's weird, okay?"

"I'll admit that. But really, it's not me. And I need to go." I tell Wallace I'll get back to him later and grab the dustpan.

Jess sweeps up glass.

"Here, I'll do that." I grab the broom from her and start funneling the shards into the pan.

She sits down at the table and locks onto her phone again.

"Jess," I say. "Put that away. It's not me, okay?"

"How can you be so sure?"

"Because I'm a nobody from Montana."

But *am* I sure?

Yes. I may have stuff—big, ugly stuff—shoved deep into a dark closet, but that doesn't mean it's me. My "things"—the bruised, ugly truths I take to bed with me each night and wake up with every morning—are vague and amorphous, like messy Etch A Sketches with wayward lines. And even though one of those truths could land me in jail, there's only one person who knows about it, and there's no way he'd say anything to anyone. Ever.

"And I'm not even in the public eye like you," I add.

Her lower lip pouts.

"Look, Jess, I promise. It's not me. It's coincidence. Let's just have a nice dinner with Sam. We'll deal with this later. Okay?"

When I get a nod from her, I ask her to grab me a trash bag and a vacuum so we can get any remaining minuscule fragments. But when I turn back to sweeping, I do it slowly, methodically, as if something tells me I should hold on to this mundane chore for a moment longer, as if my subconscious already knows that I should fight for this last normal instant before my life suddenly changes.

# Chapter 5

Sam's excited to tell us about his day while we eat, how he and his friend Oliver gathered tomatoes from Oliver's mother's garden and dropped them into her yard from high up in his tree house simply to watch them splat.

I'm happy to have him take my mind off the sketch. I smile at the image of the tomatoes in a mushy pile and the boys giggling uncontrollably.

Jess asks Sam if he got permission from Oliver's mom for the tomato mess. When he says they didn't, she scolds him, then turns to me because I'm still grinning.

"You're encouraging him," she says.

I shake my head, grab another spoonful of rice from the serving dish.

"And you're in law enforcement?"

*"Was,"* I say. "Key word." I brush away the sense that something has broken inside me—something fundamental that can never be fixed no matter what field I'm in.

"Still are," Jess says.

Sam finishes up his food and asks to be excused, and Jess tells him to rinse his plate and put it in the dishwasher.

The two of us stay at the table.

I can tell she's still bothered by this sketch business, but I want to preempt her and inquire about when she's going to get back to the podcast. As if she's read my mind, she looks down at her plate and says,

"With all this going on, I'm canceling tomorrow. I'm sorry, I know you'll be out the airfare, but at least the room is on the conference, not us."

I want to say, *Are you kidding?*

"Come on, Jess. I told you. It's not me."

"Well, even if it isn't, I want to cancel. It's not about the sketch."

*Because it's the anniversary of that awful night?* I want to ask it, but I don't. I'm very careful with her, even with Sam out of the room. I respond with two monotone words: "Then why?"

She glances at me briefly before looking down, as if to say, *You know why.*

Instantly, the mood shifts to something heavy and dense, like an old scratchy wool blanket thrown over us. I want to toss it off, let the dust flick away. I want my old sister back—the self-assured one.

A revving dread overcomes me. Is it seeing Jess like this? Or is it that silly sketch? Has my usual *mad* (which a therapist I saw in college told me had transformed from *sad* following the loss of my dad years ago, then of Sophie, then of my mom) turned to fear? What's a person supposed to do with all that sorrow? It's bound to turn to either kindling or fire suppressant, fueling flames or snuffing them out and making you depressed. I go one way. Jess goes the other.

"I don't feel up to it. I just don't feel like going," she says. "I'm not sure why I even agreed to it in the first place. That was before—"

She doesn't finish. She doesn't have to. I look down at my food.

But backing out *now*? The very evening before we're flying out?

"It will be good for you," I force lightheartedly and take a bite of my chicken. "Get you back on the horse, you know. Your fans miss you."

She goes silent.

"Besides, you can't leave the organizers in the lurch."

"People cancel all the time. And COVID's going around again. I could say I'm sick."

"You'd just *lie* like that?" *Listen to me, all angelic.* The chicken I'm chewing goes tasteless and mushy in my mouth. I swallow and take a sip of water. As if she's not talking to a sister whose words led to someone's death and whose silence led to another's. But Jess? She's honest.

The image of the woman with the earrings flashes through my mind again. *Could* it be?

"With this new sketch out," she says, "there will be only one topic on everyone's minds anyway. Trying to talk about victim advocacy and the families of victims will be the last thing people will care about while everyone's blathering on about this. Not to mention all the strange confessions that will start pouring out, just like they did with the last sketch. Do you know they've given him a name?"

"I heard. On my way over."

When the first drawing was released three and a half months ago in mid-May, not many people paid attention to it. Someone dropped a photo they'd taken of a pencil sketch of a middle-aged man with a beard and mustache vaguely resembling a younger Harrison Ford on several anonymous, untraceable social media accounts like Facebook, X, Reddit, and Instagram. Full head of dark hair, smoldering eyes, two frown lines between his eyebrows, a mouth that angled slightly upward into a half smirk. In yellow block text, all caps, the command CONFESS, OR DIE. YOU HAVE SIX DAYS screamed out from under the photo.

At first, few people noticed. The accounts didn't have many followers. And the people who stumbled across the posts assumed they were random nonsense, a bad joke.

But a little over a week later, an astute Seattle reporter who knew of the random posts wrote that law enforcement had found a man who looked like the drawing who'd been fatally shot near Snohomish.

When the story got legs, the original post got more consideration. Some said it was a colossal stretch to claim it was the same man from the drawing. But others bought it. Social media camps formed—trenches dug, positions staked out. So many "experts" who knew nothing. There was a resemblance, I always thought, but it was likely a coincidence.

The cops denied any connection. They insisted there was no way to conclude the victim matched the depiction. People assumed the journalist was making it up, trying to cash in on a little sensationalism. But because of the reporting, the anonymous accounts generated a ton of new followers.

A month later, a second sketch. It was paired with the same demand, to confess or die. And it went viral. A brooding woman with short hair tucked behind her ears, a down-turned mouth, narrow eyes, and a prominent nose. This time, way more press. Several big influencers in the true crime arena started discussing it.

By the end of that week, a woman looking a lot like the second drawing turned up murdered in Santa Monica, California. The police were vague on details.

By the third sketch, which dropped sometime in mid-July—another man, with one angled-down eye—*viral* took on a whole new meaning. Worldwide attention. All law enforcement agencies went on high alert in every town in America, especially in the West.

But after the days passed, no one turned up dead.

"Everyone's obsessed with it," Jess says with more energy than I've heard from her in a long time. "Social media is buzzing. Everyone's wondering if there's some dead body out there rotting away that they haven't found. Or," she adds, "the man dished out the correct confession and wriggled off the hook."

I may not be into social media as much as she is, but I'm fully aware of the frenzy.

"All these frantic confessions from people who think they've been sketched keep popping up all over the place," she continues. "Guess there are more than a few slightly cockeyed men out there. Who knew?" She pops a hunk of broccoli in her mouth. "Did you hear about that guy from Hamilton?" She points her fork at me.

I did. A well-known businessman with uneven eyes from a town not three hours from us, who sort of resembles the sketch, fessed up to poisoning his neighbor's trees so he'd have a better view of the mountains. It made the local paper, and the city fined him, but no one besides him really seems to think he—some nobody from an afterthought state like Montana—was the actual target.

"Jess, we already have our flights booked," I say. "You know money is tight for me. And I was looking forward to spending some time with you."

She looks at the open kitchen window as if she longs to be somewhere else. The evening has cooled with the storm, and the sharp smell of wet pine steals in and mingles with the smell of garlic from her cooking.

"And Patrick's already lined up to watch Sam. Come on, how often does that happen? And he's looking forward to spending time with his dad."

She half smiles.

"It'll be fun. We don't even need to stay for the entire conference. We can cut it short, go for just a night instead of two . . . grab a nice dinner out. I'll change our flights right now."

"You really don't think that sketch is you?"

"I don't." I grab her hand. It feels bony. Small.

"It is a crazy thought, isn't it?"

"Yes, absolutely crazy."

Jess presses her tongue against the inside of her cheek. When she turns back from the window to look at me, the lurking worry has momentarily sneaked away. "I'll go finish my packing."

# A CONFESSION

Facebook: Sara Johns—I can't believe I look like the sketch, but OMG, enough of you guys think it looks like me even though I have a little mole under my right eye and the woman in the sketch doesn't. Still, I'm scared. And I do have a confession to make . . . I hope you guys understand and don't hate me, but when I was 18, a friend and I set our friend's uncle's car on fire because he'd raped one of our friends. The car was in the driveway, and we didn't know there was a small child sleeping in the house. The house caught fire, but the child was rescued and was okay. We were never caught, but I do regret being so reckless even though he was an awful, awful person. And man, this already feels better to get this off my chest. We could have killed a child!

# Chapter 6

***Five Days***

I'm in need of caffeine and Jess informs me that she needs alone time to get her bearings before her talk, so I seize the opportunity.

Patrick showed up on time for Sam at 8 p.m. yesterday. Sam's excitement to see him sent a lump right to my throat. I heaped praise on Patrick for getting it right for a change, hoping the positive reinforcement would carry over for future visits. I changed our flights so we'll only stay the one night, rushed home to pack, and Jess and I caught a red-eye out. We stored our luggage with the hotel concierge since we were still too early for check-in when we got to the hotel around noon and have already attended a panel featuring relatives of the victims of the Interstate Killer.

Now it's late afternoon and she's due to speak in fifteen minutes. She's nervous and frazzled, but I reassure her she'll be fine, that she's done this dozens of times before.

After swearing that I'll return by the time she goes onstage, I leave the ballroom and walk through the broad conference halls toward the main lobby. It hums with the participants' energy, united in the questionable faith that tragedy and violence can be tamed with observation and exposure, like a great cat in a zoo.

It's my first time at one of these conventions. And probably my last since Jess is the only reason I've come.

The fact is, even though I became obsessed with crime in college and studied criminology before eventually becoming a police officer, I'm feeling a little silly to be among the hundreds—hell, thousands—of women and a few men milling through this convention center, ravenous to learn anything and everything about investigations, bloody scenes, and psychopaths.

The hunger for true crime books and podcasts and movies and TV series has fueled a booming industry. It's mind-blowing. Everyone now feels like a trained expert in the field, no matter if conjecture and supposition rule the day. Behind every murder, people assume there's something secret and mysterious, something stemming from grand plots and plans, when it's usually shitty, unremarkable people allowing themselves to give in to their rages and their perversions.

*Their* rages . . .

*Not now,* I tell myself. I'm here to support Jess. *Focus on the conference. On the here and now.*

The conference goers, and people in general . . . they want to zero in on the shark attacks or lightning strikes of crime—the ones least likely to occur: the violent serial killers, like this Confession Artist business.

Why? Who knows?

Maybe to help us feel like we're in control? So when we study it up close and view the details as if under a microscope, we feel like we're simply looking at the legs of a centipede instead of the rape and strangulation of a young, unsuspecting woman. Or child. As if knowing all the particulars about the crimes in the news will keep it clinical, the observation alone like a headlamp leading us through the tangled woods.

But Jess *does* study crime like it's under a microscope, and not an ounce of that practice seemed to help when she became a victim herself.

Maybe I *need* this, though. Maybe it's allowing me to escape a bit since quitting the force.

I pick up my pace, beelining it through the large busy halls. As I slide into line behind a tall man in the coffee shop, I notice a slight shift of energy out in the lobby. I look around for anything unusual.

I catch a glance at a wall of narrow mirrors lined up next to one another across the room. Our bodies are doubled—even tripled—in the reflections. The mirrors make all of us appear thinner and stretched long like rubber, like we're in a fun house. Dim, sparkly lights cast an unsettling pale, sickly glow over us.

I turn away, grabbing my phone out of my satchel. Another text from Fiona.

OMG. Why won't you call me? What do you think of the sketch?

Ha ha. Not me, I text back. In Dallas with Jess. Call you tomorrow?

But Fiona's second attempt to get my attention sets my nerves tingling all over again. I adjust my carrier bag on my shoulder and see more notifications. Another text, this one from a college friend I haven't seen in several years. John.

Girl, you aware of the latest sketch that's out there?

I swipe it away, tell myself I'll respond to him later.

Instagram informs me who's recently posted new stories. Twitter, or X, tells me I have a new follower, bringing my total to a whopping thirty-two, which is perfectly fine. I'm not on it to become an influencer. I only joined to follow Jess.

A birdlike woman with a hooked nose to match jumps in line behind me with a friend.

In front of the tall guy before me, a young man with dark hair stares at me an instant too long.

In front of him is a group of three women. They're looking at their phones, pushing satchels higher onto their shoulders, nudging each other. After one murmurs something to another, she points her chin to me.

My phone buzzes, thankfully giving me something to occupy myself with.

Wallace again.

"Hey," I answer.

"Are you at home?"

"No, I'm with Jess. At that conference I mentioned."

"You're *traveling* right now?"

"Yeah, is that a problem?"

"No. I mean, maybe. Don't you think you should do something?"

"Do what?"

"I don't know. Report the fact that you look like the woman in the sketch to law enforcement?"

"Why would I do that?"

"You know why," he says. "The earrings."

I inhale the heady smell of espresso. I don't want to think about any of this.

Wallace says something else, but I don't hear him. The chatter in the hotel is ratcheting up as conference goers transition between talks and panels. Someone's nervous laughter fills my ears while the line behind me gets bigger, everyone needing their late-afternoon caffeine fix. The crowding bodies in the mirrors grow more ludicrous.

I shouldn't have picked up. In fact, I should have set better boundaries with Wallace. To remain friends after the breakup, I never set firm parameters. Sometimes I kick myself for even getting involved with him in the first place. But we both know it's a complicated ball of string tied to Sophie, tied to both of our needs to hang on, still, even after eleven years.

I scoot a few feet forward and catch words floating by.

"I just don't under . . . Yeah, another woman." A gray-haired woman speaks to the guy she's with. "Male. Female. Male. Female. A pattern," she announces like a seasoned anthropologist.

"It's loud here," I say to Wallace. "What did you say?"

"I said I've called Kerry."

"Kerry?"

"Kerry. The *earrings*?"

The bird woman behind me clears her throat loudly.

"Oh, sorry." I scoot closer to the register. The cashier is waiting for my order. "Hang on, Wall," I say.

The tall man has moved to the side with half a dozen others, and now he's staring at me, too, along with several others as they wait for their grande lattes and macchiatos and London Fogs. Something uneasy shifts inside me.

"Grande Americano with room," I say.

I feel better to finally place my order. Performing a task as ordinary as this calms my nerves. I *am* just a regular person doing a commonplace thing at a huge conference surrounded by lots of people. Just because people are noticing that I resemble the sketch doesn't mean anything.

The barista taking my order barely registers me because, well, why would she? I'm simply an anonymous human in a crowd. Nobody knows me in Dallas or, really, anywhere. Just like I told Jess last night. I'm not in the public eye like her. I live in a small town, for God's sake, not in Seattle, not in LA, no high-profile city some crazy killer would even think of targeting.

Sure, I worked as a cop for four years, but that was all in Montana, too. I've made some enemies and have a skeleton—more than one—in my closet, but nothing of a scale that would warrant my becoming this whack job's target. So what if a few of these people are noticing that I resemble the stupid sketch?

I slide my credit card into the chip reader. "Wall, sorry. You still there?"

"Yes. Look, shouldn't you tell someone about this? Maybe go into the closest station? Tell them about the earrings?"

"Oh my gawd." Someone's voice with a Southern accent behind me in line rises above a Harry Styles song pumping out over the huge convention center, the rhythm fusing with the drone of human babble and the hiss of milk steamers.

Over my shoulder, I spot one of the women in the group of three who were looking at me, a blond woman. She's placing a hand over her heart like her compassion needs to be pushed back where it belongs. "Holy cow," she says. "She does." But when she sees me look at her, she turns away. Then adds, "I'm so glad I don't look anything like that."

Her friends' heads bob up and down in agreement.

My cheeks heat up. I feel exposed, like I'm in a middle school cafeteria being singled out. Only, it's a million times worse, because even though these strangers have no clue about me or the awful things I've done, I do. All too well.

And the idea of confessing? I shudder.

My sins are not obvious. True, the big one, involving Coleman, could land me in jail, but that one is never coming out.

I put my card back in my wallet and step away from the line to wait with the others, trying to hold my shoulders tall even though I'd prefer to melt into the floor. I put the phone back to my ear. "So what were you saying about Kerry?"

"He hasn't called me back yet. Look, are you taking this seriously enough?" He sounds anxious.

"Wallace," I say. "Everything's fine." The barista sets my Americano on the counter and calls out my name. I tell Wallace I have to go. Jess is almost up.

I shove my phone into my bag, add some cream to my coffee, and as I turn to make my way to the ballroom, I notice the birdlike woman who was behind me glance at me, do a double take, and nudge her friend. Her friend's eyes open wide and she nods twice, slowly, like she's transfixed.

The iceberg in my gut rocks.

I want to stop, grin at them both, and maybe give a little wave, allowing the ludicrousness of the moment to be just that. *No, that's not me. It's just a random sketch from some nutjob.* This impulse to roll my eyes and laugh it off feels exactly like the sensation I had while sweeping the glass last night—as if I should fight for these last normal instants.

But I don't smile, I don't wave. With a pressure building in my chest, I hurry away to go watch my sister get back in the game.

# Chapter 7

The sound system pumps pop music into the ballroom. Screens flanking the stage flash crime photos: K-9 cadaver dogs sniff their way through fields, yellow police tape cordons off run-down houses, handcuffs shackle random wrists.

Vague news headlines flash in and fade out, too: Man Gunned Down in Alleyway

Teenager Accused of Stabbing Stepmother

Serial Rapist Suspect Arrested After Police Showdown

But the audience is spellbound, attention on their phones.

The latest sketch. And why not? The Confession Artist killings tick all the right sensational boxes, and Americans gobble up the theatrics. Jess was right—what better place to discuss the latest phenom than at CrimeCon?

Conference goers brought it up in the only panel we attended after we arrived this morning, the panel with the Interstate Killer victims' family members. Jess wanted to go to it. Audience members shed tears under the cruel lights of the seminar rooms, but soon the topic switched to the Confession Artist. One posited that the new killer was after a different type of control.

I rolled my eyes at the obviousness of the statement. Well, *of course.* Tapping into shame, seeking confessions. *Of course.* When I was little, my dad told me that guilt was simply a ticket to repeat the things that you're ashamed of. The thought now almost makes me want to throw up.

Leon strobes through my mind. It's like this. He comes knocking when I'm least expecting it.

I try to tune the image of him out. I listen to all the whispering around me. Nobody seems to be noticing me, thank goodness. I don't need to get caught up in my own disturbing *Black Mirror* episode while attending Jess's talk. I keep my attention on the crime photos and headlines making the rounds on the screens. Serial Rapist Suspect Arrested After Police Showdown flashes again as if on cue for Jess.

Because that's the moment she strides onto the stage.

The crowd stills. I'm pleased to see she's found her old confident gait. It matches the music. Her bobbed, sleek blond hair I helped her curl into beach waves shines.

Jess has striking, large brown eyes and a luminous smile. Her entire aura is genuine, including her friendly, not-too-silky-smooth voice, which is why so many people love her podcast. The ache for the victims she projects is always heartfelt and real.

When the music stops and the clapping dies, Jess faces the audience.

And freezes.

Her face wilts.

The audience waits.

I sit up taller, willing her to glance at me. She knows I'm in the front row, as we planned. As I have been so many other times in her life—sitting in audiences at school plays, at her volleyball games, at her band concerts, when our mom was at work and couldn't make it, or later, in college, when Mom was too wasted to make it. I'm not sure when that sense of duty started, probably when Dad checked out of our lives. When our stepdad, Les, entered the picture. When Mom took to drinking. And Jess . . . she wasn't just younger than me, she was smaller, more sensitive, more fragile. Prone to huge mood swings as quickly and as frequently as the Montana mountain ridges catch clouds.

It may as well be me up there standing at the podium. She's not sure if her mouth will work. Humiliation waits in the wings to upend her career even more. *Come on, Jess. You've got to push through or we'll both drag ourselves home feeling worse than when we came. If you fail now, so do I. If you break more, I'm implicated further. And neither of those scenarios is good for Sam.*

Someone whispers, "What's going on?"

Another image pops into my head. It's a clip from the Rock & Roll Hall of Fame in Cleveland. My mom and Les took us. The clip was Michael Jackson at the Super Bowl. He stood with his hand touching his dark-lensed sunglasses for what felt like an eternity, until finally he whipped them off, and the crowd erupted.

But Jess is not working the crowd. Usually, she shines. Not now.

*Come on, Jess.* Her forehead glistens with sweat. Her chest rises and falls.

People begin to whisper. I shift in my seat and wave my hand discreetly in front of my chest, trying to catch her eye without too many others noticing.

Jess takes a breath in the microphone, a rasp of air punching abrasively through the anticipation. She glances back offstage as if she wants to flee like a startled doe.

*Oh no you don't.* I shoot both hands up to get her attention. She spots me. Our eyes lock. I give one slow nod and mouth, "Talk."

She stands a little taller and swallows. Her shoulders drop. She whispers one word into the microphone: "Secrets."

She scans the sea of faces. The crowd exhales.

"Secrets," she repeats with more force, "are rarely better kept locked away. Knowledge and truth are powerful tools to begin the healing process." Her deathly pale face gains some color in the overhead lighting, as if each word fuels her, one at a time, like gasoline. "When someone discovers who killed one of their family members—a child, a sibling, a parent—much of the guessing game about the monster in the dark dissipates. And that alone is an incredible relief to loved ones who have suffered deep loss."

Now that the sunglasses have come off, I realize how tense I am. My neck and shoulder muscles are rock-hard. I've considered myself her protector for so long, even though I've proved to be a failure.

My phone vibrates in my pocket.

Jess explains how she's assisted the police in finding a serial rapist from the 1990s in Salem, Oregon, a case that had gone cold but was revisited after genetic research helped find the Golden State Killer.

My phone nags. I resist pulling it out and studying the picture, afraid I might look uninterested in Jess's speech and throw off the delicate balance she's found, but I keep picturing the woman in line doing a double take of me and the others whispering and lifting their chins to me.

The concern in Wallace's voice also niggles. Wallace is not a worrywart. He's calm and poised. A performing pianist and a teacher of the instrument. A composer, too, involved in too many musical endeavors for me to list. His suggestion to visit authorities seems like overkill and makes my breath catch, but maybe he's just being thorough. Careful.

More careful than I ever was. That's his nature. A perfectionist.

And he's loyal. He doesn't fail people, like I did with him. Like I did with Sophie. Like I did with Jess. Like I did with . . . No. Not now. I can't let myself think of him.

I train my eyes on my sister.

I insisted that Jess report the assault after she told me about it, several weeks after it occurred. But she refused. It didn't matter how much I hounded her about doing it for her own sanity or how much I reminded her that pursuing a legal avenue might prevent him from doing the same to someone else.

She said that she would not destroy what she's built up by turning the press loose to pursue her during the investigation and eventual trial. She refused to be trapped forever in the public's mind as a victim, to be told that she'd been careless, that she'd drunk too much, that she'd been stupid for not keeping a close eye on her drinks in that bar. Or that she's a liar, an exaggerator, or an opportunist. She knew exactly how it would go.

She insisted that if she reported, her life would come under constant scrutiny, especially among the crime junkies who made up her core audience. She'd become a huge story, since she worked in the cold case and podcasting industry, and since her podcast was focusing more and more on victim advocacy. She'd be accused of all sorts of things: that she made it all up for more press, that she'd do anything to be in the limelight and increase her numbers. *Any press is good press,* she swore they'd say.

"Think of Sophie," she said.

Sophie. Hearing her name always feels like an angry bruise is being jabbed.

*Sophie.* As if I've ever stopped thinking about my college roommate.

Jess cited studies on how some crisis centers have ceased recommending to all assault victims that they go to the police, demonstrating that for some, engaging with the criminal justice system only further traumatized them—severely, and for life.

I couldn't say she was wrong about any of it. I'd been through it all before.

But I truly believed she should get it on the record, even though I knew firsthand that police department bias was strong. Unavoidable, even.

Still, many improvements have been made, and I told her so. And trying to push that progress along was the main reason—the big shining marker in my life—I went into law enforcement, even though it all ended up going terribly wrong.

"Jess," I had implored. "Things are different than they were ten years ago, when this happened to Sophie. Law enforcement is trained to take it seriously, to treat all victims fairly." I said this to her knowing that when I was on the force, even something like harassment wasn't handled all that well.

But this was rape. It was different. The department has an entire dedicated program and physical space in the hospital, the SANE Suite, staffed by a sexual assault examiner to provide care for victims and conduct interviews.

Still, incredibly, my bighearted little sister also didn't want to ruin Mark Coleman's life. *He needs help, not prison,* she said. She was determined to talk to him when she felt ready. To tell him that if he agreed to seek counseling, she would not go to the police.

And now he's gone, and she's backsliding.

That part scares the crap out of me. I've seen it before, when Sophie became unreachable. And once again, I feel responsible, just as I did back then.

# Chapter 8

After Jess finishes her speech, I leave her with a throng of fans and some other conference colleagues, figuring she needs the moment with her admirers, without me.

Thrilled that the presentation went well for her, I find a cluster of comfy chairs to settle into in the corner of an atrium bar on the second level of the convention center–slash–mega hotel.

I take out my phone. More texts from Fiona to call her. And two other college buddies in addition to John—Maggie and Hannah—who, like John, don't even live in my town, asking if the sketch could be me.

My pulse thrums. *Shit*, do that many people think I look like this person, or is it spreading like wildfire among my circle because one of them—most likely Fiona—put the word out? Fiona was the biggest social media queen out of all of us in college. Maggie, John, Hannah, and I hardly ever posted in comparison. Whenever we had a great group photo and someone would suggest posting it, John or Hannah would say, "Fiona will do it."

Fiona came from my hometown of Kalispell and went to my high school, and later to the same university. She was the one who loved the most to feed the slush pile of gossip back in high school and college. She was one of those friends you were never sure you completely trusted but kept in your life anyway because she was still fun and exciting and always up for doing something even if everyone else was bailing on you.

Only, for me, it wasn't because I was worried people would bail. It was the reverse. I counted on her to keep me from becoming a hermit, especially after Sophie was gone and my mom passed three years later.

Fiona was always on the sidelines in one way or another. Sure, it was usually superficial interaction, but she was still a buoy of sorts.

The therapist I saw briefly after my mom passed—an older woman with a long, severe face and crisply bobbed hair who worked for the health center's counseling services—pointed out that I had a loner streak. She wanted to know when it started. I told her it began after my dad passed away when I was in seventh grade and Jess in fourth, when I knew I needed to buck up and be strong for Jess and for my mom. But that I overcame it in high school, with Fiona's help then, too, I might add.

But it's been flaring up again since Jess's backsliding. It's not depression, like Jess is prone to; it's just a desire to be alone, to pull into myself, to not be seen and be anonymous. But mostly, to be 100 percent available for Jess and Sam when they need me.

I scroll through my photos, but I'm smiling in most of them. Those don't work for comparisons. I sit back in my chair, fluff my hair in front of my shoulders, and arrange it to expose my ears. Feeling sheepish, I hold up my phone, stare broodingly into the lens, and snap a mug shot selfie.

I'm wearing cubic zirconia studs, not the ones Wallace gave me. I rarely wear those since we've broken up. Not only does it feel a little hinky, but the truth is that I don't like them all that much, even though they are fun and sentimental.

When he gave them to me, he told me he knew they weren't entirely my style and that they were a little kitschy, a little "gift-shoppy," but thought they were apropos since we had done some hiking and camping in the mountains. He had wanted to get something earthy, something Western. And the Montana sapphires spoke for themselves with their beautiful cornflower-blue hues.

It wasn't the gems I didn't love. It's just that I'm a detective. I go for simple, and these seemed just a little extra. But a pang of remorse and sadness pings through me. They represent what could have been between Wallace and me. They represent hope and some fun, the promise of new beginnings. A phoenix rising from the ashes of the wreckage Sophie's death brought to all our lives. A way for me to move on from the guilt over what happened to her so I could expand and flap my wings more freely. Because if Sophie's own brother forgave me, surely I could forgive myself.

The noise picks up around me, catching my attention. More people have trickled into the atrium lounge—conference goers wanting space away from the crowds, or maybe they're nabbing seats before the restaurants fill up for lunch.

A bartender has appeared behind the wood bar and is taking an order from a man who doesn't look like he belongs at CrimeCon. He has the attire and physique of a rock climber. Backpack, disheveled hair, shaggier version of Russell Crowe's gladiator beard, khaki shorts with a bleach-stain spot on one pocket, and a laid-back expression that says he couldn't care less about the whole scene. The exact opposite of Wallace. Maybe early to mid-thirties, probably a few years older than me.

If I weren't so anxious, I'd lust after a guy like him, all windswept and relaxed. Calloused hands from grabbing rocks attached to actual earth instead of pale, slender ones perfectly manicured for creating ephemeral tones on piano keys that leave me feeling hollowed out.

The thought instantly shocks me—the bitchiness of it. Given how Wallace's music was the very thing that drew me to him in the first place. I ask myself, When did *this* unkindness kick in? Is this what guilt does to a person, turns them into more of an asshole?

My phone vibrates, pulling me back. Jess. Already?

"Cros? Where are you? I can't believe this is happening." Her voice is high-pitched and strained.

"What's happening?"

"One of my fans who came up to talk to me saw you with me earlier and they asked how I knew the target in the sketch. I can't believe it. I told you. I told you it was you."

"Calm down. There's no reason to get upset. One person seeing that resemblance here doesn't mean anything." I try not to think about the others in line for coffee.

"No reason? How can you say that?"

"Think about it. There are probably hundreds of people around the country having this exact same conversation right now."

"The earrings, Cros. Did you see those?"

"Yes, I have, but—"

"But nothing. How do you explain them? I didn't notice them last night, but when I studied the sketch again now . . . I just can't be—"

"They aren't uncommon. They're probably sold on Amazon."

I take her silence as a good sign. Either she doesn't know or doesn't remember they were handcrafted by one of Wallace's friends.

"Listen," I continue. "You've said yourself I look like Jennifer Garner. I'm not saying it's her, either. I'm just saying there are a lot of women who resemble other people. We've claimed for years that Fiona looks like a blond Sandra Bullock. People have doppelgängers, and Jess, we live in the frigging Flathead Valley. Do you really think someone's coming for me out there, at the ass end of nowhere? And for what possible reason?"

"It's not like Montana hasn't been discovered," she mumbles. "But maybe you're right."

More progress.

Except she follows with, "We should have never come here. I can't believe this is hap—" Her voice breaks. I suddenly feel horrible for leaving her there with her fans.

"Hey," I say. "You were great. You feel good about it?"

She doesn't answer.

"You should. You were terrific."

She heaves a sigh. "If it wasn't for you, I would have stood there like an idiot for God knows how long." She asks me where I am and tells me to stay put, tells me she'll come my way as soon as she meets with one of the conference organizers for a minute.

I look back at my fantasy rock-climber guy. He has a handsome, slightly weathered face to accompany his sinewy arms and legs. If the world were a perfect place, I could fantasize about meeting a guy like him here in Dallas, picture the sheets a mess and a bottle of champagne. But my world is *very* far from perfect.

He scans the place.

And heads right toward me.

I go on high alert.

He sits down a few seats away, as if he hasn't even seen me at all, and digs through his backpack frantically. What's he searching for? My heart hammers against my sternum.

Even if he is the perp, for God's sake, he wouldn't draw a gun in the middle of a crowded hotel—logic lost on my body as every muscle goes as rigid as steel cable.

Finally, he pulls out a phone.

I close my eyes and take a very long and quiet exhale. What is my *deal*? I shake it off and turn my attention back to the selfie I took and the drawing.

Since the sketch is in black and white, I can't make out the color of the eyes or the gems in the earrings. The shading makes it seem like the woman has dark hair, like mine, but I can't be positive. Additional texture has been applied to her cheeks, suggesting a natural blush or perhaps a darker complexion, both of which I have.

But besides the earrings, my photo is pouty and sheepish. It's missing the hardness in the sketched woman's eyes. Or is it bitterness? Maybe guilt?

There's an unattractive anger depicted in the drawing, in the rigidness of her face. She looks pissed. Like she's telling everyone to fuck off.

*Is* that me?

Looking in the mirror my entire life, have I only seen what I *want* to see? Have I even spotted *this* angry of a look on myself, the one captured in the sketch? Part of me would like to think it can't possibly be me because of this very aspect. And if it is, well, the Confession Artist is getting it wrong. My face isn't *so* obviously showing what I know has been going on inside me all year. It's not this irritated.

But deep down, I know it is.

It is because hate is similar to fear. You can't control it when it grabs you. It's primal. It can overshadow everything. It can make you complicit in shit you never thought you'd ever partake in. It can make you lie to yourself, fool yourself, keep you from knowing yourself until it's too late.

I go back to my phone.

Two more articles pop up: Next Possible Victim for Confession Artist Killer, with a question for a subtitle: Is everyone in the US who resembles this sketch potential prey?

The other: Who Have You Wronged?

Like it's directed right at me. Shit. Not now. I can't think of it all right now.

I go back to reading.

Variations of CA Has New Target keep flashing on my screen. A notification for a Reddit thread pops up, a question about what the killer is trying to accomplish.

I swipe them all away and google *dangle feather earrings with gems.* Tons of choices pop up from all sorts of stores. Thank God. Many have the gems at the very top instead of in the middle of the feathers, but I'm comforted to know that a lot of feather earrings are being sold and am confident that, with more searching, I can find some more similar to mine.

Then I hop on Twitter-slash-X.

The dumping has already begun, all the hashtagging: #ConfessionArtist, #SketchKiller, #CAConfession, #SKConfession, #PsychoKiller, #JusticeKiller, #FiveDays.

The confessions in response to the initial two sketches never came in because no one took the situation seriously. But after the first two bodies were found, the paranoia kicked up. Way up.

People who thought they looked like the third sketch started tripping all over each other fessing up to anything and everything—and on every corner of social media.

It was a shit show of folks putting it out there that they'd shoplifted when they were desperate or for the thrill, bullied someone in high school, cheated on their taxes, had affairs, lusted after their own siblings . . . I shudder to think of the huge hits marriages are taking from this psycho's cruel game.

Probably many have lost friends and maybe their jobs over some of their admissions, worrying that it wasn't worth the gamble to keep secrets stuffed away if it meant their life might be at stake.

Someone named Maggie Jo, @MaggJoWentworth, last name and all—just posted:

> #CAConfession—When I was married I used to screw this guy and his wife caught us cheating. She was one of my bf's and he was my husband's bf. We blackmailed her into not telling my husband or any of our other friends.

Holy crap. And the replies:

> Yeah, you do look just like the sketch, you're dead.

> You deserve it, Bitch

> Don't think that's what he means by confess. Better start listing actual names if you want to be absolved.

Enough of that. I move on to the next, from Kara, @KaraCrossWhite:

> #CAConfession—I must come clean about a lie I spread as a health insurance exec: I made big $$ to pump idea that Canada's single-payer system meant huge lines and terrible healthcare. I was paid to lie and I did it for a lot of $$.

I don't read the replies but tap on the posters' profile pictures and see they have similar hair and features. But noses are off, foreheads vary, hairdos differ with assorted curls, waves, and parts.

*Madness.* I want to fling my phone across the room. I do not want to be thinking about any of this when my plate is already full with my still relatively new business and looking after Jess.

But there are two people dead. It's unthinkable.

I must admit, a part of me is relieved that others *have* begun sharing their sins because that means many other women out there assume the photo might be of them, confirming what I've told Jess. But none of it makes sense. If this guy knows what people did when they were in eighth grade, why does he need them to confess only now, years later?

And me? *If* this is me? Should I sit tight and gamble that it was some other poor woman? Or should I share the thing I feel most guilty for?

No. Absolutely not. I could never let that one out. I can't do that to Jess. I can't abandon her. Or Sam.

And after the ordeal in my old job, I refuse to feel like a victim ever again.

My short time on the force—four years—was chock-full of complications. At the end of my third year on patrol, when I was preparing to take my exams to become a detective, I worked under a lieutenant named Roger Hartley.

Old school, old mentality, old ways. Cop culture. Cover-your-ass culture. Like DNA passed from adult to offspring. Cops being cops.

It was Roger Hartley who commented on the way I looked, that he preferred my uniform tight or that he'd love to see my long legs in a short skirt or shorts instead of the stock-issued pants. He bugged me to go for drinks: "Hey, gorgeous, when are we gonna grab a beer?"

When I'd say no, he'd ask if I was still planning on shooting for detective and bring up the fact that he was *very* good friends with the captain, and that he *might* just have to inform him that I'm not much of a team player. Of course, he said this with a wink, as though he was only joking around, as if he was evolved enough and woke enough to mock the idea of quid pro quo.

One day, he told me several of the guys were getting together at a nearby pub and that I should stop in, that a few of the female techs would be there, too.

He was there when I arrived.

And very much alone.

He stood and hugged me. I returned it, dropping my arms quickly, but not before catching a whiff of his acrid booze breath. His clothes smelled earthy and sour.

"Where is everyone?" I said, even as I knew I'd been tricked.

He looked at his watch. "They're coming."

There was no need to stare at the door. I knew. And I was not happy.

He downed his vodka and insisted I order a drink. I ordered a glass of ice water and told him that my boyfriend was waiting for me to have dinner, that I couldn't stay long. Hartley ignored this, said to the bartender, "Give her a pint, whatever you have on draft."

"Sam Adams?" the bartender asked.

I nodded.

When Hartley's gaze slid from my mouth to my neck, to the area between the buttons over my chest where the fabric of my blouse slightly gaped, I set my beer down and told him I needed to be on my way. He mocked me, calling me a stick-in-the-mud.

Later, after I endured his attempt at chitchat, he walked me to my car. He was sozzled. I couldn't let him drive drunk, so I asked him how he got to the pub.

"Walked," he said. "I live a few blocks from here." He pointed west. "You could walk me home." He gave me a drunk, lopsided smile that pulled his face into a rough, sloppy sketch drawn on for the evening.

I said no thanks and told him I'd see him at work the next day.

He spread his arms wide—a come-to-papa gesture—and pulled me toward him. I reciprocated stiffly, bending at the hips to give him a rigid, arms-only hug. As I pulled away, he jerked me in tighter and smashed his lips onto mine.

I snapped my head to the side and pushed him away, but not before he dragged his tongue across my cheek, like a wet, squishy slug. His hand grabbed my left breast hard and pinched. He looked calculating, as if his drunkenness had only been an act. As I drove home, I had to grip the steering wheel hard to prevent my hands from shaking.

There was no sense in reporting the grope to Captain Mercer. He and Lieutenant Hartley were tight. I was supposed to be tough, a pro at slapping down boundaries. A *cop*, for God's sake. I'd entered this profession knowing full well it was *Johnny* Law, not Jenny Law. What did I expect?

I had a friend in college who wrote a thesis on workplace harassment, and she told me, after learning that I intended to enter law enforcement after everything happened with Sophie, that the field ranked among the worst when it came to every kind of workplace and sexual harassment.

Plus, I had not been raped. What had happened to Sophie years earlier had been so much worse.

The atmosphere at the station might have been loaded with suppressed aggression, and a few of us women constantly breathed its fumes, but as far as I knew, actual sexual assault was kept in check. They knew better, and I knew the responsibility fell on my shoulders to guard myself.

Even with everything I'd been through with Sophie, I still considered it my fault for saying yes to Hartley and meeting him for drinks in the first place. That's how deeply ingrained this shit can be. And, of course, he was drunk. Everyone liked him. He was fun, he was jolly, and told ribald tales that kept the other officers in stitches.

That night I decided this was something I needed to carry around with me—annoying, bothersome, but not the heaviest of my burdens. I still believed in the system, that this was a glitch—an endless wringing out of an old grease-stained towel that hadn't been tossed away yet, but eventually would be discarded.

Turned out, though, that the next day Hartley informed me there'd been complaints about *me*. My *productivity*.

When I asked who had lodged them and what exactly they were, he wouldn't say, only that I needed to watch my performance.

I continued to stuff it all down, but I was like a pot beginning to simmer. Images of Sophie and me in the cold woods kept resurfacing. I worked twice as hard as other officers, took extra shifts and never slacked, until one day another coworker, a younger female officer named Lilly with even less seniority than me, told me about her very similar experiences with Hartley.

Prodding for drinks. Following her to her car. Insisting on hugs. And she said she was groped, too.

*That* set me in motion. I was legally bound and morally obligated to do something, to get her to the proper channels for filing a complaint. And if she didn't, I would need to report that I'd witnessed a grievance, even if relayed to me in private.

I ended up going higher than the captain, to the colonel, and reporting my experiences, too.

"You're poison now," one of the other officers informed me. I knew he was speaking for many others. "No one's gonna want to partner with you."

Lilly and I were told we had come down with #MeToo fever, even though that trend had already come and gone, at least in our world.

Someone—I never found out who—put a bloated dead mouse in my locker, turning it putrid. I found my car keyed one evening after a shift, walked out to slashed tires a few days later after dinner at a local restaurant with Wallace, and answered a call from an anonymous source threatening to burn my house down.

The backlash made me furious. The counterattack ended up shaking me more than the actual incidents, more even than the feel of Hartley's slobbery tongue on my cheek. To learn that calling out harassment in a job that's *supposed* to be about law, order, and justice would trigger these attempts at retribution? I felt like one of those high-alpine tamaracks, trying to survive on a steep, otherwise bare mountain slope, crushed into splinters by an avalanche.

I also felt a strange guilt. After all, I hadn't endured the kind of violence Sophie had encountered on that camping trip years before. I wasn't dealing with the kind of emotional and physical trauma that Jess went through when she woke in the middle of the night with her jeans pulled down and Mark on top of her, his broad, heavy frame crushing her.

Sadly, the things that happened to me didn't warrant public notoriety and universal scorn. These were muddled, everyday encounters. As much as it sucks to acknowledge it, they were commonplace. But surely they warranted some form of condemnation so they didn't create the kind of entitlement that leads to sexual harassment and rape culture in the first place.

What happened to Jess, though, just one month after all the nasty Hartley entanglements, slithered into my life like a black snake right when she was at the top of her world.

This poisonous thing had staying power. It curled around my torso and squeezed if I went more than a few hours without reminding myself of the world in which I worked. No matter what I do or how I proceed, what happened to Jess with Coleman and what followed with me and Coleman will never stop replaying in my head. But there's no way to go back, to find some wrinkle in time where I can alter anyone's actions, or even alleviate my own *if I'd only*'s.

*Luckily*, I tell myself now, *I'm a trained officer.* If it's me, this guy has picked the wrong woman. But something dark and uncertain has sunk its teeth into me—the same feeling I had when I found out my own sister had been raped ten years after Sophie was also raped.

The same sinking sensation I had when I walked away from being a cop: that I couldn't cut it. The same inadequacy that swept over me after our mom's death my senior year of college, when Jess dropped into a black hole of depression, like Sophie had, and I couldn't pull her out.

Thankfully, with time, Jess snapped out of it. This time, I'm not so sure.

◆ ◆ ◆

"Hey."

I look up, confused. The guy who sat across from me—Climber Guy—has lifted his hand. He's palming his phone with the screen facing me. "You see this?"

What am I supposed to say?

"Shit," he says, still studying me. "That's wild."

"Yeah," I agree. Usually *wild* seems like an overstatement. Not today.

"But"—he gives a one-shoulder shrug—"could be a lot of people."

"*Exssss*ackly," I say.

"You've been worried?"

"Ugh, I mean, getting texts from friends pointing out the resemblance isn't comforting. And you. Seriously, did you just look at the sketch, notice me, and"—I snap my fingers—"bingo?"

"Kinda." He squints, like it hurts him to admit it. "But that doesn't mean anything. I saw you sitting here, and I'm a little bored and looking at the news and, well, you're the only woman in my immediate view. It's not all that surprising that my eye should fall on you."

"Ouch."

"Oh no, I mean, even if you were in a crowd and not off to the side like this, I'd notice you. You'd be hard *not* to notice."

I want to roll my eyes at the cheesiness of the statement, but I can't help but crack a small smile.

"Plus"—he checks the photo on his screen again and glances back at me with his own coy smile—"she kind of looks like that actress who married Ben Affleck. What's her name?"

I shift in my seat. Is he trying to make me feel better, or is he still simply digging out from the only-woman-in-his-immediate-view remark? Whichever, I'll take it.

"Garner," he says. "Jennifer, right?"

I nod enthusiastically. *Yes. Yes.* Someone else, someone everyone can recognize. But it's an odd thought. Even though I don't want this to be me, I don't wish it on others, either.

"Well, good bet she's already ponied up for an extra bodyguard."

I have plenty enough going on without worrying about Jennifer Garner's security arrangements. "You here for CrimeCon?"

"That. And the bar."

"I'm sure there are better bars than in this place."

"I have hopes for this one. I'm a journalist. Doing a piece on how crime media is shifting toward advocacy, CrimeCon being a good place to start. And bars are always great for getting good stories out of people."

If things were normal, I'd want to pick his brain for examples of how the event was promoting such causes. Before Jess quit podcasting, she'd begun urging listeners to donate to a nonprofit demanding timely testing of rape kits by law enforcement and the enactment of more victim-notification laws.

But things haven't been normal all year, and they're as far from ordinary as you can get right this moment. And my right foot must know it since it's madly tapping the floor. I force myself to still it.

I want to discuss the sketch again, wrap my head around it, but chatting about it with a stranger doesn't make sense.

What if *he* is the Confession Artist, for God's sake? He comes off like some mountain-man creative type. With his well-muscled arms, I could see him making custom canoes or specialty furniture or having a studio somewhere in the boonies where he carves wooden sculptures of grizzly bears. Maybe he sketches, too.

He takes a sip of his drink, winces, and puts it down. "It's a little early for drinking, isn't it? But damn, these mega hotels. It's like being in an airport. You can grab one any time of the day."

"True." I stand up. "It was nice chatting with you."

"You too." He looks at me awkwardly, like he wants to add something, maybe a condolence, like *Try not to worry.*

But I walk away before he gets anything else out and call Jess to tell her I'll meet her back at the room instead.

The truth is, I have no idea whether to give the sketch another minute of thought. But I also know there's no switch I can flip to make the dark thoughts go away.

# Chapter 9

"So," I say to Jess, "you think that *if* this is me, the artist used a photo of me, or knows me personally?"

We're sitting on her hotel bed, studying the sketch together on her laptop. She's freshly showered and ready for bed in a sleep shirt and pajama bottoms.

I'm acting nonchalant and sleepy, like my ol' buddy anger isn't visiting me when I think of how this strange sketch weirdness cropped up precisely one year after the rape. I fake a yawn, but I'm not tired.

I'm wired. Even after getting up at three thirty this morning to catch the red-eye.

She tells me the artist understands the fundamentals of portraiture, especially the basics of facial proportions. "Good sketches aren't about looking at photos and copying them. They demonstrate your talent at observation mixed with adding your own style."

*That doesn't narrow the field much,* I think. So many people sketch or paint for a hobby.

"For example," she continues, "if someone has more of an anime style, they'll exaggerate some features but blend those with realistic traits to get the full effect through tone and texture."

Her tone is direct, her professional side kicking in. I love it.

"This isn't that. This is more realistic, nothing is exaggerated like with anime, and it's not cartoonish. The edges are sharp. It leans toward precision, which worries me even more. Cros?" Her voice rises in pitch.

"What?"

"It's not just the earrings." She shakes her head.

"The *what*?" I say.

"The jaw. I don't know. It's the tension in it."

Brownie points for the artist capturing *that*. How is it that my jawbone is capable of revealing so much?

"Jess." I need to switch gears. "It's going to be okay. Whatever this craziness is, I—we—will figure it out, okay? Like we always do."

She bites her lower lip. "But what is this? Why now? After everything I've . . . we've—"

"Everything is going to be fine." I put my arm around her. Her T-shirt is damp from her hair and her shoulders are bony spikes.

I have this image of her and me treating hotel beds like our own private trampolines when we were young and took trips with our mom and our stepdad back to DC, where Les arranged a tour of the Capitol building.

And Cleveland, where we visited Les's brother and toured the Rock & Roll Hall of Fame. Later, when Mom got bumped to part-time status at the hospital and Les's auto shop wasn't doing as well, we'd crowd into Mom's Honda and head to places closer: Wyoming, Idaho, Utah. If the hotel was cheap enough, Les and Mom would get their own room. Of course, this put Les in a much better mood and gave Jess and me an adjoining room with each of us having a queen. We'd hop back and forth between the two of them until Les scolded us for creating a ruckus.

Now, seeing how frail Jess is, it seems impossible to me that we've gone from those giggling girls to grown women inhabiting a world where phrases like *date rape*, *sexual assault*, and *consent* are not only common, but seemingly inescapable.

"Believe me," I say. "This is just some strange game. I promise you."

She isn't convinced. "If it *is* you, what are we going to do?"

The question hangs in the room for a moment. "I told you," I say. "I'll figure it out."

"Do you think this has anything to do with your latest case, that guy Ridgeway?"

*Robbie Ridgeway.*

Just thinking about him takes me back to my visit to him east of the mountains two weeks ago. About his own sketches on his wall, about how I slashed his tire, something I'm not proud of. It makes me wonder, could he—*is* he—finding a very creative way to get back at me?

# A CONFESSION

X: @EricLFiero #SKConfession—I realize how prejudiced I was about some people and have been feeling bad about one incident for some time. I was working my EMT shift in Huntington, WV back in 2019 and called to an address in West Huntington on Jefferson. When I arrived, the guy struggled to talk. I assumed he had taken too many opioids, like so many from that part of town.

After we got him in the ambulance, my partner and I took our time. We even chatted with a neighbor before we left. He ended up dying. Turns out he'd had a stroke. Time was of the essence, but we thought he was another loser and took our sweet time. We could have saved him. I'm sorry our prejudicial assumptions got this guy killed. I really am.

# Chapter 10

***Four Days***

Initial descent bells chime, signaling that we're over the north end of Flathead Lake.

The flight from Denver to Kalispell seems fast. Too fast. I want the trip to be longer so I can stay cocooned in the airplane, tucked safely away from the real world, which is ironic considering my cocoon is an object skimming over the steep ranges of the Northern Rockies.

I look at Jess. She works on her laptop beside me. I've refused to connect to the airline's free Wi-Fi. I can't concentrate anyway.

The flight attendant performs her walk-by to pick up leftover trash from the beverage service. I smile as I hand her my empty cup, and I'm glad there's no double take. *Maybe I am not the person,* I think for the umpteenth time since yesterday. And no one really noticed me in Denver on our brief layover, although Jess and I were rushing to grab a coffee. Plus, people in airports are intent on making their own connections. The plane lurches over a mountain updraft. My stomach flutters like a leaf in a breeze. I feel defenseless.

And unsure.

It pays to be on the safe side, though, so I make a to-do list in my mind for when I get home: Hit the shooting range to freshen up my skills since I might need to up my game in the self-protection department. Buy some kind of surveillance system for my home.

If I am the target, the killer doesn't know I've even been away. If it is Ridgeway and his minions, as Jess asked about last night, perhaps they have no idea I've left the state.

At the same time, it would be easy to wonder if I was planning to go since I've been reposting Jess's links about talking at the conference all along. And the killer—or killers—is clearly tech-savvy. Otherwise, they'd be tracked down and caught by now.

Past the lake, the Flathead Valley spreads out below us, hemmed in by the mountain ranges to the east and north while the Flathead River cuts sharp turns through farmed fields of rapeseed, wheat, and potatoes.

I close the air vent above me, hug my leather jacket tightly around me, and peer out the thick, oval window at the densely treed Mission Mountains rising to their rocky peaks. Sublime, yet stark and desolate in their vastness. *Sophie,* I think. She so innocently wanted to be part of the big unconquerable wilderness in the beginning.

I love the area, too. It's the reason I choose to live in Whitefish even though I'm only in my late twenties and might enjoy living somewhere more urban. In a way, my fixation with staying in the state is an attempt to maintain some semblance of closeness to my dad.

He was from a small town near the Canadian border called Fortine. We lived in that town when we were little. But then Dad went to Iraq, and when he returned, Mom said he wasn't the same. He yelled at her, at us, all the time, and so she took us to her parents in Kalispell, sixty miles south, when we were small. That's where she met Les.

For three consecutive years, Mom would drive Jess and me to our dad's each summer and we'd have two months in Fortine with him. He taught me how to shoot, how to hunt birds and deer. He showed me which wildflowers, like Indian paintbrush, were safe to eat, and how to find morels and huckleberries. But he went back for a second tour. After he returned, Mom said it wasn't a good idea for us to visit him anymore.

When we did get to see him for short stints, he was grumpy—often depressed. His anger triggered easily. But still, he was our father, and I loved him.

Montana too. I felt like each area of the state might unfurl its spaces for me alone, one cluster of cedars, one patch of huckleberry bushes, one chain of glacier-tinged lakes at a time. When I was in seventh grade and Jess in fourth, our dad passed away. He died of lung cancer in his early forties even though he never smoked. Talk of things I didn't understand, like burn pits and depleted uranium, saturated our lives. Things that sounded faraway and ugly.

Montana offered beauty. I knew he took solace in it, so I clung to the place even more after he passed. When it was time to apply for colleges, I set my sights on the University of Montana in Missoula because I had no intention of leaving Big Sky country, of leaving the one place I had memories of my dad.

And that's when I met Sophie and things went from semisimple to complex.

My face must show my worry, or sadness, because Jess turns to me. "Are you okay?"

"I'm fine," I say. I want to tell her more. That I'm not fine. That I feel so guilty I can barely stand myself. I want to tell her I was thinking of Dad and his PTSD and how that affected both of us. I want to tell her that I miss him. And Mom. That I miss Sophie, still, after all these years. And mostly, that I'm *very* worried about her and Sam. But I can't. Because if I do, I'll make her fragile state even worse.

A bumpy landing jars me back to the present insanity. Notifications train-wreck onto my screen when I switch my phone off airplane mode. More articles about what kind of person could do this and more confessions—some so juicy they draw national attention. There's a piece about Jennifer Garner refusing to confess anything, saying that she has nothing weighing on her conscience.

*How special.*

There's a woman in Portland, Oregon. She looks like the sketch, but her chin is pointier than mine. She's already gone public to reveal she cheated on her husband when they were on a sailing trip around the world. At port in Aruba, he wasn't feeling well. While he stayed in the cabin sleeping off a fever, she met a stranger and followed him to his house. Back home, she terminated a pregnancy she kept from her husband.

Another confession involves a female schoolteacher from a small town in Indiana who got a student drunk at a party and seduced him. The boy later dropped out of school and got heavily into drugs. She's now confessing that what she did was wrong and inappropriate and that she thinks she might have ruined the student's life.

I take in a deep breath that hitches with something shaky. With fear. Jess catches it again.

"What's wrong?"

"Nothing," I say. I have to get back to my acting, to hiding whatever crazy shit I'm feeling much better than I am. I can't keep worrying her, having her check in on me. She doesn't need that right now.

I deboard the plane with a sour sting in my stomach.

At baggage claim, Jess heads to the restroom while I stand beside lifeless conveyor belts, staring at real estate come-ons for multimillion-dollar estates in the mountains and on the shores of shimmering lakes. Big as it is, Montana—or certain parts of it—is in the process of being overrun.

I rub my gritty eyes and curse myself for allowing Jess to talk me into checking our bags when the attendant announced that the plane would be too full to accommodate everyone's carry-ons.

Wallace insisted on fetching us, something I cringed at agreeing to because, again, I should be drawing better boundaries with him. But I don't need the cost of an Uber right now.

I've just texted him to let him know we'll be out soon when someone behind me says, "Well, hey, it's you."

I whip around to see a tall bearded man standing much too close. I must appear confused because he says, "From the hotel bar?"

When I take a step back, my calf hits the side of the conveyor. I teeter on the brink of pitching backward.

He grabs my arm to stop my fall. "Sorry," he says. "Didn't mean to startle—"

My rusty cop training rocks me free of his attempted grasp. I take a ready stance, feet shoulder-width apart. My hand has even gone to my waist for the ghost of my utility belt, a reflex from a different chapter of my life.

"You were on my flight?" I say, a cold dread settling in my belly.

"News to me, too."

*What are the chances?*

"This must be"—he clears his throat into his fist—"a little weird for you, with what's going on. Truly, I'm sorry for that."

"You live—where?" I say.

"I write for *Rolling Stone*. We're doing a piece on Glacier Park and climate change. You know, shrinking glaciers, less snow, less water, threatened species, bark beetle infestations, megafires . . ."

"So not, what did you call it? Crime advocacy." My tone is accusatory.

He offers a sheepish, closed-lip smile.

"Usually, another writer has the nature beat, but he broke his femur. I was next in line, and it's not like I haven't covered nature before. I've published in *Outside Magazine* and *Nat Geo*. Wolverines in Glacier and on the GNP's designation as the first transboundary Dark Sky Park in the world. Plus, I have work on the reservations up here that relates to crime advocacy."

He sounds legit, but this so-called coincidence has me on very high alert. I'll check online to see if his writing credits are real. I'm still trying to get my heart to slow back down and can't think of how to respond.

"What brings you here?" he asks.

"Sorry, what's your name?"

"Jeremy Fisher." He tilts his head, examining me. "You okay?"

I've gone pale. I can feel it. And I hate that I might appear vulnerable. "I'm good."

"Again, I'm sorry."

"It's okay."

"Look, I'd love to get your name and number to interview you about what it feels like to, you know"—he runs a hand through his longish, wavy hair—"to resemble . . ."

He doesn't finish, like he doesn't want to offend me.

"One of the drawings?" I ask.

A half grin says he knows the request is sleazy.

I shake my head. "Not happening."

"No?"

His eyes are soft brown. Not teasing. "If I was in your shoes, I wouldn't give out my name, either."

Luckily, Jeremy Fisher's bag is one of the first two down the chute. It's black, rounded, and converts to a backpack. As he pulls it from the conveyor belt, I notice the tag. No name, just a telephone number.

*New York City,* I note. I repeat the number in my head to memorize it, but he makes a mockery of my efforts by fishing a card from his wallet.

Printed on cheap cardboard stock, no logos, no company name, just his name, title, phone number, and email address.

"If you change your mind," he says. "I'd love to do a piece, or at least talk to you about it. And maybe you'd kill two birds with one stone."

"How so?"

"If I run an article on you, you could confess in it, too."

My jaw drops. The balls on the guy.

"I wish you luck," he says, giving me one last bob of his head before he casually throws his big pack over his shoulder like it weighs nothing and walks away.

◆ ◆ ◆

Confess?

My stuff?

Absolutely not. I refuse to drag it out into the daylight.

That cannot happen.

And really, would those confessions be the types of things that would inspire vigilante action anyway?

There's the obvious guilt for convincing Sophie to come camping, but that's nebulous. And ridiculous. Wallace has never once insinuated he blames me for what happened to his sister. Their mom and dad were in shock, but they also never suggested I coerced her into the trip or anything along those lines.

And it was eleven years ago.

But the Coleman thing, that was only nine months ago. But I'm certain no one knows about it except one other person, and I am positive he wouldn't say a thing. Neither of us would squawk. It would be mutually assured destruction.

But the thought of confessing feels like a punch to my already aching gut and makes my cheeks heat up. Not just with shame but fear, too. Fear of the consequences. I could lose everything, wreck my reputation forever, lose what little career I've scraped back together, even go to jail.

I literally shudder at the thought of it all. The sourness in my stomach expands, intensifies.

I consider other smaller things, maybe because they're less painful to think about, like the petty revenge stuff and the people I've pissed off.

Just the other day, in line at the grocery store while I was buying dinner, some guy tried to butt ahead of me because he was in a hurry. It outraged me so much that I faced him down and invited everyone behind him to go ahead of me while he seethed. I knew he wanted to bite my head off, but I didn't care. Later, when I thought about it, I felt bad I'd been such a jerk.

I'm not sure how this minor habit of taking revenge on people started. I call it little punctures in the great big tire of injustice. I could blame it on the stress of being a cop, and now a PI, but it really began after Jess descended into depression the first time after Mom died during my senior year of college, two and a half years after Sophie. Jess was a freshman at the local community college in Kalispell. She had pulled out of her classes and stayed home with our stepdad, Les, staying in her childhood room and sleeping all the time.

At first, I drove the two and a half hours up from Missoula to see her every weekend. I didn't have a class on Fridays, so I'd leave right after my last course on Thursday and spend four nights with her every weekend, returning early on Mondays before my first class. It wasn't easy, especially with my senior-year course load and an internship I had with the university's office of public safety, but I couldn't stand the thought of Jess spiraling into depression like Sophie had after the rape. I couldn't even think about what I would do if I somehow lost Jess, too. Other than Les, who I wasn't all that close to, there was no one left. We were essentially orphans.

So after a month of driving back and forth, I finally decided to take the semester off and move home to take care of her. I could push out graduation to the following year, stay an extra semester the following fall.

But at home with her, I had still felt useless, like there was nothing I could do to pull her out of it.

And one time on my way back to Missoula during that month before I pulled out of my classes and my internship, I stopped at a convenience store to get some gas and grab some snacks. I watched a very impatient woman giving a young Native girl a hard time for taking too long to fill her tank. She had yelled at her, called her *squaw bitch*. Told her to grab her papoose and get moving.

I got out, went over to the woman in the car, and tapped on her window. When she looked at me, I told her to quit being such an asshole.

Of course, she didn't like that much, so she began telling me to mind my own fucking business. Called me a bitch, too.

I walked away, finished filling my tank, but when I saw her park after she filled up and went inside, I dumped my sticky cola across the back of her windshield.

And there was another time, a year or so into my time on the force, when I was renting a little house in Kalispell. I threw away my neighbor's mail because I didn't like how he kept his dog chained up all day with no walks, even when it got bitterly cold and he stayed out late in the bars.

I'd already called animal control on him, but they said the dog was being fed and watered, and there was little they could do.

I decided tossing his mail wasn't enough, so I fished it back out of the garbage, walked over to his house, and rang the doorbell. When he answered, eyes widening a little to find a cop on his doorstep, I handed him a few envelopes covered with egg-white drippings and grease stains and told him that if he didn't take better care of his dog, I'd make sure he'd never leave a bar again without me or another cop watching his every move.

My threat made no impact, so one evening, I waited outside the bar he frequented, and at closing, I tailed him, pulled him over, humiliated him with a Breathalyzer and a roadside sobriety test. I told him this was his second warning. That three was not going to be a charm. After that, I saw him taking his dog for walks with at least some regularity. Nobody wants to have to ride his bike around in the winter.

And all the other little things in my life, like the time I didn't correct the automated teller at the grocery store when I accidentally punched in two nectarines instead of three, or the time I sneaked into a movie theater without paying when I was a teenager . . . *Ridiculous* stuff.

So, I have to face it. *If* it's my face in the sketch making the national rounds, it's all about the big one.

*The* thing I've been trying not to think about, the one I constantly shove back into a dark closet: the incident with Coleman.

Someone grabs my arm. I startle again, as if I'm the most easily spooked person on the planet.

Am I?

It's Jess. "Jesus," I say. "Don't sneak up on me like that."

"I didn't."

"There's your bag."

She grabs her suitcase, and we step out into the eighty-degree weather. I take a deep breath of fresh air and look to the northeast to see the gateway to Glacier gleaming under the azure sky, two ranges bowing to each other, beckoning more and more tourists every year.

And is it possible . . . a cold-blooded killer?

# Chapter 11

We find Wallace outside. I give him a quick hug, and he holds it longer than I want. I pull away and notice he isn't wearing his usual boyish grin. His face looks pinched with worry.

It's the sketch.

"Smile," I say. It's a command I detest others giving me.

Wallace shows me his neat line of white teeth, and hugs Jess the way you're supposed to hug a friend, grabs her bag, and throws it in the Jeep.

He pushes his sunglasses up into his wavy blond hair and fastens his startling eyes—the blue practically matching the summer sky—on mine, clearly winding up for a heart-to-heart.

I give him a slight headshake that says, *Don't. Don't haul your worry out in front of Jess. Let's not talk about it now.* "I'm hungry," I say even though I have zero appetite.

To his credit, Wallace shifts gears. Suggests getting breakfast, asks about the flight, accepts my blah answer with an amiable nod. I remove my jacket in the perfect weather and toss it and my carry-on onto the back seat.

When Wallace pulls onto the highway after we drop Jess off, he heads south instead of north, where both of us live—me halfway between the small towns of Columbia Falls and Whitefish, and Wallace right in Whitefish.

"We're going to Kalispell?" I ask. It's only about fifteen miles away, but why?

"Yep."

"Where?"

"You want breakfast, right? Whitefish will be crawling with tourists."

"'Kay," I say, but I have a funny feeling. "What about C-Falls?"

*Around the same distance . . .*

"Well, this way . . . we can stop at the police station, too."

"No!" I smack the dashboard to underscore my reaction. "Not your choice."

"You don't think it's you?"

"No."

"But you can't be sure."

"This is my decision, *my* choice."

"And what have you got against playing it safe?"

"Have you forgotten I used to work there? I know what they're going to do. Not much. Not anything. There's no protection they're going to offer me that I can't provide for myself. No one there wants to get within talking distance of me. They'd throw me to the wolves if they could find a pack."

"I realize that, but still. It's good to get it on record, right?"

I don't answer.

"Look, Cros, Kerry finally called me back."

"And?"

"He said he supplied those same earrings to several gift shops around Montana."

"And did Walmart carry them?"

"No, you *know* they didn't."

I did know. It was wishful thinking. "How many did he make?"

"He said he sells about one hundred seventy-five to two hundred pairs a year, and he's been supplying them to the gift shops since they got popular about five years ago. He says they've become trendy because of the Montana sapphire. Everyone loves 'em."

"A thousand or so. That's something," I say. "And since so many visitors come through Montana in the summer, that really opens up the playing field."

Possibly, but not entirely. We both know it.

"You were a cop, Cros. So you know it's got to be good to get it on the record, just in case."

I think of *Rolling Stone* Jeremy What's His Face and how he quickly shifted from claiming to write about climate change to writing about my goofs and screwups. My misjudgments. My blooper reel. *Blooper* sounds too light, too inconsequential. It should be *fuck-up reel.*

And I still can't get over the coincidence of seeing him in the hotel bar and being on the same flight to Montana.

"If not for your sake, then do it for Jess," says Wallace.

He lets it hang. I feel the full weight of it. The implication is clear. *You didn't do enough then, so do something now.*

"Am I right?" he adds.

I think of Jess, with her insomnia and her nightmares when she sleeps. Of how, ever since the rape, she flinches if someone surprises her in the least. She's like a soldier returning from war.

I think of what happened to me at the Kalispell PD, how it doesn't begin to compare with the assaults on Sophie and Jess, but how it nonetheless made me feel powerless and inept. There's something inside me like a steady, slow bleed. Time has not done its thing. For as much as I carry it around, it could have happened earlier that day.

"Okay," I say. "I won't say you're right, but . . ."

"But?"

"Let's go to the station. I'll get it on the record."

# Chapter 12

"Crosbie," Allison Higgins, the assistant behind the glass, says. "How the heck are you? Or should I call you *Private* Detective Mitchell?"

Every inch of the place is etched in my memory.

The interrogation rooms, the metal desks, the small municipal court, the judge's chambers, the break room.

I can still hear the radios crackling and the telephones ringing, smell the cheap, bitter coffee, and see the detectives busy with paperwork.

Seeing Allison is awkward. When I worked here, we became pretty good friends, but after I left, our friendship fell by the wayside. It wasn't a good feeling. Don't friends keep up after a job change?

Allison was raised in Casper, Wyoming. She had several rough-and-tumble brothers and is used to cowboy humor. She also had a sister who had a neurodegenerative disease that made her incapable of caring for her own child. Before she was incapable of doing so, Allison's sister took her life. As a result, Allison raised her sister's son. The father was uninvolved and a drunk. I'd thought of how much I'd hate to lose Jess that way.

But when I was on the job, we were an exasperated team of two women at the bro-heavy station. Allison winced along with me at their locker room stunts and of course talked in colorful detail about all this ad nauseam throughout the workday. I'd happily answer Allison's eye roll at the juvenile jokes and puerile antics, but it was more than enduring the pranks and tomfoolery. It was the not-so-subtle club mentality. *Dudes here, ladies there.* Allison and I knew we weren't invited. It was an invisible wall of sexism. And the more you said anything, the worse it got. Nothing prosecutable. Nothing specific. All their violations landed in a gray zone, but the slights and insults were piled higher than my head.

"I'm good, Allison. And you're right, it's Private Detective Mitchell." I wink.

Allison grins back, and I realize how much I miss her, how she'd smirk and hide her laugh when we'd talk trash about the guys, especially Hartley. Our connection also involved running together, working out, and occasionally grabbing lunch.

Now, if I were still seeing the therapist I saw back in college, she'd have a field day. More isolation, she would point out. *When did this loner streak rear its head again?* she'd ask.

I knew it was me who could find any reason at the drop of a hat to retreat from friendships, and that I should resist it. And I did. For years now, I've stayed relatively in touch with the gang, even after Hannah, John, and Maggie all moved east. And Fiona, even when I wasn't sure I liked how superficial she could be.

But after Coleman, I haven't spoken at length to any of them, including Allison, in months and months. Allison and Jess even get together sometimes, but without me. They met through me when I was on the force still, and sometimes I'd invite Jess along to join us for coffee or lunch if Sam was with his dad or at school, but the two became closer after I left the department. After I isolated myself from everyone but Jess.

Allison's blond hair has gone grayer at the roots, but some of the strands refuse to cooperate with the others and pop straight up from her part.

I tell her I want to file a report: that the latest sketch looks a lot like me.

"Sketch?" she says. Then it hits her. "Oh!"

Wallace cuts in, "Not just a lot. More like *precisely*."

Allison studies me like an art critic. She fiddles with her phone and gasps. "Oh my God, Mitchell. It *does.*"

She pages someone in the back, probably Ross.

I go at the loose skin on the outside of my thumb again. "Who's on today?"

"Ewing and Stoddard," she says. "But I think Stoddard stepped out." She shakes her head like she's trying to process my dilemma. Like I'm a dead woman walking. "What do you think it all means? What will you do?"

"Not sure," I say, disappointed that Stoddard isn't in. That leaves Detective Mitch Ewing, a stalky, balding man who is good friends with Lieutenant Hartley and spearheaded the move for all the officers and techs to wear black armbands at work to show solidarity—as if that were needed—when word got around that we'd reported the harassment.

Sergeant Ross swings the door open and sees me. "Mitchell!" He flashes a big smile. He's put on some weight, his midriff expanded like risen dough.

I don't mind Ross. He has empathy. But too much compassion in a place like this is not ideal, and I often wondered how long he'd stick around. I'm glad to see he's still here.

Allison holds up her smartphone.

He squints at the sketch, then stares at me for a second, his head tilted. "Wow, I do see it," he says. "You know, I kind of *did* think it when I saw it yesterday, but I guess I figured there was no way it would be anyone from around here. But yeah, with your hair down and all."

I think of my old uniform, how relieved I was to not have to decide what to wear to work and how to style my hair each day. As an officer, I could be undeviating and practical with a tight ponytail. Since I left, though, I've found joy in changing it up, reinventing myself in minor ways with new clothes and trying different things with my hair. This morning in Dallas, I threw on high-waisted jeans with a tucked-in white T-shirt, my red leather jacket, and some high-heeled booties. But now, in this place, I feel self-conscious wearing only a T-shirt and jeans—teen-like, not someone to take seriously. I wish I'd kept my jacket on despite the heat.

"Come on in," Ross says. "Mitch can chat with you." He points to Detective Ewing's office.

Like a factory-second jack-in-the-box, Ewing pops up from behind his desk as we round the corner.

"Mitchell," he says. Mock smile. He oozes smug arrogance. "How've you been?"

"Good."

Delivered without an ounce of feeling.

"Heard you've hung a shingle. How's that workin' for ya?"

"Fine." I don't offer more. It's his way of reminding me that I scurried away under the pressure, that I'm no longer a cop. I don't want small talk. We're here for one purpose: to get this on the books in case this thing turns out to be more than some particularly twisted nightmare. I take solace in my chunky heels because they make me taller than him. I resurrect my old station stance. Shoulders back, spine straight.

Ewing points to the two visitor seats, sits down, and rests an elbow on his desk. "Sooo," he says, drawing it out, his mouth in an O shape.

"The sketch," Wallace blurts out. "Have you seen it?"

"The sketch? Oh, *the* sketch. The famous sketch. Yes, yes, I have." Ewing types on his keyboard, studies his screen.

"Look," I say. "You know I'd never step foot in here and create a hassle for anyone over something as loony as this." I pinch my earlobe. I feel the stud I'm wearing press into my finger. I don't want to tell him about the earrings right away. The earrings would make it too concrete, too real. "It's just, it's that—"

"It does look like you."

*"See?"* says Wallace for an audience of one. Me.

"But that doesn't mean it *is* me."

"No, you're absolutely right." Ewing points his pen at me. "It doesn't. We've already received other calls. Hell, every station in America has the phones ringing off the hook. It was the same the last time. And let's face it, it looks like Jennifer Garner, too, and God knows who else."

"Exactly." Listen to me, agreeing with Ewing.

"Tell him." Wallace turns to me. "Tell him about the earrings."

I give Wallace an *enough already* look.

"Earrings?" says Ewing.

"The earrings in the sketch," I say. "They're like a pair I have. They're made locally by a friend of Wallace's." I explain about the feathers. "There are probably about a thousand of them out on the market."

"Like, local market?"

"Montana local, and in very touristy places with tons of traffic," I say.

"Well, mostly," Wallace says. "But I think he's even sold some of them on Amazon and Etsy at one point."

I glance at Wallace, surprised he didn't mention that part earlier to me, but I don't want Ewing to think I've walked in here without all the details.

Ewing purses his lips and thinks for a moment. "What's the jeweler's name?" he asks.

"Bennetts," Wallace says. "Kerry Bennetts."

Ewing writes it down.

"Have you worn those earrings in photos that are public, on Facebook and such?"

"No, that's the thing. I searched my phone last night in my hotel room in Dallas and I couldn't find any photos of me wearing them. I don't think he got them from a photo that's been posted anywhere, but I don't remember when I wore them last."

"You were in Dallas last night?"

"Yes." God, why did I bring that up? I have no intention of telling him I was at CrimeCon. He and the fellas would love that, me hanging out with a bunch of crime junkies and amateur sleuths. That would be joke fodder for weeks.

"For fun?"

*None of your business.* "Does it mean anything?" I redirect him. I wonder if he has details the public doesn't know. And I've always wondered if he knows *the* thing. The big thing, if Billy Railes told anyone about how I played good soldier. Ewing is the kind of cop who would shake down Railes for the unofficial version of events, so it's possible Ewing is seeing me in a different light—ironically, a better one. Possible, but I'm not counting on it.

"Just getting the specifics. You know how it works. Or maybe you've forgotten?" A dead stare, a pointed accusation.

I ignore it. I tell him I wasn't wearing the earrings in Dallas.

"Do you have them?"

"Yes. I mean, no, not with me. I haven't been home yet. I'll check when I get there."

"Okay, let me know." He leans back in his chair and sighs, as if to say, *What the hell do you want me to do?*

I give a slow blink as if I can wipe it all away. My mom always said this tic ran in the family, that our grandmother on her side used to do it, too. That Jess and I both do it when we want to clean something out of our minds. If that's true, it's a heavy dose of annoyance I want to flush.

"Ewing," I say. "I know you're not going to order up a protective detail for me. I can take care of myself. We're just here to give you the information, to get it in a report. If something does happen to me, which I doubt it will, you'll at least have some info."

He nods in slow motion, studying me as if he thinks I might be setting a trap. God, this guy. Sitting in his office makes me realize how I've come to relish my autonomy as a PI and how much I value not being scrutinized and told what to do, even if I am worried about my ever-increasing debt.

"Okay, great," he finally says. "Thanks for that." He tosses his pen onto his desk to signal that we're done. "I'll file the report and notify the FBI, although they're swamped with these. You know that, right, Mitchell?"

"I know."

I stand. Wallace does not.

"Wait," says Wallace. "Is that it? I mean, isn't there some kind of protocol to set up? Shouldn't you give her some guidance? Direction? Should she confess something like they're demanding?"

I clench my teeth. I'd squeeze my eyes shut like a child, too, to try to make it all go away if I could, if I knew I wouldn't look like a complete fool in front of Ewing and Wallace.

"I don't know." Ewing stands, too. Gives me a quizzical look. "Should you?"

"No." I stare back. "Should *you*?"

An actual childish reply, but I couldn't help it.

"Not me in that sketch." His eyes lock on mine.

"What is the FBI advising?" Wallace says.

"Wallace," I say, making it clear in my tone that I want him to zip it. "I can answer that. Nothing. They're not advising anything. Right, Ewing?"

Ewing's eyes stay on mine, half lidded, as if opening them all the way would show me too much respect. Why couldn't it have been him in the sketch?

"Is there anything they've shared with you at all?" And here I am, talking to him again. Forcing a polite tone. "Something I should be aware of? Like, what this guy might look like? What he drives? What part of the country he might live in? Have they located an IP address?"

I need to chill. The station has gotten under my skin. So has Ewing's cocky stare. He's savoring the fact that I'm no longer a cop, that I couldn't hack it, that I won't have the decency to take this opportunity to confess to the world that I was wrong to report Hartley.

That I overreacted.

"They don't have much," is what he says. "If they do, they haven't shared anything on the network. There are no descriptions. At this point, if someone ends up dead, the local department with jurisdiction investigates as usual and shares what they find with the FBI. And it's not a two-way street. But if anything comes up, we'll be in touch. And if you change your mind, you know, about anything?"

I say nothing.

Ewing is already sitting back down, but his glare stays on me.

"Thanks," I bite off and grab Wallace's arm, past ready to be out of this place.

# Chapter 13

## Randal

Randal Askens sat in traffic on the main drag and waited for a group of smiling, excited Chamber folks to move boxes of Christmas decorations across the street so they could decorate the town.

In a few weeks, they'd have the annual tree-lighting ceremonies, transforming the tall pines to bright greens, blues, and golds.

Randal picked up his phone off the passenger seat when the screen lit up. *Damn phone,* he thought. Even though he had the ringer turned on, it never made a sound, so he ended up missing calls.

He listened to the voicemail, waiting for the last pedestrian to carry her box across the intersection. The message was from Principal Hopkins, asking him to come in for another meeting. Coach Lawry would be there, too.

God, he was so damn tired of it. It was the *Seattle Times* article, of course. The third one. It came out in the local paper yesterday, once again accusing him and the head coach of all sorts of inaccurate bullshit.

For God's sake, he couldn't help it that Coach Lawry wanted to help those kids, that he took it upon himself to open his pocketbook to help the students with travel, food, and rent. Sometimes you need to take matters into your own hands.

How were they supposed to remember every rule in the hiring handbook? How was he supposed to know that assisting low-income Black kids from Mississippi could be a violation of the Interscholastic Activities Association's recruiting guidelines?

And to paint the whole thing as *illegal*? That was downright bogus. A stretch so huge, it was criminal itself.

In fact, he was going to march right in there and take charge. No more meek, jump-through-the-hoops Randal. No more yes-sir Randal. He was sick of it all.

It had been giving him bad dreams lately. He had this recurring one where he was hunting out in the woods and kept seeing a buck he'd like to shoot, but odd shit that didn't belong in the forest kept getting in the way: couches, chaise lounges, desks, weight machines—all this crap that kept him from taking a clear shot, from even being able to move freely at all.

That was his life in a nutshell lately. Cluttered with a capital *C*. He ran his hand through his thick hair, noting that he needed a trim before the holiday party next week, and thought of the previous day's article again.

It wasn't helping in the decluttering department. The piece made all sorts of accusations, that he and Lawry had brought these boys up only to win the championship, and later stranded them without return tickets home, without assistance in helping them get scholarships into colleges as initially promised, without even help in making sure they were fed properly or could pay their rent.

He was going to blow in there and tell Hopkins that enough was enough. That both Coach Lawry and he consistently modeled respect and brotherhood. That they valued family and team cohesion. That the championships they'd won for the school didn't magically happen. They were direct by-products of the community and dedication they created.

To suggest otherwise was sheer crazy political correctness. He was going to demand that the school sue the *Times* for misrepresenting the facts.

Okay, sure, he'd admit he was a little surprised at how Lawry stranded the athletes he brought in once the season was over, not even getting them a ticket to return home. He'd leave them a little destitute and sometimes homeless, but at least they had the experience of coming to the Northwest, seeing and experiencing something different from the South and receiving the confidence that came with helping pull a team to the championships.

He steamed into the office, ready to set Hopkins straight. He smiled at Becca, who looked sad and depressed, so he wished her a merry Christmas and told her to smile.

She didn't. In fact, she looked like she wanted to tell him to go eff himself, but instead pointed him to the principal's office. She was probably still mad that he never called after their last hookup.

He silently slid past her desk into Hopkins's office. "Look, Mr. Hopkins," he started, "how many times do we have to go over this? We as a school need to issue a reply to that article in the paper, something that counters—"

"Coach Askens. Please sit. This isn't about that. It's about that incident at the team retreat."

"Shit. That again." Randal removed his hat and ran his fingers through his hair.

"Yes." Hopkins glared at him. "That again. It's about Ryan Petronis. You haven't heard?"

"No, what about him? Don't tell me they're suing the school now. I thought we had control over that, that they understood it was horseplay. Roughhousing."

"We've just gotten word." He laced his fingers together and looked down at them when he said it: "Ryan shot himself this morning."

"What?"

"At home, in his room."

Randal sat. He felt bad. Hell, he'd *liked* Ryan, but how was this *his* thing? Was this going to be Lawry's and his fault, too?

Bullshit. Just because he was in the next room, in the kitchen in the main cabin, and heard scuffling sounds didn't mean he should have interfered. He couldn't micromanage everything their boys did. He needed to allow them to have some fun, build up a little camaraderie. That was the entire point of the team-building retreat.

"I wanted you and Coach Lawry to know before word spreads."

He swallowed and nodded, kept bobbing his head up and down, trying to process it. *Jesus, Petronis. Was it that bad? Was it worth taking your life?* For God's sake, hazing was a ritual that'd been going on for hundreds of years. Thousands, probably!

Hopkins drilled his eyes deep into Randal's. "I expect you and Lawry to handle this with your boys as delicately as possible. Tell them no social media posts, no commentary, no gossip. Tell them to respect Ryan's family. Lawry's teaching a weight training class right now, but when he finishes, I want the three of us to meet to discuss strategy at one thirty. That work for you?"

He nodded. Yes-sir Randal was back. "Yes. Yes, sir, it does."

# Chapter 14

The stop at my old police HQ was less than reassuring. The looks I got around town are gnawing on my nerves. Breakfast didn't happen, but lunch did, and at a sandwich shop with Wallace, the waitress stared at me and whispered to another person, who checked his phone. Looks of disbelief. And curiosity. What horrible secret is *she* sitting on?

But it's not just the looks. It's the earrings.

A raven squawks like a petulant teen cursing me for coming home. I bought my little run-down place before prices skyrocketed, right after I joined the KPD and thought I was starting a lifelong career. The pay wasn't great, but enough to cover a monthly mortgage payment. The bank agreed.

Now the picture's muddied. I've fallen behind on my credit card payments because I figure the mortgage takes priority. Still, I'm optimistic. In addition to Clarissa Haynes's case—I'm not charging Paxton Rhoads much, since he doesn't have it—I've got insurance work to fall back on. Thank goodness for the lead on Lasserio that I got in Choteau two weeks ago.

I look out beyond the row of pines behind my house to the wide expanses of fields stretching toward the rolling, friendly peaks of the Whitefish Range, so unlike the barred fangs of the Divide farther east. I'm scanning for anything that seems out of place or strange. A few years ago, I laid down sod and distributed wood chips in the border below the house that doesn't have flowers or bushes. Now I wish I'd left the old dirt and its better ability to capture prints.

I hike my backpack up onto my shoulder and wheel my other bag to the front stoop.

The porch is also clean—no obvious disturbances.

I leave my luggage by the front door and check the front windows. They're locked and tight. There are no broken twigs or leaves knocked to the wood chips. Dust on the white sills hasn't been smudged. I inspect all the side and back windows and the kitchen door. All good.

Inside, I bolt the door behind me. Everything's in order: sofa pillows stacked as usual, pictures on the shelves unmoved, artwork on the walls straight, frames in need of TLC. I cleaned before I left, but early fall—fire season—means endless Montana dust.

I check my office on the main level and my bedroom and another smaller room—the guest room—upstairs.

In my room, I open the bottom drawer of my bathroom vanity and find the rectangular leather travel case. The case is special to me, a Christmas present from my mom—the last one I'll ever receive from her. A month after I said goodbye to her following holiday break during my senior year of college, she ran her car off the road east of town. She crashed into a tree, landing upside down. The roads were icy. She'd been drinking. She was a functioning alcoholic who could accomplish daily tasks relatively well, but not this day. The only silver lining was that she didn't hit another vehicle.

I pull out the leather case. My mom had my first initial, *C*, engraved on the top. I remove the individual pouches that contain various earrings, rings, necklaces, and bracelets. I inspect each one.

But no earrings.

*Impossible.*

I check my bedroom, feeling a weird and loopy lightness. Knickknacks from Glacier Park—a sculpture of a mountain lion, a stuffed moose—sit untouched on my dresser and beside my table. There's a pair of bookends made from the original timber from the legendary Sperry Chalet, which burned down in 2017 when a wildfire raged through Glacier. A framed photo of me with a group of my U of M friends, including Sophie, and one of my mom and Les on high school graduation day. The photo of me the day I completed Basics, which I stuffed way back in a drawer the day I quit KPD.

No earrings.

I keep a safe in my closet to hold the Sig Sauer P226 I purchased after I turned my back on police work.

I dial the combination and peer in. My Sig sits in the center on top of my passport and birth certificate.

Nothing else. I pull out the gun and squeeze my palm into the waffle grip of the handle. The weight of it instantly reassures me.

But no, I refuse to carry a gun around in my own house, especially when I don't even *know* if I'm the woman in the sketch. I shove the gun back in the safe, close the door, spin the lock.

I dig through the catchall drawers in the kitchen. Useless. I lift all the cushions on the couch. Nothing but crumbs, a nickel, and two quarters.

In the kitchen, I lean against the counter. The back of my neck tingles. The small house is stuffy, so I swing open the back door and step out. A flock of chickadees dispatch from the crab apple tree, all exacting the same angle as they fly off. The wind picks up, slapping gusts of warmth against my cheeks.

The deer have gone to town on my hostas and hydrangeas and eaten most of my geraniums and potato vine that were still hanging on into the fall. The repellent mix I spray on the beds only works when I apply it regularly. Otherwise, my plants are a delectable smorgasbord.

I walk the perimeter of my yard, where the mowed parts end and the unruly fields of wild, dry grass stretch through a heavily treed area toward the Whitefish Range. Other than deer hooves, no tracks. I walk it again, just to make sure.

Close by sits an old double garden swing. Since I figure no one will search under the rusty thing on the opposite end of the yard, it's where I hide my spare key.

I lift the left corner of the heavy iron legs. I'm relieved to find the key, dirty and ground into the soil, two earthworms keeping it company. I pick it up and shove it in my pocket.

Jess has texted me again: Are you at your house yet? Call me!

Wallace too: Home now. Call or text if you need anything.

I spin around, taking in everything, looking for anything out of the ordinary. I spot the raven in a pine tree beyond my yard, where it squawks again. A squirrel scurries down my crab apple tree, grabs a rotting crab apple, and races back up. A dog barks in the distance. An airplane flies above over the Whitefish Range, leaving a contrail that's beginning to fray. The whole scene, although typical, feels like things are on the brink of change. I remind myself that early fall always seems this way as the heat tries to hang on but can't outpace the shorter days and the lengthening shadows.

In the two days since the updrafts from the late-August heat generated a massive thunderstorm in the valley, making me race to Jess's, the air has cooled and the light is already changing. Darkness comes a touch earlier and shadows stretch a little farther across the valley floor, devouring everything.

I'm about to turn to go back inside when there's movement in a copse of aspens. I flinch. Go rigid. The hairs on the back of my neck rise.

Suddenly, a deer darts through the brush, twigs snapping. My pulse slows as I shake my head in disappointment. Is everything going to make me jump now, too, like Jess?

Inside, I grab some ice water and sit down at the kitchen table. I text both Jess and Wallace that I'm fine. *Nothing to worry about.* I tell Jess I'll call her later.

I'm tired, but twitchy. Crepuscular, like a cat gearing up for the evening hours. None of the CA's victims were attacked until their time was up, but the whole idea is unsettling enough that I can't help it.

I go into the bathroom to throw some water on my face. When I peer in the mirror, I'm surprised to see small, faint flecks of red spotting the fabric of my T-shirt near my shoulder. I examine my thumb. It's bleeding from my relentless picking, and I've managed to spot the fabric near my sleeve where I touched it when adjusting my backpack.

The last time I mutilated my own thumb until it bled was when I was being harassed on the force.

I cut the loose skin off, clip my nails, and find a Band-Aid to prevent any more picking. After I secure it, I stare in the mirror.

I still can't fathom that I'm the person in the sketch—the next target—but the headline I saw runs through my head like a news ticker: *Is everyone in the US who resembles this sketch potential prey?*

I pull my hair back from my face and bind it into a tight ponytail like I used to wear it on the force. There. I cock my head. With my hair up, as Ross had maintained, I don't resemble the sketch as much.

In the living room, I refocus on the earrings. I try to come up with the last place I wore them. It would have been with Wallace. I only wore them when I was with him. We broke up in February, so I'm positive I haven't even had a reason to look for the earrings or think about them since then.

I'd chosen a lazy Sunday afternoon when we were hanging out at my house to spring it on him. I was in sweats. I'd moped around all morning with a sad nervousness. He sensed something was up.

I'd sat him down on the couch, in the exact spot I'm sitting now. I settled in next to him with my legs crisscrossed under me, faced him, grabbed one of his pale hands, and stared at it, at his long, smooth, piano-playing fingers. His nails were manicured and perfectly pink with a white horseshoe on each tip.

"What?" he said.

I angled my head this way and that like some junior high student, and came out with it, telling him I cared for him deeply but thought we were better as pals, that I missed the simplicity of our friendship. I explained that he'd done nothing wrong at all, that it was me, that I needed to be on my own, and that I needed to be there for Jess. I rolled on, said that I was sorry, that I was afraid I'd relied on him too much during my battles at the department and again as I struggled to switch to PI work and open my own business.

It all sounded horribly trite—the sophomoric *let's just be friends* breakup—and the way I'd phrased it all made me feel like a complete ass who'd used one of her best friends to get through some tough patches.

I left out a large part of the truth—that it was me buckling under the weight of my own conscience, of shoving yet another secret behind an already-splintered door.

He shifted away, took his hand back, and looked at me curiously. His fingers twitched like he was already composing it all in his head, working at how to translate the feeling of breaking up into sound. Something aching and mournful. Or maybe even a little ravenous.

I'd responded to that quality in his music, too—something beyond hollow sadness, a sense of the insatiable, of not holding back—but I could never figure out why it existed in his creations but not in his personality. And definitely not in the bedroom.

The music is how it began. I'd known Wallace since Sophie introduced me to him that first year at the University of Montana. Wallace was a year older, in the music school. We got closer after Sophie left us, but we were never anything but friends until years later, after he'd moved to Kalispell to conduct the local orchestra. He resided in Kalispell for several years, and we'd often simply check in or meet for coffee, but one time, when we met and I confided in him about the unpleasant atmosphere at the department, he said, "You know, right, that I don't just conduct, that I still give piano performances."

I did know, but for some reason, it never seemed like it was a good time to go. I was on shift or lined up to babysit Sam.

"I have one this Saturday," he said. "Why don't you come? It would be good to get your mind off things."

This time, I didn't have an excuse, so I went. I watched him up on that stage at the community college, and out of the blue, something stirred in me. I'd only been to one of his recitals before, with Sophie that freshman year, when Wallace was performing with the university's music department.

Wallace had been a great source of pride for Sophie. She used to brag about what a renaissance man her brother was, how he was so in tune with his creative side. Back then, he seemed gangly and shy to me.

Older now, he was almost powerful up onstage. The tall, thin college student I knew had become more filled out and statuesque under the lights. His blond hair shone like gold. His serious face—his jawline—could have been cut from marble. How had I not noticed before? Did I only see this because he was up on the stage, as if the platform itself acted as a lens for me to look through, bringing him into focus?

I heard something in his piano playing that I hadn't before. Joy. Something that awakened a part of me I'd buried long ago. Something that made me hungry for human connection and affection. Along with a sharp ache, an ecstasy rose from his music.

A week later, I asked him if he wanted to go on a hike with me in the Mission Mountains. We trekked up to Cedar Lake through sweet-smelling old-growth cedars. The dusty trail turned our hiking socks gray.

We picnicked beside the lake before returning to Wallace's dusty Jeep. On the way home, we stopped at a roadside bar near Swan Lake, shaped like a tadpole nestled between the Swan and Mission Ranges. We ordered Pacificos and chicken wings and giggled over silly stuff. He made me laugh. It felt good to not think about the department and the tension around Hartley.

I found myself wanting him. In the bar, I nonchalantly placed my hand on his thigh. He looked at me curiously. I leaned over and kissed him. When I pulled away, his blue eyes stayed on mine, wide and flickering, asking, *Is this for real, Cros?*

It had taken me until that lazy afternoon seven months later to look into those eyes again and give him his answer.

# Chapter 15

Two red-eyes and the night of no sleep in Dallas have caught up with me. I'm not sure when or for how long I dozed off, but when the doorbell rings, I stand so fast, I feel lightheaded and forget for a moment where I am. I look out the kitchen window to see the light diffusing into pale pastels above the mountains. Shades of gray tunnel through the forest on the edge of my yard.

Dismissing the thought of slipping into the bedroom for my gun—*assassins aren't likely to ring your doorbell, Cros*—I go to the door, wondering if it's a UPS or FedEx delivery.

Through the glass on the door, I see a tall Black man with an erect posture that screams *official* and a white woman with short reddish-orange hair stand waiting. The guy wears a blue button-up shirt, the woman a black blazer. Both are in jeans.

FBI. But not from the office in Kalispell. I know the agents there.

*Detective Ewing.* The thought is instantaneous. He relayed my story about the earrings. It's the only reason two special agents from out of town would fly in.

When I open the door, the woman pulls a badge from her inside pocket and flips it open, revealing an FBI shield with an ID. "Crosbie Mitchell?"

"Yes."

"I'm Special Agent in Charge Greene, and this is Special Agent Alderson." Alderson flashes a smile, but Greene doesn't alter her expression. I perfected the same neutral gaze. Women in the business hone the poker face, clear and blank. Not warm, not incriminating, not cold, but not bitchy or conceited.

"So quick," I mumble.

"Excuse me?" Alderson says.

"I didn't think Ewing would notify you that fast," I clarify. "But I'm very happy he did."

"We took the first flight from Salt Lake, the local team provided a vehicle, and here we are, all in record time." He announces this like he wants a Cub Scout pin for the effort, but it's not obnoxious. There's something calming and uncomplicated about his manner.

I'm feeling relieved at their arrival. I'm not gonna lie—even though I'm not entirely convinced it's me—the looks I got at lunch freaked me out a little.

"Can't say it wasn't a little hectic," he says. "That little airport sure is crazy."

"Yeah, we're on the map thanks to Glacier."

"Your place isn't far from the airport, though. That was a pleasant surprise."

"It's convenient," I agree.

I usher them into the nook beside the kitchen. I'm suddenly conscious of my bright T-shirt with the minuscule flecks of blood. I wished I had changed it, even though the spots are too small for others to notice. I offer drinks but they decline. My ice water—now just water—and phone are still on the table, and they leave that spot for me.

After the preliminaries, Greene asks to see the earrings.

"I want to see them again, too," I say. "I flew in today. From Dallas. And the first thing I did was look everywhere and I came up empty."

They both look at each other, some secret communication—the connection I'd always hoped to have with a partner on the force if I'd stuck with it.

"You can talk with the guy who gave them to me. Wallace Scott. He went with me when we filed the report and spoke to Detective Ewing."

"I see," Greene says. "Your significant other?"

"At one point. We're friends now." Something about my quick declaration sets off a twinge of unease in me, like I'm just as coldhearted as I was when I broke up with him or, yesterday in the bar, when I thought negatively about his piano playing, like I'm somehow trying to dismiss him. But that's ridiculous, I scold myself. I'm just stating the truth.

"Have you checked everywhere?"

"I turned the house upside down."

"When was the last time you wore them?" Greene asks.

I wonder if she's on a level playing field with the men of the FBI.

"I've asked myself the same question. Maybe out to dinner with Wallace." I squint, thinking. Over the holidays we went out several times: to the local high-end golf club restaurant, to a nice place near the ski resort, to a bougie new place on the outskirts of town. "I usually only wore them when I was around him. And that was months ago. We broke up last winter, in February."

"Have you searched your car?"

"I don't think they'd be in my car."

"Do you have a place where you keep valuables? A safe?"

"Nothing hardly worth stealing," I say, "but I do have a safe for my gun and a few documents. Already checked."

We agree that we'll all spend a few minutes looking around the house when we're done talking, and I welcome the idea. I'm sure my searching skills are hampered by the anxiety of it all.

Then, a more thorough rundown. Greene and Alderson fall into a steady, even approach that demonstrates they've put thought into how they would organize my interview. Their work is admirable, and I fall into a kind of easy trance, answering their questions as best I can. Family. Schools. Friends. Hobbies. Church. Community groups. How long I've been a PI. How long I was a cop. Why did I quit. On that last point, I nonchalantly—and ironically, given my new set of circumstances—tell them I was after something safer.

Also on that last point, I fudge. I only tell them that, in the end, it "wasn't a good fit for my personality."

If they're good at their jobs, they've already dug up some background on my time on the force and how it might have contributed to my departure, but I see no reason to dredge up my history unless it pertains to the Confession Artist. And I'm not convinced that it does, even if this whole thing does hit—well, kick the living hell out of—some major nerves in me.

"Any reason you can think of that you'd be the next target? Anything unusual or odd happen to you lately?"

"No. This is the most unusual thing that's ever occurred."

"Has anyone threatened you in other ways, or have you made any enemies?"

"No," I repeat.

Greene glances at Alderson. I know what the look means. She's questioning why my answer was so final, so sure, when most people might stumble, say, *Uh, I'm not sure. I don't* think *I have any.*

I almost add "not lately," thinking of the threats during the backlash, but I can't go there. It'd be like unwrapping fish that's gotten too warm in the sun.

"I don't mean to sound so emphatic, but I've been pondering that question, you know, ever since."

"Anything you feel the need to confess, as he's demanding?" Alderson echoes.

"No," I lie. "I mean, we all have little things, right? It's not like I'm going to worry about every tiny thing I've done wrong in my life up to this point, every should've, could've, would've."

"Is there a *significant* should've?" Greene angles her head to the side, innocently, but there's something artificial in the gesture, as if she knows every personal thing about me.

"Like what?" I ask.

"Whatever comes to mind for you," Alderson says.

The nonchalance of his statement somehow ramps up how acutely awful I already feel about the things I'm not telling them, the things I *won't* tell them. Like he's just being polite even though he sees right through me. But it's probably all in my head. "Are you seeing patterns from the other victims?" I ask instead. "Stuff from their lives they *should* have confessed?"

I can tell they're getting annoyed that I'm answering questions with questions when they're here to help me and find the perp, but still, if I'm the next intended victim, I need answers as much as they do.

"Ms. Mitchell," Greene says, "we're looking into the possibility that this is a type of proclamation killer. Do you know what that means?"

I do. It means manifesto. Cause. Someone who's bought into a conspiracy, either of their own making or of some greater movement, or someone who's arrived at a breaking point.

The light in the room teeters on twilight. The whole situation feels surreal, like the three of us might dissolve away with the evening itself. I should turn on a light, but I'm frozen in place. To have these two badass-looking agents working a high-profile case, making everything even more official, gets under my skin. I'm relieved they're taking it seriously, but I'm also unnerved.

They both stare at me. Greene's pale skin looks ghostly.

"Are these earrings your first real lead?" I ask.

Another glimpse from Alderson to Greene. I want to shout, *What? Tell me. I'm the target here, not you.*

Greene flicks her head, giving him the go-ahead.

"As of now," he says, "we've got little to go on. No witnesses to any of the crimes, no physical evidence that we can match to anyone in our databases, no motive beyond that he or she has some bone to pick with the targets, and perhaps society in general, and perhaps wants us all to become a little more socially conscious about our actions."

"A little more socially conscious? And if we're not, they kill people. That's a good dose of hypocrisy."

"There's not always a lot of logic in aggression," Greene says. "People think rage is always out of control, but sometimes it's controlled."

"As I was saying," Alderson jumps back in. "It seems he might be stalking his targets in the lead-up to the killings, but we're not sure how or why he's picked his victims. We've put together lists of people the victims were in contact with in the last year to see if there's a common name that pops up, but there's nothing. If it's okay with you, we'd also like to access your phone and computer data."

"Absolutely not," I say. "My clients come to me expecting confidentiality."

Greene sighs, as if she was anticipating that answer.

Alderson looks at her before continuing. "We've scoured surveillance footage around the places the first ones were struck. We've got analysts building models of their last days, looking for patterns and connections."

"What about an IP address?"

"We have web specialists trying to pin that down, but the person's got a level of tech smarts. VPN encrypting can make it difficult to trace."

"Nothing at all?"

"It's taken some time, but we've been able to trace the first three posts to VPNs in public spaces: the first two to public libraries nowhere near the victims in Snohomish and Santa Monica, and the last from a computer at a Staples in Kennewick, Washington," Alderson says. "But that last victim—the third—whoever he was, was left alone. We believe we have a good lead on who he might be and are in the process of talking to him."

Questions run through my mind like a ticker tape, but I let Alderson continue.

"We assume that they post in a public place from a random computer that can't be traced and drive or fly somewhere else to get the victims, to throw us off. We've got people scouring all security footage of libraries in the vicinity of where the victims lived and even much larger parameters. But they're smart enough to pick libraries that don't have cameras directly on their entrances, so we've had to search nearby streets and blocks. It's tedious."

"Anything at all?"

"Nothing solid," Alderson says.

I can't tell if their tight lips are standard protocol or if they really have nothing to go on. "Any patterns? Because it would be good to know if I fit into one."

"We're working on it." Greene's eyes stay fixed on me. "We're expanding our searches of the victims' phone and computer records." She circles back: "It would be helpful to get a look at yours, too."

I ignore her.

"We're still checking into all of it," Alderson reiterates, as if every frank thing Greene says needs massaging over by his smooth voice. Maybe people perceive me the same way—that I'm too blunt. "You've seen them, right?" he asks. "They both had decent jobs, but nothing especially high powered or uber important. They weren't in politics or law enforcement, weren't big oil, Wall Street, or pharma tycoons. One was a high school football coach and the other worked for Santa Monica Community College."

"In education."

"Yes. But not you."

"And the earrings? I mean, they're not that uncommon."

"They're the first real clue we've gotten," he says. "We're trying to track down all the purchasers of the other ones sold and sending our field officers to check them out, but it's tedious. Not all gift shops keep detailed records, and even when they do, they're slow at going through everything and getting the information to us. And if people pay cash, there's no trace. But we'll let you know if we come across anyone who's purchased earrings like these who resembles the sketch as much as you do."

I swallow, my throat tight. *As much as you do.* "So, why the earrings, do you think? Why get so specific now? Do they want to suddenly be known, to give you more clues?"

"Eventually, they all want recognition."

"But surely the killer must know that the victim would contact authorities and that you'd try to catch him by keeping an eye on the bait."

On *me*.

"Possibly," Greene says. "Sometimes it's a game, and he's upping the stakes."

Like the Zodiac Killer, sending messages with ciphers to the Bay Area newspapers, mocking the detectives working his case. *Upping the stakes.* "But why so specific?"

"We don't know yet," Alderson says. "We're looking into it all. Might not even be the same person."

"I've thought of that. Someone hopping on the bandwagon. A copycat seizing an opportunity to kill me under the guise of this psycho." I think of Ridgeway.

"It's a thought," he says. "Or to frighten you. Can you think of anything you've worked on, as either a cop or a PI, that has poked a bear?"

"Plenty," I say. I'll tell them about Robbie Ridgeway, but not this moment. I want to hear more about what they've found. "But nothing enough to warrant this kind of a response. What do your analysts think about the drawings? Same sketcher or not?"

"We're working on that. As of now, we don't have evidence to suggest it one way or the other. Each artist has a signature style, so we're checking into that, if only to rule out copycats or pranksters. Either way, though, we do need you to think of anyone who might have any reason to harm or frighten you. We also need to know if you know anyone in your circles who knows how to draw, someone who's good with art."

I sigh heavily when I think of people who might dislike me. Where would I begin?

The guys on the squad? So many were complete jerks to me, but murder? I can't fathom that. Besides, the alpha males got what they wanted: my departure. All threats that a woman might get a promotion ahead of themselves have been vanquished. *Stand down, boys.*

There have been a few people I've upset by some of the things I've exposed through my PI work, and sometimes through the DNA testing and research I ordered up through Jess's company.

I've informed an adult child that her father isn't her blood parent. I've exposed that a man has two entirely different families and his wife simply thought he traveled a lot. Discoveries that have surely stoked anger—betrayed realities, emotional foundations crumbling, inheritances affected. Right up to my current Clarissa Haynes case, where she'd been working on exposing the potential pollution of a rare fen on Ridgeway's property and thwarting the sale of the land to Volanex.

There's also the fact that Ridgeway is an artist. I recall our interaction when I first entered his home and noted the prints of the naked women on his walls. I relay all this to Alderson and Greene.

Both of them make notes.

I clear my throat before I ask, "I'd love it if you could use your special FBI powers to dig a little deeper into Clarissa Haynes's death." A part of me knows it's a big stretch to ask this of them. The two cases might have zero to do with one another, but it can't hurt. And I can't shake the idea that the sketch, if it is of me, came out two weeks after I pissed Ridgeway off.

"Deeper how?"

"Pull the forensics reports from the Teton County Sheriff's Department. See what they have so far. Maybe that will give us some direction. Maybe we'll see some connection."

Alderson pushes out his lower lip and nods, like he's open to the idea. Greene's face stays set in stone, unconvinced.

"You said yourself"—I turn to Alderson—"the person who put the sketch out might not even be the same person. They might be a copycat. Don't you think it would be good to know as much as we can about Ridgeway and the murder of Clarissa Haynes since that's what I've been most involved with?"

"You're making some pretty big leaps here," Greene says. "You don't even know if she was murdered for sure."

"She was," I say. "And you should check it out if you want to be thorough."

The two glance at each other. I can see I've struck a chord. They don't want to make any mistakes. Not with a case like the Confession Artist snaring the entire nation's attention.

"We'll look into it," Alderson says. "What about other artists?"

I shake my head. A few, I think. Including my sister. But could any of them draw something so specific, so well rendered? I doubt it.

But the big lie still clings to me like someone's tightly rolled me up in a filthy film of plastic wrap. My fib to Ewing boomerangs back to me. I do have something I should feel ashamed of. It just isn't what he thinks it is. It has nothing to do with "causing trouble" for Hartley.

The worst thing, next to my guilt over dragging Sophie camping, is how I let my rage get the best of me at Coleman's place with the OIS investigator.

But there's no way I'm exposing that.

# Chapter 16

The light was thinning into a drizzly October evening, and I was nearing the end of my shift when I heard that Railes needed backup for a DV.

It was always best to dispatch two officers for a domestic violence call. One can separate and ask questions while the other checks prior history and arrest warrants, finds out if firearms are on the premises, and interviews neighbors if needed.

Railes should have waited for me so we could go in together, but he didn't have a lot of patience. And he was among those who'd hopped up quickly on the backlash bandwagon in support of Hartley. I wouldn't have been surprised if he was the one who put the bloated mouse in my locker.

*Dumbass,* I thought to myself. My anger already roiled at the base of my belly. I probably shouldn't have taken the call to assist him. My shift was almost over anyway, and Wallace was promising me a homemade lasagna at his place.

But I was closest to the scene, and other units were on the other side of town due to a big monster truck event. Plus, if I didn't take reinforcement calls due to the backlash, I wouldn't be providing any backup at all. Most of the department was now lined up against me.

In many ways, my fate was already decided.

I stepped out and walked toward the house, where shouting spilled into the cool night.

The small single-story crouched at the base of a ridge and was poorly maintained. Dull peeling paint, cardboard duct-taped over a missing windowpane, the outside stoop smelled of urine in the damp air. I climbed two porch steps to an open door and announced I was entering so I didn't surprise anyone, especially Railes.

Inside, on one side of the room, Railes was in a heated exchange with a tall, well-muscled guy with a beard and a slightly crooked nose. He had a deep, bloody scratch across his cheek.

He seemed familiar. Maybe I'd pulled him over. Maybe I'd seen him in a bar. He looked like a rough yet handsome bouncer.

"He attacked me," the bouncer-looking guy said. "Went crazy. Does it a lot. He's nuts."

The guy he was referring to stood off to the left in a corner. He was staring at me like a frightened doe. Dark bags hung under his eyes. It was hard to believe he was the aggressor as Bouncer Guy was claiming, but I knew not to read too much into first impressions.

In the middle of the room sat a tattered couch and a small coffee table. Two glasses, a bottle of Cuervo, and a saltshaker stood next to a wooden cutting board with lime slices and a paring knife. One of the glasses was knocked over. Sticky liquid pooled on the table. A white ceramic lamp lay on the dirty carpet, broken into large pieces like a cracked egg.

"You stay right here," Railes said firmly, and came over to me. I kept my eye on the bigger, bearded guy because he was amped up, his jaw clenched so tightly it looked like it might break, his hands bound up in fists. He bounced up and down like he was warming up for a sporting event. I wondered if he'd done drugs in addition to tequila.

"Couldn't wait for you," said Railes. "Too much yelling and I heard some things breaking."

"What's the story?"

"Your average kinky homo bullshit."

Railes's upper lip was raised in disgust.

His body cam was off. With some personal DV or sexual assault situations, we were allowed to turn them off or leave them in the car for the sake of privacy of the individuals involved.

Mine was on, so apparently, he was cocky or stupid enough that he didn't care about his homophobic smack being recorded for posterity.

"Care to elaborate?" I said.

"He called the cops." He gestured to Bouncer Guy. "He says Leon"—he tilted his head to the other—"went ballistic on him for no good reason. He's got scratches up and down his arms from Leon's keys and from his fingernails, too. When I came in, Leon was holding up a glass like he might throw it."

I waited. I knew the debrief wasn't over.

"He claims Leon goes wacko like this all the time and he usually just takes it since he's bigger, but this time he lost it."

Both guys watched us intently. "What's his name?" I motioned to Bouncer Guy.

"Don't know yet. Still trying to calm things down."

"Okay, well, you take him into that room." I pointed to what looked like a bedroom. The house was squalid and rough. "Get his information. Find out if he has a record. I'll get Leon's version."

Not a fan of being ordered around, Railes shot me a look of disdain.

I ignored him and introduced myself to Leon.

"What's your last name?"

"Spencer," he said.

Small-boned and skinny-shouldered, he couldn't have been more than five eight. The leftover wounds from my days with Sophie falling apart still sent raw pangs through me, and all I could think of as I approached this frightened young man was that I wanted to help him.

Thomas Leon Spencer told me he went by his middle name. He lived in Kalispell, was nineteen, and had gone to Flathead High School.

I was a trained interviewer, and I'd been studying up to take the detective's exam, so I felt fresh with knowledge. I knew to find common ground quickly, to be encouraging, so I told him I'd gone to school there, too, graduated, and moved on. "Can you tell me what happened?"

"I'd rather not." He looked at the camera on my chest, then down at his hands. He nervously fingered a key chain—a smooth, colorful agate shaped like an arrowhead and a square plastic Daffy Duck memento, both attached to a ring with his keys and a bottle opener. His vulnerability and apprehension were palpable. I was hoping he wouldn't clam up. I turned my camera off and scooted over to block his view of Railes talking to Bouncer Guy.

"Why not?"

"Doesn't feel right."

"How so?"

"The other officer. I don't think he approves of our lifestyle."

"Well, I'm not him, and this isn't being recorded." I pointed to my device to show him the little green light was off.

Leon glanced at the camera on my chest, shook his head. "You can take me to the station or whatever."

Everything inside me screamed that this kid had been abused. I needed to get him to talk. I needed to reach him, unlike I'd been able to do with my own sister two months earlier. Unlike I was able to do with Sophie. "I'm not going to do that, Leon. Not until I understand what happened here."

Leon lowered his head, stared at his key chain.

"Hey," I said softly. "Look at me. I promise we'll handle this delicately. Can you tell me why your friend in the other room called us?"

"I was the one who wanted to call. I've wanted to many times before, but I've never done it. I can't believe *he'd* call you."

"Okay, well, let's back up a little, okay? Can you tell me why *you* wanted to call for help?"

"It got out of hand. We were arguing. I could tell it was escalating. I didn't want that, so I tried to leave. I grabbed my keys and was trying to go out the front door, but he pulled me back. He tackled me and got on top of me." He swallowed hard and took a shaky breath. "He's done it before."

"Done what before?"

Leon peered around me, as if he might get his boyfriend's permission to say the things he was telling me.

"Leon," I said. "He's not listening. He's done what before?"

He swallowed hard, his Adam's apple like a mouse looking for a way out. "Pushed things too far, you know, forced things," he whispered. "When I don't want it."

His voice faded. More key chain contemplation.

A roaring sensation filled my ears. Despite my best efforts, as if I'd brought Sophie's blond-haired ghost into this small house with me, all the images from that night in the woods—our frantic running, the branches lashing against us, the gnarled fingers of exposed roots grabbing our ankles and tripping us until we at last curled in tight behind a thick, fallen ponderosa to hide—all came rushing back.

"I see," I said, pushing my own anger down. "Whose place is this?"

"His."

"Owns it?"

"Rents."

"His name?"

"Mark."

"Mark what?"

"Mark Coleman."

The name snapped on a floodlight in a dark cave.

I stopped writing. My breath caught.

That's why he looked so familiar. When Jess told me his name, I'd done searches on him. Found out about his scattered upbringing in foster homes. He had no record, but I found photos of him on Facebook before facial hair.

The black-marble eyes, the crooked nose, the high cheekbones.

It was him.

"What's his full name?" I turned back to Leon. "You know?"

"Markus Mallory Coleman," Leon said.

The *Mallory* checked, too.

I was standing in the same room as the beast who 100 percent had forced himself on my sister. The man who'd irrevocably changed her. Made her a shell of her former self, made her a nightmare-laden nervous wreck afraid of her own shadow.

The same guy who I'd dreamed of beating to a bloody pulp. The same guy I had murdered a million times in my fantasies, blowing a hole through the middle of his skull. The same one whose trachea I imagined crushing with my bare fingers.

My heart drummed so hard it felt like it might explode from my chest. I wanted to grab the tequila bottle and smash it against his skull or take one of the thick ceramic shards from the broken lamp on the floor and rake it across his throat.

I did nothing. I stood with my world still whirling and my pulse beating in my neck.

"Do you live here?"

Composure was difficult, but I faked it as best I could.

"No."

"So, when you say he forced things, you mean he forced himself on you for sex?"

Leon gripped his key chain more vigorously. "Yes," he said.

"What happened?"

He explained that Mark had ripped his jeans off, held him so tightly that he couldn't squirm away, that Mark turned him around and continued to control him with one arm. With the other he penetrated him, with his hand first, then his penis.

Sophie flashed again. Her rapist holding her down on those hard pebbles. She'd shown me the blood spots on her jeans that had transferred when she got them back on, told me that he'd ripped her pants down and jammed his fingers inside her.

And Jess? I couldn't even let myself go to those details. I shut my eyes, working hard to stay in the moment, my pulse knocking in my neck.

"I had my keys." Leon held them up. Showed me. "I just . . . I remember squeezing them so tight when he was on me." He moved the keys from one hand to the other and fanned his hand out for me like he was going to show me a jewel. Red welts traversed the white, waxy flesh of his palm. "Eventually I squirmed enough and got turned around. I scratched him. With these. And these."

Leon held up his fingernails from his other hand.

"We were both screaming. I swore I was going to call you and he said if I did, he'd hurt me worse. He couldn't believe I'd scratch his face and arms like that. He was calling me names. And I was lifting up the couch cushions, thinking my phone fell down between them, and as I was doing that, he called 9-1-1 and had someone on the line. I tried to leave, but he blocked me, and we screamed at each other all over again. When he arrived"—he pointed at the room where Railes was—"I was holding one of those glasses. I don't know what I was thinking. I was freaking out. I was scared. I guess I thought I'd throw it at him if I needed to.

"What's going to happen?" Leon said. "I don't want him to go to jail. I only want him to get some help or something."

Jess's voice echoed in my head. She'd said the very same thing.

"I mean," Leon said. "We've been dating, so it's not like it's rape or anything."

*No!* I wanted to scream as I snapped back to the situation at hand. *Here we go again, the same old justifications.* I was about to tell Leon to stay put so I could have a word with the other officer. Railes beat me to it, emerging from the bedroom with orders for me to cuff Leon.

*"What?"* Leon looked at me with terror in his eyes. "Me? Cuff me? I'm not the one . . ."

"You fucking are the one." Coleman followed. "Look at these." He held out his forearms, crisscrossed with angry, bloody scratches.

"You," I ordered Coleman, grabbing my cuffs. "Don't move."

Railes grabbed Coleman before I could get to him and pushed him back. "Stay right here."

"I was protecting myself," Leon said. Tears sprang from his eyes.

"I'm not cuffing Leon," I said. "He's not the primary."

Railes glowered at me with a seething hatred. He wasn't used to disobedience, especially from a woman. "The fuck you doing?" he said. He didn't care about making a scene. "You trying to undermine me?"

"Leon's not the aggressor."

I said it with all the calm I could muster. Even with my camera off, I had a feeling that my feet were on eggshells.

"Coleman doesn't have a record," Railes said. "He's all scratched up. Gouged."

"Defensive wounds. That guy right there," I said as quietly as I could, but my rage surged. The words came out louder than I wanted. "Is a rapist. We need to get Leon to the SANE Suite up at the hospital."

The Sexual Assault Response Team had trained forensic interviewers and nurses to get the specifics and administer a rape kit. The SANE Suite is where I should have forced Jess to go, even though she didn't tell me about her assault until two weeks afterward.

Railes looked confused, but not convinced.

"There are other things you don't know about this guy."

"What kind of things?"

"I've heard stuff." There was no way in hell I was telling Railes about my sister. Jess had been adamant about keeping it a secret. And Railes was not someone I would trust with my sister's personal trauma even if the monster *was* in the same room.

I glared at Coleman. The heat in my stare could have left a contrail through the room.

"Heard things?" Railes *tsk*'d. "We're going off crap you've *heard*?"

Coleman looked at me arrogantly, like he had the situation under control. It took every ounce of my strength to not bolt over and start swinging.

"Either you cuff him or I do," I said.

Railes shrugged. "Honestly, I couldn't care less which one of these faggots you want to take in."

I shook my head at Railes's vileness.

"Fine," I said again through clenched teeth. I started toward Coleman with sweaty palms, my heart beating furiously.

Coleman yelled, "No fucking way. None of this is my fault. I'm the one who needs a fucking tetanus shot."

"You," I roared. "On the floor. Hands behind your head."

He changed tack and went toward Leon.

"On the floor," I shouted again at Coleman.

My hand went to my Sig, not because I thought I needed it, but because I wanted it. My hands needed it. My fingers itched to put it up to Coleman's face. At the last second, some modicum of sensibility kicked in. I left it alone.

But then Railes pulled his.

He pointed it at Coleman, then Leon, back to Coleman.

"On the floor, Coleman," I screamed. "And Railes. Jesus. Put that down."

Railes ignored me, which meant my words aimed at Coleman meant nothing. Coleman was oblivious to Railes's gun and hurled abuses at Leon.

Railes shouted for Coleman to back away from Leon and get on the floor. But Coleman, like a hawk trained on a vole, stared at Leon.

"You've ruined everything," Coleman said. "You fucking piece of shit."

"Stop." Leon put his hands over his ears. "Just stop."

"I mean it," I hollered, fumbling for my Taser. "On the floor, Coleman. Hands behind your head."

Coleman stood next to the coffee table. Tequila, bottle, shot glasses, cutting board. Knife.

He faced Leon, swearing.

"Stand down," Railes yelled. "Stand down and drop it. Drop the knife."

*What in the hell was he talking about?* Coleman wasn't holding a knife. The knife was on the coffee table.

"Coleman," I shouted again. "On the floor. Hands behind your head." I wanted to tase him, watch him go stiff, fall to the floor, and shudder with pain. I wanted to trade my Taser for my gun. Why not? Railes had his out, and the bastard deserved every barrel pointed right at him.

Coleman stayed by the coffee table, five feet away from Leon. Leon wailed like a wounded child.

"Railes, dammit, put your weapon away." Out of the corner of my eye, I saw Railes start to lower his gun. *Thank God.*

I went to grab Coleman, to cuff him. But before my second step, Coleman turned back toward us, sheer anger etched deeply in his face.

That's when the shot rang out.

Coleman reeled back as the bullet ripped through his chest.

Time swallowed itself. My gut sloshed. My ears screamed in pain. The smell of nitro and graphite hung in the air. Leon bellowed in pain.

Coleman crumpled, smashing the coffee table on his way down, tequila and lime slices jackknifed into the air. The knife skidded across the carpet.

"What the fuck did you do?" Leon shrieked.

"He wouldn't drop the knife." Railes said it calmly.

"He didn't *have* a knife," Leon said.

Leon's shocked eyes went from Railes to me, boring into me, searching for support, looking for answers I didn't have.

And still don't.

I called for emergency assistance. But even as I did, I knew in that moment, even if I was shocked by what Railes had done, I wasn't sure if I cared if Coleman bled to death on his own tequila-soaked carpet.

# Chapter 17

Mark Coleman died on the way to the hospital.

Nothing could alter the truth of that.

And not a thing could change the fact that I still felt nothing but hate for him, even after learning that Railes's shot was fatal.

The drizzle had stopped, but the dark sky remained swollen with murky clouds. The chill ran to my marrow. I shivered as Ewing interviewed me. Ewing's questions were preliminary. With a fatal police shooting, an investigator from an independent agency would be assigned. But Ewing was getting a lay of the land. With one of his cops opting for lethal force, he had every right.

I felt the pressure in my chest. It squeezed my ribs, made my breath go shallow. The same kind I felt after Mom died. When Sophie OD'd. When Jess told me about the rape.

"Cold?" Ewing said.

We stood outside the house where Mark Coleman had gone down.

I shook my head.

"We can go inside," he offered.

"No, I'm fine."

I didn't want to step past the yellow police tape to return to that crummy, sad living room. Dead leaves and pine needles papier-mâchéd the lawn. There was something about the way they smeared together that made me nauseated.

"We can also go back to the station, but I'd prefer to talk to you while things are fresh in your mind." He was trying for nice and accommodating, but disdain filled his eyes, underlying the big question. Would I be a team player this time? Was there still hope for me, or would I let everyone on the squad down again so soon after reporting Hartley for sexual harassment? The wonder radiated off him like heat from a furnace.

The moment seemed to balance on the top of a point, tilting this way and that. One way meant I could snatch the glorious opportunity to send all the ugly male bro-cop bullshit down the fucking drain. The other meant I could give in to my searing rage at Coleman by minimizing what Railes had done. And I could stay the course, become detective as I had been planning.

"Fine," I said. I loathed the idea that I might give him precisely what he needed, more emboldened cop culture, more certainty that no one would crack their protective shell.

But I'd already backed up Railes in front of Leon.

That didn't mean I couldn't change my mind, though.

And so I started from the beginning, from the moment I climbed out of my car and walked up on the porch. What I heard. What I saw. What I said. What I did.

And Ewing asked me again for details on the knife.

"You mean, did I see the knife?" I said.

"Did you see him holding it?"

I looked down at my hands for an answer. All I saw was Coleman mauling Jess. It overpowered everything. I tried to slow-blink it away, but it wasn't working, just like it hadn't earlier when I was listening to Leon. The roaring still filled my ears.

"I was watching Leon," I lied. "He was yelling. He had my attention because Railes pointed his gun at Leon first. Of course I'm not sure what Railes saw."

"Okay. Did you see the victim holding the knife after he went down?"

"I only saw the knife on the floor. Maybe he dropped it as he fell."

"I need you to think clearly about this one, Mitchell."

"It's clear."

"Leon Spencer claims Coleman never had the knife, that Railes made that up."

I shrugged for Ewing's sake. My mind was already made up. "I couldn't verify that for you."

My chest spooled tighter. No, I'd never be the same after this. I couldn't tell you for sure why I lied, but it wasn't only Billy Railes's voice whispering in my ear before help arrived: *You better be a team player this time, Mitchell. Last chance.*

"Is this story going to hold up when the independent investigator arrives to review Billy Railes's use of lethal force?" Ewing eyed me as if he thought his stiff glare might either get me to crack or keep me in line for good. Make me a team player from this point on.

"Why wouldn't it?"

"Because they aren't going to ask it once. They'll ask it a thousand times and you can't give them one little opening."

"There's not much to keep straight," I said. "I saw what I saw."

It's not that I wanted to protect Railes. I didn't. I couldn't stand the guy. I couldn't stand the whole culture that produced guys like Railes. Tolerated and encouraged them, too.

But I'll admit it.

As much as I wanted to protect myself, I still wanted to get back at a dead Coleman, too.

True, I didn't want any more backlash from cops. In a weird way, I thought providing cover for Railes might earn me a ticket to the inside club, not that it was a ticket I wanted. But avoiding more backlash was only part of the story.

My reasons for backing up Railes were all too personal and something I needed to keep to myself. They were all tangled up into something ugly and raw rearing up inside me, snatching away my ability to do the right thing.

As I said, hate is like fear. You can't control it when it takes you. It can overshadow everything. In that moment, I felt Coleman got what he deserved, no matter how he got it, and nobody else should pay for it and nothing more should be made of it, even if it was at the hands of mind-numbingly stupid Billy Railes.

I knew I was as wrong as the clouds were bloated and dark above me.

Leon was a wreck by the time he was situated in the SANE Suite in town. A nurse had him in a room where I watched through one-way glass and listened over an intercom. They wanted him to talk about the rape, but he wouldn't. He was in shock, still working his key chain with intensity. I felt as low as the underside of a stray tick in a dark forest, waiting for a wandering deer.

Leon's word against mine. All I had to do was "remember" things differently when the investigator arrived in the morning.

Wallace called me, but I couldn't stomach talking to him. I texted him and told him I was held up. I focused on Leon, watching them take him through it all again, coaxing him to discuss the rape after he'd given his statements about the shooting. When he got to the part where Coleman pulled him back from the door, I thought again of Sophie. How she told me that when Josh, her rapist, was kissing her, it felt good at first.

He got a hand under her shirt and she thought that was all right, too. She was okay with things progressing—until he pulled her in way too tightly.

He gripped her arms to the point that they hurt. When she tried to squirm away, he only jerked her in tighter. Josh wasn't going to ask because he didn't want to get a *no*.

Out in the dark under those great ponderosas, hours after we ran into the woods, she whispered to me that she began to block things out. That she'd flashed to a boa constrictor, clamping around its prey, and that clicked to an old urban legend that had stuck in her mind, about a girl who loved her pet snake and would let it sleep in her bed.

She whispered the tale to me, that the girl fed the boa a rat once a day, but suddenly it quit eating. It wouldn't eat for weeks, so she took it to a reptile shop and spoke to a specialist, who told her to not let the snake out of the cage until it began eating regularly again and to *not* let it sleep with her ever again. When the girl asked why, he said, "Because it's stopped eating to make room to digest *you*."

Sophie told that story to me that night while she was racked with fear, her breath hot against my cheek, the hiss of her voice against my ear making it itch. Myth or not, the story had come to her as Josh's slobber trickled down the side of her chin. She had felt her spine grind against the small rocks under her sleeping bag.

I asked her if she told him to stop. She wasn't sure, but she recalled telling him that the other tents were nearby and that this wasn't a good idea, that one of the guys who was down at the lake might walk back up or even I might come out from the tent at any moment.

But Sophie had said she told Josh to back off. But he didn't. He kept pulling and pressing. And she had wanted it all to cease, but she couldn't fight back because she froze up.

Just as Jess had done a decade later.

Making it difficult to prosecute.

Making it possible for two rapists to strike again and again.

And now Leon—struck by the same monster who hurt my sister. But unlike in so many cases where the rapist goes free because it's often too difficult to prove when there are no witnesses, Mark Coleman would not strike again.

"Do you have any bruises or cuts?" the nurse asked Leon.

"I don't know," he said. "I don't care anymore."

My phone rang. Wallace again, likely wondering where I was and if I was coming over. I glanced at Leon and the nurse, the pit in my stomach growing larger, my rage at Coleman still ratcheting up even though I knew he was gone forever.

As upset as I was with Railes for pulling his weapon and lying, and even as the heavy cloak of guilt for not contradicting Railes's story began to descend upon me for eternity, I was glad Coleman was gone.

"I'm tied up," I told Wallace. "I can't make it tonight."

I walked out of the hospital into the cold, soggy night. Sweat trickled down my back. Drizzling rain fell on my head. My hands were wet and slick.

I kept picturing their pained and confused faces.

Leon.

And Sophie.

I pictured Coleman's body crashing to the floor.

The knife skidding . . .

It all stopped me short. Jesus, what had I done?

I had covered for Railes. How could I have done that? How could I have thrown all my morals out the window *for a piece-of-shit cop*?

The answer was obvious.

I was no better than Billy Stinking Railes.

And if I thought it couldn't get any worse, it did.

Three days later, Leon hanged himself.

In a way, Mark Coleman's murder took another life, too, when I locked arms and stories with Billy Railes.

When I told Jess, the day after the shooting, I only covered the bare bones: that there'd been a domestic dispute, that an officer shot Coleman because he was resisting orders, that he was aggressive and wouldn't comply. I didn't mention Leon. "But now, at least, Coleman's gone, Jess. He's gone," I had said.

I saw it in her face then. Not relief. Not even surprise. Confusion. And something else—a deep disappointment. Even sadness. A slumping of her entire body, like a punctured balloon. She whispered, "Now I'll never be able to talk to him."

"But what on earth were you going to say?" I asked. "There's no talking to men like him."

But it fell on deaf ears. She had gone somewhere else in her mind at that moment, like she was listening and trying to make out some strange sound off in the distance.

Two long and painful weeks later, I quit. Railes and I were both already on a decompression leave for being involved in a shooting and taking the required two weeks off. But I knew then I couldn't go back. I couldn't tuck that shame away. Jess seemed worse by the day, and she wasn't even aware of what had really happened, of how I had backed Railes. The scale of it practically knocked me off my feet, made me dizzy. Pains shot through my chest every time I thought of it. At times, I thought I was having a heart attack, but I knew it was anxiety.

And ultimately, I knew there was no way to weave that ugly, frayed strand back into the fabric of who I thought I was, into what I thought I was trying to accomplish by becoming a cop.

# Chapter 18

But I tell none of this to Greene and Alderson of the FBI. They're much more interested in my investigation for Paxton Rhoads into Clarissa's death and Ridgefield. Alderson tells me to make a list, for my own reference, of anyone who comes to mind, including clients of mine, even if I can't release that information due to confidentiality.

Let it "percolate," he suggests. As if we have time for percolation.

I tell him I will.

Nervous energy pulls me up out of my seat to my kitchen window. Pale light hangs over the surrounding landscape. I catch a glimpse of a fox darting across my lawn and back into the fields, its bushy tail bright like a statement. I turn back to the agents.

"So, what's next for people like me, who fit the CA's target?"

"First, we'd like to find your earrings." Alderson takes the lead. "If you don't mind us looking. If we can't find them, we'd like to dust, see if anything turns up."

I groan, knowing the mess it creates.

"Does Wallace Scott have a key to your place?"

"No. And I've never told anyone where I hide my spare."

"Which is where?"

"I brought it in the minute I got home." I fish it out of my pocket and lay it on the table between them.

"Okay if we look around?" Greene asks again.

"Yes, but first, can you tell me how the killer did it? As you know, the police have kept it fairly under wraps."

Greene and Alderson look at each other for a long moment. Finally, Alderson gives a shrug. Maybe potential victims get special privileges.

Yay for me.

"The man, Askens, the first, was execution-style in an empty park where he jogged in the morning," Greene says. "Three shots. One in the back, two in the head. The second, the woman, Loman, was approached from behind and slit across her throat. In her garden."

I stare at them both. A sick pit forms in my stomach.

"Why—different? Do you know?"

"We're not sure," Alderson says. "Convenience? Or they cared more about the sound with the second in a much more populated area. Or, the rage is growing, and the knife is more personal, more vicious. Worst case, there's more than one person behind this."

I swallow hard. I have three days and change left to figure this out. "Do what you need." I motion to my place. "And I'll help in any way I can."

Finally, when they're done making a mess of my house and come up empty, they take my spare key and mention they'll send someone from the county's CSI team to dust obvious places like doors and windowsills. They tell me they'll post someone from the local force to sit in the drive as a precaution.

When I say not to bother, that I'm sure the locals don't have the resources, Greene says, "Oh, they'll find them."

As if pressure from the Bureau makes everything possible.

And he's not wrong. When I was on the force, we pretended that we didn't jump when they called, but we always did.

Now that I'm alone again, my mind buzzes.

I go into my bedroom, where clothes on hangers lay strewn across my bed. I step around plastic sweater bins pulled from my closet, kneel before my safe, open it, and grab my gun. I remind myself to hit the shooting range. I take the gun upstairs to my home office and get to work.

First, I google the CA's first victims—the man from Snohomish and the woman from Santa Monica—to remind myself about them. I'm looking for any common thread I can find. The two cities are eleven hundred miles apart, but who knows? It's a stretch to think one rookie PI can spot something the FBI might have missed, but it feels good to be doing something. To get the best sense of their lives, I start with their social media.

No surprise: Their pages are overwhelmed by sympathy posts from friends and strangers. I scroll and scroll until I get to personal posts written by the victims themselves.

Randal Askens from Snohomish was an avid bird hunter. Photo after photo of his hunting trips with a group of guys dressed in brush pants and orange vests, holding their shotguns over their shoulders. A photo of a pheasant he'd mounted serves as his profile picture, the image not doing justice to the long green-and-gold tail feathers. His feed is full of comments from friends about hunting and football.

His bio boasts he was a football coach at a local high school. When I cross-check his name plus the school's name, I come up with something that raises a thrum of interest—a scandal where the head coach was accused of recruiting underprivileged students of color from Mississippi who were good ballplayers. He promised them food, rent, supplies, and pathways to college, and then left them high and dry with no support when their seasons finished.

I wonder if the assistant was in on the racket and if this is what he was supposed to confess. But that makes no sense. Why target the assistant and not the head coach, the one doing all the recruiting?

I go back to his feed and keep scrolling. I see that Askens has a sister in Texas named Ellen Atherton, who commented on one of his photos taken on the field after a win against a local rival: So good to see your smiling face. We need to chat more than once every few months.

I jot her name down.

I move on to the second victim.

Vonda Loman from Santa Monica clearly enjoyed surfing, cooking, and gardening. Well, at least she enjoyed watching other people surf: many photos of the beach, the ocean, and people riding waves in the distance.

The cooking and gardening she handled herself. Loman's social media includes photos of tasty-looking drinks in crystal tumblers, dishes of exotic food, flowers in her garden. She worked at Santa Monica Community College as a counselor and went to high school and college in San Diego.

The two victims have nothing in common that I can see beyond both working in education. Neither appears to have had children, which is a relief. Maybe the killer only picks people who don't have kids, perhaps because he lacks an appetite for stranding them.

Some of Vonda's last posts are about the sketch that resembled her: To everyone out there who thinks it's me: It's not. I have nothing to confess. I have lived a clean, honest life.

I shake my head. The poor woman. No matter what she did or didn't do, she surely didn't deserve to die at the hands of this psycho. She was someone's daughter, someone's friend, maybe someone's significant other.

*Psycho.*

But before Railes took care of Coleman, hadn't I myself imagined obliterating him? Putting a bomb under his car, maybe, and blowing him to a million pieces—that was always a special favorite, right down to imagining the red cloud of flesh and bone spraying in all directions.

It's one thing to fantasize about it, and another to do it. I got to watch Coleman die and I made sure his murderer was never prosecuted. But the moment was wholly unsatisfying. I try not to think about it, so I refocus on my attempt at looking for common threads.

I spend the next two hours digging through check-cashing and credit-application data on IRBsearch to see if the victims had similar major purchases or investment projects, ever applied to live in the same apartment or condo complexes, or bought houses in the same neighborhood at any point. Nothing hooks up.

I am as good at digging for key tidbits online as I am at looking for my lost earrings.

It's late and I can hear the wind soughing through the tops of the pines. I take a break and go into the kitchen. I study my sad refrigerator's contents to see if I'm hungry, but I'm not. I fetch a glass and run the tap.

When I look up, someone stares back at me through the window above the sink.

I jump back, dropping my glass just as Jess did the other day as I go for my ghost gun in its ghost holster before I quickly realize it's just my own reflection.

*Enough, Crosbie. Get it together.* I see myself in the glass, my chest still rising and falling from the jolt. I'm wide-eyed and wired, my face tight with worry. *Even if it is you, in the morning, you've got three more days.*

But maybe it's time I carry my gun everywhere, even if I am in my own home, at least until I pick up a security system.

The *Rolling Stone* reporter I met in the hotel and ran into again at the airport pops into my mind, sending a frisson of fear straight up my spine. "Why did I see you twice?" I whisper to the wraith in the window. "Why were you in Dallas and then on my flights of all things? And how could I have not seen you in Denver? Granted, it was brief, and Jess and I did get that coffee, but still. Could it be coincidental?"

Jeremy Fisher.

I clean the broken glass, go back to my office, and look him up.

Jeremy K. Fisher. The *K* stands for Kyle.

*Jeremy Fisher,* Rolling Stone. *Reporter-at-large.*

There are links to articles he's written, everything from finance to violent crime, sports, media, environment, and gender politics.

From Riverside, California. Graduated from Victor Valley Union High School. Graduated from the University of Montana in Missoula, where he studied journalism.

So, he does have a connection to Montana. And he went to the same university I did, but I graduated in criminology and he in journalism. But he's older. He graduated three years ahead of me. Could he have known Sophie, though? It seems unlikely. She would have been a freshman when he was a senior.

He then went on to Northwestern University's journalism grad school, one of the best in the country, I've been told.

He has a younger sister who lives in Culver City—not far from Santa Monica, where the second victim was found. Which means nothing. Fiona has a sister who lives north of Seattle, near Snohomish—is she a suspect now?

Any number of people have connections to friends and relatives in either area, including myself. Hell, one of my good friends from my younger elementary years lives in Seattle.

Jeremy K. Fisher has no Facebook account, but he's on X and Instagram. On X, he mainly reposts stuff from *Rolling Stone* or links from fellow writers. He's coy, low-key. His takes are sharp, short, and to the point.

One post: Left, right . . . The division politicians have sown is in their interests, not yours. Meanwhile, they and the big business they're associated with are laughing all the way to the bank.

The thread following that post goes on with bickering about the state of neoliberalism, free speech on social media platforms, and censorship. Jeremy Fisher replies to none of the follow-ups.

One of Jeremy's other posts reads that he'd like to be in sync with the National Resources Defense Council but that they've abandoned their mission, which leads to more squabbling about global warming, the oil industry, and a post comparing Jeremy's face to cat vomit.

On Instagram, very few selfies or photos of him at all—only shots from his travels. I use an app to set up a phony number so he can't trace the call back to me and use SpyDialer.com to bypass the ringing on Jeremy's phone and go straight to his voicemail.

*Hey, this is Jeremy Fisher with* Rolling Stone. *Leave me a message and I'll get back to ya.*

That cinches it. At least, a little. My radar is still up. Way up. I hope he's not lying. His message is generic enough, but his voice is as smooth as whiskey, and it sends the strangest opposing sensation down my spine: part warm tingle and part cold dread.

I brush the warm-tingle part away. *Be smart, Cros. Ted Bundy was a charmer, too.*

# Chapter 19

I lie on the couch. I lie on the bed. I stand at the kitchen window where I just lost my cool. I sit on the front stoop in the chilly night, but I feel exposed. The stars say nothing. My thoughts tangle.

Wallace Scott, my ex.

The missing earrings.

The FBI . . . *watching me.*

A very dead and buried Mark Coleman.

Billy Railes, who no doubt long ago counted all the lucky stars in this universe and the one next to it and wondered why in that instant I sided with Team Blue instead of Team Female Rogue. I could have sold Railes out, but instead, I handed him the hall pass of his life.

And Detective Mitch Ewing. Does he know the truth?

My open investigations, especially into Robbie Ridgeway and Clarissa Haynes, all derailed.

And more than a few times I wonder what I missed, or what remains to be learned, about Jeremy K. Fisher.

I flash to Sophie. I see her slumped over her desk, her head in the crook of her arm. Her beautiful strawberry hair fanned out, touching a sticky, half-empty bottle of Jose Cuervo near the edge. I had walked into the room to check on her, thought she'd only fallen asleep over her homework. Or wanted to believe that, but the cold, knowing dread was already creeping in. As I went to nudge her awake, I found her body had already begun to stiffen.

I wipe the image away, but it's only replaced by Jess. Jess, traumatized and a shell of her former self.

Then Leon. God, Leon. The pain clutches my chest, then rises to my throat and clenches it like there's no tomorrow.

It forces me up, so I leave the front stoop and go to my kitchen table, my thoughts stirring through all these players like a wooden spoon in a rancid stew. The pressure of knowing I only have less than four full days is not going to allow any sleep, no matter how exhausted I am.

There's a loose thread I'm not seeing. It's all a tangled mess.

The question is pretty simple. Where should I focus my fear?

I decide to get organized. I think of the crazy murder boards we've all seen on television and the murder books used to compile evidence that I learned about when studying for my homicide detective's license while still on patrol. I need an about-to-be-murdered manual. And I'm the one in the crosshairs.

Instead, I find blank sheets of paper in my office, take them to the kitchen table with a couple of inches of whiskey in a cheap glass tumbler, and start writing shit down. Every note I deem worthy earns me one sip.

The CA stuff makes me circle back to my short-lived, so-called cop career.

Did it even last long enough to call it a career? In the eyes of the old guard, *no way*. I was a washout. A dud. A loser. Someone whose tumultuous stint in uniform would be quickly forgotten by all except for the slimeball Billy Railes.

I had begun college thinking I'd become a reporter, that I'd enter the school of journalism, but after what happened to Sophie, I only wanted one thing: to make a difference in the criminal justice system. I switched my major to criminology. Became a cop two years after I graduated from college.

I had believed the system could work, despite all the stories of corruption. I believed that I could be fair, that I would model what it looked like to be a good cop.

Instead, I earned a bloated rodent in my locker, got the word *bitch* scrawled across my car's windshield in brown shoe polish, and was subjected to the daily parade of black bands tied around thick, hairy, masculine arms. Constant accusing eyes from the very institution I wanted to believe in.

Around and around.

Wallace keeps bubbling back up, not necessarily in a bad or worrisome way, but with a voice saying *Look here.* But it's just Wallace, after all, someone I've known since my college days, so I'm not sure why my thoughts keep landing on him. Perhaps because he's the one who gave me the earrings.

And the last time I wore them would have been with him. I catalog all the places we've been since he's given them to me, which leads me to think of how we got together, how his eyes seemed to ask me after our day of hiking, *Is this for real, Cros?*

The next weekend, after a night with other friends out at a bar in Whitefish, I was suddenly ravenous for him. I went for it, kissing him when we walked to his car on a dark street.

Why didn't it last? What was it about the space between us? When does a relationship go from fizz to flat? After several months, when the passion faded, all that remained was the basic, unerotic foundation of a bond conducted under the guise of a romantic couple. Where was my ability to judge potential boyfriends? For that matter, anyone?

The whole harassment ordeal at work left me feeling powerless. My sister's rape quadrupled that feeling of impotence. Of uselessness. I had already had feelings that things weren't right with Wallace, but when all this went down, he was the one person in my life who felt secure. Honestly, at the risk of sounding like some fucked-up Jezebel, not breaking up with him when I knew things weren't right, even as the relationship dragged on, was something I could control.

After I fully came to grips with the idea that we were clinging to Sophie through one another, each trying to assuage our guilt that we'd failed to do more to protect her, and I realized I needed to be there for

Jess more fully so I didn't make the same mistake, I finally broke up with him, even with him as a steady keel in my life.

Wallace said pretty much the same thing when I told him I wanted to return to only a friendship. "I understand," he said after a long pause. "I sort of knew it wasn't going to last. I guessed the ghost of Sophie would always hang over us."

That was hitting the nail on the head, all right. True, there wasn't much zing between us. The sex was fine, sometimes great, but it became as routine and uninspired as a meeting for coffee. Those problems, had we chosen to put some effort into them, were solvable. Workable, at least.

But *the ghost of Sophie*, as he had worded it, was the real weight that shattered us.

Wallace had also brought up Sophie one of the last times we had gone out as a couple. It was a benefit for his orchestra around Christmastime. The symphony had already played their set, and a chamber group was up next. Wallace decided to hit the booze since he was finished performing. I had hit it, too.

We rarely spoke of Sophie by this point. I didn't know how to handle it when he said he missed her, both of us sloshed, standing among a crowd of locals as well as his colleagues and donors. Even a few police department folks attended, which would've made me nervous enough. It was so strange to see Allison and Fiona and her husband, Trey, to step out and do something in the community. It was the first time I'd seen any of my friends since I'd quit a month ago.

"I wish she was here," Wallace said. His state of inebriation was obvious. He was wistful. I saw Allison standing in line at the bar near us to get a drink. I wanted to go chat with her, anything other than going down the road of mourning Sophie, once again, with Wallace. Why step in an emotional river thrashing with rapids? Why even dip a toe?

"You act like you've erased her from your mind," Wallace said, one of the most inaccurate accusations ever leveled in my direction. He left in a huff.

Allison quickly took his place, making easy small talk without either one of us bringing up the fact that I'd quit the force. She'd been drinking more lately and chatted about how she enjoyed Jess's podcast and wanted us to get drinks or coffee to confirm that our friendship wouldn't change because I'd left the department. But I wasn't in the mood to make any social plans beyond the fundraiser with anyone from the department, even Allison. It was still too raw for me. I fake smiled, trying to forget my gruff interaction with Wallace, then excused myself.

Then it hits me so hard I slap the table.

My clutch.

*Of course.*

I had worn a little black dress to the fundraiser that night, and the earrings. I carried my shiny purse. I'd driven my car and met Wallace in Kalispell, since he'd been working late. Fiona and Trey wanted to go to a bar after the banquet.

Wallace didn't want to because he was exhausted from all the prepping he'd had to do for the fundraiser—he said—but I knew he was irritated with me. And I with him. I felt awful that I didn't say anything sweet and comforting when he brought Sophie up, but still, I didn't want to be around him. I needed space. We'd both been too irritable.

Fiona and Trey have a child, Adriana, who was twelve months at the time. Fiona said she was with her grandma, so I could crash at their place, which I did, since I'd had a few too many at the bar to go with the few too many I'd thrown down at the fundraiser. I don't even remember taking the earrings off and putting them in the purse, but I have a strong hunch that that's exactly what I did.

I go to my bedroom, hit the light, and go into my walk-in closet. Clothes, belts, scarves, and other accessories are piled in a heap from the FBI's search. I rummage through it all but come up empty.

I glance at the time: 12:45 a.m. It's too late to ring Fiona. Or is it? It should be a no-brainer. Who disturbs parents of a young child at that hour?

I pull up Fiona's number anyway and call.

"Cros?" Through her grogginess, I can tell she's rattled to get a call so late.

"Hey, Fiona. Everything's fine. I'm fine."

"What the hell, then? It's the middle of the freakin' night."

"I'm sorry. I know. Look, I should have called you earlier, but do you have my black clutch?"

"What?"

"My little black clutch? When I stayed at your place in December after the banquet for the symphony, I left it there."

"Yeah. I remember."

"Can you look for it?"

"What? Now?"

I give her silence as an answer.

"Seriously?"

"It's about those earrings in the sketch."

"What?"

"I think they're in that clutch."

"Oh. Oh my God. Cros."

I can't tell if her voice means she's frightened for me, or excited to be a part of the story. If she'll be posting by morning how I phoned her in the middle of the night looking for the earrings in the Confession Artist's sketch. A part of me curses myself for not waiting until morning. The other part of me doesn't care. I need to know.

I hear shuffling and can tell she's out of bed.

"Cros?"

"Yeah?"

There's something in the way she lets my name hang in the quiet night that sends a shiver down my spine. I glance at my bedroom window and meet my own reflection again, as I did in the kitchen window. I see the woman in the drawing. My breath catches.

"What?" I press.

"*Is* everything okay? Are you safe at home? Maybe you should go to Jess's."

"No. I'm good." I say it firmly. That's out of the question. If I'm being stalked, the thought of bringing the killer anywhere near Jess or Sam makes my stomach do wild things.

"But—"

"No. I'm good."

"Do you want to wait on the line or want me to call you back?"

"I'll wait."

An eternity. Almost four long minutes. Three and forty-seven seconds, but who's counting.

"I sent you a picture," she announces proudly.

My phone dings.

I open the text and see the picture of them cupped in Fiona's pale palm.

A wave of relief takes hold. *Yes.* I pump my fist. "Thank you," I say.

"I found the clutch in one of the bins in my closet." She sounds fully awake. "I guess I accidentally threw it in with my stuff." Which is her way of admitting she's used it without asking me. "The earrings were in the outside zippered pocket. I had no idea they were in there when I used it last."

I shake my head. I'm such an idiot for not having remembered the event and the awkward evening with Wallace, but it was probably because I wanted to put it all out of my mind. But I'm still relieved to have located the earrings. It feels like a small win. In the morning, I'll call Greene and Alderson and let them know I found them.

"Fiona," I say. "Please keep all this to yourself, okay?"

"Of course," she says.

I hang up feeling lighter, like I'm suddenly floating in a colorful hot-air balloon. As if simply locating these earrings erases the fact that there's a psycho out there who's drawn replicas of these very earrings on ears that match mine.

But I know better. This balloon only stays afloat if I catch the CA before he catches me.

# A CONFESSION

X: @MonMon #CAConfession—I'm Monae Monzego. Here's my thing and it's HUGE! I pushed my abusive husband off a cliff twenty miles outside Florence, OR, and said it was an accident. You can google it. It was a big thing in 2016. Regret it? I'm not sure. He shot my dog in front of me. Used to hit me, choke me, call me bitch and whore. I called the police to finally turn myself in, but no response so far. I think they're getting swamped with confessions right now, but when they're ready, I'm prepared to face the consequences.

# Chapter 20

***Three Days***

Slash burning and dry morning air turn the fall sky the color of ultra-faded blue jeans. At the intersection with the paved county road, a beige, unmarked vehicle sits off to the side.

I slow down and cautiously approach. When I pull up next to it, the headlights pop on, so he's started the engine. I stop and roll down my window. He does the same.

A clean-cut, redheaded, freckle-faced guy sits behind the wheel. He's wearing the beige sheriff's uniform. I'm relieved that he's not KPD. I don't need that right now.

I smile. "You posted here to watch my place?"

"Yes, ma'am."

I can't read his badge from where I'm sitting. "You been here all night, deputy?"

"Zane. Since early this morning."

"Okay, well, Deputy Zane, I'm headed out for a few groceries at Super One in Columbia Falls, then to my office, then a quick stop at a friend's, but I'll be back. No need to follow me. I'll be in public places."

From what Alderson and Greene told me, the killer has only taken victims in either private or deserted places—Randal Askens in an empty park, and Vonda Loman in her garden.

Plus, I have some days left. Right?

So protective duty now might be a waste unless someone is stalking me and the deputy happens to pick up on that. A part of me is grateful they want to keep me safe. Another feels irritated for the intrusion. But I can't blame Deputy Zane. He's following orders and the work is monotonous.

"Thanks for doing this."

"They want me to follow your every move."

"I appreciate that, but I'd rather have you make sure no one unwanted swings by my place while I'm away."

"I have my orders, ma'am."

"Suit yourself." I have the right to refuse protective detail, but there's something comforting about it, so I leave well enough alone. I hit my blinker and pull out onto the highway, pick up speed quickly to match the traffic. I see him do the same in my rearview, and he follows me to Super One.

Inside the store, a stranger—a tall middle-aged man with a baseball cap—bumps into me in one of the aisles and sends my pulse thudding. He excuses himself. There's a high-wire tension in the air now with every step I take, every move I make. I grab what I need and get out as fast as I can.

When I go back out, Deputy Zane stands outside his car, stretching. I put my groceries in the trunk and walk over to him. I might as well find out a little about him if I'm going to have him tailing me. A Styrofoam cup sits on the hood of his car, wisps of steam dissipating in the morning air.

Zane reminds me of a guy Jess used to date after her divorce from Patrick, Sam's dad. Patrick was a long-haired, sullen guy who played in a local band.

But the guy she dated after Sam's dad was the opposite, a clean-cut redhead. But he turned out to be a jerk. He drank too much and got belligerent when he'd had too many.

I tried to warn Jess to get rid of him, and when she wouldn't, I pulled him over one time, too, like my neighbor with the dog, after

I saw him leave a bar with another woman and warned him that it was best to get lost. I didn't care that I was meddling in my sister's personal affairs. The guy needed to skedaddle, be out of her and Sam's life. Period.

He didn't exactly ghost Jess after this, but he politely ended it. I mentioned to Jess that I'd run into him, and when she asked if I'd said anything mean to him, I said I hadn't. But I think she knew I had. Thankfully, she wasn't too broken up about it. She even mentioned that if I *had* said anything to him, I'd done her and Sam a favor.

I refocus on Deputy Zane. His cheeks are flushed. I smile at the idea that he's still young enough to have perpetually rosy cheeks.

"Where next?" he says.

I ignore him. "What's your first name?"

"Andy," he says.

"Where you from?"

"East of the mountains." He looks away like he's embarrassed.

"What part?"

"Chester."

"Chester? What's the population there?"

"Less than a thousand."

"You grew up there on a ranch? A farm?"

"You could call it both."

I can tell he doesn't want to talk about where he's from, but I press on. "You went to high school in Chester?"

"No, ma'am."

"Oh, where'd you go to school then?"

"Sage Creek." Sage Creek is a Hutterite colony north of Chester, not far from the Canadian border. I've never been there, but I've met people who pay the Hutterites, an Amish-type community practicing an old-fashioned way of life, for permission to hunt pheasants on their land.

"But you left the colony?"

"Yes, ma'am."

"This your first job since you've left home?"

"I've worked others. Got my GED and my associate's at the community college. Took odds-and-ends work to support myself during that. This is my first real job since . . ."

He leaves the thought unfinished. There's sadness in his eyes.

"Good for you," I say. "Getting that all done, I presume on your own."

He rubs his forehead. He would clearly rather talk about something else. Anything else. I know the feeling well.

"You don't need to call me *ma'am*," I tell him as I walk away.

Fiona stares at me, her mouth parted.

"You have a bodyguard?"

"Don't mind him," I say. "It's a precaution. Emphasis on *caution*."

"You're worried enough that you went to the cops?"

"I did. Worried enough to get it on the record."

"Oh." She furrows her brow. "I didn't realize it was that serious. I mean, I know you're a dead ringer for the sketch and the earrings and all, but . . ."

"But what?"

"It's unreal."

"Unreal except don't tell that to the first two victims," I say. "Or their families."

"We're in nowhere Montana," says Fiona. "It's like some stupid game."

"Except for when it's not," I say. "And believe me when I say I have my own doubts."

Inside her foyer, I can see the excitement in her eyes. A memory of Jess asking me in high school why some kids, like Fiona, have it so easy pops into my mind. Jess had tried out for the cheerleading squad along with Fiona. Fiona made it; Jess didn't. Jess was heartbroken. "How can she be so popular? Friends with everyone, even the teachers?" Jess had asked.

I told Jess that Fiona did that at the expense of being real. That she was sometimes fake and didn't always follow through with people. That it was better to be sincere. I remember saying, "You don't have to try to fit in with people you don't particularly like all the time to be popular, Jess. It's okay to keep your distance."

And yet, here we are, still friends after all these years. She has always been there, but I still feel the need to keep her in check.

"Listen, Fiona," I say. "*Because* it seems like just a game, it might be tempting to pop stuff on your social media about it. I get it. It's crazy stuff. But like I said, even if it's not me, which it's probably not, it's best to play it safe."

She stares at me, her hazel eyes wide, but doesn't answer.

"Got it?"

"I told you I did last night. Want to *keep* repeating it?"

I smile at her, past the tension. "Sorry. It's all so weird. And again, I'm sorry for waking you up."

Fiona brushes my apology away. "Come," she says.

She leads me into the kitchen, a small, clean, and modern space that Trey recently remodeled. She grabs the clutch off a new white Corian counter that resembles granite or marble with grayish veins running across it.

I open the shiny black flap to expose the main compartment. An old lipstick, someone's business card, and a comb lie at the bottom. I pull back the zipper to the small side pouch and there they are, sparkly and tangled together in the corner like they're hiding. I pick one out and study it.

Seeing it up close, however, is bad news. It makes me realize the drawing is very accurate. A blue centerpiece in the middle of the silver feather. And even though the sketch is in black and white, the ones in the drawing are still eerily spot-on. I place the earring back in the pocket with its mate as Trey enters the kitchen holding Adriana.

Adriana reaches out for me, and I hold her little hand and smile.

"Crosbie," Trey says. "How you holding up?"

I hate that expression with a passion because it always seems designed to make you melt into a puddle, not to bolster you.

"I'm good."

"Yeah?" He studies me with concern. Pity, even. And something else, curiosity mixed with disgust, like he's wondering what I've done. If he only knew. If Fiona only knew. "You going to confess something?" he asks.

"Everything's fine." I say it like I believe it. I think I sound convincing. "I need to get going, though. Thanks for this." I hold up the clutch.

"No need to thank me," says Fiona. "It's yours. And, Crosbie?"

"Yes?"

"Sorry—I know you're in a tough spot."

"Unless I'm not."

But now, I know better.

"I'm sorry you're going through this."

"Thanks," I say.

"Be careful out there, okay? Even with a cop on your butt, be careful."

"Got it," I say. "You bet."

# Chapter 21

Zane is two cars back, trailing me. As I pull into my drive, he pulls into the same spot where I found him when I left the house. I'm happy to be left alone and need time to think before the all-powerful FBI arrive.

My happiness is quickly zapped. A black Lincoln Navigator claims part of the driveway in front. Standing outside their vehicle, Alderson wears a pleasant smile, and Greene her usual earnest indifference. She removes her sunglasses as if to take a better look at me in the daylight.

Clouds have moved over the sun, dimming the early-day glare and casting an enormous blanket of shade over the mountain slopes. Greene's hazel-green eyes take on the color of yellow moss in the diffused sunlight. Alderson keeps his Ray-Bans on.

"Johnny-on-the-spot," I say.

"You have 'em?" Greene asks, holding out a hand like we're engaging in some drug deal.

"In my purse."

I fetch the earrings and hold them out in my palm. The clouds slide by and the bright sun makes the silver sparkle and the sapphires deepen to near black. "No use in dusting them," I say. "My prints were all over them to begin with, and so are my friend's. I'm certain they haven't left this purse since I used it almost nine months ago, when I forgot it at Fiona's."

Greene holds out a baggie from her blazer pocket, and I slip the earrings inside. She studies them through the plastic for a second before handing them to Alderson.

He gives them a long look before tucking them into his shirt pocket, but not before throwing a wide-eyed look to Greene that says I'm screwed.

"We're going to need the full name of your friend and everyone she lives with." Greene's face is solemn. "And we need to talk more. Can we go in?"

"I have groceries." I walk back to my car, open the trunk, and grab two large canvas bags stuffed to the brim. A red-tailed hawk sails above the field to the north, hunting mice. I feel the agents' eyes on me, watching my every move.

"Need some help?" Alderson asks.

"I got it, but you can close the trunk for me." I take one last look at the circling hawk and inhale the faint, sweet scent of prairie hay wafting from the fields, brown from the past summer's heat.

Inside, I have no patience for pleasantries. I turn to them, my arms folded. "What would you like to talk about?"

"We'd like to sit down," Greene says. "If that's okay."

"I'm fine right here."

Greene sighs but doesn't respond. She isn't going to confront my obstinacy, which I take as a bad sign.

I transfer bananas and apples to a white ceramic fruit bowl on my counter. I don't want to be a jerk, but I can't seem to help it. To let everything proceed entirely on their terms hints of surrender.

"Have you come up with those names we need?" Greene asks.

She's referring to the list of people with a possible reason to want to harm me. "I'll grab it for you in a sec."

Alderson leans casually against the counter, his arms across his chest. He's rolled his crisply ironed sleeves up. Greene stands dead center between the U-shape of my counters.

"Before I get it," I say. "Has anyone else contacted the FBI? Who thinks they might be the one?"

"There's a woman in Texas we're checking out. She looks a lot like the sketch. And a lot like you." Greene scrolls through photos on her phone and holds it out for me. "But she doesn't have the earrings."

The woman does resemble me, more than any of the others I've seen so far online, more than Jennifer Garner, more than the woman from Oregon who confessed she had an affair while her husband lay sick in the cabin of their sailboat.

This stranger resembles me more than Jess does, which I find surreal. It's oddly comforting to know there's someone else out there. "Does she own any earrings that might be somewhat similar?" I hand the phone back to Greene.

"I mean, she has lots of danglies, but nothing precisely like the ones in the sketch."

"Has this Texas woman confessed anything?" My own guilt and the fact that I have zero desire—or intention—of confessing anything make me feel like something rises up and lodges in my throat. Like shards of my own conscience. I swallow it down.

Greene shakes her head. "But she's thinking of doing an interview with the press to generate a bunch of interest in her, hoping that if more people are aware of her out in the world, she'll be more protected. Swamped by reporters and such."

I cringe. Who in their right mind would want that? I think of the media spectacle it will create and how it will change her life, how people will always consider her the CA's potential victim from here on out, how it will inevitably draw the attention of other stalkers and online bullies.

One of my first cases as a PI was with a twenty-three-year-old woman in the Flathead who'd become the target of an online bullying campaign for no other reason than her success. She'd grown up gaming and become a bit of a sensation on Twitch. Simply becoming popular among gamers made her the subject of online harassment. A handful of gamers began coordinating attacks, creating countless new accounts with fake names across multiple platforms with the sole purpose of making her life miserable. They issued death threats and harassed family members. I didn't have the means to ID and monitor those stalkers making the most violent intimidations, so I contacted the local FBI, and eventually, they shut the key accounts down.

As far as I know, no one has posted anything about me on social media. My friends have only texted or DMed me or each other since the sketch came out. Fiona mentioned on her Facebook account that she has a friend who resembles the sketch, but even she has enough sense, perhaps because of my warnings to her, to not tag me or mention my name.

Greene notes the sour expression on my face. "Going public isn't an entirely horrible idea, Crosbie. Like I said, it's more difficult for a stalker or a killer to strike if everywhere you go, a certain number of people can ID you."

At the suggestion, something hot shoots through me, like the sun is suddenly burning ten times hotter directly over my head. For one tiny second, I had considered appeasing whoever is up to this crazy cat-and-mouse game of shame. It'd be fresh, gleaming meat for the press. But of course, if I confessed, there'd be consequences. Serious ones.

For me. For Railes. For Ewing, maybe, too.

But it's not only the consequences. It's the shame, red hot as a flame, searing me to my core. I can't bear the thought of the public knowing me that way. Of Jess, Wallace, Fiona, Hannah, Mark, Allison, my stepdad . . . everyone in the police force. Of the community and the world. The friendly guy—what's his name, Mr. Tyson—at the bakery in Columbia Falls. Joan at the county library. Dr. Jones at the Women's Health Clinic. Dr. Ammera at the dentist's office, Mr. Dahlton, my favorite teacher in high school . . .

And I'd have no work. How would I make a living?

But as always, I swing back to Jess. How would she take it when she wanted closure so badly and I helped rip it away from her? Would she ever forgive me?

Not just my future, but my relationship with my sister and Sam dries up like dead leaves right before my eyes. I see the debris of them sweep away in the wind in flurries. It makes me dizzy, like the walls of my kitchen are swaying around me like a ship in a storm.

I wonder briefly what the Texas woman might have to confess, but I don't ask. I've been seeing enough already online to make my head spin.

But even if I wanted to confess, I have Jess to think about. We would become victims for life even if I didn't end up being the CA's intended target. The media would skin us alive. They would uproot and scrutinize every incident in our lives beyond my deplorable decision to protect Billy Railes.

I can't fathom putting Jess through the viciousness of the press after everything she's endured, especially since one of the main reasons she refused to report Mark Coleman in the first place was to avoid their savage bites. She watched me go through it with Sophie years before, when social media wasn't half the beast it is today. And I was a nobody. Thanks to her rising career in podcasting, she's a much more prominent figure than I'll ever be.

"And you think that's wise for the woman in Texas to do that?" I look to both my FBI protectors.

"Can't deny she'll be surrounded by reporters," Alderson offers. "They'll post up right outside her front door for a while—and while they're there, it would make it more difficult for the son of a bitch to grab her. Plus, if she confesses something, he claims he'll leave her be."

"But you don't even think it's her, do you?"

They both stare at me, not answering, eyes searching.

"Because of the earrings?" I say.

"We think we need to take this very seriously with everyone and anyone who could be the target," he says.

"But honestly. Do you think it's wise for this woman to go to the press? For me to do the same?" I can't fathom the thought.

"Ninety-nine percent of the time," Greene says, "the press makes our job harder. But we don't know. She could be safer with the spotlight on her. For you, though, we have a different idea." She pauses, letting that sink in. "And it involves some information we want to share with you. So please, can we have that seat now?"

# Chapter 22

## Vivian

Vivian came home from class to a sour smell in her apartment. She leaned over the sink to take a whiff of the garbage disposal and checked the trash bin. She couldn't identify the culprit, so she did the easy thing and tied up the bag and took it out to the dumpster behind her complex.

The sky was an enchanted blue, but Vivian didn't feel magical. She felt numb. In fact, she'd just been in a second-year psych class at her community college in Kalispell—five hundred miles from her hometown of Snohomish, from her mom and dad—and had learned a new phrase: *absence of affect*. It's what therapists call someone who is devoid of emotion or even understanding, usually in response to trauma.

It had been almost a year, but she still felt the urge to text Ryan right there and explain the phrase to him. Ryan liked it when she shared new tidbits. It had become a habit of hers in the early months when she'd gone away to northwest Montana to live, ski, and attend the community college.

Ryan was always the brains in the family. He was three years younger. He asked questions about things on her mind, even silly stuff. He never teased her about them, even the stupidest stray thoughts.

One time when she was in middle school and he was still in elementary, she asked him why a glass of ice water doesn't overflow when the cubes melt. He'd smiled kindly and explained how ice expands and is made up of mostly air, so it doesn't change the volume. It simply displaces water.

And when he was only four years old, he memorized every country in the world and its capital. And by the time he was eight, he was an insect freak. But you couldn't ask him anything or you'd be stuck forever listening to him go into great detail about his favorite aquatic bugs (namely stone flies, which survive in low-oxygen or oxygen-free conditions).

Eventually, it became a joke between them. She began sharing any matter-of-fact thing about life she came across. Hey Ryan, do you know the name of Odysseus's dog?

He'd answer, usually correctly. He'd text back something scientific he knew. Hey Sis, do you know that floodplains are among the most biodiverse landscapes on earth?

Now she looked to the northwest, toward Glacier Park, to see mountains like those jagged teeth of the plastic dinos he played with when he was little. It was cold out and she wrapped her arms around her waist after she closed the dumpster lid in the alley. She wasn't sure she wanted to go back in. She wasn't sure what she wanted.

She looked back to the mountains. Blue bled up from the peaks, and the higher she gazed, the paler the sky.

Her boyfriend, Logan, had gone up to Big Mountain to skin up. He'd asked her to come, but she'd said she had classes. She couldn't skip. The psych teacher told her she needed to make a choice: start attending or pull out before the drop date.

She didn't have the energy to go skinning. She imagined Logan's neck glistening with sweat despite the cold. She pictured his thighs pumping with each slide of his ski up the steep terrain of Tony Matt, the main run that shot up from the resort like an arterial vein.

Logan never sat still. She wondered how long he'd put up with her while she wallowed in this inertia. *Hey, Ryan, learned the other day that* inertia *means the opposite of how it sounds. It's* lack *of motion. Lack of activity, not energy* in *motion.*

Vivian shivered and turned to face her apartment complex. It was one of the newer ones, part of the generic sprawl creeping across the valley. She often thought about all the field mice and other critters that got displaced when they tore up the land to build it.

Her parents had agreed to pay the rent and living expenses if she committed to giving college a try. She had picked Kalispell for the community college and access to skiing in Whitefish.

That's honestly all she wanted to do: get a job in the service industry and get certified to teach skiing. In high school, she'd dreamed of being on the slopes all the time. That had been her dream ever since their family had taken their first trip to Salt Lake City when she was seven, to ski Park City, Alta, and Snowbird. *Hey, Ryan, did you know that tree wells are spaces under spruce trees that have unconsolidated snow that can kill you if you fall into them?*

Her mom and dad used to dish out those condescending smiles whenever she'd mention her alpine goals, as if they were only humoring her. In their minds, it was a no-brainer that she'd go to college. That was expected. She would attend, paving the way for Ryan. But that was unnecessary. Ryan was college bound, no matter what. Until he wasn't.

And her parents now? After they'd fought so hard for her to enroll somewhere, anywhere, did they care if she stayed with it anymore?

When she was home over Thanksgiving, her parents had barely spoken to each other. Mom seemed upset over how much Dad drank. Mom wouldn't say it outright, but Vivian could see that there was a new disgust in her face when she looked at her father—one that never existed before Ryan's suicide.

And Dad, he had learned since Ryan's death not to say anything out loud. But Vivian could tell he was impatient that Mom hadn't been out of the house in months. She walked around like a zombie.

Suddenly college, something Vivian had initially felt forced to do, presented itself like a lifeline. When the teacher said she should maybe drop the class altogether, a fear so sharp and cold rose inside her that she went speechless. When she was confident she could speak without her voice cracking, she promised the instructor that she'd do better.

As Vivian came closer to the outdoor staircase of her building, she saw a gal from school park her Honda Civic in the complex's lot. Vivian almost stopped and waited in a slice of a chilling shadow to let her go up the stairs first, but then it would be obvious she didn't want to interact. It was the truth, though. She wanted to retreat to the dark cave of her apartment.

But when the woman saw Vivian, she flashed a cheerleader smile and waited until Vivian caught up at the base of the stairwell.

"Hey there," she said, squinting into the bright winter sun. "It's Shona. In case you forgot."

"Yes. Hi." Vivian knew her from one of her classes during her first year at Flathead Valley Community College. Shona was in the nursing program and worked hard. Much harder than Vivian. She was a non-trad student, as everyone called them.

They chatted about school as they climbed the steps. As they arrived at Shona's entrance, she said, "Want to come in? Have tea or coffee or something?"

Vivian looked at her, still squinting in the sunshine, her cheeks rosy from the cold. In Shona's polite offer, there was something motherly and inviting, something suggesting to Vivian that she didn't have to bear this world alone. She accepted.

Shona's layout was exactly like her own—one bedroom, a bathroom, and a small kitchen separated from a tiny main room by a counter that allowed exactly two stools.

But Shona had made her space much homier than Vivian's. Shona had prettier furniture and a nice fuzzy area rug with earthy tones. She'd hung abstract artwork—something generic and cheap she'd most likely purchased from Target, but it looked nice. Vivian was the type who'd rather go without than make do with something chintzy. In the end, she lived starkly, while most of her friends' surroundings were at least comfy and attractive.

Vivian and Shona pulled off their boots. They hung their jackets on coat hooks by the door. Shona motioned to one of the stools at the kitchen counter while she went to the other side, grabbed the kettle, filled it with water, and heated it on the stove.

"You're in nursing, right?" Vivian asked.

"Not exactly. I'm on the phlebotomy track, but I have to take a lot of the nursing classes for that." Shona angled her head down, like she was studying her. "I haven't seen you around campus that much this year."

Vivian wasn't sure she wanted to acknowledge her absence from classes, from social events in general. She knew that Shona knew about Ryan. When it first happened, a little over a year ago, she had come up to her after class and told her that she was thinking about her and that if she needed anything at all to let her know. That she'd keep Vivian in her thoughts and prayers.

"How are you doing?" Shona grabbed two cups from her cabinet.

Vivian smiled. It felt foreign and forced. She couldn't deny it, though; it was good to be in Shona's presence. She was genuinely nice. She would make an excellent phlebotomist, Vivian thought. One look at her smile and anyone would surrender the pale, blue-veined underbelly of their arm to her.

Shona put tea bags in the cups, took a lemon out of her fridge, and began slicing it as they waited for the kettle to whistle.

"You have a boyfriend?" Shona asked.

"Been seeing him for over a year now." Vivian had met Logan in mid-November of her first year at college. The relationship started a month, she thought, before it happened, but she did not say that to Shona.

"That's nice. You met him at the college?"

Vivian explained they'd met on the mountain when she was buying a ski pass, how they were in line next to each other.

"So he's a student?"

"No, bartender. And ski bum."

"Must be nice," Shona said.

"Yeah, he pretty much does what I came here to do, only I'm not really doing it." Vivian told Shona how she'd wanted to come here to work and ski, how she'd made a pact with her parents about college.

"Your parents. They're faring okay?"

"I guess. I mean, it's hard."

"I'm sure."

"It's, well, it's all so complicated."

"How so?" Shona's eyes were large and doe-like. Vivian wanted to fall into them, the way she used to stare at her mother's eyes when she was little and scraped up after a tumble.

Vivian thought of her mom again. She was a genuinely pleasing person, like Shona. But her mom, well, was too genteel to stand up to their father when Ryan had said he didn't want to play football. Their dad insisted it was "nonnegotiable."

He decreed it and therefore no bending or breaking his rules.

This rule's logic went something like this: Boys need to play on a team so they can learn how to be a part of something bigger than themselves, so they learn how to cooperate and experience camaraderie, which in turn makes them successful humans.

Their dad had played football in high school and college. He was convinced it had taught him how to succeed. As a software engineer who'd helped launch numerous start-ups, he said playing football taught him how to be a team player. He insisted his son should have the same experience. No, the same *opportunity*.

But Ryan didn't see it as that. He saw it as a sentence. During summer break, when Vivian was still home after her senior year in high school, when Ryan was entering his freshman year, she could remember the arguments. Ryan insisted he didn't want to play any sports at all, and her dad said that was not an option. Ryan would come to Vivian to complain, to say that Dad didn't get him, didn't understand that team sports weren't for him. She had tried to explain to him that it wasn't such an awful idea. Secretly, she—athletic like their dad—had thought it would benefit him for all the same reasons Dad had mentioned.

Plus, she wanted more for her baby brother's high school experience than always being the geeky kid. She wanted him to be accepted the way she was, to have ready-made friends that came with a team, maybe put some muscle on his lanky frame and some color to his cheeks so he could get a girl.

She didn't say all this to him, but she'd thought it.

Ryan moved on to their mom, hoping she would strike a compromise. "How about I join a club, like the kids that work on the yearbook?" he'd suggested. "Or even the speech and debate team. You know how much I hate to be in front of people. That I'd be willing to do that shows you how much I don't want to play."

Mom had smiled sweetly at him. "You could do both. Or even all three," she said. "But you know how your dad is when he sets his mind to something."

Later, he entered Vivian's room while she got ready to go out with friends. She was getting tired of his protests. They had ended up in a fight, and he had called her a daddy's girl, saying she went with everything he said because she was "superficial."

Now Shona handed Vivian a steaming cup with the tea bag already in it and a spoon and a wedge of lemon on the saucer. She grabbed honey from a cabinet and set it before Vivian.

"That honey's from the Flathead," said Shona, "and they say you should always have local honey because it helps your system get used to all the hay-fever triggers around here."

Vivian squeezed the plastic container and watched the golden gel stack up and swirl into her spoon and slowly ooze over into the cup. Vivian was fairly certain that if she asked Ryan about it, he'd tell her it was a myth, that local honey doesn't ward off anything.

"You were saying," Shona said. "It's complicated?"

"Grief. It's complex, because everyone has their own stuff to deal with as they process their own loss, but at the same time, they have to deal with the other person's shit, too. I think all the signals go haywire. It's why so many couples don't make it after . . ." Vivian petered out because a lump had suddenly formed and congested in her throat.

"I totally understand," Shona said. "Your parents? Are they getting any help? Doing any counseling?"

"It's touch and go, as you can imagine."

"I can't, really. I just can't, them losing their son like that and how that must put a type of poison into the relationship."

Poison? The word had made Vivian flinch, as if Shona had jabbed her with one of her phlebotomy needles.

But there was also something freeing in how Shona didn't shy away from the topic.

"That's one way to put it," Vivian said. "You should see how my mom looks at my dad. So much anger. And he at her with nothing but disappointment. It's, I don't know, it's so sad."

Shona's eyes were wide and understanding. "You know." She held out a palm. "There are groups for this kind of thing. In one of my community health classes, we had a woman who runs a grief group come speak to us. I could get you her name if you wanted."

"Nah, that's okay. I mean, I'm fine."

"Okay, well, there are other resources, too. Stuff online, books. We've had all sorts of guest speakers come into my class. Some are super interesting. I can look into some stuff for you." She smiled.

Vivian felt guilt rise in her, like she was betraying the only family she had left, deceiving her parents, who she knew were in so much pain, like she was. To quell the swelling guilt, Vivian tried distracting herself by thinking of the guest speaker due to visit her own bio class in the morning. It didn't stick, though. The fact was, sitting here with her new friend, it felt good—damn good—to talk, like she was dislodging sediment in a floodplain. Shona's voice, in fact, her whole appearance was like that golden honey she'd drizzled into her tea—smooth and comforting.

*Hey, Ryan, is it true that locally made honey helps your immune system against resident allergens?*

In her own apartment, Vivian felt hungry and dug out a frozen pizza from the freezer. When it was ready, she ate it at the counter while she read from her textbook. She left a few pieces for Logan, who she knew would be ravenous when he came over after work.

But he didn't come over. He called and told her he'd been invited along with some of the guys on a backcountry winter camping trip. Too good to pass up. They were leaving early in the morning, and he needed to get his gear in order.

Vivian sighed quietly so he couldn't hear. She felt abandoned, but she knew that was irrational. She told him to have fun.

Whatever newfound energy she'd discovered after talking to Shona drained away. A part of her was glad he wasn't coming; another part was caught in a purgatory between empty fatigue and a nameless desire to do something, anything, but she had no idea what.

*Hey, Ryan, I know you know what* dysthymic *means.*

The next day around the same time, Vivian looked out her window to the parking area below as Shona pulled up. She grabbed her pack from the back seat of her car, swung it over her shoulder, and walked gingerly over the icy lot to the staircase.

Vivian gave her time to settle in, then texted her and asked her what she was up to. Shona replied, The usual, with an emoji of a textbook. What about you?

Twenty minutes later, Vivian was back in Shona's kitchen. Shona made a mini pot of coffee with a powerful aroma.

"Figured we needed the caffeine." She poured Vivian a cup as she took a seat at the white counter.

"Perfect." Vivian smiled.

Vivian told Shona that Logan had gone camping. "It's like he's made to be on the move," Vivian said. "Like my dad."

"Outdoorsy?"

"Not like Logan with the backcountry, but he was a jock in high school and college. Track and field, football, and basketball. All the team sports. He got one of those all-state awards. Played football in college, too."

Shona laughed. "Sounds like my dad." She explained how her father was raised in a small town in eastern Montana, Havre, and that he went to Montana State University in Bozeman, where he became a linebacker for the Cats.

Vivian must have made a funny face because Shona said, "What?"

"I don't know."

"What?"

She let it out. She told Shona how her father had forced Ryan to join the JV team, how her mom didn't stick up for Ryan and was always so silent. How all the teams went on a preseason retreat to build camaraderie up at a camp with all these cabins on Whistler Mountain.

"That sounds fun. Didn't your brother enjoy that?"

She poured it out while Shona listened.

She had been going into one of the bars on the main drag in Whitefish. She'd finally met some other local instructors—two girls her age—on her own, not through Logan. She'd met them at a preseason instructor meeting, and they'd invited her out. Both, on the offseason, worked at a lodge on the lake right below the ski hill.

Vivian couldn't wait to pick the instructor's brain. She had driven to the small town twenty minutes north of Kalispell, parked by the train station, and was walking toward the bar where she was to meet them when her phone buzzed.

It was Ryan. She'd picked it up, thinking it would be quick. She knew he was at the retreat. "Hey, little bro, what's up?"

"Um, not much." He sounded nervous.

"What's wrong?" she asked, irritation creeping up in her.

"Uh, nothing. Just wanted to talk."

"How's the retreat?"

"Fine. I mean, it's . . ."

Vivian usually would have pushed, asked, *It's what? What's the problem?* But she was already running a little late and she didn't want the others to leave the bar to go to another before she got there.

Instead, she said, "Good. Okay, glad things are fine."

He went silent.

"Ryan?"

He didn't answer.

"Ryan, look, I gotta go. But is everything okay?"

"Yeah," he said, but he didn't sound like himself. That was the first time she wondered if maybe it wasn't such a great idea for her dad to push him so hard. She knew it would only take a bit of prodding to pry him open, to give him permission to vent.

She knew he needed that—except, at that moment, she did not want to stand out in the cold and listen to him complain. She did not want to have to give him a pep talk when the new girls were waiting for her. This was one of their father's unspoken reasons for making him play, she was sure—to make him more confident, more self-sufficient. More manly. Maybe it was high time. He was fifteen, for God's sake. Time to start bucking up.

She hopped over a puddle of water in the road. "Look, Ryan," she said. "Have fun. And try not to overanalyze everything. I've gotta go. Friends are waiting for me."

"Right," he said. "Have fun."

Weeks later, after the retreat, Ryan still wasn't himself. Eventually he broke down and admitted to Vivian what had happened that evening. He told her that the reason he'd called was that he was nervous because he sensed the JV team hazing shit he'd heard about was bound to happen that night.

So, it had been a cry for help, Vivian had thought. A sinking, sick feeling had overcome her when she thought of how she brushed him off.

A part of him, he revealed, had wanted to tell her, to have her call their mom and insist she go fetch him. Another part of him wanted to not be a baby. To tough it out. To be picked up would have only made things worse.

Toughing it out was exactly what he did. He made Vivian swear not to tell a soul about how they'd broomed him, all in good hazing fun. His insides still hurt from it, he told her.

Her guilt ballooned. She insisted he should go to a doctor, but he refused. When she said that she needed to tell their mom what had happened to him, he broke down and swore he'd never forgive her, never speak to her again if she breathed a word to anyone. Vivian couldn't bear to make things worse than they already were.

Vivian said to Shona now, "He was never the same. By December, he took his own life."

"Oh my God," Shona said when Vivian quieted. "That's so, so terrible. So incredibly awful. Your poor brother. I feel so bad for him." Her forehead was creased with anguish. She set her hand over her heart for a moment, then placed her cool, delicate palm on Vivian's wrist. "And you never told anyone?"

Vivian's eyes filled with tears. "He asked me not to. He begged me not to. He was so afraid that if it got out, he'd be bullied endlessly at school. And he would have been. I didn't want that to happen to him, either."

Shona shook her head in disgust, and Vivian waited for her to say something about the hazing, about the team, about the coaches, about what a horrible sister she was to not report it to someone, but she didn't. She said, "And your dad?"

"What about him?"

"Jesus. What a jerk," Shona said with disgust. "What an ass to push him to do that. Why couldn't he have honored who he was—your brilliant brother, who had other interests?"

Shona wasn't trying to be mean. In fact, she could have been so much more vicious by spotlighting Vivian's own negligence in the situation, but suddenly Vivian wanted to jerk her hand away. She looked down at Shona's white fingers, imagined them gingerly inserting the tip of a thin, cold needle. She brought her eyes back to Shona's, wide open and full of a combination of distaste and pity. Her pulse began to race. She wondered if Shona could feel it beneath her palm.

She waited for Shona to remove her hand, but she didn't. It felt like a handcuff, like she was trapped. She wanted to flee out the door and run back to her apartment.

The guilt rose up in her like bile again, fierce and acidic, the coffee surging up into Vivian's mouth. She jerked her hand away and covered it, managed to swallow the bitter brew back down, the sting of it lodging in her throat.

"You okay?" Shona asked, her voice like sunny lemonade.

Eleven months had gone by since they'd found Ryan in his room, gone from this world forever. Vivian would always remember that phone call. She would never stop going over it.

What if she had stayed outside that bar, ignored the chill in the air and the cold seeping through her boots, and talked to him? Really listened? What if she had called her mom and demanded that she go pick him up, insisting that he was in danger? Would her mom have done it? Or would her father have instructed her to stop babying him?

And what if she had told her parents about the brooming? Would they have gotten the appropriate help for Ryan?

The questions plagued her. Like a rogue mudslide, they dragged her down. Suffocated her. She'd never know the answers. But what she did understand, deep in her heart, was that she'd failed Ryan. She'd betrayed him.

Vivian stood. "Thanks for the coffee. I need to get back. So much studying."

"Oh, I know, right? But before you go, I have something for you." Shona looked around in her backpack and pulled out a sheet of paper and held it out. "It's a list of resources. Like I mentioned."

Vivian took it, thanked her again, and walked back to her place.

# Chapter 23

"One of them is close," says Greene. "Here in the Flathead."

"One of them who?" I say.

"One of the more active participants in the social media chatter," says Alderson. "Our tech guys spotted it."

"Where?"

"The public library," Greene says. Her moss-colored eyes return to a duller hazel in the kitchen light. "We don't know who he is yet or if he's the same person who's posted the sketches online, but his behavior is suspicious. The comments? They have a ring of righteousness to them, and they're all defending the killings."

My gaze drops to the grooves in the wooden table. Dread feels like the worst case of nausea.

"And it's closer than we expected. As we mentioned, the sites where the killer's dropped the actual sketches have been at least a good day's drive or a flight away from where they ended up committing the crimes. So, this could be a good thing; if they're staying in the pattern, it could mean it's not our person. But if he or she is breaking the pattern, well, not so good. But obviously, any activity in northwest Montana worries us."

"Any keyboard warrior could jump on the righteousness bandwagon, especially these days." We've settled at my kitchen table, which looks small against Alderson's hefty frame. "What makes this guy so suspicious?"

"The number of times the user shows up," she says. "It's excessive. Obsessive, even. Same generic username with numbers, but different IP addresses. Doesn't post from the same place. In fact, we're having a hard time locating the user."

"But have you pinpointed where the sketch was dropped from in the first place?"

"No. And that's why we have orders to get you somewhere safe."

"And where would that be?"

"A safe house."

"A Motel 6? What?"

Greene stares at me flatly, but Alderson half smiles. "Something like that."

I pick at the Band-Aid on my thumb covering my mangled skin. Heat rises in my face as I think of leaving my home and hiding out. How helpless would *that* feel? Pacing and killing time in some depressing motel room?

*No!* I want to yell.

"For how long?"

"Until we feel the threat has passed."

"How will you know when that happens?"

They don't answer because there is no answer.

"It may never pass if they're set on getting me, or I don't give them the confession they want. So it doesn't make any sense. I'm not going to *hide* somewhere. I have work."

I think of Paxton Rhoads, Clarissa's brother. And my new lucky number—the latest workers' comp claim I need to keep checking, which involves observing Aaron Lasserio, Ridgeway's old ranch hand who's moved to the Flathead. I need to watch him putz around his house and follow him around on his daily routine. Even if I discover nothing more from Lasserio about Clarissa's case, at least when I deliver that report, I'll get paid just enough to make my mortgage and utility payments this month and the next. I can't duck out and do nothing. "The FBI covering my mortgage while I hide out?"

Greene purses her lips like a librarian irritated with loud talkers. A white streak of sunbeam shines in from the kitchen window, lighting up her freckles and exposing wrinkles around her mouth and the pale, tissue-thin hoods of her eyes.

The thought of the killer in the area, stalking me, turns my blood cold, makes my limbs go heavy and numb, but leave my home? Sit back and trust them? I can't stand the thought of twiddling my thumbs in a safe house. And my finances can't take the hit, either.

"No," I say. "Deputy Zane out there, and whichever deputy replaces him when he gets off. That's all I need."

"With all due respect to Deputy Zane and the others," says Greene, "a local deputy might be nothing more than a speed bump for the perpetrator. And when did you last have some training in the field?"

It stings, but she has a point. I don't answer. A raven caws jarringly from outside, as if to protest or even mock me. I don't tell them that it's been a couple of years.

"We'll have more of a chance of catching this guy if I'm out and about," I say.

"We'd prefer not to chance that," Alderson says.

But they give up. There's no point. They can see it in my face.

"All right," says Greene. "Let's look at this list."

I've included everyone I could think of who might be pissed at me for the work I've done in law enforcement both with the KPD and on my own. People who became particularly enraged when I arrested them for DUIs or for public disturbances like fighting in the streets. I've included the names of several husbands and boyfriends whose houses I was called to on domestic violence calls where the woman went ahead and pressed charges or, at the very least, applied for a restraining order. One guy named Tanner Florenza followed me one evening after work from the station to the Super One grocery store and threatened me out in the parking lot after he received notification of the order. He screamed at me that I'd ruined his life.

I left off Mark Coleman because that would involve revealing what happened to Jess. And Railes. And me.

And I already filled them in on Ridgeway, even though the last thing I need is the FBI snooping around right now, making it harder to get decent information from such hermetically sealed communities.

But I can't deny the staticky voice of fear in the back of my head whispering, *What the hell are you doing? If this is really you, you only have a few days left.*

They study my list and listen to my synopses and ask all their questions and take notes on each person.

Greene asks it so casually, out of the blue: "Why did you quit the local force, and what happened with your roommate, Sophie Scott, when you were in college? Sophie was your boyfriend's sister?"

After all this time, it still stings to hear Sophie's name uttered in the past tense. And Wallace's in the same sentence.

"Former boyfriend," I correct them, but it doesn't feel good to say it.

"Yeah, well, it seems there was a bit of press about it back then, and obviously, we're looking for anything that this killer might glom on to."

"I'm sure you've heard about the harassment I underwent in the department?"

"We have."

"Well, I quit the force because I was tired of the boys' code, sick of the role I was jammed into, some messed-up combination of victim and pariah." I don't want to go into how intense the backlash was.

I don't need to sound whiny before two federal agents about how taking a stand for what you think is right can end up making you even more of a victim. "As far as my roommate in college goes," I say, "you're right—there's more than enough online."

"But we'd like to hear it from you, if you don't mind," Greene says.

A flash of Sophie and me ducking behind a thick, gnarled log floods my senses: the astringent smell of damp pine, the delicate feel of papery lichen. The cold, wet mud soaking through my jeans.

Alderson and Greene eye me curiously. "You okay?" Alderson says.

When I don't respond, he adds, "We want to figure out if the killings might have something to do with revenge for abuse of power differentials, some type of harassment or sexual assault. Randal Askens in Snohomish was a coach, and Vonda Loman worked in education, as a counselor. Each was someone with power over kids, someone with influence."

I could've told them that from my own superficial digging. And probably 90 percent of the people at CrimeCon, too.

"Askens was involved in a recruiting scandal with the head coach," Alderson adds.

"I read that," I say.

"The third guy, though," Alderson continues, "that's where things fall apart, or at least we lose traction. For all we know, he could be in his house, his cat nibbling on his ears.

"We did find one guy related to the third go-round," he continues. "He contacted us, like you—reported to his local police in Spokane. In our opinion, he resembled the drawing the most out of any of the folks who came forward. But nothing happened to him, so we can't say for sure if it was him. He had a scare, out in the woods. He thought he saw a gun and someone behind a tree stalking him. But it's hard to say for sure it was the killer that frightened him. But he's also from the Northwest. Doesn't work in education, though. Works for Carssen as a drug rep. His sales territory includes parts of western Montana and Idaho."

Now we're getting somewhere. Here's something no CrimeCon attendee knows. "This guy," I say. "If it was him, he's still in a position of influence. Able to convince doctors to use his products, who then can convince their patients to use his company's products. What was his confession?"

"Exactly that. At first, he admitted to being a glorified drug peddler after the sketch first came online. But after, he had that scare and felt like he was being stalked right at the end of the six days. Basically, he got more desperate, so he put a more thorough confession out there, spilling all the details of what he felt he did wrong and also giving his reasons, or rationale, for why he went astray. Said he was sorry and that since those days, he's resigned and gotten a job selling appliances."

"And the stalking stopped?"

"Yes. So, if it was him, the more complete confession did the trick."

My pulse picks up. I look to the window, avoiding Alderson's dark eyes and Greene's apropos hazel-green eyes boring into me. But again, a thorough confession on my part, motive and all, would involve Jess. To confess would produce what she needs to avoid—my suffering little sister being thrown smack-dab into the limelight. I clutch the edge of my chair with my right hand to stop myself from furiously picking at my thumb with my own forefinger, even with the Band-Aid on. Nausea builds in my gut. "Was the coach dealing?" I switch gears back to the victims, wondering if this is related to drug peddling. "Was the counselor?"

"We're looking into all of that."

"Has the former drug rep given you his phone and computer records?"

"Like you, he refuses." They tell me that they're having him make lists of anyone and everyone he's confided in about any possible thing he feels guilty about and anyone who he's angered.

"I'd give you access to my data if my job didn't involve confidentiality."

"So we forge ahead," Alderson says. "And right now, we need to know more about your history."

I look out my window again. A squirrel chirps frantically, like he's defending a stash of nuts. I want to mimic him—to get busy doing *anything* but sitting here talking about my past with these two.

"That's a bad habit," Greene says.

"What?" I say.

Greene points her pen at my hand.

I look down at my thumb, where the Band-Aid is stretched and folded under. Apparently, gripping the chair to keep me from self-mutilation failed. The Band-Aid has slid to the tip and now exposes the raw skin it's supposed to shield from my other nails, despite how short I've clipped them.

"Yeah, I know." I rip the ravaged bandage off, get up, and throw it away in the can under the sink. I remember Sophie scolding me the same way, and I feel spooked, as if she's speaking to me from our dorm room years ago.

The same old tired guilt that goes with the memory, still hot and sharp as a blade, pierces me.

"You okay?" Greene asks, watching me as I sit back down.

I nod, do a slow blink, and tell them all about it, how eleven years ago, when Jess was a high school sophomore and I headed off to the University of Montana in Missoula, two hours south of Kalispell, I met Sophie.

I give them broad strokes, how she was my roommate, how great she was, but for me, it all comes screaming back in vivid detail, like it was yesterday.

Sophie was from Nebraska. She had a heart-shaped face, blue eyes, and a bubbly personality with little crinkles at the outer edges of her eyes. She loved to laugh, and I felt I'd won the roommate lottery.

When I told her I was born in Montana, she pumped her fist in glee. "Yes! A *Montanan*. I *wanted* a local. You can show me how to live in the mountains."

I was all in. I felt powerful. Reinvented. She made me think of my dad and the times we'd spent in the woods.

We hit it right off, and I didn't miss Jess so much when I was with her.

We used to go on walks by the river, where the late September days pulsed with life as students played soccer and Ultimate Frisbee and residents walked their dogs along city paths. One late afternoon, we'd been casually watching four guys toss a Frisbee around. Watching but *not watching* when it sailed our way. I caught the orange disc as one of the guys barreled toward us.

Almost as if I was the target.

He was tall and muscular. He smelled like sweat and freshly cut grass.

Ruse? Accident? Or fate? It didn't matter.

We joined in, meeting them all: Derek, Seth, Riley, and Josh. Josh was the one who nearly crashed into us. Josh and I exchanged numbers. He invited me and Sophie to a party that weekend. There were always parties.

I took great pains in getting ready. Sophie laughed at my primping. At the party, I found Josh to be more friendly than pushy. He wasn't too eager, which I liked. A lot.

The following weekend—in early October—Josh texted me about going camping. He said to invite Sophie, too.

Sophie declined, blaming schoolwork.

"Come on, Soph," I pleaded. "You can sleep under the stars like you always wanted. In the mountains of Montana, no less. If you stay behind, you know you won't get to it until Sunday night anyway."

"We don't *really* know them," she said. "Do we?"

"Come on. They're nice. And you said you wanted the real Montana experience."

Sophie's long strawberry hair fell across one shoulder. She was gorgeous. I could see why Josh's friends wanted her there.

"We can take care of each other." I picked at my thumb with either excitement or nervousness.

"Stop that."

"Stop what?"

"That." She pointed at my hand. "That's a bad habit. You stress more than I do."

"Does this mean you'll go?"

She looked away, like she was embarrassed by something.

"What? What's the problem?"

It was in that moment she confided that she was a virgin, that she wasn't sure about being around a bunch of guys for an entire weekend. Four of them, two of us. She felt naive and shy.

"Soph, don't worry. Maybe you need to put yourself out there a little more. Not be so guarded."

She shrugged.

"What? A little risk is good for the soul, right?"

She flashed a smile. "Promise me we'll get back on Sunday afternoon?"

Three days later, we drove into the Mission Mountains Wilderness and hiked up four miles to the calm waters of Crescent Lake.

The view was magnificent, the lake hemmed in by subalpine pines and the jagged ridgeline of the Mission Mountains above. It made me giddy. My dad would have absolutely loved the place.

My enthusiasm was heightened by my deep crush on Josh. I giggled over everything he uttered, even if it wasn't funny. Sophie jabbed me in the ribs to make it clear I was being too obvious. Suddenly, she was the relationship expert.

Sophie and I pitched our tent farther away from the guys' for a bit of privacy. Braydon, new to the group, and Seth unloaded booze from their backpacks. Whiskey, beer, vodka, tequila, and juice for mixers. Their packs must have weighed a ton. Drinking commenced immediately.

It was too cold to swim. Derek and Riley fished while Josh and Seth and I started a fire and roasted hot dogs. We were the only campers. The guys took it as a sign to blast the portable speakers. Serenity? Nonexistent.

Worse, I was not the target of Josh's eye. It was Sophie. I had missed every signal from the get-go.

I tried to get Sophie to walk around the lake with me, but she wanted to stay by the fire with Josh.

I went alone. Down at the water's edge, a perfect reversal of the mountains was reflected in the calm surface. I found a big rock to sit on and watched the glassy surface. Geese flew over in formation, a few on the left end out of line and fraying the V. A bald eagle sat up high in a pine tree surveying the lake, his bleached head winking in the sunlight. I tucked myself down behind a rock and tried to read a paperback novel in the dwindling light. But the loud music was too much.

I didn't want to admit it to myself, but a huge part of me willed—ached for—someone, Sophie especially, but any of them really, to come fetch me, to encourage me to join in. And the sense that I wanted that so badly made me feel weak, like a deep dig that hit something already bruised inside me. I stubbornly looked out over the lake, disturbed only by rings from fish rising to the evening mayfly hatch. I didn't want to feel this way, like I needed others. Like I wasn't just fine on my own.

When I returned to camp, the empties were strewn about and the guys started to crash. I told Sophie we should hit the sack.

"You go ahead." She slurred her words. "I'm awake."

Josh had his arm around her. She leaned into him, eyes at half-mast. She kicked a stray coal into the campfire. Smoke billowed.

"I might sleep outside," she said. "Under all this."

Above, the night sky was an inky bowl splattered with stars, the Milky Way running like a burst vein through the center.

Sophie looked ethereal in that moment, either strong like a fire goddess or fragile like she might dissolve into the smoke. I sensed a touch of dread, but I couldn't separate it from my jealousy. And why? Did I want a drunk roll in the hay? Try to steer Josh my way? If the tables were turned, would I have let Sophie sleep alone in the tent?

I went into the woods and peed, got in the tent, zipped the fly, and crawled into my sleeping bag. I closed my eyes and tried to block out the blasting music.

Later, the night was still and quiet when I woke to Sophie frantically prodding me. She was gasping for breath. She grabbed me through the bag and shook me awake.

"We have to go." If terror had a smell, it rode on her breath—something acrid and urgent. "Now, Crosbie. Please, please. Get your boots on. *Now.*"

I found my flashlight. Her eyes were wide, tinged with fear.

"I'll explain later," she said.

"A bear? Did you hear something?"

"It's Josh."

The urgent tremor was like a jolt of electricity to my sleepy head. I slipped on one of my boots.

"He's at the lake, but he's coming back."

I tugged on my other boot as fast as I could, leaving them unlaced. I grabbed my jacket, snatched the flashlight, crawled out of the tent after her, and followed her into the dark.

I tell Greene and Alderson how we fled and spent the rest of the night in the woods. How we stumbled over logs and roots after we turned my flashlight off because we heard some of the boys talking and realized they were looking for us. How we kept on, away from their voices, away from the lake and down slopes and ridges, hopefully toward the highway, but we ended up going too far down into a drainage basin. We curled up together to stay warm.

The next morning, I remembered something my dad told me years before when hiking in the North Fork of the Flathead. He said that people make a common mistake when lost in the mountains: They keep going down, thinking that's correct, but they end up too low, in basins far away from the trails and roads. Often, if you go back up, you can find the path. So we picked our way upward, and eventually we hit a path traversing a ridge. We followed it and made it to a dirt road that led us to the Swan Highway, where we got a ride into the closest town and called a friend, one of our dormmates. Back safe in Missoula, we went to First Step, a resource center at one of the hospitals for victims of sexual assault, to have Sophie examined.

I tell them how, after a few days, Sophie finally decided to go to the police. They informed her, before they'd even spoken to Josh, that it would be tough to prosecute because there was a lot of alcohol involved and things got blurred. He said, she said. Et cetera. They brought him in when he returned with the others, but nothing came of it. Sophie told me she wanted to return to college life and pretend it didn't happen.

She wanted to act like everything was carefree and fun, like our first few weeks in the dorm. But it had become anything but.

One month after that night in the mountains, after my philosophy class, I returned to our dorm room. Sophie sat cross-legged on her bed staring out the window. She wore an old green, baggy sweater that hung loosely on her bony shoulders. Her hair fell around her shoulders, greasy and lank, and the autumn light falling across her face exposed some creases in her forehead that I'd never noticed before, as if she were no longer a college student but a much older woman.

I wanted to cry. What was happening to my roommate? I should have prevented this. I should have never talked her into going camping, should never have encouraged her to be more open and, with that, implied willingness. If I could only press rewind, I'd do it all differently.

I set my books down and sat on my bed, facing her. "Aren't you going to go to your math class?"

She shook her head. "Not today."

"Sophie." It came out as a sigh. "You need to go to your classes. If you don't, you're going to flunk out."

"I'm not sure I care."

"Of course you do."

"I don't know what I want anymore."

"You can't go on like this. Not eating, not going to class." *Crying all the time.* "It's going to keep eating away at you. If you press charges," I said to her, "at least you might feel empowered, like you're taking control of your own situation."

"I just don't know if I can talk about it," Sophie said. "I mean, to everyone in court like that. In a trial and everything. I can barely talk about it here. Talking about it just puts me right there, in it again."

Suddenly, with tears streaking down her cheeks, she looked like a child. She nodded to me with wide, hopeful eyes, trusting that I was correct, that it would make all the difference.

# Chapter 24

"But it didn't," I say to Greene and Alderson at my kitchen table. "The cops told Sophie that it would be difficult to prosecute but that it was up to her whether she wanted to go ahead and press charges."

This draws out a surprised eye lift from Greene. Nowadays, all cops should know better than to scare a victim off from pressing charges. Protocols have been put into place, and most agencies, even smaller ones, are aware of them.

"Yeah," I say. "Things have changed since then." *Or are supposed to have changed, at least.* "But Sophie—with some prodding from me—had decided to go ahead and press charges. And once it all came out, the backlash around town and the college was more overpowering than I anticipated. It was relentless. And we had to contend with the fact that Josh was an athlete, one of the university's top golfers, there on a scholarship.

"Not only did we become these foolish, stupid girls—a couple of ditzy freshmen idiotic enough to go camping with a pack of boys and a ton of alcohol—we were also accused of making the whole thing up. They said we'd gotten lost in the woods and wanted to cover up our own stupidity for wandering off on our own."

I go over it all again with them, how Sophie was called a liar, a slut, a whore who'd gotten laid while on a frosh camping trip. The implication always circled back to our poor judgment.

When booze came up about Sophie and me, it was that we were stupid for drinking in that situation. When it was mentioned in relation to Josh, it was framed as an excuse: *Poor guy, he wasn't in his right mind,* since he was under the influence. *If he hadn't drunk so much, he'd never have misread the signals, if there even were any in the first place.*

And the question that got the most press: How could it have been rape if Sophie didn't call for help? All the other boys attested to that: She hadn't yelled for anyone, so she must have wanted it. Otherwise, it made no sense. For goodness' sake, with all those guys around, why in the world wouldn't she cry out if she didn't like it, if she felt threatened and didn't want it to happen? "And," I say. "Why wouldn't she, at the very least, call out for her friend, asleep in her tent less than"—my voice falters, so I pause for a second, swallow hard—"fifty feet away?"

I shake my head like I'm just pissed and angry and try not to show the sadness welling and lodging in my throat.

*Less than fifty feet?* It's still charged, visceral, for me to think about it. To say it out loud.

"But you know from your jobs," I say, "like I do, that it's common for rape victims to feel paralyzed, find themselves unable to scream, to feel like they're in a nightmare in which they're trying to run but cannot move. You know this?"

I look from Alderson's dark-brown eyes to Greene's sharp green ones. Neither one answers, but it's not a question.

"Two years later, when we were juniors," I say, "Sophie died by suicide before the whole thing even got to trial."

I see no point in loitering on Memory Lane any longer, reliving all the mundane details about our existence as Sophie had grown ever more anxiety-ridden and depressed. How she overdosed on a high dose of fentanyl pills and half a bottle of tequila.

"But I don't see how any of this history could possibly tie into what's happening now," I say. Again, the words *amorphous, nebulous* pop into my mind. Although this event helps form the triad—Sophie, Leon, Jess—of my weighted conscience, it was ten years ago and far from the line I crossed with Railes.

"The only thing I feel guilty for with Sophie is urging her to go camping in the first place." *And that her first sex was literally rape. That I urged her to not be so guarded. That I* pushed *her to press charges in a town known for putting their athletes first, for having a good ol' boys culture.*

I should have known better. And that's why I didn't press even harder with Jess, even though I knew some things had changed in the past ten years. That the local hospital in Kalispell had, at least, instituted a SANE Suite.

"You were young," Alderson says.

I throw him a sharp look because what he says scratches at the underlying wounds. Even though I just admitted feeling guilty for going camping with Sophie, it still makes me furious that we should have had to say no to an invitation to go with some guys out in the woods in the first place. That we couldn't go and enjoy ourselves because the danger of having one of them force themselves onto one of us might be too great. How absurd and disgusting that we should have even *had* to "know better."

But there's no reason to go into that. Reality isn't always fair, and as a police officer and a private detective, I've seen enough unfairness to fill up acres and acres of sewers.

"Still, like I said, I don't see how any of it pertains to what's happening now, unless you think Josh Lyster has a vendetta against me, which would make zero sense, all these years later. And unless he was tied into the other victims."

"No, we've checked. He's not. And Sophie's family? Wallace? He was her brother?"

"Yes."

"When did you begin dating him?"

"Not until years later, when he moved to the Flathead to play for the symphony."

"And it didn't work out?"

"We broke up this winter. As I told you."

"And he knew you encouraged Sophie to go camping when she didn't want to?"

I nod.

"And he knew she was inexperienced with guys and you encouraged to, as you said, to *not be so guarded*?"

"Yes, but have you spoken to him?"

"We have."

"So you know there's nothing to worry about with him?"

Alderson and Greene stare at me, expressionless. Too blank, like they're trying hard not to show their hand.

"What?"

"Nothing," Greene says. "You need to be careful around everyone right now. Understand?"

"Yeah, I do. But I need a favor."

"What's that?"

I tell them that I can't be an effective PI if I show up out there as a detective with a caravan in my rearview mirror.

I instruct them to tell Deputy Zane to follow my lead. Keeping an eye on my house is one thing, but tailing me everywhere is another.

A bit reluctantly, they agree.

What I *don't* tell them is I'm certain now, for sure, that I'm the one. I'm the target. It's not only that they're privy to someone locally who's been aggressive and obsessive online, and that they want me in a safe house, too, it's that I can't be in denial anymore about these earrings.

Sure, a lot of tourists could have bought them. But the fact is, no one who also looks like the sketch who's either confessed or contacted authorities has claimed to own a pair exactly like them, even with over a thousand of them out there.

I go cold all over.

I've been fighting it since the sketch came out. I haven't wanted to voice it yet in my own head, but I no longer have a choice.

And that also means I'm certain as hell that I won't be confined to quarters.

# Chapter 25

After they leave, I check my phone.

Three calls from Wallace.

Four from Jess.

No voicemails. I call Jess back.

"So, they've been there twice?" Jess asks. Her tone is laced with anxiety.

"Yes, but it doesn't mean anything. They're checking on others, too. There's a woman in Texas who may be the target."

Fiona told Jess I called in the middle of the night. I don't have anything to say to make that part better. "Yes, it was bugging me. But still, that doesn't mean you should worry."

"There's no way not to. Look, maybe I should come over."

"Absolutely not. You stay put with Sam. Promise me, Jess—for Sam—that you're not coming over."

"You are worried, then?"

"It never hurts to take precautions, for Sam's sake." I'd like to go to her. But there's zero chance of calming her down, especially given what I now know. "Look, Jess, I plan to stay away. Until this is over."

She doesn't answer.

"And I don't want you to come here, either. Okay?"

She still doesn't answer. I can hear her breathing rapidly, though.

"Okay?" I press. "For Sam's sake?"

"Okay," she says.

I pull up next to Deputy Zane and repeat what I told the agents, that I'm heading out and I think it's best if he keeps an eye on my place. I also ask for his number.

He seems giddy to please me or perhaps happy we're on the same page and he's doing something valuable.

Suddenly, I want to protect him. Tell him to find another job. Something safer.

"One of those agents told me what you wanted," he says.

Surprised Greene and Alderson have honored my request, I thank him, give him a thumbs-up, and drive away.

First, I hit my office. I don't plan on staying, but I want to make sure everything is in order there and grab my file on Aaron Lasserio, who I still plan on surveilling before the day runs out.

I park in the lot and look across the street, where a cluster of old grain silos from a bygone era hover like sentries guarding my office complex. The silos are slated to have a trendy new restaurant built on top of them now that the west side of town is beginning to gentrify like the east side did years ago.

I step outside and continue to look around. Everything seems normal. Cars pass leisurely by. A woman walks a small dog down a sidewalk. Someone hammers something in the distance. The sounds of traffic from Main Street several blocks east. But I sense something anyway, that strange feeling that someone's watching. The hairs on the back of my neck are on edge. I chalk it up to the situation I'm in. Of course. Of course I'm bound to feel like this. It's only logical given my circumstances.

And I have less than seventy-two hours. Not even three full days anymore. Two and a quarter at this point.

But Alderson and Greene said the potential third victim, the Carssen drug rep, believes he was stalked out in the woods before his time was up. Is the killer that sneaky? That stealthy?

I go in. The sign on my door reads MITCHELL INVESTIGATIONS LLC. Inside, the first thing that hits me is a framed poster Jess gave me when I opened the office. It's a quote from Blaise Pascal:

**JUSTICE AND POWER MUST BE BROUGHT TOGETHER SO THAT WHATEVER IS JUST MAY BE POWERFUL, AND WHATEVER IS POWERFUL MAY BE JUST.**

Justice. Power. I wonder how anger fits into the equation. And sadness. Deep fucking sadness.

I lock the door behind me and look around the rest of my little space—at the dieffenbachia on the shelf below the poster, at the framed school pictures of little Sam on my desk, at the candle that's supposed to smell like ocean mist.

Everything seems normal and in place.

I sit at my desk for only a minute to find Lasserio's file before locking the place up again.

◆ ◆ ◆

Next I hit the shooting range to sharpen my skills and get the added bonus of some stress relief from blasting away at targets.

I go to an old-fashioned facility west of town located in a large field at the base of the mountains. I'd rather not use the newfangled digital training simulator the force uses. It's also open to the public since local tax dollars paid for it, and it was the only way to get the $900,000 facility approved, but I'd prefer not to run into any ex-coworkers.

Besides, last time I went to use the new one, about three weeks after the Coleman incident, the simulator served up a domestic dispute on the three-hundred-degree array of high-def surround-sound screens. Lucky me, I walked in to find a man pointing a gun at a young woman's head, screaming at her. Her baby cried from a car seat propped on the counter, and a frightened toddler crouched, wailing in a corner.

I pleaded for the virtual man to put his gun down, suggested we could talk things over and not make things worse, but all I could do was think of Leon, Railes, and Coleman. My palms went instantly wet, and my voice quavered. I wasn't forceful or nearly convincing enough. The man shot and killed the woman and began firing at me. My heart pounded in my throat as I froze. He shot me twice in the stomach. By the time I walked out, I thought I was having a heart attack. I was drenched in sweat and my legs barely worked.

Now, at this shooting range, I look around the parking lot and only see one man arriving in his car. He's paying me no attention.

I enter the hut, sign the form, pay, and go outside to the range, where one familiar man looks like he's packing up.

*Are you kidding me?* It's Lieutenant Hartley, the one who lured me for drinks and slimed my face with his tongue. Could this week get any worse? I almost turn around.

"Mitchell." He greets me like the whole ordeal never occurred. "Freshening up your skills?"

"Yep," I say. "Don't you use the new facility?" *Or is that too high tech for you?* I want to ask.

"I like it out here. Peaceful," he says, pulling his lips in for a tight smile. The old acne scars on his face appear deeper and more purple in the sunlight. "Other than the pistols firing, that is. So, tell me, how is it?"

I don't ask, *How's what?* because I don't sense an ounce of sincerity behind his ugly grin.

"Huh? How is it to be hunted instead of being the hunt*er*?" His lips stay open like a fish's when he stresses the *er*.

I shake my head, say nothing, move down the firing line to the very end of the range, as far away as possible. I feel his eyes on me.

I wonder if he's referring to what happened with Railes and Coleman, as if we hunted those boys down on purpose. What does it matter?

Suddenly, I miss Allison. She was a welcome buffer among the guys, even during the worst of it. When I'd mentioned Hartley's name and she could tell I was frustrated, she'd said, "Try putting a picture of him on that bull's-eye." I laughed, imagining Hartley's fuming expression if he walked in to see his own face on a target frame. I think of my friends in general. Wallace isn't cutting it, and Fiona? I'm not sure I trust her 100 percent. My words to Jess back in high school return again: *You don't have to try to fit in with people you don't particularly like all the time to be popular, Jess. It's okay to keep your distance.*

*Distance.* That word. Again, my therapist's question—*When did this loner streak rear its head again?*—rings in my ears.

*Distance.* It seems to have become my motto with everyone but Jess and Sam since the night with Railes. Lately, I've separated myself so much that I'm not sure I trust anyone at all. It strikes me how much of a loner I've become over the past year, even without the onset of this sketch business. I think of my mom and how she became a hermit near the end, how she was choosing the bottle over her friends, over Les, over even her daughters.

I don my earmuffs and eyewear and wait for the range operator to give the green light.

There are only three others in the firing line, and all wait patiently. For some reason, my heart speeds up as if I haven't done this a gazillion times before.

"Commence," the operator orders. We all start blasting away at our targets, pistols and rifles cracking until we're told to cease, and the silence falls among the pines. The familiar scent of gunpowder swirls. My heartbeat slows, and already, I feel better. I've been fairly accurate, with only a few shots more than five inches off my bull's-eye.

I shoot three more rounds, falling into a bit of a transcendent headspace, more than a few times picturing Hartley's face on the target. Or Railes's. Or Coleman's.

When I imagine my own face, I shudder and call it quits.

*Not yours, Cros,* I tell myself. The face of the killer, that's the one to imagine.

And what the hell does *it* look like?

# Chapter 26

Workers' comp cases often involve a level of IQ that leaves me wondering about the quality of public schools today, and Aaron Lasserio is another shining—check that, depressing—case in point.

I've surveilled him enough for the past week and a half since I got the go-ahead from Graham Insurance several days after returning from Choteau to know that he stayed home with his girlfriend last Tuesday evening but went to a poker game on Wednesday at a bar down the road from his house. I'm assuming he might keep the same schedule this week, and since it's late Tuesday afternoon, I figure Lasserio is in for the evening.

After I left the shooting range, I went to Target, bought a multicamera system, and went home and installed the cameras around my place: at my front and back doors; one on my garage; one on a post at the main entrance, where Deputy Zane is stationed; and on both sides of my house, where I have my bedroom and office windows. I hated running my plastic up even more, especially so soon after the Dallas charges, but since hiding out in a safe house isn't an option if I want to continue working and have a shot at catching this guy, this is a wise choice.

Parked under a large maple tree down a little from Lasserio's house, I'm relieved to *finally* be at work. I refuse to get distracted. I am *not* dropping my Lasserio stuff or the Ridgeway investigation. I am not, if I can help it, going to let another man get away with harming another woman.

But it's hard to sit still. In my rearview mirror, I catch my own big eyes. They're lit up by the unnatural buzz of adrenaline trying—but failing—to mask my exhaustion from the past two sleepless nights. Three, if you count the red-eye out of the valley.

I check my new home-surveillance app and see that everything around my place is quiet—the front stoop is empty, the driveway clear, the back porch and yard peaceful.

I roll my window down for some fresh air. The early-September sun throws long, moody shadows. Some kids are playing in the yard of the next house over, but the other homes are quiet. It occurs to me now that I've forgotten to eat all day, and my stomach is gnawing away at itself. I fish a granola bar out of my console and munch on it while I open my laptop and connect to my phone's mobile hot spot.

I wish Greene and Alderson would have given me the name of the man who is still alive, the drug rep from Spokane.

I study the third sketch again. Except for the one slightly wonky eye, there's nothing that distinctive about it. That is, no specific detail like my earrings. His shirt collar is nondescript and he has no necklace, hat, or other identifying detail like a mole.

I search the Carssen Pharmaceuticals website, but there's no information on the individuals or their territory sales forces. That leaves me with LinkedIn and a search of all the Carssen reps I can find. Most of them have profile pictures, so I can discard the ones who look nothing like the sketch. Carssen is a big outfit, so scrolling down is a slow process—a fresh source of irritation—when my eye is drawn to movement at the Lasserio house.

The front door has popped open and Aaron Lasserio steps through it carrying what looks to be an old microwave. He lugs it down his front steps and across his yard, sets it in the back of his pickup, then goes back in, leaving the front door open.

After a few minutes, Aaron emerges again. This time, he and his girlfriend are carrying a midsize dresser that could be oak and looks burdensome. I snatch my phone and video their journey to the truck. His light-haired, tiny girlfriend rests her end of the dresser on the driveway while Aaron, with his curly mop of dark hair and ripped jeans, leans his end against the tailgate. Aaron hops up into the bed like a twenty-five-year-old Olympic hurdler, grabs his end again, and sets about gallantly hefting the dresser up without her assistance. It's a pretty manly display, especially considering the limitations he listed on his insurance claim.

He jumps down from the bed, slams the tailgate shut. His woman goes back into the house, and he climbs in behind the wheel of the truck and backs out. I follow him out of the neighborhood to a run-down storage business south of town. I followed him twice before Jess and I flew to Dallas, both boring and fruitless trips, and never to a unit. The place seems right out of the seventies or eighties. There's no coded entry gate, no security cameras that I can spot, and no front office. Just a sign out front with a number you can call to rent a unit. I pause on the shoulder of the main road to give him a minute, and go in.

It feels so freaking good to be doing something, but I'm constantly checking my rearview mirror, too.

In the third corridor from the entry, I spot his truck parked halfway down. I continue to the next aisle as if I'm looking for my own unit and creep down to the end, place my car in park, get out, and sneak around the edge of the last shed to peer around the corner and up the row where Lasserio stopped.

Lasserio is unlocking a unit on the opposite side. After he jerks the padlock free and lifts the mini garage door, apparently oblivious to the harsh squeal, he disappears inside. I'm already shooting video when he reappears. He's toting a beige backpack in his grip. He looks up the corridor and turns back toward me. I yank myself back, unsure if he's spotted me.

Lasserio goes back inside his unit with his arm extending out like he's about to drop the pack back inside it. A second later, he comes out all nonchalant and whistling, no longer carrying it, his hands in his pockets.

He's looking away from me to the car that has stopped about ten sheds up from him, where a tall woman steps out and starts fiddling with her padlock. He's changed his mind, I think. He came to take the pack out, but the car has interrupted him. He doesn't want to be seen with it.

Lasserio watches her for a moment, shakes his head in irritation, locks up his unit, and hops back in his car.

I dash back to mine, throw it into drive, pull across his row, and go to the next two over in case Lasserio takes a U-turn to the left instead of to the right to go back toward the exit. I don't want him to end up behind me. I drive to the end and wait for him to pull out. When he exits two rows over, I follow him out again and onto the highway.

This time, he drives farther south to a green-box dump site, one of the county's designated solid waste disposal areas. I'm still wondering what was so special about that pack that he needed to ditch it before the stranger saw him with it.

The dump is enclosed by a tall chain-link fence with the dumpsters arranged in a U shape. He unloads the dresser with minimal effort, all recorded for posterity on my camera.

Next, he grabs the microwave, also with ease. Once I check the weight of his jetsam, I'll know by precisely how many pounds he's exceeded the max he claims he's able to hoist. This "case" is a breeze, but it will pay the bills. I find myself more concerned about what he left at his storage shed and why he abandoned his mission when another person arrived.

I wait near one of the first dumpsters in the U shape on the opposite side and act like I'm trying to organize some recycling in my back seat as he backs out, swings around, and drives out of the site. He doesn't look my way.

*Nobody* is looking my way because the place is empty.

Good.

After his taillights are out of sight, I pull over to the spot he vacated, get out, go to the side of the dumpster, and nudge the dresser to get a feel for its weight. It's even heavier than it looks. I prod it again, estimating an easy sixty pounds.

I take a photo of it, using my flash, since it's getting into the thick of dusk. I try to lift the microwave that he's placed next to the dresser, even though the sign instructs that appliances need to go to the main dump north of Kalispell. It's an old model, so roughly as heavy as a VW Bug. I find the product information plate on the back and snap a final shot. It'll be easy to find the actual weight online.

I've pocketed my phone and turned to head to my car when lights from another vehicle swing across the dumpsters and halt on me.

The driver stops in the entrance.

Kills the lights.

The hairs on the back of my neck prickle. What the hell? Why turn the lights off?

The night isn't completely black—the sky above the horizon has turned a pale lavender—but the glare has momentarily blinded me. I readjust to the fading twilight and keeping an eye on the mystery car, begin to cross the thirty yards to mine.

But I freeze because the lightless mystery car begins to head slowly toward my SUV. Its tires grind on the gravel. It pulls to a stop on the other side of my car so it's hidden and I can't see the driver's seat.

I stand still, waiting for them to get out and deposit a bag of trash.

Nothing. No movement.

My hand goes to my gun, even though it isn't there. I left it in the SUV, under the driver's seat. So much for getting myself all tuned up at the range.

Crickets chirp in the dry surrounding fields and the breeze brushes the tops of the cottonwoods in the distance. The rancid scent of garbage fills my nose. Cars from the highway swish by, and I think I pick up the soft click of a door opening, but I'm not positive. Did someone slip out? I didn't lock my door since I was only going to be gone for a second to take the photos.

What a fool. With everything going on, and after stubbornly telling Greene and Alderson that I was more than capable of defending myself, how could I be so careless? To top it off, I didn't even mention to anyone that I was coming here.

I pull my phone out and debate making a call. To? Greene and Alderson? Zane? What would I say? There might be a bad guy at the recycling center? By the time anyone got here, whatever's going to happen will have happened.

Again, a dark figure shifts around beside my car, but I can't tell if it's walking over to the bin to unload something or staying beside my vehicle. The evening has faded to a steely, dark gray. I continue to strain through the dark to see. I'm not fool enough to stroll back to my car without knowing what they're up to. But now I'm starting to get angry. Screw this.

Fully shielded beside the dumpster, I yell, "Hey!"

No one answers.

"Hey!" I repeat. "I'm with KPD," I lie. "Step away from my vehicle and state your name."

Still, no answer, but I hear a shuffle, and this time, for sure, a car door shuts. My muscles lock, my breathing stops.

"Stop!" I yell out again, and as I do, another truck pulls in, lights sweeping across the lot and across both our vehicles before landing on one of the dumpsters on the other side of the U.

I can't see the mystery vehicle even when the truck's lights dust across it because it's still hidden behind mine. Its headlights flash as it starts. Suddenly, it peels out and speeds away, lights off and no illumination on the back bumper. No plate is visible, but I can tell by the shape that it's a medium-size, dark-colored SUV, like mine.

I have a quick decision to make: stay and watch which way it turns at the end of the drive or run to my car to follow it. I need to know if it will head east or west, so I watch.

As it turns west onto the main road, its headlamps flick on. I can make out its side. It looks like a Ford Explorer but I'm not positive. It could be a Toyota 4Runner like mine.

When I get to my car, I check the back seat with my phone light. It's vacant. Front seat, ditto. My gun is under the front seat where I left it. I grab it and circle the vehicle, checking to see if my tires are slashed.

I steady the light on each tire and then lift it to the side doors. My blood turns to ice, and suddenly I'm acutely aware of every sound in the oncoming night—the cars in the distance, an owl *hoo-hoo*-ing from afar, scurrying sounds from a small animal in the dry field behind the nearest dumpster.

My body spools into a tightly knit knot.

In white marker on the side of my passenger door, two words are scrawled:

**IT'S YOU.**

# Chapter 27

## Vonda

*Goddammit,* Vonda cursed. Martha was bringing another walk-in.

She checked her watch. Past 4 p.m.

She wanted to leave a little early, get home and out in her garden before dinnertime. Reply to more of the crazy messages she'd been getting all week from friends saying how much she looked like some stupid sketch a wacko had put out on the internet.

Like she had either the time or inclination to futz around with online games, especially since now there was another student to contend with.

Martha brought the girl, Hannah Jenkins, to Vonda's office.

With her burgundy-colored hoodie on, Hannah slumped into her chair without saying a word.

The only thing Vonda felt like asking her was, *You going to take that goddamn hoodie off your head? You going to sit here in my office all disrespectful like that, hiding in your hoodie, not looking me in the eye?*

And yet. And yet: *You're here because you want my help, aren't you? You're going to tell me about how you're depressed, how you miss your mommy and daddy, how the girls in your dorm aren't treating you right. You're going to want me to do the impossible: make it all better, give you the confidence your helicopter parents never gave you.*

Vonda drew a deep breath. She released it in a sigh she tried to keep quiet. "So," she began in the sweetest voice she could muster. "What brings you in?"

"I don't know," Hannah said, shrugging off her question.

And Vonda was off—launched once again on the school counselor's tiresome dance, trying to pry it out of them, one basic question at a time. *Where are you from? What year is this for you?*

If their parents had forced the student to come in and see her, this would not be a productive chat.

If they came in on their own, they might talk eventually, but not until she wrestled it out of them because they were always too meek or hazy or immature to simply lay it out.

God, it was exhausting. Vonda dreamed of opening a counseling practice for adults, for halfway functional grown-ups willing to dive into their issues.

But even now, at the end of her flipping rope, there was something about the mix of innocence and arrogance of college students, cheeks still puffy with youth and eyes filled with both uncertainty and determination, that got to her. Even when they thought they were more sophisticated than they were, and it grated on her nerves when they did, she enjoyed the challenge.

She could see enough of Hannah's face to see she had flawless skin. Her upturned nose was smooth, with none of the pimples inflicting so many of the students from the awful cafeteria food they shoveled down. "Can I ask, was it your idea to come see me?"

"Yeah. I mean, I guess."

*Which is it?* "I'm asking, did you come in because you wanted to, or because someone suggested it?"

"I mean, both."

*I mean, I mean,* Vonda repeated in her head, giving an internal eye roll. *I mean* was the present-day *like* filler of the past. Not that *like* had gone anywhere.

Maybe instead of pulling weeds, she'd smoke some when she got home. Or have a few edibles.

"Someone suggested you come?"

Job #1 was finding out if their parents or friends sent them, if anyone at all knew of their plans to see the school counselor. Not for any therapeutic reason, but because it flagged their eligibility for Vonda's little side gig with Davis, which didn't work if anybody in the subject's personal circle knew of the visit. She bobbed her head encouragingly at Hannah and waited her out, expecting her to continue averting her eyes and avoiding anything approaching decent conversation.

Hannah surprised her by being direct.

"I'm here because"—she sat up straighter—"because my math teacher has been coming on to me. I feel like my grades are at stake if I don't play nice, and I don't like that. I'm here to report him."

Vonda sat up taller, too. Where had *that* come from? Usually, they were all so meek, so timid and afraid. And if they'd come in on their own, she could reel them in, gain their confidence, hook them up with Davis for additional counseling, a little pharma-therapy, and everyone would be happier.

But here this hooded girl had guts for a change and stated her problem head-on. And she didn't use *I mean* even once. Vonda gave her a little standing O in her head. Maybe there was hope for this hollowed-out generation after all.

Vonda pulled a notepad out and started taking down Hannah's statement. Hannah claimed her Algebra 2 instructor, Mr. Caras, had taken to cornering her in the hallway and in the parking lot after evening classes. He stood too close when he spoke to her, sometimes even touched her hair, pushing it behind her ear. "An extremely intimate gesture," Hannah said. "Don't you think?"

Vonda looked down at her notepad, writing it down instead of answering her, surprised by her articulate question.

Hannah forged on, telling Vonda that lately he'd begun suggesting they go for drinks to talk about her performance in class, saying she might need some extra help with the formulas and equations.

Vonda continued to treat Hannah's statements gently and with care. It was dangerous to have a student report something and not take it seriously.

Hannah looked at Vonda, wide-eyed, when she'd finished.

Vonda assured her that she'd done the right thing coming in. When Hannah asked what came next and how they'd be dealing with the situation, Vonda told her not to worry. That there was a process and that she would handle it with care so that there'd be as little backlash as possible.

But Vonda knew there was very little that could be done that wouldn't make the girl's life hell. Vonda would speak to Mr. Caras and get his take. In all her years here, she'd only gotten two other complaints about him. He was a great guy. And very intelligent.

But so was this student. She was *not* a candidate for Davis.

Despite the hood yanked down over her face, she was too sure of herself. Davis needed them meek and unsure. The easier to convince that the drugs would make them better—and the easier to persuade to go out with the men who paid Davis.

Not this girl, though. Vonda patted herself on the back for recognizing it.

She couldn't have said why, but it dawned on her at that moment that this crazy social media sketch thing her friends were bugging her about might possibly have something to do with her work with Davis.

But that was ridiculous. Paranoid. What? *Confess?*

Confess that she sometimes referred certain girls to a qualified, trained psychoanalyst?

The state gave the guy his license, not her. It wasn't her problem what he did with his patients. She didn't do anything but get these girls the help they needed.

And what's a woman in a criminally underfunded helping profession to do? The cost of rent in Santa Monica was insane. Sue her if she'd found a way to make some extra dough on the side through referrals. And Davis had helped a lot of students, too. A *lot*. The ones who couldn't be helped . . . well, couldn't be helped by her. That was his call.

There'd been only one time she was aware of where things had gone off the rails, when the girl had too much of whatever they gave her and the guys who paid Davis for her ended up having to drop her off outside the doors of an ER in Santa Monica a few months back. That had sounded like a mess. She'd ended up in a coma for several days, Vonda thought—but wasn't positive on all the details.

What was her name? Summer? Or Somer? From Montana?

Vonda knew she hadn't *died*, or did she? She couldn't remember if she followed up on the story. So many deaths around LA. How in the world would she follow them all? But no, surely, she was still alive. So all was well that ended well. Okay, maybe that wasn't the correct phrase for the outcome, but in the end, nobody got too severely hurt.

And these girls, they were so stupid sometimes. If they couldn't figure out on their own that their doctor was getting them hooked on a drug, maybe it was time to learn a lesson or two.

But this girl before her now—no, she wouldn't be seeing Davis.

She didn't seem depressed. The opposite. She seemed out for blood. Maybe her grades weren't as good as she claimed in Mr. Caras's class. Maybe she just wanted to stir up trouble for him. Maybe she was simply being a drama queen.

Vonda made a note to check her transcripts, to speak to Mr. Caras to get a peek at Hannah's grades. Get the skinny on this hooded avenger.

They'd have a good laugh about how sensitive the girls were these days. The whole thing would blow over. The student would thank her in the long run. Even if her story checked out for the most part, pursuing it wouldn't be worth the hassle. It was a harder, slimier game than they all thought—the he says/she says tug-of-war.

And there were much better games to play than dragging some poor professor through the mud over silly accusations.

Hannah wouldn't be the first student she'd saved from such nonsense.

When she finally left work, Vonda was feeling good. Even slightly smug about the favor she'd done for the girl.

But fuck if the way life had been treating Vonda lately didn't snuff out that sense of satisfaction within a matter of minutes as, driving down Broadway, she noticed a truck, a blue Ford with a black topper, looming behind her. She vaguely remembered seeing one like it a few days ago on her street. And she was positive she'd seen it pull out behind her as she'd left the college parking lot.

*Chill,* she told herself. This *was* SoCal. Think how many thousands of trucks like it were cruising the streets of the greater LA area right that minute. The whole area was crawling with vehicles, like insects, at any given moment. She was paranoid because of this stupid sketch business. When she got home, she'd delete those emails. Wouldn't even waste time answering them.

Sure enough, when she got home, she didn't see any sign of the truck. And she followed through—opened up her computer and purged her inbox of every last sketch-related message.

Such a relief.

After she changed into old khaki shorts and a T-shirt and went outside to garden, she noticed the sky had turned an ugly skim-milk color. The temperature had dropped. She went in and grabbed an old cotton sweatshirt, then a rake to take care of all the cherimoya leaves that had fallen onto her patio and part of her lawn.

When she bought the house, the Realtor told her that the cherimoya was a tree native to Ecuador, not California. As if she cared. Now she wanted to get all these irritating broad leaves off her patio and the tiny yard.

While she raked, she came upon a dead robin. Its bill and head were bloody, as if it had flown beak first into something hard. She turned to look at her kitchen window, and sure enough, a splat, like a Rorschach test, bloomed on the center of the glass.

*Stupid bird,* she thought as she raked it away with a pile of crunchy leaves. *Away you go.*

Her shoulders ached. She thought about going back inside, maybe having another of the edibles she'd grabbed before coming out. She left the pile of leaves and the dead bird beside her patio and decided to pick a few weeds around her sunflowers.

She looked up at the sky and squinted. Even though it was overcast, the sunlight still pierced through and felt like a hot iron pressing on her shoulders. "Goddammit." She peeled off her sweatshirt. Probably would have to put it back on in another sixty seconds when the sun disappeared again.

Everything seemed to aggravate her lately. She thought again of the hooded girl in her office. Of the other girl in the hospital. Reminded herself to google her when she got inside. What was her last name? Somer what?

And what the hell, she'd also check to see if there'd been more hoopla with this sketch business.

She pulled weeds until her knees ached. But right as she decided to quit and scooped her last handful into her gloved hands, she heard a scuff behind her.

Before she could turn, her head was yanked back. Something cold and sharp pricked her neck.

"You move and you die," a cold voice said. The voice surprised her, but only for a second before terror rushed through her in a wave. She froze, afraid to move with a blade pressing right into the nape of her neck, her skull cradled in the crook of someone's arm.

"You know why this is happening?"

She was too freaked out to answer, but she managed to get a *no* out. But a big part of her *did. Oh Jesus. Oh God.* Maybe it wasn't some social media game. "The drawing?" she got out.

"Why didn't you confess? You don't think you've done anything wrong?"

She couldn't breathe. She dropped the weeds she was holding, started to bring her hands up to pull the knife from her throat, but she felt the sharp metal pierce her flesh.

*Oh God*, was this real?

Was this happening?

It all felt so otherworldly, but the tight grip around her head and neck felt more authentic and focused than anything ever. This was no joke.

"I can confess now," she blurted, hearing her own breathiness. "The referrals? I mean, those were just . . . I mean, what he did with them, that wasn't my call."

The voice in her ear said, "Fuck you. It's too late."

She felt an excruciating pain slice through her throat and a flood of blood gurgling up.

# Chapter 28

I'm in my car out at the main highway, but I'm too late to know if the author of the **IT'S YOU** scrawl has gone north or south where the highway meets an intersection a little ways down the road. And I still don't know if it was one person or two.

I drive back to the dumpster site and catch the truck that arrived while we were both there. He's pulling out. I flash my lights, roll down my window, and wave for whoever's driving to stop. A graying man lowers his window.

"Did you happen to notice the make of the other car that was next to mine when you came in?"

"You mean over on the other side?"

"It was the only other car besides mine when you drove in."

"I want to say it was some sort of SUV. Too dark to see the color or make of it, though. They steal somethin' from ya?"

"No. Just a little graffiti." I smile and roll my window up before he can ask more.

He gives me a salute-like wave and drives on.

I go to the spot where I first parked and search the area again. The ground is too hard packed and well trodden for any distinct footprints or tread marks.

I hop back in my SUV and check my phone. More notifications pour in, including several alerts from my new surveillance app.

When I look at the surveillance feed to my front entrance, I see Deputy Zane out of his vehicle speaking to about three people.

I dial Zane's number.

"Crosbie," he says. "You okay?"

"I'm good."

"It's late. Where are you?"

"Just finished some work. Who are those people you're talking to?"

Zane sighs loudly. "You're not going to like my answer."

"Why?"

"Reporters."

"What? How did they get involved?"

"I don't know. Apparently, some stories have come out with your name."

"Do not let them anywhere near my home. I'll be right there."

I flip to one of my news apps. At the top are several *Top News* national headlines regarding politics, Russia, and Ukraine, a weather update about a hurricane in the Atlantic, and below those—second down from the top, after some headline about Kevin Costner—it reads: Sketch Artist's Next Victim Possibly ID'd.

*Damn.*

My pulse pounds in my ears as my world shrinks and spirals into more of a madhouse than it's already been. As I click on the article, a call from Jess takes over my screen.

"Jess," I answer a little breathlessly, but still try to conceal that I'm reeling over the marker on my car.

"Where are you?"

"Heading home."

"Oh my God, Cros, no. You can't go home. This has gotten crazy. Have you seen the news?"

"Only the first headline on *The Daily Beast*. Did they mention my name?"

"Yes, and there are photos of your earrings. I have no idea how they got them. There's a picture of you wearing them at that banquet you went to with Fiona and Trey. Looks like it started with *TMZ* or *Page Six*."

"Fiona," I say.

"She wouldn't do that."

"Would and did. Probably sold the photos, if it's *TMZ* or *Page Six*." I know how those news outlets work. Although paycheck journalism isn't a big thing in the US, it still occurs when a rag wants a good story with fresh photos and finds someone eager to cash in.

"You don't know that it was her."

"Come on, Jess. Who else?"

"Maybe it was the department. You stopped in there, too, right?"

"Possibly." I think about it. There were a lot of cameras that night at the event, but the earrings? That level of detail, about me? "Hold on a sec."

I change screens, keeping Jess on speaker, and pull up *The Daily Beast* article. I scroll down to see close-ups of my earrings on top of a white, marble-like countertop, exactly like Fiona and Trey's new one. A flame of rage ignites at the pit of my belly. I can barely hear Jess talking, and when I tune back in, she's saying that it's beside the point who gave them the photos, that what's more important is making sure I'm safe. "If you won't come here," she says, "we need to figure out where you need to go."

"I'm not going anywhere. I'm going home."

"You can't."

"Yes, I can. If anything, this makes my home even safer." I explain to her what Alderson shared with me earlier today about the woman in Texas, and how having reporters around might deter the killer.

She thinks about it. "I don't like it, Cros. Look, I know this doesn't seem real, like it's some bad dream, but those two others, they're dead now."

"And I promise you, I'm not going to be one of them."

Silence.

I'm disliking how she's taken to going quiet on me. This no-response thing is new for her—one more aspect of her that's changed.

"Jess?"

Still nothing.

"Jess, did they . . . is there any mention of you being my sister in any of the articles you've read?"

She doesn't reply. Tension creeps higher. Finally, she says, "No, not yet, not in the ones I saw. But I'm sure there will be soon."

"God, I'm so sorry."

"Look, it's not your fault, and they have no need to dig further into my life."

"But they might call you and come to your house to ask you questions about me."

"I know, and I'm prepared to shut them down."

She seems stronger than usual, and I feel my chest loosen slightly. She's almost sounding like her old self for the moment. "Okay. I'll call you when I get home."

I hang up and put my car in drive, snapping back to wondering who followed me out here and scrawled the ugly message on my door.

I race across the valley, knowing that if things haven't already gotten wacky enough, they're going to change even more now. I crack a window for some air. The lights of gas stations, car dealerships, pot dispensaries, dog kennels, and other storefronts slide by in a blur along the highway from Kalispell to the north end of the valley. The stretches of dark fields beyond them, usually comforting, suddenly seem menacing.

The Flathead Valley, and the surrounding wilderness, is my haven. It makes me feel whole, wipes away my past troubles, and for years now has helped make my dad's and mom's deaths and what happened to Sophie seem like clouds stretching over the mountains—in sight, but far away. But now, cast into this strange, deepening technological nightmare, the serenity of nature and all its balance and rebirth seem like a load of crap.

When I come to my gravel drive cutting through my own pitch-black field, I find Zane standing outside his car, his lights on, talking to a knot of five reporters, all carrying cameras with long lenses and huge flashes. There aren't that many local reporters, so I'm thankful it's not a mob.

I pull in tight next to Zane and park. The reporters waste no time. They crowd around him and my car, firing questions at me like darts through my barely cracked windows.

*Crosbie Mitchell, do you believe it's you?*

*How scared are you that you're next?*

*What do you need to confess?*

*Are you going to confess?*

Flashes explode in my face as they take pictures of me behind my windshield. I'm glad the reporters are either in front of me or behind Zane on the driver's side. The writing on my car is on the passenger door. None of them have seen it or will be photographing it.

I wave Zane in closer and speak through the narrow opening of my window. "I'm going to drive in. Do not let them near my house. And if more arrive in the morning, whoever comes on shift after you, please make sure they also understand that my house is off-limits. Okay? Can you handle this?"

"Yes, ma'am," he says. He turns, spreads his arms out like the wings of a giant bird, and begins pushing the reporters away from my car so I can drive past. Suddenly, I'm beyond thankful to have him around.

When I get into my garage, my heart settling once again from the invasion of the press, I take pictures of the side of my car where the message is and call Alderson to tell him about what happened out at the dump site.

He scolds me like a tardy child, saying I shouldn't have been out at dark alone. He asks me to send the photos and instructs me not to touch anything on that side of the car so that they can dust for prints and take samples of the marker as soon as they can get someone from forensics, probably first thing in the morning.

I lock myself in my house, go straight to my computer, and find all the articles. Jess is right. So far, they haven't made the connection that Jess, the semifamous podcaster and DNA sleuth, is my sister. Jess is also correct that it began with the tabloids, specifically *TMZ*. They mention my name, that I live in the Flathead Valley, that I was a former police officer, and most saliently, that I own a pair of unique earrings that perfectly match the ones in the sketch.

God, I want to wring Fiona's neck. The fury is disorienting. I don't even know the time. Maybe I should resist the impulse, but screw that. I pull up her number and call.

"Crosbie," she answers, her voice sheepish. "I know what you're thinking, but it wasn't me."

"Fiona, seriously—"

"I know you didn't want it out there that you have those exact earrings, but Trey . . . he, I mean, well, Trey said that it could only protect you in the long run. That the more attention you get, the safer you'll be. And Cros, things have been hard financially, we should have never done that remodel, and daycare's gotten—"

"Fiona, stop."

She does. What follows is a long, freighted silence. What am I going to do, threaten her and Trey? Yell and scream at her that she's violated my life? Tell her that she's robbed me of my own choice to handle this the way I think best—that I would've preferred to gain some momentum in my own investigation before the press got involved?

"Fiona," I say at last, with all the calm I can muster, "it wasn't for you and Trey, of all people, to decide for me how this thing goes down. You should have asked for my permission."

"But Trey said you'd be safer, and—"

"Fiona," I say, "you're not listening. You should have asked."

"But Crosbie, you have to understand that we thought it was best to get it out there," she says, still not apologizing. "Rip the Band-Aid off."

If I could wing my phone into the wall and see the screen shatter into pieces without it costing me anything, I would. I used to get the same rush when my stepdad roared at us and I felt like I couldn't yell back. I was fearful of pissing off my mom, worried she would accuse me of sabotaging their marriage. I feel that same rush now.

"And you," Fiona continues. "You don't seem like yourself."

"What's that supposed to mean?"

"You know," she says. "Always focused on Jess. We figured you could use a little help doing what's best for you, keeping you safe."

Heat explodes in my cheeks. The hand holding the phone begins to tremble. I want to scream into it until she incinerates on the other end. Instead, I shake my head and hang up.

What a jerk to use my sister as an excuse for doing a greedy, self-serving thing. I understand now why my uncertainty about Fiona as early as in high school was justified.

My heart pounds and my mind whirs. My phone pings steadily. Announcements flash on the screen and seem to throb, hounding me until I swipe them clear. I catch glimpses of them without opening them:

If you're a piece of shit, might as well fess up.

Just kill yourself now.

The truth will set you free.

What evil thing have you done? You deserve to die, PigBitch #ACAB

Even . . .

OOOOH . . . I love a dirty woman. Will you marry me?

Shit.

Allison and a few other friends call, and even my stepdad, but I don't answer any of them. With our mom now gone, I hear from Les no more than three times a year—on my birthday, Christmas, and Thanksgiving—and as far as I'm concerned, it's a miracle that we have that much contact.

I need to think, but my phone screen pulls at me like an undertow.

I open Facebook to see more messages piling up. Strangers berating me, telling me I need to confess my sins and make myself right with God, not just the killer. That, of course, I deserve to die—that there is no way I didn't do horrible things, if I was a cop. All Cops Are Bad . . . #ACAB after #ACAB.

And about me, they're right. I have no excuse. I did fall into the trap. Adhered to *the code* after all.

Other messages offer condolences, addressing me like I'm their best friend and conveying how sorry they are this is happening to me. One person asks me what I plan to do with my Facebook page after the Confession Artist kills me, as if this issue would of course be top of mind. But suddenly, it is. I can't help it—I envision my phantom self, living on virtually in bits of data after the Confession Artist manages to fire a bullet into my brain. My virtual heart pumping with each email and notification popping up for months and months, still trying to sell me everything the algorithmic fields suggest I buy.

It was the same with Sophie. Condolences mounted up after her suicide from people across the U of M campus and the town, too. People addressed her specifically and personally, as if she could write them back to thank them or could pop in a thumbs-up to acknowledge them. Hearts, praying hands, and happy faces peppered her page—a sad, hollow outpouring, after all the vitriol she'd endured. I tried to convince Wallace to delete her pages on Facebook, Instagram, and the then Twitter, but he didn't know her passcodes. Neither did I.

When I looked it up, I found that you needed to provide a scanned photo of the death certificate to each of the platforms to either memorialize the page or have it deleted. Wallace never bothered, and eventually, we quit visiting her sites, though I still get reminders about her birthday once a year and occasionally receive a shared memory photo.

*Enough about the damn past,* I berate myself, wanting to throw something like I wanted to in the car, anything—my phone, my laptop, a coffee cup—across the room. I shake it off. *Time to get to work.*

I've stood up from my kitchen table to go into my office when my phone makes a different, disconcerting *ping*. I realize it's the surveillance app, alerting me to movement on one of the cameras. It's the one I set up to cover part of the driveway. I open it, expecting a furry creature, but instead, the dark shape of a human passes.

I jolt back, my blood rushing, my heart in overdrive. I grab my Sig on the kitchen counter. My hands have barely quit quaking after talking to Fiona, but my gun hand, at least, goes rock steady when I squeeze the stock.

I kill the lights in the kitchen and dining area. I don't plan on giving whoever it is the advantage of a clear view into my home. I creep across the wood floor on tiptoes, trying to move as stealthily as a cat.

When I get to the front door, I stand between it and one of the side windows, hold my gun before my chest with a cocked elbow, and crane my neck and peer through the side of the window.

Beyond my porch light, it's pitch black, like a dark blanket has been spread across everything beyond my little world. I squint and will my eyes to penetrate past the glow, past the shadows and shifting shapes of trees in the breeze, but I can't see anything more.

I listen.

All is silent.

My old training comes back. I hold the pistol close to my gut with elbows bent and brace it with both hands, wrists firm. Scuffling footsteps make their way across my gravel drive toward the house.

The room goes airless. The walls of my living room feel like they're closing in on me. I'm holding my breath.

As the footsteps reach my front steps, I hit the porch light and throw open the door.

# Chapter 29

## Gus

Gus got up at 5 a.m. for his day out in the woods. He checked the weather online so he and his men would know what to expect on the dirt roads. Fortunately, it was going to be a little dryer than it had been, but the mosquitoes would still be out in droves because there'd been so much spring rain.

It affected how he dressed for the day, although not that much. He still wore mostly the same old stuff—his steel-toed work boots, Carhartt pants, insulated flannel overshirt under his reflective vest—the get-up that Somer used to tease him about, calling him a Montana hick. And when he'd dropped her in Santa Monica, leaving her to go to the community college, she asked him to not wear a flannel shirt and boots—even though the ones he'd brought weren't his work pair—on the day of the orientation.

Now, when he thought of that metropolis, his stomach lurched. It was all he could do not to vomit. Instead, he packed his box lunch, poured the strong coffee he'd made into his thermos, and headed out for the day before the sun rimmed the eastern mountains with rose-gold streaks.

The Benz Lumber logging roads were on the north end of the valley, not far from the ski resort. They were rutted out and filled with standing water, but he and his men would plow through it. They had a lot of work to get done, and they'd already taken too many breaks on account of late-season snow followed by torrential spring rains that made the soil prone to rutting under the heavy equipment.

One of his men got a skidder stuck in the mud, immobilizing work for days. Plus, there was a clause in the Benz's contract with the state that if any topsoil was disturbed enough to affect Whitefish Lake, all operations needed to cease until the soil dried and became stable enough not to filter sediment downslope.

The area hadn't been logged in some time because of these issues, Benz opting instead for the heavily forested areas they owned farther away where there were fewer hoops to jump through and the clear-cutting and demolition of swaths of trees didn't horrify the snowflake tourists or stir up a political hoo-ha in town.

But now, there was no choice left. Developments were pushing deeper into the woods, the ski resort was expanding, and fires were getting worse each summer, so the head of Benz Lumber decided it was time to clean the woods up, harvest some of the old-growth ponderosa that made the company money.

Gus would meet Danny and the others at the entryway to the Benz logging road, where they'd parked all their equipment—the skidders, fellers, bulldozers and harvesters—for the night. Gus made a stop at the gas station to fill up his cans because some of the guys had quit early the previous week when they ran out of fuel. They hadn't obeyed the rule of making sure they always came out into the woods with extra.

Help these days. He'd eventually have to bring in TP so he could wipe their asses for them, too. In the old days, his men never would have showed up without all the necessities. But that was another lifetime ago. Everything was another lifetime ago for him now, demarcated by the before and after the very moment he got word that Somer had gone into that coma and solidified two weeks later when she passed. His existence since felt foreign and blurry, like a bad dream that would never end.

The trouble wasn't only the amount of mud on the road or how wet the soil was. He'd been logging for twenty-plus years. He never once flipped a feller, even on the steepest slopes. No, the trouble was these black holes of thought he tumbled into, these all-consuming reveries where he would lose time.

Sometimes he'd go blank for a few minutes, but other times, a dark rage of fantasy would envelop him. Like, really black. First, the edges of the forest would go murky, like a burning photograph, and into charred view would come he, himself. And in that scene, he'd be repeatedly striking the men who'd left her outside the hospital with a Pulaski axe, the kind he'd wielded when he used to fight fires straight out of high school.

He'd swing down on their skulls, cracking and crunching their bones into pieces. And the wet red-and-pink mixture of bones and brain matter would fill up his mind and erase his pain and memories of her and how those men—the "unknown assailants," as the police officers had called them—left her outside the ER with an ungodly concoction of drugs pumped into her system.

Whoever they were, they'd had the foresight to remove the license plates on their vehicle before pulling up to the hospital. But somehow, in his fantasies, he'd tracked them down and exacted violent revenge. And when he was finished with them, he'd also hunt down that bitch at the school who was supposed to help students, not deliver them up to the scum of the earth. He had no proof to give the police about this woman, but Somer had told him how she had recommended that doctor.

Somer was excited about him, told her dad he was brilliant and kind. Said she trusted him. Gus hadn't even warned her to be careful about any of them, because why would he? That woman was a school counselor, and the man was a psychiatrist. Somer would be in good hands, he had thought. He mentioned those two to the cops, but they'd seemed more focused on the men who left her at the ER—understandable on one level, but not on another. It was the people behind the scenes making bad things happen that should pay.

The reverie was in full bloom while he cut through some thin-diameter lodgepole pines until he felt a tipping sensation. He snapped out of it at the part where he was down on one knee with the axe raised high behind his right shoulder, getting ready to swing it another time into the man's broken skull.

He came to in time to realize he was falling off a pile of wood into a deeply rutted hole in the wet soil. After all these years, his reaction was swift, and he turned the Tigercat off on its way down. He felt his stomach rise to his throat and adrenaline surge through him as the Tigercat plopped into a pile of soft, wet dirt.

He sat for a moment with images of Somer flashing through his mind.

He saw Barbie dolls, broken crayons, plastic unicorns. He saw her fuzzy, stuffed puppy dog with the chewed-up ear; he saw her stuffed seal, turtle, and monkey all lined up on her bed; he saw her dark eyes and timid smile and her yellow barrette pinning thick brunette locks; he saw tangled hair with pink bubble gum stuck in it and him cutting it out with scissors while she cried. He felt her sitting in his lap while he rocked her to sleep until the sound of the chain saws from Danny and Henry not far away brought him back to the reality of his situation.

He tried to get out of the feller, but the door wouldn't open.

Eventually the buzzing roar ceased, Danny and Henry running over.

"Man, you okay?" Danny called.

"I'm fine. Just can't get the damn door open."

Danny hopped up onto the machine and pulled at the door.

The three men stood there surveying the situation, the sharp tang of soil, pine, and fuel all around. The feller lay on its side, like a dinosaur lying wounded in mounds of mud. "We should grab the excavator," Danny said.

Gus agreed. "We can hook the line to the side by the rim there and winch her right outta that rut."

"Let's do it, then," Danny said as he headed over to grab the backhoe.

After they pulled the feller back upright onto its broad wheels, Henry got back to work, but Danny stood for a moment longer looking at Gus like he had something to say.

Gus removed his hard hat, took off one work glove, and ran his grubby fingers through his sweaty hair. Mosquitoes buzzed and he swatted at one behind his neck. "Thanks for getting me out," he offered to Danny. "First time I've done that."

"Sure." Danny looked at Gus carefully. "You all right, though?"

"Yeah. Wasn't paying attention."

"You sure?"

"Yeah, why?"

"I don't know, with everything. I mean."

Danny's eyes filled with the kind of sympathy that Gus didn't want to see. All those expressions only did one thing: They reinforced reality. Gus hoped Danny wouldn't ask about his drinking.

"I know how hard it's been," Danny said. "But if you need to take more time or something, you should."

Gus resisted the urge to grunt, *I'm good.* He was afraid if he said anything, he might cry right there in front of Danny, among the mud and the dripping trees, among the new lime-colored tips of the pines that Somer used to caress between her fingers. The freshness of it all threatened to soften his wrath and replace it with sorrow. That would be unbearable.

"You've been pretty"—Danny winced, seeking the right word—"distant." He shook his head as if no, that wasn't right, either. "I mean, I just don't want to see you get hurt. It's a safety thing. You know that better than anyone."

"I do." Gus inhaled the tangy, pine-saturated air around them. All of it so *alive*. How could she be gone? "You're right. I need to focus. Sorry. Like I said, never flipped one before. Ever. Guess everyone deserves a first."

"Sure, but if you need to talk . . ." Danny hit his own chest as if to say, *I'm a good listener.*

"Appreciate it, man. Right now, though, I want to check to make sure the oil levels are okay and finish out this day."

When Gus drove home, he could feel that tipping sensation in his gut and how his heart plunged. He heard the drone of a saw in his ears. A pressure built up in his head and hammered behind his eyeballs.

When he'd hit the ground in that feller, his entire world had pitched over—and he was still falling, still hitting bottom, over and over. But this wasn't a jobsite accident. This was reality. There would be no soft landing. There would be no getting out of it. It was a black hole of rage mixed with sorrow. He was tumbling down, crashing and falling, crashing and falling.

By the time he got to his driveway, he'd begun to weep at the thought of going in, of spending another evening alone in the house where he'd raised Somer after her mother left them. He kicked himself again: *I should have never let her go to that city, so far from home. I should have never let her talk me into it.*

After he dried his eyes, he sat in his truck and wondered, *What would Somer do now, in my shoes? If she was the one left behind?*

*She'd google something to find a solution,* he thought. He smiled thinking about how she'd grab her phone and say, *I'll figure it out. It's not that hard when you have the entire world at your fingertips. You need to keep up, Dad.*

He sat for a moment longer, staring at their little blue house, then fumbled for his phone out of his pocket and typed in one word—*rage*—to see where Google would take him.

# Chapter 30

My porch light illuminates a man blinking into the light's glare a few careful feet from my stoop. Hair pushed back behind the ears, facial stubble, holding something by his side with one hand and the other held palm out as though in surrender.

It takes a second for my brain to catch up, and when it does, it's a jolt in my chest. Oh my God, it's him. *Rolling Stone*. Jeremy Fisher, the man from the airport. Holding a . . . what? A six-pack?

Why the hell is *he* here? My mind spins from all the chaos. The same person I saw on the day after the sketch came out shows up unannounced in the dark?

My breath punches out louder than it should in the still air.

Plus, the look on his face suggests he's clueless about my state of worry, but then maybe that's the point, his entire ruse.

"Crosbie Mitchell," he says, squinting into the light. "That you? I'm not here to hurt you or cause any trouble."

I step out, still holding my gun up.

"Whoa." Jeremy takes a big step back. "Is that necessary?"

"Do you really think I'd answer the door without making sure I'm safe? Why are you creeping around out here this late?"

"*Creeping* is a strong word."

"I don't see your car. Where is it?"

A tentative smile. "As I'm sure you're aware, your entrance is well guarded. I figured I'd park on the next road over and walk across the field."

"And why in the hell would you do that?"

"To talk to you before the others do." He gives me the same sheepish squint he gave me in the airport.

"How do you know where I live?"

"Once your identity came out in the news, it really wasn't difficult. Can we talk?"

I press my lips together and think about it. The inhales and exhales through my nose are still too loud. I part my lips and try to breathe more quietly and calmly. I don't trust him, but I do need to know more about him. If I suspect Jeremy, which I do, then I should talk to him, find out what he wants. Keep my enemies close.

I do the math: In the morning, there will be only two days left. Discovering what he's after here and now saves me time from tracking him down later, if I need to.

"I brought microbrews. Local ones. And other than that"—as if he's read my mind about what else he's carrying—"all I've got with me is this notepad and pen." He points to his jacket pocket with his free hand. "May I?"

"Slowly," I say.

He half kneels like he's balancing on a surfboard and places the beer down on the gravel, then equally gingerly opens his fleece so I can see the inside pocket and pulls out his notepad and pen.

"What do you want?"

"Like I said, to talk to you first. About your story. You know I deserve first dibs, right?"

"Deserve?"

"Come *on*." He motions to the field he's apparently come across. "There were divots and gopher holes. I almost ate it twice." He flashes a wry smile. "And I was carrying this." He glances at the beer. "And, you know, you almost shot me. That ought to be worth something."

He's undeniably disarming. Plus there's the strong angle of his jaw, his golden eyes, and how his eyebrows grow fuller on the outside edges—something I wouldn't have guessed would appeal to me. But I think of that word—*disarming*—and it occurs to me that maybe he didn't use the field simply because Zane is guarding the front of the place. Maybe he doesn't want me to see his car because it's a dark-colored SUV like the one out at the dump site, and he's been keeping an eye on me since we arrived from Dallas.

My mind frantically whirls like a top. I'm more convinced than ever now that the drawing is of me. I saw this guy at the conference, of all places. And then again at the airport in my own small Montana town? What are the chances? It seems much too coincidental.

Maybe he doesn't know I didn't get a good glimpse of his vehicle or its license plate and has come here because he thinks I'm now a loose end that needs tidying up ahead of the six-day allotment.

"Where were you before this?" I ask.

"At my hotel, reading up on you."

If he's faking it, he's quick. And a good actor. "And what did you find out?"

"That it looks like someone you know sold you out to the press."

I keep studying him. The night feels charged. Crickets trill loudly from the surrounding fields and my porch lights are attracting bugs. Bats swoop in and out of the shadows beyond the glare to hunt insects. He studies me back, his eyes wide with either concern for the gun pointed his way or sincerity. I can't tell.

*Keep your enemies close.* "It's cold out here," I say at last. "Hang on." I grab my phone out of my pocket with my free hand and hold it up and snap a photo of him. "There," I say. "Now I'm going to text this to the deputy out front, so he can identify you if he has to."

"Fair enough."

Glancing up to him and back down to the phone, over and over, I pull up Zane's number, attach the photo, and tell him that everything's fine but that I want him to know I have a visitor.

"Also," I tell Jeremy. "You should know, when I heard you outside, I called him, so he might be here any second."

A lie, but it would have been a good idea, though I was glad he was still at the entrance keeping the others away.

◆ ◆ ◆

Once inside, Jeremy stands by the front door, still unsure of himself—a good sign, I consider. I usher him into the dining area next to the kitchen.

"You going to keep that pointed at me all night?"

"Maybe." A part of me does feel bad. No one likes to have one of these trained on them. "Sorry. But given the circumstances . . . And you were an idiot to sneak up like that, with everything that's going on."

"I'm aware. But these are the hazards of the job. Gotta take some risks. I'm sure you understand, being a PI and all."

There's boldness, and there's crazy, I think. "Have a seat." I motion to the kitchen table, and he follows my direction. I remain standing while he twists the cap off one of his beers and holds it out to me. I stare at him, not moving to grab it.

"Don't like?"

I take it but stay by the counter facing him, still holding the gun. A few sips won't hurt, and I could use something to calm my nerves, which are thrumming like a high-voltage wire. "Thanks. You know I'm not giving you any kind of a confession, so what do you want from me?"

"Why not? It could save your life."

"Gee, I don't know, maybe because I have no idea what I've done that needs confessing. What? That a friend dared me to steal a piece of candy from the drugstore when I was a kid?"

"Hmm. That's the worst secret you have?"

"No." *God no.* "But you get my point. I could scour my life, as anyone would in this situation, but there's nothing that stands out," I say. He doesn't need to know that I've considered every wrongdoing I've ever committed—from my minor infractions to the times I've threatened people, like my neighbor when I pulled him over, or Jess's ex-boyfriend when I warned him that it was best to stay out of her life, or poured cola over a rude woman's car window—I've done all this even while knowing that it all, every human bit of it, pales in comparison to how I failed Sophie, and Leon, and my own sister, and myself, through my complicity with Railes.

But no one knows about the big one except Railes himself.

I take a deep drag on my beer.

"But the point is"—I wipe the back of my hand over my lips—"even if I had anything to fess up to, there'd be no way I'd confess a damn thing before I developed some kind of understanding of what this person's after. Maybe if I could get a grip on why he's doing this, I might have a clue as to what kind of a confession he's looking for. Until then, there's no point in me or anyone else throwing stuff out there." I take another, daintier draw on my beer. "Plus, I don't plan on smearing my life all over the place. Not my style."

"Got it, but still, are you telling me there's really nothing?"

I cock my head nonchalantly, pretend the guilt isn't throbbing so loudly inside me that it's deafening, and give him a look that says, *Of course there's a minor thing or two, but I wouldn't tell 'em to* you.

"Look, I get that you don't know me, but I think I can help you."

"Well, *that's* nice of you. How, exactly?"

"If you read my stuff. I mean, I'm not saying I'm a Pulitzer-winning journalist or anything, but I will say that I do my best to be honest, respectful, and thoughtful. I wouldn't just throw anything out there for the clicks or kicks. We don't even need to write about your confession. I want to do a story on *you*, what it's like to be in this awful, *awful*"—he shakes his head with what looks like actual sincerity and stares me in the eyes—"situation. I write about human beings, not subjects. And my hunch is that you're a decent, nice person and don't deserve this." He points his beer toward the front of the house. "Not many other journalists out there are going to do that, I can tell you. They're going to rip your life to pieces and throw the scraps to the wolves. They're going to speculate, exaggerate, flat-out make things up that are twisted bastardizations of the truth. You get that, right?"

"I do."

"Check out my stuff a little. And give me an exclusive. I'll turn it into a feature that counters all the asinine stuff that will keep erupting until this guy is caught."

"And how do you plan to do that?"

"By writing a considerate, careful piece on you. All you need to do is tell me about your life."

"You probably already know about my life—that I was a cop, that I quit the force, that I'm now a PI." I wonder how many other things he's come across. Does he know about what happened in the department?

Does he know about Sophie? My pulse picks up. I want to sink into the counter behind me, become a part of it. I set my beer down and reflexively rub my face with my free hand as if I can hide it from him—shield any tell—but I act like I'm only doing so out of exhaustion.

"I know a few things, and if I go by what's purely on the web, I could find a thousand ways to pump enough speculation into every one of those things to make you look like you deserve to be in that sketch. In fact, that's already being done. But you and I both know that's not the case."

"What, that I don't deserve to be in that sketch? It's not the case for me, or for any of the victims, no matter what they've done." I wince internally, thinking of Coleman's body hitting the coffee table and falling to the floor. Hadn't I thought over and over that he deserved what he got, the reason I took the mum's-the-word stance? How is Jeremy so sure I don't deserve to be in that sketch?

"True. But you have the right to have a cleaner, clearer picture of yourself out there."

Do I, though? I've far from earned it. "You don't even know if I'm the actual target."

"That's honestly beside the point," he says. "What's interesting to me and titillating to the rest of the world isn't whether it's you or not, but how it *feels* to be you. How it feels to be someone who's a dead ringer for the drawing, to be in—no offense—but, you know, in the crosshairs."

"It feels like shit. There: There's your scoop."

This earns me an eye roll.

"Listen," I say. "You said you don't think I deserve it, but you don't know me. You have no idea who or what I am. How do you know I don't?"

He takes a swig of his beer, his eyes still on mine. The way he's studying me makes me feel like no one has really ever looked at me before, like he's seeing all the bad stuff in me, and maybe an ounce of the good, too. "Just a hunch. I did a bit of a deep dive on you before I came out. I know about your roommate in college."

This drives something sharp and hot through my chest.

"In fact," he says, "I went to school in Missoula, a few years ahead of you, and even after I graduated, I remember hearing about the whole thing with your roommate, Sophie Scott, and that golfer. And you're right, I also know about you quitting the police force. Like I said, right now, the people out front are already cooking up ways to twist that a hundred different ways. Trust me, it'll be red meat for everyone who wants to smear you and sensationalize this. If you check your phone right now, you'll see new stuff already coming out and it's not even morning yet."

I study him back, hoping I display enough dispassion in my eyes to convey that I'm in control, that I'm an investigator, and he is on the other side of who and what I inspect daily. But he doesn't shrink or look away because ultimately, as a reporter, he is one, too. And he's shamelessly trying to rake up my deepest regrets. And if I don't supply them to him, will he find them anyway and expose me whether I give him an interview or not?

And if he's the killer, maybe even kill me if I don't confess, not just to him, but to the world.

"What makes you think I care about all the horrible things that people are going to write about me?"

"Crosbie," he says like he's known me for a long time. "You're human, right? Eventually, everyone cares."

"What I care about more is catching the person who's playing this cruel game."

"Right. That's a given. But you know, the surest way for you to protect yourself would be to come clean about your demons."

That hits like ice on an exposed nerve. I shift from one foot to the other.

"I thought you said you weren't interested in those. That you're interested in my life, who I am, who I've been?"

"I am. But we all have demons. Every one of us."

"Exactly. So that's what makes this thing so frustrating, because it seems so random. And yet, it can't be, so there must be a reason I've been targeted. And that means there's a way to find this guy. So no, Mr. Fisher—"

"Jeremy, please."

"Okay, so no, Jeremy. I'm not spilling my life for you or anyone else. I'm going to find who is doing this. You can print that if you want."

"And you've got the guts for that? For facing down this killer with only the help of that deputy you said you called? The one who still hasn't shown up?"

I squirm again, shift my stance to hide it. I almost mention the agents to prove it's not only Zane and me, but I catch myself. That would be sloppy. "If you must know, I knew I could handle you by myself." I hold up the gun and squeeze its grip, attempting to appear more confident than I feel.

"Fair," he says. "But in case it's not clear, what I'm saying is that you ought to confess something—hopefully the right thing—and I think it should be through an interview with me. I think that's what will save you from this killer."

My breathing goes shallow. I hope to God he doesn't notice my chest rising and falling. *And if you* are *the killer, how special, you get my confession face-to-face.*

The silence between us feels strange and intimate, like he's pinpointed something deep and personal about me. But he hasn't, has he?

I take a sip of beer to hide my unease. As I lower it back down, my phone trills.

"Your deputy?" says Jeremy.

"In fact, yes." I exhale—maybe a little too loudly.

Deputy Zane is agitated. He tells me there is a man at his checkpoint who insists he's a friend, harmless, and known to me. "Wallace Scott," says Zane.

Wallace. Why would he come over so late? Does he have something important to tell me, something that's going to make this awful day even worse? Either way, I'm grateful he's here.

Because Jeremy is making me more and more anxious. And I can't help but wonder if that's his intention.

# Chapter 31

"Send him up," I tell Zane. "It's fine."

"Who?" says Jeremy.

"An old boyfriend."

Jeremy doesn't need to know the relationship isn't all that ancient or that he's *that* roommate's older brother.

"Are you okay?" asks Wallace when I greet him out front. He's a bit breathless. "Jesus, it took me five minutes to get that deputy to even call you."

"Wallace, it's late. What's up?"

"I didn't see the news until tonight. I'm sorry I didn't come earlier. We rehearsed late for the show this weekend."

"It's fine. I'm fine. You didn't need to come."

I'm going to set much firmer boundaries with Wallace, even if it hurts his feelings. Wallace walks up to the door right as Jeremy comes up behind me.

"Who's he?" says Wallace.

I introduce Jeremy, saying that he's a reporter.

Wallace studies Jeremy with a *what the heck* look. "It's late," he says to me. He's giving Jeremy the stink-eye along with his rutted brow.

"The news didn't break until this evening," Jeremy offers.

Wallace glances around the driveway. "And where the hell is his car?" he asks, as if Jeremy isn't standing right next to us.

"He walked over."

"Walked? From where?"

"Over there." Jeremy points across the field. "My car's on the neighbor's drive, off Dillon Road."

"Jesus." Wallace shakes his head.

I've never seen him this angry and impolite before. "Wallace, it's fine."

"No, it's not fine. Are you kidding me?" His voice is loud, overriding the loud trill of the chirring crickets in the dry fields. "Jesus, Crosbie. Your life could be in danger, and you're inviting strangers in? You need more protection. One cop at your entrance is clearly not enough."

*No, clearly, it's not* zings through my head as I stand here and talk to two men late at night during one of the most bizarre and threatening weeks of my life.

Wallace looks at me, then Jeremy. Confusion and anger still fight for center stage in his eyes. "Can we talk for a moment?" he says to me.

I need to be careful, and if Jeremy stays and we continue to chat, I'll have to keep fighting off his prodding for a full-fledged interview. Wallace showing up is a stroke of luck because he provides the perfect excuse to shoo Jeremy away. But the hairs standing up on the back of my neck won't lie down.

"Of course," I say to Wallace. I look at Jeremy. "Jeremy was just leaving."

Jeremy smiles wryly at me, tips his head once like he gets it that I'm using this to get rid of him. "You mind?" He motions to the kitchen.

"No, help yourself."

He walks back to the table, pulls out his notepad, bends down to scribble something, and tears off the page. He doesn't pick up the rest of the six-pack, which was what I'd assumed he'd returned to fetch. He grabs only his open beer, saunters back over with the bottle dangling in one hand, and holds out the piece of paper to me with the other.

"Do me one favor, okay?" He dips his head at the slip. "Read this."

"What is it?"

"The title of an article I've written. To show you I'm not a hack."

He closes the gap between us, and I sense, more than see, Wallace tense up. *I* tense up. His light-brown eyes, with the fans of tiny lines on the skin around them from time spent squinting in the sun, stare squarely into mine. This is the closest Jeremy's stood to me since I saw him in the baggage claim area, and I feel his presence too keenly. It throws me off-kilter. I take the note from him.

"Stay safe," he says. Our gazes stay fixed for a second longer than normal, and he slides out the door to head back across the field. Watching him disappear into the dark, I'm thinking: *Should I trust that all he wants is a feature story? Or is Jeremy Fisher playing me?*

"What was that all about?" Wallace asks as we go back inside.

"Just a reporter wanting an exclusive interview with me now that Fee-fucking-ona and Trey have gotten the press involved."

Wallace winces at my sailor mouth. He says, "You sure it was them?"

I tell him that I'm positive, and explain the situation with Fiona and Trey. "I guess they took photos of them. Plus, Trey had an old picture of me at the banquet, too."

Wallace's forehead wrinkles in confusion until something dawns on him. He looks away. I see a sadness in his expression, and I realize my mistake—I've not only admitted how long it's been since I've worn the earrings but callously demonstrated that I cared so little about them that I left them in a purse at Fiona's all this time.

God. I don't have the luxury to worry about whose precious feelings I'm stomping on right now. My mind whirs. I have so much to think through, including what happened with my car at the dump site and the fact that Jeremy took the one thing that would have his DNA on it if we ended up needing it.

"Wall, look. I'm sorry. I—"

He holds up his hand to stop me. "It's fine. We haven't been seeing each other for months now. I don't expect you to wear something I gave you." But I can see it in his eyes. He's calculated it out. The banquet was two months before we broke up.

"It was just me being absent-minded," I offer. "A lot was going on back then."

He waves his hand. "We should concentrate on the problem at hand. I mean, you're not giving that ass an interview, are you?"

"No," I say. "I'm not."

"Good. I don't see how that can help anything."

I'm not so sure about that. For a split second, a part of what Jeremy claims he can do is almost appealing, as if it would be interesting to see how someone might assemble all the pieces of my life together into a cohesive whole instead of all the unflattering tidbits and conjectures that are probably already beginning to circulate. It's not that I think I'm biography-worthy; it's that the thought of someone other than me making some sense of all my awful shit is almost tantalizing. To have the company of others looking at me through the same lens of self-loathing and failure as I do.

But it's only for a brief moment that I entertain this. It's simply not going to happen, because, in the end, it all comes with enormous consequences.

And realistically, there is nothing I could do anyway to ease my conscience or atone for my deeds. What's done is done. It's my job to lift myself out of my own dreadfulness and the haze of my own guilt like everyone else does, one day at a time, all possibly while sitting in a cell.

I'm about to tell Wallace that although I appreciate his opinion, I'll decide on my own how I want to handle the media, but my phone buzzes.

It's Alderson.

"I need to get this," I tell Wallace. I bring the phone to my ear as I walk down the hall and into my bathroom for some privacy and shut the door behind me.

"Crosbie," Alderson says. "Is everything okay?"

It's soothing to hear his voice. I'm glad it's him and not Greene on the line.

"Yes," I say. "You've seen the news?"

"Yes, and Zane filled us in, too. And he mentioned you've had two visitors, one he didn't know about until you texted him, and the other your ex-boyfriend?"

"That's right."

"Not exactly airtight security."

"They're just two guys," I point out. What am I, Zane's and the other deputy's PR person?

"So how did he get to your front door?"

I fill him in on how Jeremy walked over and is gone now. I tell him that Wallace is still here.

"He's there with you right now?"

"Yes."

"Is he leaving soon?"

"Yes, why?"

"You can't afford to trust anyone right now. I want you to exit out the back door, circle around, and get to Zane. I'll call him right now."

"What?" I whisper so Wallace can't hear. "I'm not doing that. It's Wallace, for God's sake."

"Listen, Crosbie, we've been doing some more digging. And there's a few things you should know."

"A few things like what exactly?"

"Like the fact that Wallace has been out of town on the dates of the other two victims' murders."

That stops me. I can never keep track of all the places he travels for his gigs, but I haven't thought of it. Why would I? It's a ludicrous idea. "In the same exact place as the victims?"

"Within driving distance. Seattle and Los Angeles."

"That's nothing." I swipe my hand before me. "He travels all the time for concerts. He's in demand. He's an amazing musician. I'm sure if you check each of those concerts, his whereabouts can be accounted for."

"We have checked, and there are some large blanks in his schedule. He arrived way earlier than necessary for his gigs and left a good two days after he wrapped up each of his performances."

"Again, that means nothing." I see myself grimacing in the bathroom mirror. "Wallace is that way." I keep my voice down still. "He likes to take things slowly, absorb his surroundings—unwind before and after events. He doesn't like to feel rushed, and he enjoys the places he travels to. He loves Montana, but he relishes it whenever he gets away to anyplace with some urban culture, where he can take in other musicians, museums, plays." But even as I say it, the thought that he, more than anyone, would know what I did with Sophie and have reason to hate me for it takes root in my mind.

"We figure that's what he'll claim, but the facts remain."

"You haven't spoken to him?"

"We wanted to talk to you first. We're visiting him in the morning. We'll keep you posted. In the meantime, you need to be extra careful with everyone you come across. Trust no one."

"Look, I'll have him out of here in five."

"Okay, but if I don't hear back from you in six, I'm calling Zane."

I go back to the living room, where I left Wallace, but don't see him. I turn the corner and find him beside the fridge, leaning against the counter with one hip, his back to me. I'm about to ask him if he's hungry, like I normally would, but another part of me hears Alderson's voice.

*Six* minutes. Get him out of here in the next few minutes so I can get back to work.

Then he turns, and I see that he's holding my gun.

# Chapter 32

I stop dead, then take a step back.

Wallace stares at me with a look I can't parse. Could be, *How in the world have you become some sicko's target?* Or, just as easily in the senseless world I've been thrust into the last few days, *I could shoot you right now.*

The dark metal of my weapon—the weapon that should be in *my* grip—contrasts with his creamy fingers. They're immaculate, and I see them gliding over his piano keys. The gun in his palm is 100 percent at odds with the image.

*It's just Wallace,* I tell myself, but the hairs on my arms stand straight up. I'm holding my breath.

"It was right there on the counter," he says. "All the times I've been over, I've never seen it out." He's inspecting it now, turning it this way and that. His blue eyes are intense, but focused, like when he's composing or playing. *Has* he held a nasty grudge against me for convincing Sophie to go camping? Did she share with him that I encouraged her to be more free-spirited? If she did, he never breathed a word about it over all these years.

"You know how I feel about gun safety," I say, holding my hand out. "A gun is never a solution to any situation when I'm off the job. Rarely on the job, either."

He inspects it some more. I can see the tension in his jaw, the muscles tightening under the pale skin of his throat.

"Wallace." I shove my hand closer. A sick sensation mixed with dread rushes to my head. Could it be him? Has he hung on to and nursed resentments over Sophie until they reached a breaking point? Could he just pull that trigger right now here in my kitchen? "Give me the damn gun."

He pulls his head back in surprise. A nervous laugh escapes. "Jesus, Crosbie. What? Oh my God. You really think I could hurt you?"

"No," I say. *Maybe.* I don't know what to think, who to trust, anymore. "But give it to me."

He shakes his head in annoyance and sets the gun on my palm, but his eyes stay on mine. It's so much more than irritation. In the sharp, bright blue of his irises, I see the rage. Even hate, like the teeth of an open-mouthed shark breaking up through dark waters. I pull my head back, oddly even more shocked with this than at the gun pointing at me.

"Wallace?" I whisper it more than say it, like I'm trying to understand if he's the same guy I've always known standing in my kitchen.

"Crosbie," he says firmly, like a parent scolding a child. "What have you *done*? *What* do you need to confess?"

*"What?"* Hearing these two questions leave his lips—the *sureness* that I've done something awful—jars me horribly, goes right to my deepest shames.

I can practically see him thinking, *What has this person who I've been involved with*—intimate *with—done?*

Or maybe, *I know what you did, how you lured my sister out to those woods with a pack of guys,* encouraged *her, for God's sake, to not be guarded, pushing her right into the arms of that monster so her first time was fucking* assault.

The pain is unbearable. I feel lightheaded. More nausea climbs. I take a strained breath. But then the anger trails. The damn anger. But it's easier, so, so much easier than the agony. I curl my fingers so tightly around the handle of my gun that it feels like they might break. How dare he ask me that right here, right now, after fondling *my* gun. Does he not realize how insensitive it is?

Or is that the point?

"Wallace," I say as calmly as I can muster. I need to get him out of here. "I get you're trying to help. But I'm exhausted. I need a shower and some sleep. Also, I think it's best for you to stay away from me for a bit, you know, for your safety."

"I'll be fine. You don't need to worry about me."

My anger—and worry—keeps rising.

"I need some space." I bark it out. "You know, to focus so I can figure this thing out and to be there for Jess, too. It's not like this has been easy for her, either. As if she hasn't had enough going on and to have her sister thrown into this mess."

He gives me a cold, hard stare. His lips whisper something I can't make out. For a moment, I think he's said, *Fuck you, Crosbie.*

"What did you say?" I ask.

He glares at me for a moment. "I said, *fine*, Crosbie."

He wheels away with one hand over his shoulder in agitated farewell and storms out the front door.

I let my body fall back against the counter. I suddenly feel heavy, shattered.

*Wallace is a good person,* I tell myself.

*He's Sophie's brother. He's a decent man.*

Who am *I*—the guilty one, the bad one—to get mad at him for asking me what terrible things I've done? For asking me for the truth? It's my pattern. Remorse. Then rage. Then guilt crashing right back in because I don't like who I am in these moments. Or maybe in any moment at all.

And behind it all, Alderson's words still ring in my ears: *Trust no one.*

I lock the house. I check every window. I check the security cameras. Once, twice, three times.

In the bathroom, I turn the water on scalding hot and let it run until the room is thick with steam. I lather up and let the water prick and sting my skin. I will what happened at the dump site to wash down the drain with the suds and try not to feel like Crosbie Mitchell, woman in crosshairs. Failed ex-cop. Bruised from the guilt of not protecting her college roommate. Betrayer of Leon's trust in the system. The very cause of his suicide. And someone who caved hard when it came time to fall in line with Code Blue because secretly, I was fine with my sister's attacker being eliminated from the world.

I make myself stand under the water without flinching. I let it sear my skin, desperate that it might burn away all that I hate about myself. When the tears finally come, they're not just for Sophie and Jess, they're for Leon.

With cheeks flushed and my skin red and enflamed from the hot water, I throw on a T-shirt and some pj bottoms, pull my hair into a tight bun, and go into my office. I'm exhausted and wired, but fatigue won't win this battle.

I get to work catching my killer.

First, I pull up the video I took at the storage facility of Lasserio exiting with the backpack and doing a one-eighty. The pack is difficult to see in the distant footage, and when I enlarge it, it's grainy. I send the video to Clarissa's brother, Paxton, asking him if he recognizes the pack. It's late, so I don't expect an answer right away.

I switch gears and find pictures of the previous Confession Artist victims and tape them to my office wall. I find as many family members and friends of the victims as possible from their Facebook and Instagram interactions and write all their names down. I print out all the articles I can locate related to Randal Askens's high school and Vonda Loman's community college, as well as everything I can find related to Askens and Loman on a personal level. There's not much of the latter beyond some address listings and divorce announcements on both. That's something, I guess. Besides working in education, divorce is another thing they have in common.

I study my prior list titled "Commonalities" and write down *Occupation: Field of Education* and *Divorces. West Coast* as residency. I cross-reference their lists of family members and friends to see if there's any crossover.

No such luck.

I start another spreadsheet with the four of us.

Yes, *us.* I write my own name out in full at the top of one column, pretending I'm a dispassionate investigator, not someone desperately working to manage their own fate.

It's a queasy feeling, lumping myself in with the victims or would-be victims.

Under *Loman*, I write *Counselor, college students.*

Under *Askens—Coach, high schoolers.*

Under *Unnamed survivor—Pharma sales rep.*

Under *Crosbie Mitchell—Ex–police officer, PI.*

I study the articles, looking to highlight the ones that contain something at least a little scandalous.

For Askens, it's clearly the recruiting scandal. I jot that down in his column. It's clear to me that Askens was not the lead in the recruitment process—the head coach was—but still, I decide to call the school in the morning.

For SMCC, Loman's school, I find two vague references to a scandal, professors who maintained personal web pages that condoned teenage sex and military violence on one of the college's servers for game-authoring courses. But most of the information comes from blogs, so it's difficult to tell if any of it is legitimate. No official complaints have been filed with authorities.

I pull up the third sketch again and resume my search of Carssen sales reps on LinkedIn. I keep at it until my eyes are gritty with fatigue. I rub them and think about going to bed, but first, I plug in the title

Jeremy Fisher jotted down for me and up pops the link: Crimes Without Leads in Jurisdictional Minefields.

The summary reads: "On Montana's Crow, Blackfeet, and Flathead reservations, families of missing and murdered Native women ask, 'Where's the attention for our young women?'"

I click the link, and my fatigue fades rapidly. Jeremy's prose dances, keeps me flowing paragraph to paragraph. The research is impressive. He's not only spoken extensively to parents and grandparents of those who've gone missing, but he's interviewed the US Attorney for Montana, Justice Department officials in DC, local sheriff's departments that share jurisdiction of the Blackfeet, Crow, and Flathead reservations. He's interviewed Native American sociologists from Stanford and Harvard, tribal police, tribal councils, the federal Bureau of Indian Affairs, the FBI, and more. He adds specifics that show he's paid careful attention to their culture, noting that the drummers sometimes use fishing rods instead of reeds on their drums because the touch is better, that dropping a feather from one's headdress brings bad luck.

Most importantly, he discusses the effects of such tragedies on the families and the tribes, on a people who feel unseen, unheard, and powerless within the US. He discusses how the tribes' lack of access to technology continues to keep them under the thumb of the US government and even US businesses who track everything they do and purchase, and the crimes they commit.

About two-thirds of the way down the article, he quotes Palmer Edmonds, an elder, as saying, "Until our tribes acquire our own technology to track our own crimes and our own missing persons, we'll never be able to solve our own problems." Edmonds is the very man Paxton Rhoads told me I should speak to because Edmonds had breakfast with his sister, Clarissa, the morning of the day she drowned. But when I contacted him, he blew me off, saying he was too busy. And Paxton can't get me in front of him either because Paxton dated his daughter, and they were slated to get married, but Paxton ended up cheating on her and broke her heart. The wedding was called off, but Edmonds has never forgiven Paxton even though Edmonds remained friendly with Paxton's sister, Clarissa, until the day she died.

But Paxton has told me that Clarissa mentioned to him that Edmonds told her to stay out of the Ridgeways' affairs, that they were bad people, that he'd gotten sideways with them in the past and they'd made his life miserable. Several years before, when he'd led a protest against drilling that the Ridgeways backed on sacred land butting up against their private acreage, one of their henchmen roughed him up badly. They told him if he ever got involved in their affairs again, the beating wouldn't stop until he was dead. I suspect it's also part of the reason Edmonds doesn't want to speak to me, and not just that he has a bone to pick with Paxton. He doesn't want to get involved, knowing it relates to the wealthy, powerful Ridgeways, and wants to avoid getting roughed up again.

Selfishly, I wonder if Jeremy might be able to help me more than I initially thought since he's obviously trusted by the Montana tribes, including the Blackfeet Tribe. And by Palmer Edmonds.

When I finish reading, I shut down my computer, feeling raw. Jeremy wanted me to read this to show me that I'd be in good hands with him. And he has achieved that. I am impressed. At the bottom of the article, it mentions that he's won several awards for the piece, which doesn't surprise me. But what he doesn't know, couldn't know, is that he has also pinged a bruised chord inside me by discussing sexual assault against these women.

In the article, he points out what I already comprehend from my law enforcement work: that Native women are three times more likely to experience sexual violence compared to white women, that homicide is the fourth leading cause of death for those under twenty, and that those numbers are surely skewed by the fact that it's estimated that the causes of untold numbers of those deaths have always been misclassified as suicide, overdose, or exposure to the elements.

I place my forehead against the butts of my palms, squeeze my eyes tightly shut, and press for all I'm worth, trying to squash away all this madness. Here are all these literally lost women, including Clarissa, who receive no attention, and here I am, popping up on people's screens across the nation because I'm a white woman who *might* happen to play into a sensational, viral-ready string of crimes.

And Jess, a white woman raped by a white man, was afraid to press charges, scared to prosecute because bringing something like acquaintance rape to trial rarely works in the victim's favor. Yes, she had a better chance of getting something done than most of the women Jeremy writes about, but still, she refused because it's so difficult and uncertain.

I shake my head like a dog to clear my thoughts. I must think about the now and protect my own world, so it doesn't fall to pieces.

I look at my thumb. It's red and mangled by my own self-induced damage. Worn down as I am, I wonder if maybe I should let Jeremy interview me, not to disclose what happened with Sophie or Mark Coleman, but to share something, anything, to appease the killer.

# A CONFESSION

Facebook: Philip Inglewood—I'm a general surgeon in a small OK town where we don't even have an OBGYN and have a slightly crooked eye. I'm confessing that I waited too long to administer care for a woman needing a DNC. She miscarried, had trouble clearing the fetus, and was sick but I couldn't tell if her life was in danger for certain. She needed a DNC, a very common procedure but now under scrutiny in many anti-abortion states, especially OK. The medical staff were nervous to assist. They didn't want to be held legally responsible for helping without clearly knowing whether the mother's life was at stake, whether her body might fight off the infection. We waited eighteen+ hours before operating. Too long. She was septic and her organs were shutting down. I blame the state for this, but I blame myself, too. I shouldn't have been so scared to be held liable. I should have helped immediately. She did not need to die. Now, her two other children don't have a mom.

# Chapter 33

***Two Days***

I wake up early. Pale light has erased the first layer of darkness, leaving my yard still and dusky, the mountains in the distance barely discernible.

I brush my teeth with haste, dress, gather my waves into a bun, barely toast an English muffin for breakfast, and get to work.

I hop back onto LinkedIn, scouring profiles for faces that resemble the third sketch. I can hardly believe it, but within ten minutes, two-thirds of the way down the long list of Carssen Pharmaceutical employees, I get lucky. The hair and eyes are strikingly similar. The face in the photo is broader, the cheeks in particular fuller, like the guy was heavier when the photo was taken, but everything else fits—the slant of the left eye, the texture of his hair, the shape of his jaw.

Plus, the man is from Spokane, where Alderson said the potential, would-be third target contacted the police.

Timothy Mooney. His profile says he is an appliance salesman for a small company in Spokane, but he used to be a sales rep for Carssen, which is why it came up under my search for Carssen staffers. I get his email off the appliance company's website and a phone number to the sales department he works in. I call it and get a recorded message, so I leave a voicemail for him to call me back.

As the world begins to wake up, my phone pings steadily. I ignore it until I can't. I have shrapnel notifications from every app. There's a text from Wallace, too, screaming at me in all caps: KEEP ME UPDATED. I guess he didn't hear a word of what I said about needing some space. Suspicion shoots through me, but I tell myself this situation is making me crazy.

I have another voicemail from my stepdad and, worryingly, one from Linda Holbrook from Graham Insurance, the company that hired me to check out Aaron Lasserio's claim. I call the agency back since it'll only take a minute.

"I'm glad you called, Linda. I can have Aaron's report by the end of the day."

"Listen, that's not why I'm calling." She clears her throat like she's nervous.

"Oh?" I sense bad news, but I'm hoping she wants me to start on another workers' comp case.

She says, "We don't think we'll be in need of your services anymore."

My fingers tighten around the phone.

"We're cutting back," she adds.

I close my eyes. "Is this about this sketch business?"

"We think you need to focus on that right now. You know, keep yourself safe."

*I also need to pay my bills!* I want to shout. But even more, I ache to unleash a string of curses on Trey and Fiona.

Instead, I take a breath. "Okay," I say. "I'll be sending you the report before the day's over, and I think you'll be happy with what I've discovered about Lasserio. And as far as this other situation, I won't need more than a few more days to focus on it. Let's chat again then."

After what feels like an endless silence, she says, "I suppose, but, you know, it's not *just* about your safety. I mean, it is, of course, that's the most important thing, but it's also that, well, you know."

"No, I don't," I say and wait.

"Well," she finally adds. "It's also about what it says. You know, about you."

"What it says about me?"

"I don't know how to say this, so I guess I'll just come out with it. But what it says about your integrity. Or *lack* of it. There must be some reason you're being targeted."

I feel a sharp sting right to my solar plexus that settles into a deep ache in my belly. The comment hits dead-on. Linda's right. It's not that I don't know it, it's just hearing it from someone I rely on for my bread-and-butter work assignments makes me shrink even more, like I'm sliding and fading into the floor. "Linda, please, let's chat again in a few days."

"Okay, I guess," she mutters. She offers, "Stay safe."

"Will do," I say. "Bye-bye." Like we've had an entirely normal conversation, like she's told me to have a nice trip, instead of suggesting I'm a terrible person while telling me to stay alive.

I've shifted my focus back to Randal Askens when my phone vibrates again. It's Paxton Rhoads.

"Hard to tell given how far away the image is," he says about the pack in the video I sent him. "But from what I can see, it looks familiar, like it *could* be Clarissa's. Is there any way to get a closer look?"

"Possibly," I say. "I have a few connections. Do you recall if there's anything distinguishing on her pack, like had she written her name or initials on it or something?"

"I know she ironed on a patch of our tribal flag on the canvas flap."

"That's something." I replay the video, enlarging it and trying to see a spot of sky blue, the color of the Blackfeet Nation flag, but it's too grainy and I can only see one side of the pack. "I'll see what I can do and call you later."

I pivot back to Randal Askens. It's finally late enough in Washington, so I call the high school in Snohomish. It's an hour earlier there, only seven a.m. I figure school starts around eight, but someone might be there. No answer. I hang up on the recorded voice that comes on the line and go get another cup of coffee.

I do another half hour of research, and as soon as the clock hits seven thirty Pacific time, I try again.

This time a woman answers with a chipper voice. "Becca Parson."

"Hi," I say. "I'm Randy's sister, Ellen Atherton, formerly Askens."

I made a note from Facebook that Randal has a sister who lives in Texas named Ellen Atherton. She called him Randy in her post and said that they should talk more often, so it seems a safe bet that chipper-morning-person Becca has never met her. Also on Facebook, I saw that the service for Randal has been postponed until later in the fall, when more of Randy's family members, including a brother who lives in England and a favorite uncle in Tokyo, can attend.

"Oh," Becca says, surprised. "Randy mentioned he had a sister. Are you in town?"

"I'm in Dallas. Just calling to, well, I don't know. I guess it's been so hard to wrap my head around all this craziness. I was thinking if I called and spoke to someone where Randy worked, it might help me process, you know."

"Of course," she says, heaving a richly empathetic sigh. "I'm so sorry for your loss. We all miss your brother so much."

"Thank you. I appreciate that."

"So how can I help?"

"I don't know. There's nothing specific, really. It's just, you know, the FBI . . . they've been grilling me, and they've asked all sorts of stuff about your school."

"We've been bombarded with calls, too."

"It's so hard, but it's understandable. Right?"

"It's the reporters who are the worst," she says.

"They've been calling me nonstop, too. Some of them are asking about this . . . this recruiting scandal thing? Randy never mentioned a word about that to me."

"He didn't?"

"No, and I, well, I thought that maybe someone there, at your school, could talk to me about that to help me process. It's so awful, to know that he was targeted like that and to not understand the kinds of things he was wrapped up in." My own words ring in my ears and remind me again of Linda's assumptions about my character. "Did you know him well?"

"A little. We dated once."

"Oh."

Crap. Becca might be a little *too* familiar with Randy.

"It was a while ago. It never went anywhere, but we were pretty good friends."

"That's right. I think he mentioned you."

"He did?"

"Yeah, but like you said, it's been a while."

"It has." She sighs again. "I was mad at him at first. You know, your brother could be quite the player."

"I hope he didn't hurt you."

"No, it was fine." She's brushed it off, but I can tell she wasn't over him.

"What exactly was Randy's role in this scandal thing that the FBI keeps asking me about? I don't understand. Was he more involved than the head coach?"

"I wouldn't know about that, even if he was."

I don't believe her. She seems well plugged in. "Yeah, I'm sure the higher-ups have kept a tight lid on it."

"They have," she says, and sighs loudly.

"What?" I push.

"Nothing," she says. "It's, well, for years, we've run this place like a tight ship and rarely ever had a glitch. It was such a pleasant place to work. And now, for the past two years, it's been crazy. We finally put that recruiting thing to rest, and then the Petronis thing happens, and now, for God's sake, one of our very own coaches is the target of a *serial killer*. You couldn't even write that in a book and have someone believe it. How does that happen, for goodness' sake? Hopefully, bad luck really does come in three and we're done now. But gosh, I'm sorry. Here I am droning on about our problems when your family—"

"It's okay," I say, tingeing my voice with as much sorrow as I can muster. "I'm sure things will get better from here on out for your school. But you mentioned the second thing. The Petronis thing?" I google the name *Petronis* plus the school's name while I ask. A few social media hits and other links, including an obituary, pop up. "What was that about?"

She goes quiet, as if she realizes she's said too much, and I think she's going to cut the call short, but she adds, "He didn't tell you about it?"

"No. I mean, we didn't talk as much as we should have. Just every few months. You know? Siblings. It's something I wanted to change, and now . . ." I let my voice falter like I'm too choked up to go on.

"So much tragedy," Becca adds with a thick voice like she might cry herself.

"With this Petronis thing, too?"

"Oh God, yes. It was another very sad thing. A student took his own life."

"Oh." I pause for dramatic effect. "Yes, maybe Randy did mention that. How that rocked the school and the community." I scan the articles that have loaded on my screen and see an obituary for Ryan Petronis. "So, so sad," I say, scrolling farther down and stopping at a photo of the boy in a football uniform. Such a little guy. "He played football, right?"

"Yeah, he did."

"Randy knew him?"

She goes silent. Finally, she says, "Ryan was a JV player. Randy often worked with and supervised the JV team. But don't you worry, Ellen. Your brother was nothing but a good coach and a good friend to all the boys."

"Of course," I say, thinking that response is oddly defensive. But that might stem from all the press that's been hounding the school, looking for reasons for a killer to target him, as Linda at my soon-to-be ex-client's firm was doing with me.

"Look, I should get back to work now. If you need to talk more, you can call anytime," she says sweetly.

◆ ◆ ◆

I stare at my phone, swiping away all the announcements that I can tell involve me. I see blips of the headlines with the words Confession Artist, Sketch, Victim Revealed, and, last: Crosbie Mitchell and Her Traumatic Past.

*Ughh.*

I focus on Ryan Petronis's social media. Photos and comments reveal he was involved in science club, enjoyed chess, played trumpet in the band. An interesting, curious, creative kid. I can't find anything that mentions Askens's name in relation to Ryan, but the tingle in my spine tells me to not give up.

I add *Ryan Petronis's suicide* under Askens's column. There are few high schools in America that aren't experiencing an alarming number of suicides, so it seems unlikely that this is the link. Nonetheless I jot down *Other suicides* and add the names of two students who have taken their lives at both Askens's high school and one at Loman's community college.

I also list the ones from my orbit: Greer Mathews, a kid who shot himself in the basement of his parents' home, a case I was called to while on patrol with the force. And a few years earlier, Sienna Peterson, a high school senior who crashed her car into a rock divider. I was first on the scene for that one, too. Sienna had sent a text to a friend saying she'd decided to take her life in that precise manner.

And . . . Leon. The unintended, unexpected fatality stemming from Coleman's death.

I can barely summon the courage to even think about it. It's too devastating. Too raw. I don't think even time will ever distance me from the crushing pain of knowing I had a hand in it.

A friend found Leon hanging from a beam in his basement apartment. Ewing handled the scene because, clearly, it would have been a conflict of interest for either Railes or me to be called in if we'd even been on duty and in the area, so I was not involved. Though of course I tormented myself then—and not a day goes by that I don't still—with the thought that I very much was.

I write Leon's name under my column. I find that Leon Spencer's mom died when he was seven and he was left with his dad, a guy named Burt Spencer, who liked his booze—a detail I had already gleaned after Leon hanged himself and I tried to figure out if there was going to be a service. When I checked, the guilt crushing me so heavily that I wasn't even sure I had it in me to attend, I was selfishly relieved to see that there was no service open to the public. That, if there was anything at all, it was private. There was nothing in the local paper about it other than the mention of a young male adult dying by suicide. But at the time, I gathered from my search that his father, Burt Spencer, had accrued two DUIs.

I don't let myself wonder about what kind of life Leon had very often. It's too painful. My throat constricts like it's gathering in and molding all my mistakes into a hard, twisted ball of barbed wire.

And now, I don't have a second longer to think on it either because my phone buzzes.

It's Jess.

"Oh my God, Cros. You have to get over here."

I begin to remind her that I don't want to draw attention to her place, to her, to Sam, but I stop. Dread tightens my stomach. She sounds frantic. "What is it?" I ask. "Is the media harassing you?"

"No. But someone's been here."

My insides go cold. "Who's been there?"

"Someone's written something on my windshield."

# Chapter 34

There are already days when I'm finding it hard to live with myself, but what if something happens to Jess or Sam?

"Come on, *come on*," I implore the Subaru in front of me, panic clustering up high in my chest.

My hands shake on the wheel.

The highway center strip turns from solid to dashes. I throw on the blinker, slam on the gas, and whip around three cars as a pickup barrels toward me. The driver is enormous, hairy as a Sasquatch. Not a good day for him to play chicken with me. He slams on the brakes, and I knife back into my lane, leaving his horn blaring in outrage.

When I get to Jess's, she's outside sitting on her front step. Even from a distance, she looks pale and stricken. She runs toward the driveway as I pull in next to her sky-blue Subaru Outback. I can see that there's white text on her windshield.

When I step out, Jess is already there, in my arms, grabbing me. I hug her back, her body frail and rigid against mine. Whatever life the Dallas event instilled in her has all drained away. She feels like a twig that might snap if I squeeze her too hard.

I look over her shoulder to her car again and try to make out the lettering, but I still can't see it clearly. I pull her away from me and go have a look.

Across the windshield is scrawled **YOUR NEXT**.

Ridiculous first thought: Do they not know their contractions, or is the grammatical error a ploy? Fury follows, though, rising up and wedging tight in my chest. I scan the neighborhood. It's a peaceful, idyllic area with cute houses that have white shutters and nice paint jobs near some open fields and pine forests.

"Where's Sam? Is he okay?"

"Yes, yes, he's at school. He carpooled in with the McMurphys today."

"When did you see this?"

"Right when I called you. I was cleaning up the kitchen after sending Sam off. I'd made him a lunch, and when I looked out the kitchen window . . ."

"Did you see or hear anything last night?"

"No, Allison was here with us for dinner, but she left early, around eight, before Sam's bath." It stings slightly to know that Allison and Jess have become closer than Allison and I were. But I don't have time to think about all the ways I've failed Jess and Allison right now and how Jess is turning to other people to fill the hole I've left.

"But I heard dogs barking around one a.m.," Jess says. "They're always barking at something, getting worked up over a deer or raccoons. Took me a while to get back to sleep, and I slept lightly after that. Around two thirty, a car door slamming shut snapped me up in bed."

"And?"

"I got up and looked out my bedroom window, then went to the kitchen and saw taillights pulling away."

"What kind of car?"

She squints. "Medium-size SUV, maybe. It pulled away slowly, not in a hurry or anything, so I figured one of the neighbors had a visitor that left late in the night or maybe someone needed to leave early for the airport."

"Did you notice the license plate?"

"Not the numbers, but it was a Montana plate, one of the solid blue ones. I didn't think to take in the numbers. I didn't think I needed to"—she looks back to her windshield, her voice cracking—"until this morning."

I put my arm around her. "It's okay, Jess. I'm going to figure this out."

"No." She twists away from me and hugs her sweater back around her waist. "Just stop." Her voice sounds choked—the words barely getting out, but when they do, they sound like she's coughed them up from deep inside her. "Would you please quit acting like you have it under control? You *don't*."

I set my jaw. I'm exhausted. Not only from this hideous week unraveling before me, but from all the past months since Jess's rape. She's still living a nightmare, but I'm sick of tiptoeing around broken glass. I want to scream, *Jesus, Jess. I can't always be taking care of you! I need to take care of myself this time, this one time. Can you let me do that without laying into me?*

But no. That would be entirely unfair. She didn't ask to be involved in this terrible thing any more than I did. And Mark Coleman? She certainly didn't ask for that.

"Realistically, Cros," she says, "who do you think is behind this?"

"I don't know, but *realistically*?" I say, circling back to her choice of adverb.

"Yeah, please, Cros. None of this *I'll handle it* fantasy anymore. Tell me what you and law enforcement are doing about this crap right now." Like she's firing her words from a nail gun.

It stings to hear her doubting my competence, but I swallow it down. I'm doubting it myself, aren't I? "Come on," I say. "Let's go inside."

"No," she says, digging in. "Tell me. As if I wasn't having a hard enough time before this cropped up. You're making it worse—acting like you've got it all handled, and you don't. Like you didn't when you went to Mark Coleman's that night."

The final blow knocks my breath away. I knew intuitively that she was unhappy with what happened to Coleman, had even mentioned that she felt robbed of achieving some closure because she planned on confronting him when she was ready. *Now I'll never be able to talk to him,* she had said when I told her about the shooting.

But for her to throw it in my face right now, this week, when I'm the target of some sicko, is entirely surprising. My teeth hurt with the pressure of my frustration, my guilt, but I say it as calmly as I can muster: "Look, nothing is certain, Jess. But I'm working on good leads. So are the agents."

She doesn't budge. She stares at me for a long moment, scrutinizing me.

"Come on," I say.

◆ ◆ ◆

We sit in the living room. Sam's toys are scattered across the floor—a spaceship made from Legos, and the same small herd of dinosaurs.

On the coffee table is his box of Creature Cards I found for him online. They're prized possessions for him because they no longer make them. I worked hard to find a used set in good condition. They're a tad larger than index size and come organized by category in a filing box: Toxic Terrors, Monsters of the Deep, Monsters of the Past, Tiny Terrors . . . Sam cherishes them, partly because he loves to read and organize things, and partly because they're a gift from me.

The Wendigo and the Teke Teke—the scariest ones, the ones he always wants me to read to him when I come over—are displayed on the table. I have no idea how they don't give him nightmares, especially the Teke Teke, a Japanese myth about the ghost of a young girl who was cut in half by a train and now drags herself around looking to slice others in two with a scythe. Sometimes Sam drags himself across the carpet, pretending to be her, and I act all terrified, running and hiding.

Jess sits on the couch, her eyes still stretched wide by fear and nerves. I see she's chewed her cuticles and her usually neat nails are bitten to the quicks. *Runs in the family . . .*

Seeing her like this, wrenched into the same bristling bundle of fear and pain I saw her in the night she relived the rape when she finally told me about what Coleman did to her, lifts a surge of bile up my throat. I swallow it back and say, "I'm going to get you some water."

In the kitchen, it's all I can do not to kick the bottom of the fridge. I can't afford to act out like a child, but what am I supposed to do with this rage—and my conscience—ballooning inside me? My eyes burn with it, but I need to keep my shit together, for Jess's sake, for Sam's sake.

How could this nightmare now involve them? I squeeze my fists so tightly that even my short, clipped nails leave half-moon imprints in my palms. I take a deep breath and grab a glass, run the tap, and wait for it to get ice cold. Jess hates tepid water. I can hear Mom's orders to this day, to not forget to put ice in Jess's water glass.

Standing with my index finger under the stream, I face myself down: *What* is *your plan, Crosbie?*

Maybe Jess is right. Maybe this is pure self-deception, acting like I know what I'm doing.

There's a ping from my phone. My security app is picking up movement. I pull up the screen and see Greene on my front lawn. It's Alderson I choose to call, but Alderson walks into the camera's view and holds out his phone to Greene.

"Alderson's talking with one of our techs right now," Greene says. "We're at your place to examine your car."

"I see that. Smile for the camera."

She turns and glares up at the one set above my front porch. "Where are you?"

When I tell her about Jess's windshield, she says, "Stay there. Don't go anywhere. We'll be right over."

Jess is scrolling on her phone screen when I go back into the living room.

"Don't do that," I say.

"Too late," she says flatly. "Here." She shoves her phone at me.

I take it with a sigh. The speed of news is staggering. There's a video of me and my car racing by that pack of reporters and Deputy Zane going viral on TikTok. *Oh, good:* It shows the graffiti of **It's You** scrawled on my car.

I shake my head and hand her phone back. "Whatever," I say. "Trust me on this one, Jess. Turn off your notifications or you'll drive yourself crazy."

Her skin has taken on an unnatural pallor. She takes a sip of water. Her hand quakes.

When she places the water back on the coffee table, I say, "Do you know if your neighbors have any security systems or cameras?"

"Yeah. Maybe."

"Anyone usually home now?"

"I'm not sure, but I think Mr. Johnston goes to work a little later in the day."

"What does he do?"

"He's a manager at one of the restaurants in Whitefish."

"Which house?"

"Two houses to the left on the other side of the street."

"I'm going over. Do you have a hat I can borrow?"

Jess digs in the front hall closet, finds a baseball cap promoting a local ice cream shop. I grab it from her and open the front door and run smack into Wallace.

"Oh," I say, confused to see him at my sister's house. The small flame of worry I've been feeling since seeing him with my gun in his hands erupts into a larger fire.

"And hello to you, too," he says, extending his arms to give me one of his overbearing hugs.

I take a step back and stare at him with an obvious question written across my face: *What are you doing here?*

"I wanted to check on Jess," he says, reading my expression. "After what you said last night. You know, that she was having a hard time."

The back of my neck prickles.

But I think he's not entirely ignoring my request for space. It's Jess he's checking on, not me. "She's okay," I say. "I don't think she needs anyone here right now. She needs rest."

"I brought these for her and Sam." He holds up a white bag. "They're from a new bagel store in Columbia Falls. I know how much Sam loves sesame seed."

I take the bag. "I'll tell her they're from you." I usher him to his car and watch him drive away and go back in and set the bag on the counter. I then call Alderson and tell him I'm going to the neighbors for a moment and hang up before he can protest.

Then I tell Jess that I'll be right across the street at the neighbor's front door and to text me or yell to me immediately if she notices anything odd or she's worried about anything at all, even Wallace.

"Wallace? Why?"

"Just because," I say. I don't want to worry her further, and I'm not even sure where my own trust levels hit right now. I wonder if I can leave her alone, but it's broad daylight, and I don't plan to go in and have coffee with them. "I need to know who's coming and going," I say. "No matter who it is."

# Chapter 35

As I walk across the street, I spot the camera at the corner of the house near the front porch. I'm hoping their system, if operational, stretches all the way for a full street view.

A hedge of lilac bushes on the side of the house lost its blooms months ago and is dropping pale, yellowing leaves. Off on the edge of the lawn is a crab apple tree that has spread its crimson berries over the ground, some of them broken and picked upon by birds. The air smells crisp, like fresh laundry.

Mr. Johnston answers the door along with a big black-and-tan Bernese mountain dog who barks gruffly. Mr. Johnston calls him Osso and shushes him. Osso obeys, sniffs my hands.

When Mr. Johnston asks how he can help, I tell him that I'm the sister of his neighbor across the street and am wondering if they had their surveillance system on during the night because my sister's car was vandalized.

"The Morris kid up the road is a sophomore in high school, and I hear he's been pranking his neighbor lately. Guess he tapped into their Wi-Fi and activated their printer and typed a bunch of creepy stuff as if he was a ghost."

"Clever." I smile. "Do you mind if we check your video footage?"

He looks over my shoulder, trying to see what's been done to Jess's car. In his early sixties, he has slicked-back hair and an Errol Flynn mustache. Khaki pants and a crisp white shirt suggest he's soon off to work.

"You can't see it from here," I tell him. "It's marker on the windshield." I scratch Osso behind one ear. He nuzzles his head into my leg. This dog's affection is the best thing that's happened to me in days.

"Well," he says, "don't think my cameras pick up your sister's house. Why doesn't she park in her garage?"

"She's been using it for storage. Anyway, I was thinking the camera out front might catch a bit of the street."

He studies me a moment too long. I tuck a stray strand of hair back under the side of the hat. I'm grateful for Osso, as loving him up gives me an excuse to look down. And away.

Finally, he says, "Well, that's a worry."

*You think you've got worries,* I want to say, but refrain. "So yeah, I was wondering if your setup recorded any activity in the middle of the night."

"This neighborhood doesn't see much of that kind of thing. Though there was a garage break-in last summer, which is the reason I got the security system."

"Smart," I say. "Is it okay if I have a look at it?"

"Let me go grab my phone. Want to come in?"

"No," I say. "I'm good out here."

When Mr. Johnston returns, he begins scrolling, both of us standing on his porch. I'm standing at his side, breathing in his Old Spice and squinting at his phone's screen. Boring flashes of a still, quiet street streak by. At 2:20 a.m. there's a flash of motion and he slows down. He pushes the time bar slightly back. My pulse races. I wait patiently, but God I want to grab his phone and do the driving.

"Yes, yes," he says. "Around two forty."

"Can I see?" I hold out my hand. It takes effort not to grab it from him.

"Let me get it to the exact spot again." He fiddles with the rewind again. "Here, 2:38, to be exact."

A dark vehicle with its lights off slides down the block, passing Mr. Johnston's house but not stopping. I can't make out the license plate, but I can see that the car is an SUV because one of the streetlamps provides a touch of illumination. Right near the end of the clip, it's slowing down, creeps almost to a stop, and most likely halts beyond the camera's view.

"Looks like it's pulling over, about to stop," I say. "Probably didn't want to be directly across from my sister's. What are your neighbors' names?"

"The Harmses."

"Do they use a camera system, too?"

Mr. Johnston smiles. "They certainly do. Ol' Artie always needs to one-up me with everything. I bought a Trager last year, and he got one a week later. When I installed my cameras, I could've set my watch to him. He did the same within days. Only thing Art hasn't been able to keep up with is the fact that I have a hot new girlfriend and he's stuck with Louise." Mr. Johnston chuckles.

I smile politely, surprised he's trashed his neighbor's wife like that, but thank him, give him my email address, and ask him to send the video to me.

Art Harms is the opposite of Mr. Johnston in about every way. He's round, sweaty, and reeks of nicotine.

He's wearing a T-shirt that was once white but has turned the color of tobacco.

When he answered his door, a woman's voice—Louise's, I presume—called from deeper inside the house, asking who it was, saying something about the UPS guy leaving treats for Malley. Mr. Harms now picks up a yapping chihuahua into his arms. Malley, I surmise, seasoned detective that I am. I wonder if Mr. Johnston got Osso first, and Arty could only talk Louise into a lapdog.

At first, Mr. Harms is leery about my request, but when I tell him that his neighbor happily assisted, he thinks on it for a moment. "Wait here," he says.

I stand in the entryway. Harms doesn't seem to mind that the door is wide open. When he returns without Malley, he's got his smartphone and a pair of readers. Louise appears behind him and she's holding the dog. I say hello and do my best to keep my face averted.

"Not quite sure how this thing works," Art says, peering through his glasses at his phone. "To be honest, I'm not sure we even need the damn thing. All it does is notify us every time a deer or a mountain lion traipses through in the night. I had to turn the notification ding off so we could get some sleep, which kind of defeats the purpose."

"May I?" I hold out my hand. "I'm pretty good with these."

The screen shines with grease and grime, and I already want to wash my hands. I pull up the Ring app and find the images from the front camera. Bright sunlight shines across the front yard, taking in the entire lawn and the curb at the very edge of the frame. My heart sinks, because even though the curb is visible, the camera is poorly aimed. It's not going to pick up much other than possibly tires and the vandal's shoes.

I scroll until I get to 2:38 a.m. The front and back tire of the left side of the SUV come to a halt by the Harmses' curb. I watch intently. All is still. No feet emerge from the vehicle. After about a minute, the door swings open. Ankles and shoes only. Dark tennis shoes. They head to the back of the car, which would be the direction to Jess's.

Art pesters me if I see anything, and I tell him there is a car and that I need to wait to see if I can catch the license plate when it drives off. I can already see, though, that I won't be able to. The best I can hope for is another view of the guy's shoes. Also, with better technology, the FBI wizards should be able to identify the make and year of the vehicle by its wheel wells.

I'm patiently waiting for the night stalker to return when Louise says, "Now wait a minute."

Out of the corners of my eyes, I can see that Louise is examining my profile.

"Now hold on," she says, louder. "Excuse me?"

"Yes?" I say, still staring at the screen.

"I know you," she says. "We know you."

"Well, yeah," I say. "I've been in the neighborhood before."

"Oh, so we've met?"

"No, I don't think we have, but I come around a lot to visit family. I'm sure you've probably seen me around."

"I see."

I'm pleased to have dodged that one, but within seconds, Louise says, "Wait, no." She's a dog with a bone, and I'm the bone. "It's more than that. You're that girl. The one in the sketch. You're her, aren't you? Artie, isn't it? It's her, right?"

Art tilts his head down to look over his readers to study me, too, but I keep my face lowered because while they've been figuring out who I am, the black tennis shoes have come back across the screen. The door opens and one foot goes into the car.

Louise is closing in on me, studying me like a bug pinned to a science fair exhibit. She smells like cheap perfume and a different but no less pungent flavor of sweat. I can feel her breath on my cheek. But I don't budge. I'm intent on the screen.

Right before the other shoe follows, and I assume he's going to shut the door and drive off, a small object—maybe the marker he used—drops to the sidewalk.

"You *are* the one, aren't you?" Louise breathes excitedly onto my face. "That's how I know you. Girl, you're all *over* the news these days. You're a national phenomenon!"

"Look, please." I back away from her, farther out to the edge of the covered entryway. A richly appreciated cool wind has picked up and sweeps the Harmses' aromas clear of me but threatens to blow my cap off. I hold it down with one hand and stare at the screen in the other as an arm with a sweatshirt sleeve pushed up to its elbow reaches down and grabs the object. I take my hand off my cap to rewind the footage and pause on the image. It takes me a few tries and I can feel my cap about to lift off my head, so against my fervent desire I step back into the doorway of Art and Louise's house, away from the wind and into their noxious atmosphere. It's marginally preferable to having the cap fly away while I work the phone with both hands.

It takes me five more tries, and Louise won't stop asking me about my situation. How it feels to be me. What I'm doing to protect myself. What I'm going to confess.

*What have you done?*

"Please," I finally say. "I need to concentrate on this for a moment."

Finally, I manage to stop the video on the frame with the arm stretching down. I enlarge the screen as much as possible and there, in a grainy, blurry image, I make out a blotch of something dark peeking out from under the cloth. A shiver shoots up my spine. "Jackpot," I whisper to myself, ignoring the Harmses, who are arguing with each other now. Artie tells Louise to be quiet and to leave me alone. Louise insists I'm the one all over the news and they should call law enforcement or a reporter.

A tattoo. It's only a smudge on the screen and much too faint to make out, but I'm sure Alderson and Greene's tech guy can figure it out. On the man's wrist, there's a bracelet or band.

"I'm going to need to borrow this for a few hours," I tell Art and Louise right as Alderson and Greene's black SUV pulls into Jess's driveway. "And no, I'm not the woman you think I am, but if you spread rumors that I am, you see that black SUV that pulled up?" I point to Alderson and Greene.

Louise's eyes are huge.

"I will tell them to come have a talk with you both about the consequences of meddling in a law enforcement matter."

# Chapter 36

I tell Jess to stay where she is while I let the agents in. No introductions are necessary because Greene and Alderson have already questioned her extensively, asked her to turn over some samples of her artwork, and had their experts analyze it. No one has cleared her yet, and while I realize they need to be thorough, it's infuriating to see resources wasted that could be focused elsewhere.

When I give Greene the name of one of the guys I know from the county sheriff's office who's good at image analysis, she assures me they have their own guy.

"Well, in case you need someone local."

They head over to speak with Mr. Johnston across the street and in no time send the video attachment to their own tech, probably someone in Salt Lake City at their field office.

When they come back in, they ask Jess all the same questions I have, tell us that a tech from the Flathead County CSI unit will be by any minute to dust both of our cars for prints and collect samples of the kind of marker that was used. Then Alderson asks me to step outside.

"This vandalism stuff feels personal," I say before he even tells me why he's brought me outside alone.

"Yeah, well, that's a given. We know that it's not random."

"No, I mean, it feels even more personal than that. It doesn't seem like the Confession Artist's MO. Was there any sign of him leaving messages or anything like that for the others?"

"No, but that doesn't mean he's not suddenly changing up the game, adding to it, like with the earrings. It's a mistake to assume they'll slavishly follow their scripts. And they could've left them for the others and we simply don't know about it. They can't exactly tell us now, can they?" His brow furrows and he adds, as if answering himself, "But friends and family members of the victims didn't report anything to suggest he did, so it seems unlikely."

"Exactly," I say. "So why this time? Why bring Jess into it, too? It's weird. Plus, the grammar—that *your/you're* business. Would he get that wrong? None of the other messages online have any mistakes."

Alderson smiles. "Everybody slips up, don't they? I mean, it was on a windshield."

"It feels off."

Louise Harms is out front, holding Malley and watching us with concern.

"Do me a favor," I say. "Give that woman over there a serious stare."

Alderson does so without hesitation, and I can see the whites of Louise's widened eyes. He turns back to me. "What was that about?"

"Just punctuating my threat to her that she shouldn't call any reporters."

"Gotcha," he says. "Pattern or not," he continues. "And as frightening as it is for your sister, this narrows things down. We're going to need a crossover list of all the people that you and Jess have in common, have worked with, have socialized with. Anyone remotely who overlaps your two orbits."

"That's a lot of people, since she's my sister. But yeah, I agree. It narrows things considerably. One good place to focus right off the bat: She's made a number of referrals to me, and I have asked for her company's help on some of my jobs when I've needed to track lineage."

"Okay, well, we'll need that immediately. But in the meantime," Alderson says, "I have something I need to tell you."

*Hell. I don't need another jolt of bad news.*

"We questioned Wallace Scott extensively this morning," he says. "We released him, but we're not convinced he's clear. He was alone, sightseeing and eating dinner out in both Seattle and LA on the nights the victims were killed. He's provided receipts for the restaurants where he ate, but the time stamp would have allowed plenty of downtime to find the victims. Plus the receipts were a little too handy, if you catch my drift."

"But have you found one single connection between Wallace and either Askens or Loman?"

"That doesn't mean they don't exist."

"Come on, Alderson." I sigh. "You guys can do better than that."

He doesn't answer.

I want to argue. Say, *Maybe there's some coincidental stuff going on here, but surely you're not going to find evidence that he has a connection at all to the victims.* But suddenly I'm uncertain. I feel like my entire foundation is crumbling beneath me.

"Maybe we won't," he allows. "But we're not done digging. And you should know that he can't provide proof of his whereabouts when they were killed."

"What do you mean? What does he say he was doing?"

"Wandering around the cities. Taking in the sights. But he can't even provide a coffee shop or bar receipt for the time frames we're interested in."

"I know for a fact that Wallace loves to walk. A lot. What about intersection cameras?"

"You trust him that much?"

I think about him showing up last night and again this morning at Jess's house, no less. He didn't mention getting questioned, but I didn't give him a chance to. "I don't have any reason not to."

"What about his sister? You said yourself that you wish you wouldn't have talked Sophie into going camping. Maybe he blames you."

I think of the times when I've sensed anger from Wallace over Sophie, and how he's kept it in check. I recall the night at the banquet when he was so furious at me. *You act like you've erased her from your mind,* he'd said, resentment smoldering in his eyes. And last night, the downright fury in his glare. The *fuck you, Crosbie,* which I'm sure is what he really whispered.

But still, what in the world would Wallace have to do with some coach from Snohomish, Washington, and a counselor from Santa Monica Community College?

The same worm of doubt I had last night wiggles in even deeper. I never kept all that close track of who he saw or what he did when he traveled. The thought that there are so many things I don't know or understand about someone I've been so intimate with suddenly terrifies me.

"If there's a connection," Alderson adds, "we'll find it. Maybe they've been to his concerts. Maybe they've been to a bar near one of his performance venues."

"Maybe," I say weakly.

He pivots back to Jess's house, and I do the same.

"The video," I say, like I'm grasping for hope. I desperately do not want to think of Wallace in this light, but I can't deny that the thought of him harboring so much anger—even more anger than what I'm capable of—and in such a controlled fashion, gets under my skin and lodges there.

I point over to Art and Louise's. "Someone was here last night. An actual person, targeting my sister. And I can, at the very least, tell you that Wallace does not have a tattoo on his arm."

"I hear you, but we're still going to take him into the county building for additional questioning."

I think of Wallace getting taken into the cold room I used countless times. I know every crack in the walls. I picture the departmental rumor mill flying into gear once it gets around that Greene and Alderson have brought him in, because it will. From my experience, when the FBI used the county's space for interrogation in Kalispell, it wasn't uncommon for any of us on the force who wanted to pop into the observation room to view what was going on. I cringe at the thought of Ewing watching my ex-boyfriend. "Don't you think that's overkill?"

"You know as well as we do that an interview goes much better at the station."

"Only when you want to add pressure," I say.

"Your cop skills remain intact." Alderson dips his head.

# Chapter 37

It takes an hour for Jess and me to review all our clients and any potential overlapping names. Alderson and Greene take the list and tell us they've arranged for a protective detail for Jess and Sam when he's with her. He's still at school and the agents have instructed them to not let Sam leave with anyone other than Jess, Patrick, or me.

"Hope Jess makes better use of hers than you do," says Alderson with a smirk. Not funny.

A tech guy named Ray, someone I knew from my time on the force, finishes gathering evidence from our cars. I stay out and chat with him until he leaves.

Once he's gone, I head inside to look for supplies to clean both our cars. I want to find Jess and ask where she might keep rubbing alcohol, but when I call out her name, there's no reply. The living room and kitchen are both empty.

"Jess?" I call out again.

I open the kitchen door that goes out onto her small back patio. It's gusty out, but a lattice board blocks the wind that sweeps in from the fields, not unlike the ones behind my house. The wind scatters dead leaves across her patio.

No sign of Jess. I try to quell the stabs of fear shooting through me. I'm sure she's around.

I go down the hall by Sam's room and a half bath. I poke my head into the smallest of the three bedrooms, which Jess uses as her office. All is quiet, so I continue down the hall to Jess's room. The door is closed.

"Jess?" I tap on the door. "You in there?"

I open the door and step in. Jess is curled in a fetal position on her bed, face buried in a pillow.

I'm relieved she's fine, but then a prick of irritation follows. But as usual, not for long before the same flood of guilt washes over me.

I helped create this. And for me to want her to buck up, to be stronger than this is not only unreasonable, it's selfish.

"Jess, what's going on?"

She shakes her head into her pillow.

"Trust me, they're going to find who did this."

She props herself up on one arm and looks at me with puffy red eyes. "It's everything, Cros. It's too much."

"I know. It's a lot to handle." I want to make more promises, but her words earlier to quit acting so confident ring in my ears, so I wrap her in my arms and hold her. She doesn't resist the comfort.

"I wish I could *sleep*," she says. Jess has had trouble sleeping ever since the assault, and I'm sure this week isn't helping. "But I can't. I keep seeing him, keep feeling his hands on me every time I shut my eyes. I just wish I could tell him what he's done, how he's wrecked so much, but I can't."

For the gazillionth time, guilt falls over, pressing me down. But to hear her say it out loud again gives me the sense that I'm sinking below the earth, dirt filling my mouth and throat, choking me. I practically want to run to the sink and spit and spit. To wash my mouth out repeatedly. "Try to relax. I'm not going anywhere. I'm going to clean that crap off our cars, okay?"

She puts her head back down.

When Mom died and Jess had holed up in her bedroom and I took the semester off to be with her, one night, she lifted her head, half asleep, and said, "You're the best sister a girl could have."

She was eighteen. I was twenty-one. I was afraid I'd never make it back to Missoula to finish my criminology degree. But so much more terrifying was the thought that Jess would keep getting worse, like Sophie.

But by the end of that long fall semester, she pulled out of it. She started back into school at the community college. She caught fire there, kept it up at the University of Montana for her BS. In Missoula, she met Patrick, Sam's dad, and got pregnant her sophomore year, when she was only nineteen. I had just graduated and was applying for a position with the local force in Kalispell. I was worried the pregnancy would set her back, but it didn't. She insisted on having the baby, and even becoming a young mom didn't deter her.

She was three months pregnant when she finished her sophomore year. She married Patrick that summer. After Sam came along, she stayed strong, even after she realized Patrick was too young and wasn't going to be very helpful. They divorced within a year.

And I was there to help her. To pick up the slack.

She was even able to build on her BS for her MS, also from the University of Montana, which segued smoothly into her business, which boomed. An amazing ride. I was so relieved.

It didn't bother me that I put some of my own ambitions aside to go into the force and stayed in Missoula—a town that carried so many awful memories for me—an extra two years working odds-and-ends jobs before returning to Kalispell so I could help look after Sam while she studied. That I had been ignoring the heavy plunge of my own heart to help her through, the pain of losing our mom leaking into every part of me like I was made up of broken pipes.

I was just happy it was working out for Jess. That she had come out of her debilitating state. I knew I could apply anytime for the department in Kalispell, and that's what I finally did two years later, when I was twenty-four.

And then Mark Coleman came along four years later, and all that effort—on both our parts—slipped down the drain.

I go look for some rubbing alcohol and also her medicine cabinet in the hallway bathroom for some Advil to treat my sleep-deprivation headache. There's only a bottle of bright-red, sugary-looking kids' liquid Tylenol for Sam. Not finding any adult Tylenol or ibuprofen, I go into the kitchen and riffle through Jess's pantry. Nothing. I go into her office. Nada. Jess might have secretly turned to healing herself through faith because her drug supply is nonexistent.

I scoot over some loose papers and file folders scattered on her desk in case the bottle's hiding, but it's not. Who doesn't have pain reliever on hand? I poke around the credenza her printer rests on, but there's nothing but a cluster of framed photos on it—mostly of Sam, one of Mom and her, one of Dad and both of us when we were little out at his cabin, and one of me and her on the summit of Logan Pass in Glacier Park.

I open her top desk drawer but find only pens, notepads, paper clips, neon Post-it notes, stamps. The next drawer down is deeper and holds boxes of envelopes, new pens, and pencils.

I sit back and consider that the bottle is probably right next to her where she's dozing or in her attached bathroom. My head throbs. I take a seat in her chair, resting my elbows on the desk. I am about to tiptoe back into Jess's room to look when a file poking from underneath several others catches my eye. On the tab, I read the letters PETRO . . .

I pull the file out.

PETRONIS, RYAN.

A zing of adrenaline makes my spine go straight.

Why does my sister have a file for Ryan Petronis, the boy who died by suicide at the high school where Randal Askens coached football in Washington State?

Jess is a gifted investigator, I remind myself. This coincidence isn't *that* surprising. It makes sense that she'd get there as I had, so I relax and wonder if Jess called the secretary at Ryan's school, as I had done. Hopefully she didn't pose as Randal Askens's sister, too.

I open the file and begin to read.

Jess has notes on Ryan's parents, Rick and Cindy Petronis, and his sister, Vivian.

Jess, no surprise, is ahead of me.

Ryan's sister, Vivian, attends the community college in the valley.

This is something—a tentative link between the place the CA's first victim worked in Washington and Montana. To the very area I reside in. The college must be Jess's connection to the boy's sister.

At the top of one of her pages, Jess has written in bold, ***Hazing That Is Not Hazing***. She's underlined it several times. I read more of the story behind Ryan, how he was broomed by several of his teammates at a football camp retreat in the Cascade Mountains.

My back is stick-straight, my head in a fog.

Vivian must have divulged quite a bit for my sister to have so much personal information on Ryan Petronis. But why hasn't Jess said anything to me about her research? Her *digging*. About her connection to this girl?

It doesn't sit right in my gut.

If I know my organized sister, she will have dated her notes. Sure enough, at the top of the first page, it reads March 22.

This information launches me out of my chair. Jess has been gathering information on Ryan Petronis since *March*?

*For the past five and a half months?*

Nearly two months *before* the first sketch even dropped?

The walls of her small office close in on me.

Why was she gathering information on a boy whose coach was in the adjacent room when he was assaulted by a group of football players, the same coach who was one of the Confession Artist's first two kills? How could she have known about the boy two months before the nation even knew about Randal Askens?

# Chapter 38

I stand in the doorway and watch her. She's no longer curled up with her face smooshed into her pillow. She's stretched out, nose up. Finally asleep, she breathes rhythmically and deeply. She looks peaceful, but I'm going to ruin whatever few brief moments of calm she's found through sleep.

Jess looks frail, too. She's lost even more weight and her cheekbones are even sharper.

I draw and release a deep sigh and have begun to make my way over to her when the doorbell rings. Jess flinches awake and sees me.

"Stay put," I say. "I'll get it."

I hurry back into Jess's office and drop her file where I got it and go to the front. I peer out the windows to see who's there. Alderson and Greene. And the officer assigned to Jess and Sam. They introduce me to her. Turns out she's from the Kalispell Police Department, not the county, like Zane, my protective detail. I don't recognize her, but that doesn't mean anything. The department is getting bigger as the valley grows, and in this situation, involving the FBI, they'll use resources from whichever department they can.

"You guys can't get enough of me, can you?" I say.

Alderson chuckles. Greene still doesn't find me amusing and doesn't even crack a smile, but both sets of their eyes are energized. I wave them in.

"Where's your sister?"

"Trying to get some shut-eye."

"We need her, too. Our tech guy has sent us close-ups of the tattoo."

Jess is in the bathroom throwing water on her face. I tell her who it is and what it's about while she dries up with a towel. "I'll be right out," she says.

Alderson doesn't wait for Jess. "In addition to the overlap list you created for us, we've added all the individuals you arrested while you were on the force," he says. "We need you and Jess to look through it and identify anyone Jess might have also known in some way."

A flash of Coleman hitting the ground, a bloom of red spreading from his chest to the carpet, the knife on the floor when he smashed the coffee table on his way down. It all comes zinging back into my mind, even the tequila and lime slices flinging into the air like they're in slow motion. The smell of nitro. The metallic scent of Coleman's blood.

Of course, Coleman was never arrested. Railes took that opportunity away from him, so even though Jess and I both knew him in *some way*, he is not on the list and is not an issue here and now.

They've taken seats in Jess's living room like they belong. Greene on the sofa, Alderson in the easy chair. I'm sitting next to Greene to leave space to my right for Jess. Greene shifts closer to the armrest as if I'm invading her space. She grabs her laptop while Alderson opens a briefcase and fishes out some paper.

He hands me a printout and pulls out another one.

"Here are names of all the people that your sister worked on at Rotical in which either of you enlisted their help or they enlisted yours once you opened your PI practice. Study each name and tell us if there was anything that occurred that could make any of them angry. And we need you to tell us if there's anyone suspicious that you know of who is not on the list."

In addition to Paxton's name, the list has only about ten other names.

"Or anything that jumps out at you for any reason at all would be useful," Alderson continues. "You both know that with investigative work, sometimes the smallest, oddest thing can lead you somewhere."

Jess walks into the room as he hands me the second paper. I try to read her, but her face is blank, still drained. The sky outside has become dark and bruised, so I ask her if she can switch on the light so we both can see the lists better. I get through the second sheet of names quickly and hand it to Jess. There's nothing about anyone that strikes a chord with me other than Paxton. Then I study the one with all my arrests, which is also short. When I see no connection to Jess in any of these names, either, I ask, "What about the tattoo?"

"Yep. Just came through." Greene angles her laptop toward me.

It's a little blurry, but it's a rough, almost hieroglyphic capital *R*, depending on how you view it from the position of his arm. On the image, because his arm is reaching for the ground, the letter is upside down, but if the owner of the tattoo were looking down at his own arm, it would be right side up.

"Have you seen this before?"

I squint at the screen.

Greene clicks a button and enlarges it.

"Son of a bitch," I say, shaking my head in annoyance. "The Crazy R."

"Clearly an *R*," Greene says. "But *crazy*?"

"Yeah, I remember it from when I went to the Ridgeways' ranch. Just a few days before the sketch came out. The *R* is supposed to be viewed by others, so it's meant to be upside down. An upside-down letter in ranching often means *crazy*. It's basic, almost a cave-like design, because to brand cattle you have to keep it simple since you're burning hide. The more complex, the bigger the risk of infection."

"The Ridgeways?" Jess asks. "You mean Clarissa Haynes's case?"

"Yes," I say.

Alderson turns to Jess. "This whole Ridgeway thing. Crosbie has told us about Clarissa, and we've got someone from the agency pulling records of Teton Valley's investigation of it. But how exactly do you know him?"

"Clarissa and her brother, Paxton Rhoads, contacted me initially because of my work at Rotical to see if they actually were blood relatives in addition to being foster siblings. Later, after Clarissa passed away, Crosbie advertised her new PI services on my show. So Paxton called me to see if I thought she might be able to help him. When I spoke highly of Cros, he called her."

"And this guy"—Alderson points at the screen—"whoever he is, has Ridgeway's ranch logo on his arm?"

"Yes, apparently," I say.

"Does Ridgeway have a tattoo like this?" Greene asks.

"No, not on his arm anyway. When I went over to the ranch to talk to him, it was a warm day and he had his sleeves rolled up. I'd recall if he did."

"Did you notice if anyone else there on the ranch had one?"

"I didn't see anyone else besides Ridgeway." I think about surveilling Lasserio the night before. He was wearing a long-sleeve thermal-type shirt. His sleeves were down the entire time.

"Did you look into the forensics reports from Teton County on Clarissa's investigation like I asked you to?" I ask.

"Yes, actually," Alderson says. "They grabbed moldings of the tire treads at the trailhead in the area Clarissa was last seen. We're having them reanalyzed, but there's nothing conclusive yet."

I'm delighted and surprised that the Teton County Sheriff's Department cared enough to pull moldings in the first place. As long as there weren't too many other tracks in the area to make them useless, the evidence might prove useful. I think of that pack Lasserio took back into the shed. If things weren't so crazy today, I'd have already made it back there to snoop around.

I tell Alderson and Greene about it, show them the video, and suggest they use FBI muscle to get access to that shed before Lasserio returns, probably this evening after his Wednesday poker fest. That is, if he's not too drunk to drive. "I've already called the storage business owner," I say. "Lasserio isn't even renting it. It's registered in Robbie Ridgeway's father's name, David Ridgeway, who is no longer alive."

"Interesting," Alderson says. "Establishing probable cause over a guy carrying a random backpack out of a shed isn't feasible, but I'll see what we can do."

I know he's right, that my video of a guy moving a pack around means nothing, but I can't get over how suspicious Lasserio looked and the way he got so nervous when a stranger pulled in.

Alderson fishes around in his notes until he finds his information on the Ridgeway lead. He makes phone calls while Greene taps away on her keyboard. Jess excuses herself to take a shower, and I go outside to finally scrub our cars.

After about forty-five minutes, the agents come out with Jess trailing them. They announce they have three people they plan on contacting who currently or have recently been ranch hands at the Crazy R Ranch.

Before they get in their car, Alderson tells us both not to hesitate to contact them if we think of anything else or notice anything suspicious at all. He directs it to Jess more than to me, probably because he senses she needs it more than I do, since I've been getting used to the drill. "And," he adds, handing her his card, "you might want to consider renting vehicles for a few days. Especially you." He points to me. "Now that you've been filmed coming out of your place, everyone knows what you're driving."

I brush it off, but I know he's right.

I stand beside Jess as they drive away under the darkening sky.

"Jess," I say. "We need to talk."

"Oh." She looks at her phone. She's holding Alderson's card, her brow tight with worry. "But I have to pick up Sam from school." She glances at her car. "You got all the writing off. Thank you," she says. "Is it okay to drive, though? Maybe we should both swing by the airport and grab rentals, as he suggested."

"That's not going to matter. They know—" I stop. I don't want to worry her more than she already is.

"They know what? Where we live?"

I nod.

"That's obvious."

I don't reply.

"Jesus," she says, shaking her head angrily. "What have you gotten us into?" She's glaring at me with an anger I haven't seen since we were younger and in the throes of hormonal teen rages.

It's a good question. What *have* I gotten us into? But her glare rankles me. Classic Jess—try to support her and make her happy, only for her to seize on the one thing that might indicate I'm making everything worse.

"You're *not* telling me something," she says.

"No," I say fast, fetching the bucket of water I've been using simply so I can turn away from her. I wonder if I sound like I'm lying, but at least I seem 100 percent sure. She's spot-on that I'm not telling her things. It's cliché to say someone will never talk to you again, but with Jess, I wonder. She already seems so on the edge. I can't disappoint her further by telling her that I played a critical role in taking away what she saw as a path to her own healing, talking to Coleman and offering him forgiveness as a direct line to her full recovery. That I *helped* Railes get away with taking that from her, even if it was in an indirect way.

All of it feels like it's rushing up like acid in my throat, choking me, keeping me from speaking.

"Cough it up, Cros."

I swallow. "Nothing to tell."

"You've been strange lately. You know it. I know. But never mind." She turns from me. "I have to go."

"Wait," I say, dropping the bucket as I follow her inside. She stomps in and heads to the kitchen, where she grabs her purse and looks inside to make sure she has her keys. "You want to talk about strange? Do you want to tell me why you have Ryan Petronis's file in your office?"

She looks up at me. There's a dawning in her eyes.

"What? You were snooping around my office?"

"I was looking for some Advil. I didn't realize you had things you needed to hide."

"There's absolutely nothing I need to hide." Her voice is cold and hard. Almost detached. It surprises me. I have a flash of wonder if there really could be an inky pool of darkness, a hole in her soul, developed from what Coleman did to her.

Lord knows one developed in me.

But no. No way. Jess would never be involved in these murders. There has to be an explanation. "Then why do you have so much personal information—information that you haven't bothered to share with me or Alderson and Greene—on a boy whose coach was the target of a serial killer who is now stalking me?"

She sighs loudly. "Okay, look, I met his sister, Vivian, at FVCC in the late winter," she says. "I gave a presentation on DNA analysis to one of her biology classes. After the class, she came up to me to tell me she was a fan of my podcast. We got to chatting, and she started telling me about what happened to her brother."

"And so?" I fold my arms across my chest.

"Initially," Jess says, "Vivian didn't tell anyone about what happened to Ryan because he'd asked her not to, but eventually she shared it with her family, thinking they might hold the school accountable. But the parents decided not to do anything because they didn't want to create a scandal and to tarnish Ryan's name even more when they were already in deep grief over his suicide. Months later, Vivian decided she no longer wanted to keep it a secret, that she wanted to expose it all. She wondered if I'd do a show or a series on hazing that's not really hazing, but physical abuse and sexual assault. She wanted to shed light on it all, even though she knows her parents don't want to drag Ryan's name through the mud."

I knew there had to be an explanation. And it makes sense, but still, it's all too crazily coincidental and too close for comfort.

"What did you tell her?"

"That I'd look into it. And I did. Those were my notes."

"Why haven't you told me about this connection to the case? Why haven't you told anyone about it?"

Her face is pained, like she might cry, but she quickly shuts it off. She lifts her chin and stands taller. "I'm sorry. I don't have time for this right now. I need to get Sam."

"Jess," I say as calmly as I can muster. "My life is at stake here. Why didn't you tell me about this?"

"Vivian is fragile," she says. "She's a kid who's lost her brother and she feels responsible. I didn't want to sic the cops on her. I don't think she could handle it. I called her to ask her if she was okay with me telling law enforcement and she said she'd think about it."

I stare at Jess in disbelief. In some ways, she's echoing the very thing I thought about her—that she couldn't handle Alderson and Greene breathing down her neck. And yet, still, it's unconscionable that she'd keep this from me. "But what if she's the one? The one you and I are hunting down?"

"That's exactly it." She says this with venom. "She's not. There's no frickin' way she has anything to do with these crazy killings. It's coincidental and there's no way I'm unleashing the cops on her without her permission. You don't understand, Crosbie."

"Don't understand what?"

"You don't get it, being on the other side of things. Being in law enforcement."

"And that's supposed to mean I can't understand someone's pain? That I'm a bully?"

"Forget it. Look, she promised me she'd let me know by the end of today. And I don't want you to tell them, either, until I hear back from her, okay?"

"I'm not promising that."

She stares at me with loathing, her chest heaving. "I have to go." She rushes past me to her car, hops in, and backs out without glancing my way.

◆ ◆ ◆

I'm reeling. The seething in Jess's eyes rocks me to my core. I stay on the curb, my feet frozen in place as I watch her drive off. *Is* it just anger? Or is it hatred, too? Does my own sister *hate* me? And why now? Does it boil down to the stress of this crazy situation?

Ever since Mark Coleman, it's like something has crawled in and rotted in the crawlspace under a floor Jess and I share. I decide she's not talking about my job. I decide my own guilt is making me so crazy I can't even read her clearly anymore. What she probably wants to say is that I can't understand because it wasn't me who was raped, that I can't possibly get it. She has a point that I can't fully comprehend, but that doesn't mean I don't have empathy.

Who does she think I am?

Maybe that's the problem. Maybe she's simply picking up on what I've been doing with myself all these months . . . Soaking up and mimicking my own self-hatred, not so unlike Sam when he gets whiny and needy, sodden with his mother's anxiety.

But it makes me wonder what my own sister actually thinks of me. All this time, I've been trying to protect her. Help her. Be a sort of big-sister shield for some of the worst, unexpected moments the world throws down. And Lord knows we've had a boatload of those, from Dad's illness and passing to Mom's sudden crash, to Coleman. But maybe she resents me. Maybe she hates me for it.

I put the bucket back in Jess's garage and my mind turns to her office. I wasn't snooping before, but now that's exactly what I plan to do. Part of me is terrified I'll find something on Vonda Loman, too, but the other part of me believes Randal Askens is a coincidence. All sorts of correlations crop up when you live in smaller communities. There's a saying I've heard applied to both Montana and Wyoming, that each state is a small town with very long streets.

I'm relieved when I don't find any notes on Loman. I'm also calmed when I go through a bin full of her latest artwork—most colorful watercolors. The sketches in the bin are all of fishing boats or canoes out on still lake water, red and orange kayaks stacked by docks, people fly-fishing on rocky riverbanks with sunsets blazing over the distant hills or through background trees. There's not one single sketch or portrait.

I walk out of her office reassured but confused. And deeply bothered. It especially stings, given how I'm always putting her first, that Jess didn't think my life being at stake outweighed her need to protect Vivian.

# Chapter 39

I rush home, rattling Deputy Zane with my speed until he realizes it's me, to grab a pair of lock cutters and my firewood axe. Within minutes, I'm back at the sketchy storage business south of Kalispell. I want to get there before Lasserio finishes his Wednesday afternoon poker. I'm hoping he didn't return this morning to retrieve the backpack.

All is quiet, with only one man in an old Ford unloading who knows what. Americans who own too much shit. If your three-bedroom house doesn't have room, you probably don't need it. Think of the money that could be saved and better spent on, say, therapy for idiots like me.

When the Ford pickup leaves, the place is empty. I search again for cameras and find none, so I park in the same aisle as the day before and walk around to Lasserio's—or Ridgeway's—unit.

The padlock is tight. The next unit over has no lock, and when I roll up the door, it's vacant. And no magic side door like adjoining hotel suites. Me and luck? I can't even remember how it feels. Waiting for Greene and Alderson to get a warrant won't cut it.

I suck my tongue fiercely against my front teeth, contemplating it. I know from my time on the beat that these units are flimsy. In the days before storage businesses sharpened up and installed security measures, break-ins were common.

I could take an axe to the flimsy wall or use lock cutters on the shank. Either of these things would make me a thief, right along with being a liar and a crooked cop. I feel a pit in my stomach like a steady drip of acid. The insurance agent's question about my character burns like a heated pair of eyes staring me down.

I go back to my car, get in, and check my phone. My connection from the county forensics unit hasn't called me back yet. I try him one more time.

When the tech, Ray, answers, I sigh. "Oh thank God."

"Thank God what?"

"Nothing. Don't mean to be so dramatic. I'm under a time crunch here."

"Under*stand*able," Ray says, drawing it out, like he's showering me with sympathy in the one syllable. More acid drips into my stomach. This burn is all disdain and bitterness, of being vulnerable, of being cast as a victim and being treated like one by everyone I know. But more than that, I don't deserve one single ounce of sympathy from anyone.

"Have you looked at that video?"

"I've got some close-ups for you. I'll send them to you now."

I thank him profusely, hang up, and wait for the email to come, trying to ignore more of the social media notifications still piling up, but good God, they're humming around me like gnats.

Finally, the file comes through. I open it. In the enlargements—a beige, canvas-style backpack, just as Paxton described Clarissa's. And in one of the enlargements of the flap is a patch of blue.

I think of calling Greene and Alderson and sending them the images, asking them to find a way to get a search warrant for this storage unit ASAP, but I know that will take more time than I can afford to waste. Plus, even if they could establish probable cause, by the time they get the warrant, Lasserio will have probably come and removed the pack.

Another drop of acid. I know what I'm going to do. I've already crossed the line. I get out of my car and look around for good measure to make sure I haven't been followed, to check that there are still no security cameras anywhere, and to scan for anything unusual at all, like a peephole in an opposite-facing shed or a door not completely shut.

When I see that there still aren't any cameras around and everything looks normal, I return to the aisle my car is parked in, put on some nitrile gloves, and grab my bolt cutter.

Inside the shed, it's dusty and crammed full of boxes, plastic bins, and old horse tack.

Right on the floor, closer to the left wall of the unit, is the pack, right where Lasserio dropped it.

I pick it up and inspect the outside, my ears tuned for any new vehicle approaching. The patch is the Blackfeet Tribe's flag with black-and-white eagle feathers creating a circle surrounding a map of their territory, all against a blue sky.

Inside, there's a long-sleeve thermal shirt, a light raincoat, and a Nalgene water bottle, which certainly carries Clarissa's DNA. In a different compartment, a kit of test tubes, pens, markers, a wildflower identification handbook, a notebook, and . . . a sketchbook and drafting pencils. That seems odd, although it's possible Clarissa sketched wildflowers and landscapes. I inspect the front cover. It's made out of leather and has a watermark on the cover. It's the same logo as the tattoo. A wave of chills travels up my spine. Why would Clarissa have a sketchbook with the Ridgeway watermark in her pack?

I open it, illogically thinking I'll see rough drafts of my own face, but there's nothing there, only torn-out sheets. On the remaining blank sheets, the watermark sits at the top of each page. I put it back in the pack and leaf through the notebook to see notes on the fen . . . on various plants like the sundew and animal species like the Northern lemming. I'm about to open the wildflower identification book when I hear a car pull in.

Shit. *Was* I followed? I throw the notebook and wildflower book back in. I wanted to look through the dusty boxes, too, but I don't have time.

I make a quick decision to take the pack with me rather than leaving it for Lasserio. The snipped lock will tell him plenty anyway.

I hurry out, scanning left and right. The car I heard is nowhere in sight.

Without turning my back to the corridor, I slide Ridgeway's shed door down. I scan all opposite-facing units again, still looking for anything out of place: a partially open one, a peephole that someone could look through, anything . . . I spot nothing, so I hurry to my car in the next aisle over.

But right as I round the corner, I clock a blue Chevy 4x4 idling next to my car.

Shit. Security guard?

But no one gets out of the truck. And within several very long seconds—with my heart pounding so hard I feel like it's going to knock me right into the unit I'm standing beside—the Chevy drives away.

I give it another half a minute so the truck can make it to the exit, then run to my car and drive away.

A few miles up the road, when my pulse is back to normal, I think of how I need to show the pack to Paxton for him to positively ID that it belongs to his sister even though her name is on one of the notebooks. There's no time to wait for DNA results on the water bottle, but it could help if I, or maybe even Alderson and Greene, who are already looking into the case as I asked, can get the DA interested in investigating Ridgeway's and Lasserio's connection to Clarissa's death.

I also think of the article *Rolling Stone* Dude asked me to read and all the inroads he's made with the Blackfeet. People on the reservation seemed to trust him enough to give him detailed information on how they saw the tribe's missing and murdered Indigenous women situation. More details than I've ever been able to gather. Maybe he's come across something on Clarissa's case. And at the very least, maybe he could get Palmer Edmonds, the Blackfeet elder, to talk to me. I can't let it go that there's something I'm missing about the Ridgeways. About Clarissa's murder. And how the sketch might simply originate from Ridgeway and his goons so that if something happens to me, it gets pinned onto the real Confession Artist.

The idea that the real CA might never even have had me in their sights at all makes me feel lighter, but I still don't trust Jeremy. And I'm not sure I really believe that the CA isn't targeting me. I can't escape the bruised cloud that's settled over me, that might never leave me until lightning from it strikes.

I decide to call Jeremy and try to nudge in on his connections on the reservations. Calling him makes butterflies swirl in my stomach. I can't decide how much is because of my attraction to him, or how much is due to the crazy coincidence that he was in both Dallas and now the Flathead Valley.

But I do it anyway.

"This is Jeremy."

"Hey," I say. "It's Crosbie."

"Crosbie." I can hear the smile on his face.

"Where are you?"

"In the park."

"Which part?"

"West Glacier."

"Perfect. I'm heading to West Glacier myself. Can we meet?"

He says he's tied up with some other folks for a bit, but that he can meet in an hour and a half.

"That's fine. I have some things to do beforehand as well."

After he agrees, I call Paxton and ask him to meet me in West Glacier, too. Both in a public place, to be on the safe side.

# Chapter 40

Forty-five minutes later, I'm sitting with a cup of coffee in a café on the outskirts of Glacier National Park. This is a bonus because up around Glacier, cell service isn't great, so people who've been in the park for days aren't paying a ton of attention to the news. I profile everyone who looks at me a second too long, which is hardly anyone. Maybe Jess's pink-and-blue ice cream hat is really a Harry Potter Invisibility Cloak.

But before Paxton arrives, I suddenly find I'm wrong. As in, dead wrong. Which is a funny phrase if you think about it. Because if you literally were dead every time you were wrong, it might be a whole different world. I'm not laughing.

A set of three women have come in and taken a table across the room, but after one of them motions with her head to me, the rest all rubberneck it to get a look. When one of them turns to the table behind her and whispers something to a man and he cranks his neck around to look, too, I've had enough. They're all too close. I feel claustrophobic. I throw a five on the table and walk past them with all eyes gunning for me. As I exit, I hear one of the guys saying, "Wait, aren't you . . . ?"

When I pull out and drive into the village of West Glacier, I check that there are still a lot of tourists milling about and that I won't be isolated if I conduct my meetings here or inside the park. I figure I'll have just as high a chance of being recognized in the village as I did in the café, so I go through the entrance gates off the park. I want to thread the needle of diluting the crowds enough to decrease the chances I'll be recognized while still keeping enough tourists around to feel safe.

I find a brief patch of service and call Paxton. "Change in plans," I tell him. I call Jeremy and repeat the info.

I drive to the quaint village of Apgar, perched at the southwest end of Lake McDonald. I find a parking lot past the docks among about ten other cars.

At least here the café walls and the whispers of people aren't closing in on me.

Still, I check to make sure I've got my gun securely fastened in its holster under my light jacket. Then, I wait, trying to relax enough to draw in a deep breath of the fresh pine and the smell of breeze off the cold lake.

Paxton arrives, driving a flashy black Lincoln MKZ that looks out of place among all the SUVs, Jeeps, and generic rental cars in the lot. He parks beside me and hops in my car.

I show him the picture I've taken of the pack. "That's hers," he says, excited. He wants all the details. I make up a fib. It doesn't matter.

"What's in it?" he asks.

"Test tubes, notes. Paxton, did your sister draw?"

"Not that I know of, but maybe she drew pictures of the plants she studied. Why?"

I tell him about the sketch pad with the Ridgeway logo. In the back of my mind, I'm wondering if the pad belonged to Ridgeway or one of his guys who might have drawn a picture of me and simply shoved it in Clarissa's pack to get rid of the evidence along with her things. "Would she have had a sketch pad of theirs?"

He stares at me and shakes his head. "I have no idea. I mean, maybe, if she was out there trying to interview him and forgot her own notebook. Maybe she borrowed one?"

When he asks if he can have it, I tell him that I'm going to have it analyzed and it's best not to mess with it.

"And Palmer Edmonds?" I ask about Paxton's ex-fiancée's father, who met with Clarissa the morning she drowned. "You still can't get him to chat with us? Even for Clarissa's sake?"

Paxton shakes his head. "I've left messages and even gone to his house. He refuses to call me back or see me."

I'm about to wrap things up with Paxton when I see a white Chevy Equinox with a single driver.

Jeremy. Dammit. He's a good twenty minutes early. The last thing I want is for him to know anything about my clients.

Jeremy misses the entrance to the lot, so he drives to the end of the road to swing back around. I rush Paxton off, telling him I'll be in touch. I stand outside my car as Paxton drives away, rechecking my gun—even though I know it's exactly where I put it before he arrived—when Jeremy pulls in.

He parks next to me, where Paxton had parked. His shaggy hair is tucked behind his ears. He's wearing a button-down, clay-colored shirt with the sleeves rolled up, revealing tanned arms and confirming my memory that he has no tattoo of an upside-down *R*.

He grins as he approaches. "Who was that?" he asks.

"None of your concern."

"One of your cases?"

"I can repeat those four words if you didn't hear them well enough."

"So it was one of your cases."

"And if you keep prying, I can go back to my main job of simultaneously lying low and finding out who is trying to hunt me down while the clock ticks down to my own personal doomsday."

"Easy," he says. "Easy, easy."

"Nothing about this is that."

"Understood."

"Then leave shit alone when I ask, okay?"

"Got it," he says. "By the way, nice hat," he offers with a flash of a smile.

My cheeks heat up. I'm embarrassed that this man who I'm not sure I even trust yet has this kind of pull on me. "Not very effective, though. Which is why we're here instead of the café."

"Ah, I see. Too many gawkers."

"You've been camping?" I ask.

"And hiking," he says. "Sorry if I'm a little scruffy. Wasn't expecting a call from you." He leans one sinewy arm on the top of my car. "What brings you my way?"

*My way?* Like he owns Montana and the glorious Glacier National Park?

"I read your article."

He waits.

"It's good. Congratulations on the awards. Especially the National Magazine Award. Impressive."

"Thank you. Does this mean you're going to let me interview you?"

"I'm still mulling over the idea."

It's a lie.

"So why did you call?"

"I was interested in the work you've done on the reservation. You know Palmer Edmonds well?"

"Well enough to get his take on the situation with the missing. Why? What does he have to do with the pickle you're in?"

"Nothing." *At least, not that I know of.* "But he has something to do with another case I'm working on."

Jeremy leans his entire back against my car and listens intently. I tell him about Clarissa Haynes without using her name, and that Palmer Edmonds had breakfast with Clarissa the day she went hiking, but that he won't speak to me, and refuses to speak to Clarissa's brother, Paxton. I tell him why.

"Aha." He smiles again. "So, you want to use me to get in front of him because Paxton hasn't been able to?"

I give an innocent shrug.

"What do I get in return?"

"Depends," I say. "If you can get Edmonds to talk to me about Ridgeway, I might consider giving you that exclusive."

I can't *really* fathom the idea of going through with it, but I can't think of another bargaining chip in my possession.

"*Might?* That's weak."

"It's better than nothing. And it might help me figure out what happened to this poor drowned woman." I don't tell him it might also provide another avenue to figure out if the killer, or at least a copycat of the killer, is affiliated with the Ridgeway Ranch in some way.

He thinks about it. "I know who you're talking about. Clarissa Haynes, right?"

"Yes."

"Sad case," he says, and he looks sincere. "Who hired you to look into her death?"

"Someone who cared for her."

"The guy with the black Blackfeet Nation Pikuni license plates who just drove away?"

Again, I shrug.

"Okay. I can try. But why are you running around alone? Shouldn't you have a bodyguard or something?"

"And pay him—or her—with what? And the real danger doesn't kick in until my six days are up."

"Which is the day after tomorrow."

"You're keeping track?" A wire of tension travels up my spine. I casually run my fingers across my gun.

"The whole nation is. But still, Crosbie, your life is at risk. Are you taking this seriously enough?" He pins me with his eyes, like he's known me for years. It's the same intense way he looked at me when he handed me the note the night before. I can't read it. I can't read *him*. Is it born from good ol' basic genuine interest in me or is it something else entirely? I can't tell. Everything is too messed up. Too crazy.

"Yes," I say, staring back. "Of course I am."

"Why are you going about business as usual?"

"What else am I supposed to do?"

"Oh, I don't know. Maybe go on a vacation somewhere safe, somewhere nobody knows about."

His concern feels real. It melts something inside me. I feel the pressure of tears threaten behind my eyes but push them back. My mind is frayed from my interaction with Jess. I'm still trying to make sense of the coincidence of her speaking to Ryan Petronis's sister, Vivian, the sister of the boy who was raped during a football team's hazing ceremony under the supervision of the coach who ended up being one of the CA's victims. And of Jess not telling me about it. What I need is one of those walls to hang photos and draw dashed lines or solid lines around connections and possible connections. What I need is time to think it all through—even probe deeper into my conscience and consider all the consequences if I confess, and how to plan to catch the killer if I don't. Is it possible to upload all your facts and suspicions to AI and have it point you in the right direction? Probably, and *that* thought creeps me out, too. It's all making me uneasy and a little crazed, but I don't need to let Jeremy see the mess.

When I'm confident I can speak without my voice cracking, I say, "There's been a part of me that's been in denial. I mean, it's hard to swallow something like this. And even after having it sink in, a part of me still wants to believe this is a stupid internet trick and a colossal coincidence that two of the people in the joke both ended up dead, but I know that's wishful thinking. There's no situation where two people matching two of the sketches both end up murdered."

"What about that deputy outside your house? Is he doing his job? I mean, your boyfriend had a point. I got to your house fairly easily."

"Wallace isn't my boyfriend." I feel silly for correcting him so quickly. "But Deputy Zane is making sure no one unwanted swings by or is waiting for me when I return."

He studies me with narrowed eyes. "There's a lot you're not telling me."

An echo from Jess.

Another car pulls in. Two couples. Older. Hats, tennis shoes, fleece jackets. It's a calming, happy scene, but something about it makes me feel alone. With time banging its mean clock like a heavy metal drummer, it's the opposite of what I can afford to do right now. Or even if I could afford to be part of it, I know the feeling of serenity would be wasted on me. Too much baggage. I wish I were any one of them.

A part of me knows better than to confide in Jeremy, but I can't help it. He has a way of making me suspicious and lowering my guard at the same time.

I fill him in about the messages on my car and Jess's and the tattoo pointing in the direction of the Crazy R. When I'm finished, Jeremy tells me that as soon as he gets somewhere with better cell service, he'll make calls on my behalf to try to hook me up with Edmonds.

"In the meantime—and I don't mean to assume too much—but you seem anxious. How about a walk? A few deep breaths?"

He bobs his head, pointing to the beach.

# Chapter 41

The sun is setting behind us. Pink light feathers over the majestic mountains of the Great Divide across the lake. The aspens are just beginning to turn, gold and yellow leaves making a collage at the base of the lower hills, their brilliant leaves glimmering in the glow of sunset.

I'm not entirely sure why I've agreed to the stroll, but perhaps it's because it feels beyond good to have someone recognize just how difficult the past few days have been. And remain.

One of the couples who walked down to the beach is standing on the shore and looking out, taking in the scenery of the peaks reflected perfectly in the lake. The others are a little farther down, examining rocks on the shoreline.

"This is why I live here. I fell for it all a long time ago when I'd spend summers with my dad. He loved being in the woods. There's something about it all that reminds you to not take yourself too seriously. That we all have the same short . . ."

"Same short?"

"Time on earth, I was going to say, but that sounded a little too ominous, under my circumstances."

"I know. I was going to say that you're one lucky lady, but I rethought that, too."

"That's okay. But you know, luck has nothing to do with it. A lot of people don't get to live in a place like this out of luck. It's a choice, and with it come a bunch of sacrifices, like making good money." I laugh. "And getting a good Pad Thai."

"True," he says.

We lock eyes. His face is ruddy in the light and cold wind. I peer out at the lake's surface rippling from a breeze, shattering the smooth, picture-perfect reflection of the peaks. I wrap my arms around my waist and shiver.

Every detail pops beyond vivid. Every fresh scent of pine, aspen, wet rock, and distant chimney smoke claims me. I wonder if having your life threatened makes it all zing to life. Or if it's simply the magic of Glacier Park. I've forgotten how when you get around such immense surroundings, your senses naturally heighten. Or maybe it's the addition of Jeremy and his good-natured intensity, and the way his light-brown eyes, practically golden with their flecks of amber, are taking me in when I look his way again.

"You're cold." He steps closer, puts an arm around me, and squeezes me gently.

A static charge makes me stiffen. I check that the couple is still close. They are. I move my right hand to my gun. Habit. Or . . . ?

But he feels strong, and after a second, I let myself have this one moment. I lean into him, go slack. It's been a very long few days.

I look away from the towering peaks on the north end of the lake and face him. His eyes are the color of pecans in the pale light. My attraction to him is undeniable. But I wonder, if I were to date someone like him, how long would it take before he saw through me? Saw who I really am?

"I do have a thing or two I should confess. One big thing in particular."

I had no intention of saying these words. It's as if the past hours have teed them up in my larynx, ready for them to leap out.

"Yeah?" He takes his eyes off the water and turns to me.

For a moment I want to take them back, swallow them down, but then something wilts in me. "I'm willing to tell you about them, about it, if you're still interested." The words in the crystal-clear, pure air shock even me. Where are they coming from? I've kept these things to myself forever. Why now? Why him? A journalist of all people?

I know why. Besides wanting to save my own skin from the Confession Artist, I can't deny that the pressure is getting to me. It's too big, like it's all going to blow if I don't release a tiny bit. I envision a pressure cooker with all kinds of knobs at the top, and my hand reaches for one and twists it ever so slightly to release a small hiss.

And telling him, in an odd way, seems easier than sharing it with someone I'm close to, like opening up to a bartender or a hairdresser instead of your own family. But because Jeremy's a journalist, I'm not entirely positive I will follow through or, if I do, exactly how much I'll share, but surely I can expose some of it, maybe how I felt about dragging Sophie along camping.

"I most definitely am. I'm in town for two more days, and tomorrow's your last day to get something out there, right?"

I'm not sure how I feel about the excitement in his eyes . . . Predator zeroing in on his prey? Or decent, helpful guy who's happy I might finally come clean?

"I have a few things I need to take care of first."

"Okay," he says. "What's changed your mind? You haven't had a scare like that drug rep guy, Mooney, did out in the woods?"

I pause. My breath hitches. *How does he know about that?* I want to ask him, but I stop myself. My mind whirls. I try not to appear surprised or confused as I tick through it.

Tim Mooney *did* confess along with a bunch of other men who looked like the sketch. And yes, he contacted the police, both of which a good journalist could figure out.

But the scare? Tim Mooney confessing because he became frightened near the end of his six days and felt compelled to divulge more . . . that was not public information. Only the cops in Spokane and the FBI know that, and there's no way they'd share that with Jeremy or any other journalist.

And clearly they haven't, or it would be all over the internet already.

I pull away from him as naturally as I can, so it doesn't seem abrupt. I have an immediate strong urge to get to my car and drive as far away from him as I can. This guy goes from warm and fuzzy to cold and creepy faster than a spinning top. I'm not sure what to make of it. Alderson's voice rings in my ears: *Trust no one.*

But I tell myself to be cool, that that would be a gross overreaction to something very inconclusive. I could ask him how he knows. Right here, right now. But if he knows because he was the guy stalking Mooney out in those woods, there's no way he's admitting it to me. Then I'll have played my hand.

As nonchalantly as I can, I shuffle a few steps away from him. I keep myself focused on what's before me: the blue, brown, and wine-colored river rocks below the clear water, the strong breeze ruffling its surface, the peaks on the far end of the lake, the leaves on the cottonwoods beginning to yellow in the early fall, the weight of my gun tucked into my jeans.

Jeremy picks up a small, smooth pebble and side-tosses it so that it skips a good six or seven times across the water.

Again, so normal. So natural. His muscles at ease under his fleece. But is it a facade? I take the opportunity to slide farther away from him.

He turns and looks at me funny for a second, then smiles at me in his carefree way. "You're antsy to get going, aren't you?"

I force a sweet smile back, but my stomach feels like it's twisted itself inside out. Whatever feelings I was having for Jeremy have turned to a syrupy sludge churning in my guts. Again, there's nothing definitive, but still, it's a significant detail I don't like at all.

I kick myself for being so stupid. How could I trust this stranger who's been on my back since Dallas? Since the day I saw the sketch?

"So, when would you like for me to interview you?"

"I'll let you know soon," I say, "but right now I should get going, and you need to make those calls." I wave to the parking lot. "After you."

He starts back toward our vehicles, his feet shifting on the pebbled beach as he takes each step. I follow a few paces behind, trying to navigate the rocks myself while not taking my eyes off him.

# Chapter 42

Fiona has tried calling again. Wallace, too. But not Tim Mooney. One message, though, leaps out: Glacier Elementary.

Sam's school.

*"This is Wanda Collins from Glacier Elementary. I have you down as a contact for Sam. I'm calling because school got out a little over half an hour ago, and Sam is still here without a ride. I didn't hear from his mom or dad regarding this matter, and I haven't been able to reach her or Patrick on their phones. If you could please call us, that would be great."*

Fear shoots through me. I call the school but it's long past closing hours. Voicemail. I hang up and call Jess. She doesn't answer. Voicemail number two. I can barely live with myself now, but if something happens to Sam, I'll die.

My heart hammers against my chest. If someone has targeted Jess's vehicle, they know who she is, where she lives, and they could easily target Sam, too.

"Jess. Call me. I got a call from Sam's school, and I have no idea what's going on. Call me. Immediately."

I hang up and listen to Fiona's and Wallace's messages in case they know something I don't, but neither seems to have anything important to say other than that they're checking in and still worried.

I drive faster than I should, gripping the steering wheel, panic closing in on me. My heart feeling like it's going to beat itself right out of my rib cage.

◆ ◆ ◆

It's dark out when I pull up. The lights from Jess's kitchen and living room shine onto her front lawn. I'm about to bolt out of my car and run inside when I see her cross in front of the kitchen window.

"Thank God," I say out loud. But Sam? Where is Sam?

But even as my mind is registering that Jess would never be calmly shuffling around in her kitchen if Sam weren't there, I see him, too, through the main room's larger windows. He's in the living room on the couch, his head bowed, looking at something.

I close my eyes and sag back into the seat. The fact that they're both safe washes over me like a wave. I squeeze my eyes tighter to keep away threatening tears.

A memory from when Jess and I were little pops into my mind. We were playing unattended with some miniature toy cars Les had provided us from his office at the back of his grimy auto shop, the thick smell of oil and gasoline around us.

We pushed the little models around on the pavement beside his shop, real cars surrounding us like giant, ticking beasts. We made little zoom sounds as we laid tracks in the gravel. Road dust covered our fingers and clothes as we crashed the little models into one another, pretending we were bad drivers.

But eventually, I got bored and wanted to push mine farther away, to venture out on my own, away from Jess.

"Wait," she called. "Where are you going?"

I didn't answer her. I was sick of her copying everything I did.

I shoved my little Mustang along, away from her, toward some gravel off to the side of the lot.

Suddenly, our stepdad's voice roared.

I turned to see him snatch Jess up by the arm as an old Ford pickup backed up to the spot she played. He held her tight against him.

"What the hell's wrong with you?" He glared at me over her shoulder. He squeezed her arm so furiously that he left welts on her pale skin. "You're both so pathetic. You," he said to Jess, "always letting yourself get hurt. And you . . ." He pinned me with his glare while Jess wailed by his side, her arms tiny and thin in his clenched, oil-stained hands. Tears smeared her cheeks. "You should protect your little sister, not get her hurt."

Those words—straight from that dusty lot—seem to have followed me down every turn in my life. And still, I'm doing a poor job of it.

When I open my eyes, I notice a car parked across the street in front of the Johnstons' house. Behind Jess's car is an unmarked sedan. The same police detail that showed up earlier today with Alderson and Greene.

I walk over, tap on the window. "When did they get in?"

"About thirty minutes ago."

I ask her if there's been anything strange going on. She shakes her head, bored as they come.

When I walk in, Sam launches himself at me from across the living room and wraps my waist in a big hug. "Aunt Crosbie," he says to my belly, still pronouncing it *Cwasbie*. He's in his green-and-black dinosaur pajamas, his little belly popping out.

Tears leap to my eyes. I'm still staggered by my relief that he's okay. And yes, his mom, too, though I have a bone to pick with her. Why didn't she call me back when I was panicking on the drive over after getting that call?

When he tries to release me, I don't let him go and take one more whiff. He smells like a combination of lavender and something fruity, like bottled innocence and sunshine. When I finally let him go, I drop to my knees, tousle his hair, and ask him about school. He tells me it's been good and wonders if I'll come read his Creature Cards with him.

"I will if it's not that scary one about the Japanese girl," I say, pulling my face into a mask of terror.

"That's the best one!"

"Well, maybe." It's all I can do not to haul him into another embrace, but I don't want to scare the poor kid.

But the pressure that's been building like megatons of water against an unstable dam creates a fissure in me. Taking risks, like letting Jeremy into my house and meeting him in a semiremote place, is one thing. But if I'm endangering Jess and Sam, too, by my unwillingness to confess and bear the consequences, that's quite another. As I look at my nephew's innocent, sweet face, I decide that I need to start somewhere. And that's with Jess.

"Give me a sec to talk to your mom. You go pick out the cards, okay?"

He agrees and is gone like a shot.

I find Jess in the kitchen, washing dishes. "I tried calling you. Why didn't you pick up?"

"I just saw," she says, flashing me an unfocused glance and refocusing on the plate she's sponging off. "I've been making dinner for Sam, and I had to get him in the bath."

"I left messages to call me. Immediately."

"Yeah, I just saw."

"Jess, the school called."

"I'm sorry. I got held up. There was an accident on LaSalle."

"You should have called to tell me."

"Sorry," she says, moving on to a big pasta pot. She hasn't properly looked at me yet. "I didn't realize they'd called you."

"Why is your car in the street?"

"Those agents informed me that there would be an unmarked car across from my house. So, when I saw it when I came home, I pulled in in front of them to speak to them before going in. After we chatted, I decided to leave it there. Figured someone would be less likely to mess with it with them right behind it."

"Good point," I say, staring at the side of her pretty face. I can't read her. It's one thing to not be able to read Jeremy Fisher. It's another entirely not to be able to read my own sister. It's like everything with her has gone haywire. The old Jess would have called the school if she was just five minutes late. One night after the rape, she told me that she wanted to take her own skin off and climb out of it. It almost feels like that's exactly what she's done.

I return to the living room and sit on the couch with Sam and read several cards, moving from actual creatures like the Giant Orb Spider and some dinosaurs to scarier mythological ones like the Wendigo and the Kraken, at which point Sam begins to rub his eyes. Jess comes in from the kitchen and declares that it's time for bed. Sam fights her, saying that he wants to fully see me off when I leave. It's our little ritual, when he stands at the big living room windows at the front of the house and waves at me until my car is officially out of sight.

Jess tells him "Not tonight" and takes him to his room. Twenty minutes later, she returns while I'm picking up Sam's stray toys—minus a Star Wars Lego project in progress.

Jess sits, places her face in her palms, and rubs. Hard. When she looks up, she says, "Look, Cros, I'm sorry I didn't tell you about Vivian."

"It's okay," I say. I don't want an apology from her. I want to give one.

Yes, it dawns on me. I really do.

Maybe not to the world, but at least to her. It's time. Her anger at me feels like it's growing, like it's taking on a life of its own, becoming its own monster stalking the edges of our relationship. It's as if she senses that I'm the cause of all the toxic things in our lives. And I guess I am.

After the flood of fright I felt after receiving the message from Sam's school, I have to start somewhere. I need to confess, ironically, as the Confession Artist wants me to do, at least to her.

"I'll tell those agents about it if you think it's wise," Jess says. "I'll have to give Vivian a heads-up, but she's not going to be able to tell them anything that I haven't already told you."

"They should know about the boy and his connection to Askens," I say. "You know that, right?"

Jess begins to weep and shake her head. She's brittle. A soft breeze might take her down. I want to weasel out of what I've suddenly decided I need to do, but the tug to protect her pulls fiercely.

I won't back down. I can't. Not with my guilt building, wanting to burst past its dam, knowing that my dirty secrets might be putting them in danger, too. Plus, there's a tiny voice whispering in my ear: *Your sister, the one who was helplessly crying in her bed just earlier in the day, is not* that *helpless.* This morning, I wouldn't have thought so, but after seeing those files in her office and how she held that information back from me, I'm wondering how much of her I've misunderstood. But I need to plow forward, for her, for me.

"Jess," I force myself to say, "there's something I need to tell you, too."

She stops crying and swipes at her eyes. "What?"

"About Mark Coleman."

"What about him?" Her voice goes higher with fear, as if he's in the kitchen grabbing a beer. Her eyes widen, her nostrils flare.

"It's just—" I shake my head. Swallow hard. The cartwheels going on in my stomach make me feel like I might vomit.

"What?" Jess stares.

"It was my fault Railes shot him." I spit it out. "I was so angry when I found out who he was. I went for my gun too hastily. Railes saw me and pulled his." But even as I'm saying it, I know it's not quite right. It *is* what happened, but Railes . . . he would have gone there anyway, regardless of my actions. I know it in my gut.

No, the real problem stands with what happened later. This is just warming up, trying to build on the courage of saying the first thing out loud.

"But it was self-defense," she says. Confusion and shock scroll across her face. She pulls her head back like she's already distancing herself from me before she even knows the full story.

I let a long moment fill the abyss to hell. And back. I don't breathe. My stomach curls into an even tighter knot while my head goes dizzy. "Railes shot him in cold blood," I say. "Railes claimed Mark had a knife, and when the investigator came to question me . . ."

"What?" The confusion changes to desperation, which alters her face into someone I don't recognize.

I take a big breath like I'm about to leap off a cliff. My heart goes from a fast-paced thrum to a forceful bang. It's too late to back out, to not say it now.

"What?"

"I lied."

"You lied?"

"Yes. I wanted him dead. Because of what he did to you." The words out loud in the quiet room seem to ricochet back to me and coat me in a film of slime. Jess's shocked expression worsens the sensation. But I deserve every bit of her reaction.

But, but . . . I've finally done it. I've said it out loud for the first time ever.

She shakes her head, looks down, tries to take it in.

"And Leon, his boyfriend? He was distraught about Railes lying, but everyone kept focusing on Leon as victim of a rape. He wanted me to back him about Coleman not holding the knife."

"But you didn't," Jess says. There's so much shock and surprise in her eyes that I want to crawl into the couch cushions and disappear.

But still, it's there. The tiny release of pressure. I can feel it. Just a small stream of release after keeping the secret pent up for so long. It's there. My heart is still beating hard, but it slows a little.

"I didn't."

"But why? Why would you protect Railes? You don't even like those guys."

"I despised everything about them. And in a flash I joined them." Speaking this part out loud makes my heart speed up again. Shame prickles every inch of me. My cheeks burn with it. "It's incomprehensible.

Reprehensible," I say. "I hate myself for it. I don't know exactly how I came to it other than it was all twisted up in my anger at Coleman and what he did to you. And . . ."

"And what?"

I close my eyes. I can't face her stricken expression a second longer, but I know I can't stop short. I open them. "This part is hard to admit."

"What part?" More horror is growing by the second in the flabbergasted intensity in her wide-open eyes. A new wave of shame builds and unfurls like a wave inside me, pushes up through me to my head.

I shake it to dislodge the rush of it. And to avoid saying it. I'm not sure I can say it out loud to her. Surely, I think, I've already told her enough.

"What part?" she presses.

I shake my head again.

"Crosbie, *what*?"

"That I didn't want to screw up my chances of making detective."

She pulls her head back again, more fully this time, like a turtle. But a turtle doesn't show disgust, and her eyes swim with it. "But you ended up quitting anyway? After you lied for Railes?"

"Yes."

"But why haven't you told the truth about it since you quit?"

I thought I just said the hardest part, but I realize what I'm about to say is even worse. *This* is the hardest thing to say to my sister. But this part, it's less about the shame. The guilt. This is about the nuts and bolts of how it will affect me, her, and Sam altogether. I'm going at my thumb again, and Jess swats my hand hard to signal for me to stop. She could have slapped my face. It would feel the same.

"Cros? Why?"

"I'd go to jail, Jess. Obstruction of justice. Lying to the independent law enforcement agent. Not to mention that Leon took his life. Do you think one minute doesn't go by when I don't think that if I'd told the same story as Leon, that if we took on the swamp thing that is Billy Railes, that Leon might still be alive?"

Tears push to my eyes. I press at the corners with my fingers. I'm tempted to grab Jess's hand, but she must sense it and stands up from the couch. She looks at me with more revulsion and incomprehension.

"For God's sake, you don't even *work* there anymore." Her voice is high-pitched. Frantic but layered with hostility. "You could have at least told me after the fact. If I'd known the whole story, maybe I'd be processing this a little differently instead of feeling like the rug got pulled out from under me not once by Coleman, but again by Railes for killing him and taking away any chance that I—or even that Leon—had to confront him or deal with our grief in our own ways."

I still feel like shit, like crawling into a hole, but my anger bubbles up through it all. I want to yell back at her, *No, no, I know you, and you wouldn't have processed things any differently! You'd be the same. Remember how you were after Mom died? You wouldn't get out of bed. You couldn't function. And maybe if you'd reported him from the get-go instead of being so afraid of how it would affect your popularity online, he wouldn't have done what he did to Leon.*

But I'm here to lay my sins down. To apologize, not make things worse.

"It was selfish. I was embarrassed that I'd covered for Railes. Ashamed. And I kept thinking that I handled the situation with Leon and Coleman so horribly not only because of my anger over what he did to you but also because of what happened to Sophie."

"Enough!" Her voice booms so loudly I'm sure it's probably woken Sam. "Enough about Sophie. That was years ago." Her stare pierces me with daggers.

"Okay, okay, sure, yes, it was." But the comment stings, burrows deep inside me. I have spent years roiling in guilt in the wake of her rape, of her suicide. Is it fate that I would create something even bigger in my life to feel shame about? Or have I been trying to make it right through Jess?

It's the first time it's hitting me . . . the question suddenly neon bright, pulsing around my head like a strobe: How much of my actions, all my attention to Jess, especially since we've been adults, has been shaped by my guilt over Sophie?

"Jesus, Crosbie." Jess continues. "Would you listen to yourself? Who do you think you are? God? You don't have that much power over people. You have no idea what Leon was thinking." She sits back down, her shoulders hunched. "Can you please leave?"

"Jess," I say. "Please, can we—"

"No. I'm tired," she says, her voice firm. Drenched in dissatisfaction. In disgust.

The house is quiet, hushed, like it's waiting with me. Waiting for more. My pulse ticks out a beat in my neck like my whole body is a giant clock.

But nothing more comes.

The shift from her anger to pure disappointment—the anticlimax of it all—makes me feel even smaller and more horrible, but I know it's exactly what I deserve.

# Chapter 43

On my way home, I wallow in the pain like some sorrowful creature in the night. The lights of houses and storefronts seem to float in space, unmoored. My head and chest hurt from all the nerves and anxiety that have been flooding through me on and off the past few days and culminating so fiercely in my heart and head while I sat still on Jess's couch and took in her repulsed face.

But behind the exhaustion and raw pain, another question forms. Having taken a practice run with Jess, can I let the whole world know?

The thought of it still rocks my being to the core. Nausea gathers in my gut like it's throwing a rally when I think of not just Jess knowing, but the entire world. The revulsion in Jess's face will be duplicated a millionfold—in the endless expressions of people everywhere I go—in the way everyone views me for the rest of my life if I come clean for the CA. Not to mention that I might go to jail.

And yet, and yet . . . I can't deny that small release of pressure I felt coming clean to her.

And if telling her is a starting point, and I feel a modicum of relief, then maybe, just maybe, giving the Confession Artist what they want would not just ensure the safety of everyone I love, but save my life, too.

And maybe, just maybe, make me feel an ounce better in the process.

My driving slows as if my body is getting mucked up and sluggish with the thoughts of confessing. I consciously pick up my speed when I see my phone light up. It's Tim Mooney calling me back.

I pull over into a Town Pump parking lot. With a scratchy voice, he says he got my messages and tells me that he's been following me closely on the news. He expresses his condolences and relays how frightening it is to be targeted like that.

"Are you certain you were the target?"

"I can't say for sure," he says. "I don't know, but I confessed and I'm alive. And no one else turned up murdered. I have a wife and kids. After it became national news, I figured I better not fuck it up."

"So, you put it out there that you felt like a glorified drug peddler and you were sorry for that?"

"Yes." He clears his throat, but his voice still sounds scratchy. "But there are other things. I'm sure you know. You go through everything in your head. I mean, I'm not a perfect guy by any means. We all make mistakes, right?"

"Definitely." *Yes, yes, yes.* It echoes through me but also makes me sick that I'm identifying with this person who I've clearly also judged and condemned for doing something scummy and unadmirable enough to become the CA's target before me. His confession, I recall, was all about consciously and deliberately peddling a fentanyl inhalant to doctors and getting them to prescribe it en masse while slowly upping the dose to get people hooked, all the details I read in his confession after Alderson and Greene filled me in on him and I figured out who he was by searching the Carssen drug representatives on LinkedIn.

"And we have no idea who we piss off in the process. I mean, as a sales rep, I was just trying to do right by my family. But for what it's worth and in a weird way, I feel like I've become a better person these days. I'm not saying the wacko is good or anything like that."

I think of the moniker: the *Confession Artist.* So, okay, it sticks in my craw to say so, but it appears one person's life might have been a little enhanced due to this person's idea of "artistry." The sliver of relief I experienced from telling Jess barrels full circle back to me.

"I understand. But what made you think that it was that one thing and not something else?"

I almost don't want to know the answer. The only reason I'm asking, I tell myself, is that it might provide a clue or some connection to the killer. But also niggling at the back of my mind is the other thought—one I'm barely able to consider because it feels like I'm putting my hand on a hot burner when I do.

I want to know how much he shared because it also helps me figure out just how much *I* should if—and it's still a big *if*—I decide to confess.

*If* I do, I face a felony conviction. Most likely jail time. And if I don't, I could be murdered. I could die. My breathing goes shallow just thinking it. My head aches and pounds right along with my heart.

Luckily, he launches into describing his former sales practices, so he doesn't hear my rapid breathing. He describes throwing the parties, encouraging doctors to prescribe to more than just cancer patients so that they'd broaden their base of users. "I'm not proud of any of it," he says. "Like I said, I sort of fell into the company ethos at the time. But"—he sighs—"I'm well aware that patients got hurt."

I open my car window to let some cool air in, trying to ignore the crucible staring me down. I take a big gulp of it, then ask another question. "Any idea who would've been motivated to go after you?"

"No, the list would be long, right? If you took every doctor involved and went through all their patients, I mean, who knows who could be angry about one of their loved ones getting addicted? About how that affected their lives."

"Do you recall hearing about anyone in particular? Any overdoses?"

"I heard of a few."

"Do you know their names?"

"I'm sorry to say I don't. But I can tell you the regions."

"Please do." These are specifics I can focus on, details I might be able to use. Just holding my pen poised above my notepad calms my breathing a little.

"There were a few in Idaho. Two in Coeur d'Alene, one in Wallace, and some in Montana, too. Two in Missoula, one in Stevensville, some in Arlee—on the reservation. And one that I know of in Ronan, also on the reservation."

"And no one contacted you about these? No one wrote you an angry email or anything or complained to your company?"

"No one emailed me directly, and the company, well, they've gotten thousands and thousands of complaints. I think the FBI is scouring through those to find ones that came from these regions."

Mooney tells me he needs to get going, wishes me luck. But before he gets off, he says, "I haven't seen you confess anything yet. Have I missed something?"

"No, you haven't." Again, a throbbing dizziness grabs hold of my head.

"You probably should, with the little time you have left. I'd hate to read in the news, well . . ."

*An article about my murder.*

"I'm considering it." Saying it out loud does something to me. At first, I'm not sure what, but then I realize that behind the fear, behind the unimaginable shame of exposure, it's the same release I felt with Jess, a slight slackening of the knot in my gut.

"Well, if and when you do, make sure you confess the whole thing, not just the tip of the iceberg." He reaffirms what the agents told me, that he put a half-assed confession out early in the week. But when he felt he was still in danger, he delivered a more extensive version.

The thing Jeremy also knew but shouldn't have.

"I spilled all the slimy details about bribing the doctors and getting them to up dosages on their patients," he says. "And giving my personal motive for acting like such a shit—you know, family pressures, debt. Needing more money and going along with the company ethos. It was the confession you most likely read—a whole two pages long. I poured my heart out. And that's when I also went to the cops, convinced it was me."

"Have you spoken to any reporters about how you got a fright, how you felt you were being stalked?" I already know the answer—if he had, it would be in the news. But there's a slight chance Jeremy's contacted him but hasn't reported on it.

"No, only the authorities. They told me to keep that part quiet. Said it was always good to keep some stuff under wraps when so much national hype was involved. I'm only sharing this with you because, well, you know why . . ."

"Yeah. Because I'm in the same boat you were in not long ago."

I pull back onto the highway and speed up to get home. I need to start investigating Jeremy Fisher more. Much more.

When I get home, it's late. The reporters have all left. The turnoff for my driveway is quiet. Too quiet. Too empty.

No Deputy Zane. Or his car.

I stop, climb out. The quarter moon hangs like ice in the dark sky, tingeing the fields silver.

I turn off my car, listen some more. A wash of dread pours through me. Where's Zane? And if he's not here, what waits for me at my house? An entirely new knot—one made of cold, dark terror—coils around my sternum. I pull my gun from its holster.

I don't have many choices, so I turn my car back on and drive slowly up to my house. My headlights spray across Deputy Zane's unmarked car in my drive, the front door ajar as if he'll be right back.

Crouched in the field, the house is dark.

I get out of my car. "Zane? You here?"

My car's engine ticks. The fields are silent with no scurrying rodents or chirping crickets. Even with the slight moonlight, patches of darkness in my yard seem to fold this way and that. I get out my phone, turn on the weak flashlight.

I call out again. Dread sends every nerve in my body tingling. Why is Zane not here? I look around for him, still scouring the woods for him or anything or anyone lurking in my periphery because I can't help but wonder, is the Confession Artist near?

Have they gotten rid of my protective detail? A new fear spreads like spilled ink in my mind.

This time, a voice drifts out from around the side of my house. "Here."

"Zane?"

I'm sure it's him. The voice is strained, so I run to the side and look around, but don't see him.

"I'm here," he calls again. *Backyard.*

I hurry around to the rear, scan with my light in one hand, my gun in the other. I spot him sitting against my crab apple tree.

He's paler than a ghost and is holding his hand over the apex of his chest above his heart.

"Been shot," he says.

"Oh my God, Zane." I kneel down. A patch of blood blooms outward from under his palm, and every time he inhales, a small sucking sound emanates from under his hand. I start to call for help.

"Already did that," he says, his breath raspy and irregular. And sure enough, before I say anything back, I hear the sirens.

He keeps his hand over the entrance wound, but I know from my training that I need to get pressure on the exit wound if there is one, and most likely there is. I peek at his back to find a larger spot blooming with much more blood. I don't want to set my gun down with the CA stalking me, but I need both hands, so I put my gun in its holster and press my one hand tightly over the hole, feeling the wet blood under my fingertips and how hard he's struggling to breathe. I place my other hand over his to provide a counterpressure and to help keep the pressure strongly on the wound, which, from the sucking sound, must involve one of his lungs.

"Saw a light. In your field," he tells me. "Drove up to—" He squeezes his eyes shut and winces and breaks into a coughing fit.

"Shhh," I tell him. "Don't talk right now. They'll be here any second." My mind races. I try to keep my face calm for Zane, but my eyes dart from him to the woods to the house and back to him.

*You're out there, somewhere? Aren't you? You're out there watching.*

"Saw a guy snooping around your garage," he tells me anyway. "Had a face mask on. I called out. Fired at me." He spits blood that runs down the side of his chin.

"Shhh," I say. "Stay still." I squeeze harder from both sides. "They'll be here any second."

"Shot back but he ran. In there." He lifts his chin to point to the woods beside the house. He scrunches his face up from the pain, clenching his eyes shut again. I look to the woods again, try to stare into the trees like dark-hooded ghosts are weaving in and out among them.

"Andy." I use his first name, trying to get him to really tune in. "Don't talk. Don't move."

His eyes droop at half-mast. He looks like a child, and my world spins. How could this be happening? Fear for him on top of the dread the CA is out there somewhere rushes up inside me. My heart might explode. I cannot bear it if this young man dies or is incapacitated. I do not want to see him, practically a kid, still fresh off the Hutterite farm, pay for my mistakes. My lies. I can barely swallow. I feel useless and responsible.

More than that, I feel menacing, that I'm the culprit of too many awful things. I want to ask him, this innocent, critically injured young, young man, *Zane, Zane, can you do bad, bad things and still be an okay person?*

Of course I can't. I don't. I wait with him, pleading with the universe that he'll be okay while I scan the forest like a stressed animal for any sign of someone, wondering if the killer is out there watching, observing, or if this is Ridgeway's doing and his goons are long gone.

I follow the ambulance to the hospital and stay in the reception area until I finally get some news from Alderson, who's been filled in by a nurse. Deputy Zane, he tells me, is in intensive care with a collapsed lung. The surgeon has inserted a chest tube. He is fortunate the bullet missed major blood vessels.

I slump into a chair in the waiting room, relieved that he's stable but thinking of my impetuousness. I think of how I took that backpack from Ridgeway's shed. Was that why someone was snooping around my garage? Is this all because of Ridgeway?

Either way, all my decisions cause pain.

I don't want to see anyone else get hurt.

I want to keep Jess and Sam safe.

I want to catch whoever killed Clarissa.

I want whoever shot Zane to pay.

And even if I'm simply some copycat's victim, I want to help catch the real CA even after I'm in the clear.

I make up my mind: I'm going to confess, and I'm going to do it thoroughly whether I'm the target of the real CA or someone like Ridgeway copping in on his game. Damn the consequences. It's time I pay the price.

At first, the thoughts just feel like words running in my head, like something I won't actually do. Of course I know, and feel, how awful what I did was. But sometimes I can detach, can be outside myself looking in. Like one part of me—the side that did such an awful thing—is on one side of a window, and the other, larger part who saw myself above such terrible acts—observes that awful part of me through a thick pane of glass. It's the only way to cope.

I feel that now, like I'm watching myself—blurry and unreal—through a window. Observing myself in the waiting area trying to decide how to proceed.

But I tell myself there's only one me, and that me needs to make myself do the right thing, make the words—*I'm going to confess*—real. If not for myself, then for everyone around me.

"You need to bring Lasserio in for questioning," I stress to Alderson and Greene in whispers. "You need to focus on Ridgeway more." I tell them I showed Paxton the video Ray sent me, and he confirmed it was his sister's pack. I don't share with them it's in my trunk at this very moment.

Alderson takes notes. Greene looks at me, wondering what else I'm holding back. "What would they want from your house?" she asks.

"I'm not sure," I lie.

"Okay," she says. "We'll get Lasserio in for questioning. You know, a safe house—"

I stop her with a firm head shake. Not a chance.

"Go home and get some sleep, then. You look exhausted."

"Little tough to sleep these days."

"We'll have someone else posted at your drive, and we'll make sure to have some eyes on the other road, Dillon Road, behind your place where the shooter probably came in from."

I think of how Jeremy hoofed it across that field and feel angry they didn't already post someone there, too. Maybe if they had, Zane wouldn't be in the ICU.

But I know it's easier to be mad at them than to face my own looming guilt list. I force myself to face it and think of the pack in my trunk. Alderson and Greene turn to go.

I stand alone in the center of the hall, watching them walk away. Alderson broad and tall. Greene shorter and lithe. Their steps echo on the bare floor like the fibs pulsing in my mind. These fibs. All these little fibs. And the huge ones, too.

I hear Zane's lung wheezing in my ear.

I need to stop. They're almost to the elevator at the end of the corridor. Two frickin' federal agents trying to help me. And what do I do? I lie to them, even with Zane fighting for his life. Even after I've decided I'll confess. Even when I'm going to have to face major consequences. So what if I add a stolen backpack to the list. How does it make an ounce of sense to keep that one back when I'm going to fess up to the big stuff?

"Wait," I say.

They don't hear me and keep walking.

"Wait," I say louder.

They both turn.

"There's something else."

"What?"

"I have the pack from the video I sent you. Once I get it to a friend of mine at the crime lab, I'll have it confirmed that Clarissa's prints are all over it. Plus, there's a water bottle in it if we need her DNA."

"How do you have the pack?"

"I'd rather not say."

"Jesus, Crosbie. You broke into Lasserio's shed?"

"I knew the chances of you getting a warrant were slim, and even if you got one, he would have taken it by now. I'm guessing he was searching for it at my place and that's how Deputy Zane got shot."

Greene and Alderson share their unspoken partner glance.

"And in the pack," I say, "are dark drafting pencils and a sketchbook with the Ridgeway Ranch watermark on it."

"What does that mean?" Alderson asks.

"Not sure. Paxton isn't sure whether Clarissa drew or not, but he said she might have sketched flowers on her job, but it's weird that the leather has the Ridgeway Ranch watermark on it."

"Where is it now?"

I gesture outside. "In my trunk."

# Chapter 44

At the entry to my drive, I don't bother to ask the new deputy's name. I don't want to know. I'm still feeling too raw over what happened to Zane, but when I grab his number, he gives it to me anyway. Deputy Carter.

By the time I turn my car off in my garage, it's very late. I step outside into my drive and take stock. The cops and forensics have wrapped things up and departed. Police tape still circles my backyard where Zane went down. Crickets have begun chirping in the fields, as if they know Zane is safely tucked away in the ICU.

Still, I can't shake the sense that eyes are on me.

But the sense of being watched, of being paranoid, is logical given my situation. And now, a shooting on my own property. Intensifying everything. Making what has been surreal and bizarre up until this point all too material and devastating.

I continue to scan the area. My house is still and dark. I never even went in. I followed the ambulance straight to the hospital. Now the sliver of the moon that was dimly casting some light has dissipated as it has sunk lower and farther west. Blackness envelops the fields, and tree branches in the forests play tricks on my eyes. The awful sucking sound from Zane's wound stays in my ears.

Perhaps Leon's or Sophie's ghosts are out weaving like wisps among those skinny pines, watching me. Perhaps even Mark Coleman's. And shit, the living—Ridgeway, Lasserio, even the CA . . . ? I shudder. Any one of them could be out there right now watching me, hunting me.

I tell myself I need to get to bed, force myself to get some sleep so I can be alert these last days. The home stretch. But as I turn to go in, a snap of a twig breaks through the night. I whip out my gun and freeze, waiting.

I've been here before. It could be anything: deer, elk, mountain lion, fox, coyote . . .

I stand still, my eyes and ears straining to see or hear something moving.

Then another sound. A crunch of underbrush.

I lean forward, toward the woods, but everything goes still again. I continue to scan the forest, my gun ready, elbow cocked. Darkness seems to separate and fold, my eyes straining to make out what's between the dense trees. Suddenly, a faint ping rings out. But barely.

A phone, a notification coming through? Or am I overstressed and overtired? Overwired?

I keep scanning, trying to spot some kind of light from a device or any movement at all. I stay perfectly still, like I'm having a standoff with the night, with the trees, with ghosts, with even the looming, dark, ridged mountains.

Then, more rustling, something fleeing, scuffling through the underbrush, bashing through branches.

Adrenaline courses through me as I run closer to the edge of the forest. My pulse pounds in my ears. I search for the white tail of a deer, listen for the pounding of hooves. I see or hear neither, but that doesn't mean it wasn't one. But it sounded bigger, like a human or even a bear.

And the ping? Did I imagine it?

I call the new guy, Deputy Carter, they've posted out front and ask him to call the guy they've finally posted out back by Dillon Road and tell him to have that deputy patrol the area, to search for any cars parked on the outskirts of the forest or any of the surrounding roads or driveways, especially on Dillon Road where Jeremy walked in from.

Then I grab my Maglite from my car and slowly walk across my yard, into the woods toward the place I heard the sound. The light bounces off the ground, off the branches and bramble, off the trees and their boughs. Game trails thread through the forest floor. Deer and elk pellets scatter about here and there. Off the edges of the beam, darkness pools around me, but I see nothing unusual.

The late-night cold is sharp edged. Autumn nestling in more forcefully. I feel impossibly small, a speck among the fields and before the dark mountains.

I've decided there's not much more I can do when my light catches something white, something caught up in the spindly branches of a small gooseberry bush.

I walk over and inspect. It's a tissue. A simple piece of trash. It could have come from anywhere, but it looks intact, fresh and white, recent. One of the cops searching the place after the shooting could have dropped it.

I go back, grab some gloves and a Ziploc to bag and tag it.

# Chapter 45

## Lauren

It had been a slow afternoon at the restaurant where Lauren worked. Ironically, it was a Mexican restaurant smack-dab in the middle of the sovereign nation of the Confederated Salish and Kootenai Tribes in Arlee, Montana.

The tourists stopping in had long ago quit noticing or caring that she was a Native woman running tacos, burritos, and chimichangas out to the lacquered wooden tables. She had turned off the sound system, closed the place down early so she could head home after the lunch shift. On the front door, she hung the sign her husband, Marco, had made for her. It read: CLOSED FOR THE EVENING. GONE TO SEE THE WARRIORS PLAY. GO WARRIORS!

She thought of the person who'd come into the restaurant earlier, someone Lauren had seen before at her Tuesday night grief group in town and now more regularly in the restaurant.

When the restaurant was slow, the two talked about a lot of things, including how the rehab facility several miles up the road wasn't quite working. It made Lauren feel a little better. After all, it cost too much for most tribal members to use the place, so it had become a haven for the privileged. They also talked about what happened to Lauren's daughter, Nalia, and the idea that Lauren should find a way to expose the injustice nationally.

That nothing would fully alleviate Lauren's pain, but *doing* one small thing might help a little.

A gale tore at her as she crossed the parking lot. She put her head down and charged forward, navigating through slushy puddles of ice and snow. In her car, Lauren turned the musty heater on and sat for a bit to warm the engine up before driving.

When she did, it only took five blocks to exit Arlee, a town where about half the residents were Salish. It's the place her people came after they were pushed out of the Bitterroot in the nineteenth century. With the grocery store and coffee shop and art gallery behind her, she passed trailers and small houses before the landscape unfurled to fields swollen with ice and snow.

Lauren sighed, trying to switch some toggle inside herself to turn on the joy and anticipation everyone else would be fat with come game time. She tried to transform her anger to eager excitement for her son's sake. And for her husband's, too. She knew when she got home her husband, Marco, would already be wearing his red T-shirt with the Salish phrase for "Proud to be a Warrior Parent" scrawled across the chest. Pinned next to that would be a button showing their son, Wade, wearing his jersey and a wide smile.

She *was* proud, too. She really was.

Wade was one of the best players on the team. And on the rez, Indian ball was everything. Basketball gave the town hope. It gave *Marco* hope. The gymnasium was the number one gathering spot for the community, a place where the old could honor the young and where the young gave back and made people happy—something the tribe felt was the greatest gift you could give.

Plus, playing basketball was a ticket out for some of them. It could be for Wade, too.

Marco was hanging his dreams on it, that Wade would get a scholarship to the University of Montana or to another state school.

Lauren wasn't as hopeful. She knew Marco always said that a Native kid had one shot and one shot only at most of the state schools. Some of the recruiters even asked beforehand if the player was Native or not because once in college, so many struggled without the support of their community and would drop out.

So Lauren was conflicted. She didn't need the only child they had left to get alienated from them in white-bread college life and descend into alcohol abuse like far too many other famous Native American players had. Or worse, start taking those little light-blue pills that were designed to look like a prescription, like OxyContin.

But mainly, the reason she couldn't get excited boiled down to the damn anger. She wanted to rise above her conflicted feelings and be brimming with joy for Wade, but she couldn't get there because of this seething rage that never seemed to leave her.

Lauren's aunt Darla always used to say that Lauren had inherited her optimism, but it had left now, blown out like a rubber tire on the highway.

It had been four years, and nothing was going to change the fact that her firstborn was still gone.

Five years ago, prior to all the pills that were flooding the reservation now, Tim Mooney had rolled into Ronan and basically bribed Dr. Winnipeg into prescribing the deadly inhalant version of the drug and upping the dose so he could get more money from his company.

She knew this because Abigail Winter, Winnipeg's PA, had told Terry, Lauren's dishwasher at the restaurant. She told him about all the parties, about the process of titrating—of upping the dose even when the patient didn't need it to be increased. About all the wining and dining in Missoula at fake educational seminars on this powerful inhalant containing fentanyl, an opioid up to a hundred times stronger than morphine, which Winnipeg had prescribed Lauren and Marco's Nalia for neck pain after her car accident.

Lord knows how many patients he got so addicted that, when the feds finally cracked down and he quit prescribing, the patients turned to the cheap street drugs to fuel the habit he'd cultivated in them.

Three years later, after Nalia had turned to the street stuff and Lauren caught on to her addiction, Lauren desperately searched for local resources with Indian Health Service to treat her and found hardly any options. No surprise there, given their meager funding.

The day before Nalia passed, Nalia told Lauren that her boyfriend, Dakota, had proposed to her. They'd both cried, and Lauren didn't want to ruin the moment by asking if she was ready for such a thing when Lauren suspected she was still using.

Later, when she got up the courage to ask and Nalia said she'd stopped months before, Lauren was skeptical. But that night, Lauren dreamed of her daughter's wedding, dreamed she was making meat stew and fry bread for the guests.

The next morning, she found their daughter face down on the floor, no longer breathing. Lauren screamed and called the ambulance, but Nalia was long gone when they arrived.

Some days were worse than others. On the days it was bad, Marco would keep telling her that she needed to let it go or it was going to make her sick. She thought of the visitor again, with the terse smile and aching but penetrating eyes. How they mentioned that if Lauren did find a way to expose it nationally, she should expose the enablers, too, while she was at it . . . the ones on the sidelines who never are held accountable. *All the enablers in all their slithery forms need to gain some serious self-awareness. Everyone out there ready to avoid being burdened, ready to pretend they're not complicit. It could go all the way down the line to the ladies at church, but starting with the ones right by their sides is a beginning.*

Lauren agreed. She had pictured a bunch of intertwined rattlers vibrating their tails on a hot day, like in the den she'd come across on the Bison Range north of Arlee when she was a kid. It struck a chord with her because Tim Mooney was a sideliner and she had a special cache of rage stored up for him, almost more than she had for Dr. Winnipeg.

She tried different things to quell her fury. She took long walks. She joined in on community jump dances. She meditated. And she worked harder, scrubbing the fryer longer and more vigorously until she got tendonitis in her elbow. Nothing worked.

Lauren got involved with Trisha, the tribal police investigator she met when Nalia passed, to help distribute flyers. After the tribal council created a task force to respond to the opioid crisis, Trisha took the lead and began to hold seminars to educate the public on how to give naloxone, since more and more fentanyl was taking root on the reservations. Hopefully people could at least help their loved ones if they found them unresponsive, like she'd found her own daughter.

This was a good thing, but it didn't take the rage away.

The wrath was like a flock of birds. Sometimes it flew in unison and made precise patterns against the bloodred clouds, and sometimes it scattered everywhere in messy, senseless swirls. Today, it flew in concert, the birds spiraling and swooping together and darting forward with a mission, with a new plan against the gray, cold sky.

She wanted to share the idea with Marco, even if he would be distracted as he got ready to leave for the game.

As she drove by more pastures with cattle, she saw a flock of chickadees depart from a snow-covered swale. She kept her eye on them. They rose and turned together in a tight arrangement, dissolving against the dark ridge behind them.

The road curved through more ranchland until eventually she reached their own place, a one-story ranch-style home that hunkered below a timbered ridge rising east of town. The Jocko River flowed through their land.

Marco's truck sat outside. She parked and got out and filled her lungs with the February air. When she shut her door, another flock of birds—this one huns—dispatched from a hedgerow of tall grass sticking out from the snow off to the side. They darted out at an angle. Lauren watched the flurry of cinnamon-colored, whirring wings and admired how they also all rose of one accord.

An omen, she thought.

Marco was sitting in his lounge chair, chatting on his phone. She'd been wrong: He wasn't in his red T-shirt yet.

She presumed he was talking to Arlen Whitewolf, who he always spoke to before the games. Arlen's son was on the team, too. They were discussing one of the players on the Loyola-Sacred Heart team the guys would be playing, someone named Edison Woodward who was known for his speed and a pull-up jump shot that was difficult to guard.

"That's okay," Marco said. "Wade's faster. No one's gonna read his moves. Trust me, they're gonna pull it off. Our boys don't play selfishly like them white boys. Or so boring." He laughed and winked at Lauren. "This Woodward, he's obviously their star, but our boys'll be on him."

She gave Marco a kiss on the head, went into the kitchen, put the go-box in the fridge, and made some tea. She sat at the kitchen table while she waited on the kettle.

After he hung up, he came in and asked how work was. She said it was a little slow, which was good since she had closed shop early.

He opened the fridge, fished out the container she'd brought him, and looked inside. "Thanks for this," he said, but only closed the lid and put it back into the fridge.

"Tired of enchiladas?"

"No," he said. "Too jittery to eat. They *have* to win this one."

"They will," she said. "Like you told Arlen."

He smiled.

"I was thinking," Lauren said with some trepidation. "About that drug rep that Terry told me about. About how he bribed Nalia's doctor. I was thinking—"

"Lauren." His lips formed a tight line. "Do you have to do this now?"

She swallowed hard. "I guess not. It's only something that popped into my mind when I was doing research on the web last night."

"How many times have I told you to quit going down that rabbit hole? The internet is *not* going to help you. It's going to make you more upset than you already are." He leaned a hip against the counter and crossed his arms. "We need to focus on Wade. How many times I gotta tell you? Native kids got one shot. We need to support him, not dwell in the past."

Lauren looked down at her hands, one squeezed into a tight fist, the other wrapping around it so Wade couldn't see how white its knuckles were.

Marco dropped his arms and held his hands out to his sides. "Survive the past. Survive the present, Lauren."

She was so sick of that saying she could pull out her hair by the roots. It was what everyone had said to her since she was small, partly a reference to intergenerational trauma from colonialization, when the white men forced all their youth into the Catholic schools back in the early 1900s. Back when they told them that the devil was in all of them. But also a reference to all the alcohol, drugs, and suicide so many tribal members dealt with presently, which was, of course, obviously related to all the brutality, policies, and racism that followed colonialization.

Of course, that was all absolutely true and important, but *survive the past, survive the present* sounded so fatalistic to her. Like her people were just trees, with no choice ever but to face into the storm.

"But," Lauren said, "I'm not sure all this focus on basketball is the best thing for Wade. What if he doesn't do well in college? What if he drops out like that Crow player did? What if he gets depressed and turns to—"

"He won't. And there's no guarantee he won't turn to worse things here on the rez." He doesn't need to say, *Like Nalia did.* That's already in every breath, every word, every breeze, every drop of water, every object on their land and in their home and headspace. “If he goes to college, at least he’s tried. You want that, don’t you?”

“Yes, but I don’t want him to get lost.”

“Lauren, it ain’t a perfect world. World used to have endless buffalo, but sure don’t now.”

“I know it doesn’t.” She could scream. She didn’t want to think about buffalo or basketball. It was avenging Nalia’s death she wanted to talk about. Why didn’t Marco feel the same way? Why wasn’t he as angry as she was? “But surely, there’s something we can still do to—”

“To what? Get justice? Bring enlightenment to folks who ain’t never gonna get enlightened? Where you even going to start to focus? Whole system’s broken. You’d have to go way, way back to right any wrongs. You’d have to take such a long view, it’d make no sense. None of it.”

Lauren fell quiet.

“Lauren.” Marco’s voice had grown gentle. Tears might well up in Lauren’s eyes on a different day just hearing the kind shift of it. But now, she was smoldering with rage, so she had no trouble damming the deluge of aching sorrow. “So many of us have lost children.”

She knew he was referring to the cluster of suicides two winters ago. More than a “cluster.” Twenty-one. So horrific. So many brokenhearted parents and families.

“And now,” he said. “All these overdoses. Why don’t you still go to the grief group on Tuesday nights? That’s what so many of the other parents are doing.” He picked up his phone and checked the time. Brushing her off again. He was right, though. It was probably getting close to leaving time if they were going to get decent seats in the gym. He needed to go get his shirt and pin on.

“It wasn’t helping.” Lauren answered his question anyway.

“What?”

“The group. It wasn’t helping.”

“Maybe give it another try?”

She looked down at her hands again, squeezed her hidden fist so tightly she could feel her nails biting into her flesh. There was no use in explaining any of her ideas to him. She could tell his mind was on the gym. He could probably already feel the pulse of the crowds in the bleachers, hear the honor song of the drums for the seniors, see the red Flathead Nation flag on the brick wall with its crossbow, white feathers, and tepee. What was she thinking, bringing this up now?

Yeah, he was right. She didn't need his approval, anyway. It was one tiny thing she could try, and like he said, things were worth attempting. It wasn't like she was moving mountains. She was simply going to find out a little more about this exposure idea.

And the birds. They were flying in unison today.

# A CONFESSION

Instagram: @Simone.Murray3—I worked at an assisted living facility in Strongsville, OH. I didn't mean to let this one old woman lay there in her own urine until she got bedsores. I couldn't deal with her moaning. Her daughter used to get so angry at the facility. At me. One bad night, I didn't check on her at all, and when her daughter came to visit the next a.m., I finally went in. She had passed. I would like to apologize to the family that I didn't help more, that I wasn't kinder. I should never have taken a job in this facility. I'm not cut out for that kind of work. I really am a compassionate person. Let me know if this is enough, please! I don't know what you want!

# Chapter 46

***Last Day***

All-too-lucid dreams plague me during my restless few hours of sleep.

The boa Sophie described to me that night out in the woods pursues me, burrowing through a hole in my mattress, spooling its long, thick muscles around me. I'm paralyzed, unable to breathe or move.

Something trills in the distance. I want to shake loose and get to it, but I can't. The snake has me pinned. The sound sharpens, closer to my head. The reptile hisses in my ear, prepares to swallow me whole. Finally, through whatever magic the chime possesses, the serpent pops free.

I look frantically around. I'm in my bedroom. The ceiling fan comes into focus. The ring occurs beside me.

"Did I wake you?" Alderson asks.

"Yes," I say, rubbing my eyes, still thick with sleep.

My thoughts rush to wounded Zane. Andy. Just a kid. Andy Zane. I look at my hands to see if there's still blood.

"Can you come to the station?"

I squint at the time. It's seven. I've slept three hours. Still wired after coming home from the hospital, I searched online. I found the apartment where Vivian Petronis lives between Kalispell and Whitefish. My plan is to find her today. My eyes sting with exhaustion.

"Why?"

"Remember the guy we told you about who registered a ton of activity tracking you here locally?"

"Sure."

"We looked into his followers."

"And?"

"One guy who commented on a number of the guy's posts has a bunch of photos of himself on social media, and he has a tattoo of an upside-down *R* on his forearm. His name?"

"Yeah?"

"Aaron Lasserio."

At the county building in Kalispell, I sign my name at reception, step through the metal detector, and collect my bag on the other side. Greene greets me with her usual serious expression. She should give lessons in inscrutability to an aloof cat.

"Follow me," she says.

She takes me to a room I know well. It's got a table and two chairs and a small window. I take a seat. It's a spare room, not an interrogation room per se, used for various tasks like looking through mug shots or taking complaints.

After I give her the tissue I found in the woods and tell her about the ping I *thought* I heard, Greene says, "We'll check it out. Now, I want to show you some photos. Specifically, Lasserio. To confirm he's the guy you've been surveilling." She sits and pulls an eight-by-ten photo out of a file. "Is that him?"

"Without question."

I stare at his round head topped with unruly hair and protruding ears. The image of Zane slumped under my tree won't leave my head. The awful sounds from his lungs play like an earworm in my head.

"You aware he's got a record?"

"Yeah, arrested three years ago for aggravated assault."

Montana law draws a distinction. *Aggravated assault* is serious bodily injury with a weapon. *Assault* is bodily injury without one.

"Beat up some poor Indigenous guy, a Blackfeet man, in a bar over in Cutbank with a pool stick," Greene says.

*Palmer Edmonds,* I think.

Greene adds, "Lasserio used to work for the Crazy R Ranch, and we think he's still got connections to your man Robbie Ridgeway in Choteau and Dupuyer."

"What about the local guy who was posting from the library—the one whose social media accounts Lasserio was chatting up—and the others with the suspicious activity?"

"No real leads," she says. "So far, they all check out and have alibis."

"So now what?"

"Alderson and I are about to speak to Lasserio. If there's anything else you haven't told us, now would be a good time."

She's irritated with me for breaking into the shed, as she should be, but she's not bringing it up this morning. Good. I know there are complications with using illegally obtained evidence in an interrogation.

"Feel free to use the video I took if it helps pressure him."

As evidence, the video is fair game. I remind her about the flag stitched on the flap, which ties it to Clarissa. "You need to find out if he's working for Ridgeway," I say. "Doing his dirty work. Can I observe?"

"We knew you would ask, but no."

"Listen, I've been in that room many times before," I say. "It's not a big deal if you let me observe. I'll stay out of your hair and might pick up on something that's useful."

She leans back in her chair, her jaw tight. Her stare blades right through me. "Go grab some breakfast close by. I'll talk to Alderson about it, and we'll get back to you."

I'm not hungry, but I buy a bagel and coffee at the café anyway because I've hardly eaten much of anything in days. I keep my head down with Jess's hat low the whole way.

I'm worried sick about Zane.

From my car, I call the hospital to inquire on him. I'm not family, so I don't get anywhere. Even in a small town, HIPAA is a bitch. I hang up and wait. My Americano tastes as bitter as I feel.

I look in the rearview and see my own cheekbones, now sharp as blades. My sleep-hungry eyes are dark, round coins. Haunted. My hair is a tangly mess. I want to either laugh maniacally at or cry for the fool who thought she would never pay a price for joining the messed-up funny farm of police who protect their own. At any cost. How do you take an oath that you will discharge your duties as a cop "with fidelity, honesty, with commitment to serve and protect . . . I do solemnly swear" and turn your back on that promise the second it benefits your personal agenda?

Wallace called me twice while I was meeting with Greene, wanting to know what I'm going to do. I'm too preoccupied to call him back. Wallace ends his last message with a tinge of irritation: *Okay. If you don't want to talk to me, that's fine, but I will see you soon.* I can't tell if it sounds like a threat or an olive branch.

*I will see you soon.* Is the *soon* loaded? A chill shoots up my spine. Then it makes me grind my teeth.

Jeremy? Wallace? My head spins with all the lack of trust.

But what *am* I going to do now that this Ridgeway thing has some legs? I had decided I was going to confess, but that will lead to a waterfall of shame and consequences.

And if this is a copycat situation, I won't have to face the nation, face all the consequences. I can keep chugging along, trying to grow my business. Do my best to make things right with my sister. Keep it between me and Jess, where it belongs.

The thought brings a huge dose of relief. That it could all be okay after all. A thrill shoots through me at the notion that, poof, it could all just go away. That perhaps the real CA has decided to no longer strike, and that Greene and Alderson will nail Clarissa's murderer, this copycat, all in one swoop.

Something murky and toxic roils inside me. If I survive this, how long can I live this way? With these corrosive secrets? Is it enough for only Jess to know them? Can I go back to life as it was?

And still, even as I feel this churn—like I'm filling up with candies that have too much saccharin and leave you feeling gross and unsatisfied—I still want to get out of confessing desperately. For me. For Jess. Coming clean, like Mooney said, involves doing it thoroughly, with all the reasons and rationalizations, good, bad, and otherwise. And Jess doesn't want her personal life out there. It's the very reason she didn't report the rape.

It's been twenty-five minutes, which is nothing in cop-interrogation time. It takes longer than you'd expect to get someone in a room, settled and chatting.

I'm impatient. I hop out and walk to the front entrance, coffee in hand. I pace by the door, thinking it over, feeling like a kid shut out of an adult dinner party. I want to talk my way into the wing where the observation room is located, but my lack of a security badge means I'm nobody.

I spot Ewing walking up the sidewalk. *Ugh.* Besides the killer coming up behind me with an axe, Ewing's the last person on earth I want to see right now.

He hoists a stiff, fakey-fake smile into place. "Mitchell."

"Ewing."

"What brings you in here? Are you okay?"

He almost looks concerned. I want to laugh. "I'm fine."

"Everything okay with the, uh"—he clears his throat—"situation you're in?"

"Everything's fine."

"I hear some guy involved in one of your PI gigs is getting questioned." He motions toward the glass doors.

I know word travels fast but remind myself to talk to Alderson and Greene about running a tighter ship.

"Is that why you're here?"

"I've got some other business to take care of," he says. "But you know we always offer to help the FBI out. Teamwork. Right?"

I don't answer. *More like spying.*

"Guess you weren't big on the whole teamwork thing, though," Ewing says.

"Excuse me?"

I heard him clearly. But I'm surprised he's gone there. Then again, not: He never had a problem saying what was on his mind, even if it made him a rude jackass.

He stares at me. Studies me. "Have you been eating?"

"Yeah," I say, and think of the uneaten bagel sitting in the car.

His lips pull together softly and his head lists to the side, as if something in him shifts. His hard gaze relaxes.

Is it pity? I dislike it more than his judging stare.

"Look," he says. "I'm sorry. I'm sure this is a bitch of a week for you. I was sorry to see you get identified in the media."

Again, I don't answer. Why is it I can never think of any decent comebacks around this man?

And because I don't answer, he continues. "I am sorry." He looks at his watch, which must have the date on it. His fingers tick up in order, one to five. "Your last day, right? And you haven't confessed anything. Are you going to?" His eyes drill into mine. Is it curiosity or is there that same old warning in them? I can't tell.

"Not sure." I take another sip of my coffee. "Probably not." I haven't fully come to a decision on this, but it's not for Ewing to know what I'm thinking. I'd rather have him think I have nothing specific on my mind *to* confess.

"Gutsy. Hopefully this is the guy. Wouldn't that be something? Catching the Confession Artist out here in little ol' Kalispell, Montana? Or more likely, you being targeted by some copycat. No less someone involved in your own work." He grimaces. "Hell, you never even being the *real* target of the actual Confession Artist, now there's a story."

I give him back a smarmy smile like I, too, think it's all worth a laugh. Ha ha, joke's on me: Crosbie Mitchell's not even worthy of the *real* CA.

Does he have any idea what a relief that would be?

"What are you doing out here? Aren't you going to watch this guy get interrogated?"

"You've forgotten. I don't have clearance anymore without my badge."

"Ahh," he says. "Well, you're in luck." He flashes his. "Follow me."

*What the hell?* I have no idea why Ewing would be going out of his way for me. Is this my reward for backing the blue with Railes? If so, I feel even worse. I want to shake the slimy feeling suddenly clinging to me like a coat of acid, corroding away at me second by second.

But also, I'm reading something else in him.

Something sincere, like there's an ounce of his conscience bubbling up. An ounce of generosity. Perhaps regret?

Either way, I'm happy to swoop up the break.

He shows his badge to the palace guard and says, "She's with me."

I follow him into the elevator and walk beside him down several halls to the observation room. Ewing knocks on the door.

Alderson opens it, and I'm glad it's him and not Greene, who's told me to stay away.

"I see you've enlisted local help," Alderson says when he sees me standing behind Ewing. "Persistent, aren't you?"

"That she is," Ewing says.

"Is Greene in there with him now," I ask, "or are you still letting him stew?"

"Greene's with him now."

"Can we come in?" I say.

"No, you can't."

"Why? I'm the target here."

"She has a point," Ewing adds.

Alderson rolls his eyes but doesn't shoo me away. "Wait here a sec," he says, and shuts the door.

I lean back against the cool hallway wall and look at Ewing. "Why are you helping me?"

"Because I feel like it. Because no one should be in the situation you've been in this week." There's a sincerity in his voice. It dawns on me that, maybe—just maybe—he's got some guilt of his own to work through.

But I also want to say, *No one should be in the situation I was in with Hartley and all the harassment at work.* I eat my words, though. Getting into an argument after his generous favor here makes zero sense.

"I'll leave you to it," Ewing says. And walks off.

Alderson reopens the door. "Where's what's his name?"

"Just left. What's going on?"

He holds the door to the observation room open and I step in. I immediately look through the one-way. Greene is with Lasserio, staring him down, apparently waiting for an answer to something she's asked.

"Have you gotten anywhere with him yet?" I say.

"Yes, quite a bit," Alderson says. "When we showed him the video of his arm grabbing the marker and told him we knew it was his tattoo, he came clean on a few things." Alderson fills me in on what they've learned: that Ridgeway had hired Lasserio to keep an eye on me when Ridgeway learned I was investigating Clarissa's death. When he realized I was a dead ringer for the sketch, he seized the opportunity to keep me freaked out and distracted.

"When we showed him the video at the storage unit," Alderson says, "he said he knew you were tracking him. So he called his brother, Sawyer Lasserio, to come and scare you. When you didn't look sufficiently frightened out at the dump site, they both went by your house intending to try something there but ran into all the reporters. That's when he and Sawyer changed tack and decided to go after your sister."

Seeing the baffled *that is completely bonkers* expression on my face, Alderson laughs.

I'd like to return the laugh, but everything inside me goes cold. If they simply realized I looked like the sketch and then acted, that means the real CA is after me.

But Lasserio could be lying. It still could be them who put the sketch out.

"None of it was very bright or logical," Alderson says. "When we asked Lasserio why they didn't simply let the six days play out instead of getting involved, you won't believe what he said."

"What?"

"That he wanted to take the opportunity to prove to his boss that he was worth more than Ridgeway gave him credit for."

I shake my head at the stupidity. "What's he not saying, though?" I'm still clinging to the idea that he and Ridgeway put the sketch out.

"A lot. Have a listen for yourself." He waves to the interrogation room. "She's hit a brick wall asking him about last night."

"If he shot Deputy Zane, he's in for a whole lot more than trouble around damaging private property."

"Running errands. Getting groceries and gas," Lasserio says to Greene from behind the glass.

"Your girlfriend says she doesn't know where you were last night, that you weren't home with her, so let me repeat, where were you?"

"And let me repeat . . . gas, groceries."

"Are you sure about that?" Greene asks. "Because we were at your place. It didn't look to us like any new groceries were bought recently."

"It's stuff you wouldn't notice. Soap and stuff."

"You have a receipt or two?"

"I don't keep receipts. I used cash."

"Which stores did you go to?"

He goes silent.

"So," Greene says. "You have no alibi for yesterday evening around the time a deputy was shot at Crosbie Mitchell's house?"

"Don't know nothin' 'bout that." Lasserio folds his arms over his chest.

"All right. Let's change gears. The other video? Tell us about the backpack you were bringing out of your storage shed. Whose pack was it?"

"Mine," he says.

"What was in it?"

"Tools."

"Hmm." Greene exaggerates looking perplexed. "That's strange, because we have reason to believe the pack belonged to Clarissa Haynes, the reporter."

"It's mine."

"Where did you get it?"

"Don't remember."

"What was in it?"

"Told you. Tools. Screwdrivers, measuring tape, and stuff."

Greene goes around and around with him until she says, "Let's take a break, shall we."

She stands and exits, leaving Lasserio to stare at the blank, white cinder block walls.

Tension clenches in my guts. I want to confront him about the pack to the point of bursting. But I don't let it out. I keep my calm.

# Chapter 47

When Greene enters, she sees me and says, "Of course you're here. Why am I not surprised."

"When you go back in, tell him you *know* it's Clarissa's. That her prints are all over it. I know this is just a start, a foothold, and maybe only solves Clarissa's murder, but if we can gain some traction with the murder and take down Ridgeway, maybe we can figure out if this has all been set in motion to simply copy the CA." I realize I'm speaking too fast, the tension curled inside me unspooling in any way it can.

"Whoa," Greene says. "You broke into Ridgeway's shed, and now you want us to stick our necks on the line while interrogating him, making illegally obtained evidence part of the record?"

"Yes," I say, relieved that Greene is finally stating it out loud instead of giving me the eye. "You can blame it on me, say I dropped the pack on your doorstep, but we need to find out why they had it in the first place, and we need to find out why there was a damn sketchbook with the ranch logo on it and sketching pencils in the pack."

Greene looks to Alderson. He gives her a curt nod. "We do need to understand their role in all this. If these guys put out the sketch of Crosbie, we are wasting our time in trying to find the real CA."

"Okay, but." Greene turns to me before storming out. "For the record, I'm not worried about getting in trouble. I'm worried about not being able to get a DA interested in looking into these possible murderers, because the evidence was obtained illegally."

It should sting, but I'm too numb to even feel it.

◆ ◆ ◆

"Let's cut the crap," Greene tells Lasserio. Round two. "We've verified that the backpack is Clarissa Haynes's."

He stares wide-eyed, so I can tell he's a little taken off guard.

"You need to tell us how is it that you have her backpack, and you need to tell us now." Her voice is stern and means business—probably fueled by her anger at me—but Lasserio doesn't know that. He sits up taller like a schoolboy being reprimanded. He squirms in his seat and looks to the wall.

"Found it," he says.

*Change of story . . .*

"Where?"

He pauses before he speaks. Formulating the next fib. "Some bar."

"Some bar?"

"Yeah, in Choteau. She must have left it behind."

"Before you keep lying to us," Greene says. "You need to know that we will check out every word you say, and all of these lies *will* be used against you."

He stews, fidgets in his seat. Says, "Okay. On Ridgeway's property. I found it on the ranch. Not far from the area she was interested in, by that swampy part. She must have left it there when she was snooping around. It's not our fault she left her pack on property she was trespassing on."

"When? When did you find it?"

"I don't remember the date. Earlier this summer."

"What about the sketchbook inside the pack?" Greene asks.

"No idea."

"Why does it have the ranch watermark on it?"

He smiles. "She probably swiped it from Ridgeway. Little thief."

"Bullshit." My anger launches me to my feet. "After he killed her at the river," I say, wishing my voice were loud enough to pierce the soundproof room, "he took it. Then, like a dumbass, he put it in his shed. But when I came snooping around and asking questions, Ridgeway told him to get rid of it, so he went to pick it up but got nervous to be spotted with it when the other car pulled in."

"Probably, but we can't prove that. It's all speculation on your part," says Alderson.

I stop pacing and refocus on Greene. She says, "What was the sketchbook being used for? Did you or Ridgeway use it to draw Crosbie Mitchell's face?"

Lasserio thinks before flashing a wicked grin. "What makes the stupid bitch think she'd get on some national killer's hit list anyway? She think she's that important?"

They hate me enough to do it, but *did* they? Did they draw me and have the smarts to put it on the web without the FBI being able to trace them? I have a sinking feeling that they didn't, that the real CA is out there. The one who drew my face, my earrings.

"Does that mean you're admitting that you guys copied the killer—that you and Ridgeway put out the sketch yourselves?"

He continues to smile slyly. "I think I'm done talking now. Don't I get a phone call?"

# Chapter 48

The *stupid bitch* isn't unhappy, but she's nowhere near relieved, either.

This might all stem from Ridgeway and his men and not from the real McCoy CA, which would be a huge relief, but there's still no way to know for certain. A wicked grin and a call to an attorney is no proof of anything.

Alderson and Greene tell me that Lasserio has alibis for both of the CA's first two killings, that they are still doing a thorough analysis of those claims. They feel confident that Lasserio is telling the truth based on what they know already about his whereabouts on the key dates, but all this means is that they're not the original CA. It doesn't prove they didn't copy the CA to scare me, to get away with murdering me and pinning it on the original.

My hands are bundled in tight fists as I listen. My shoulders taut. I hadn't realized how much I've been clinging to the idea that my sketch came from Lasserio and Ridgeway.

Because it lets me off the hook.

But still, it doesn't make complete sense. "What about the earrings?" I ask. "How could Ridgeway know about them? I only began working on this case this summer, and Fiona has had my earrings since the winter."

"We found it on Fiona's husband's Instagram account," says Alderson. "What's his name? Trey?"

"Yes."

"It was the same photo Fiona sold to the press. Of you at the banquet."

"I searched my name's images and nothing under Trey came up."

"Different search engines produce varying results," Alderson says. "Some turn up more options."

I'm angry at myself for not checking more closely, but I exhale a sigh of relief. It could still be Ridgeway. "I searched Fiona's and other friends' accounts but didn't check on Trey's. I didn't know he had one." I pick up my phone.

"Don't bother," Alderson says. "He's deleted it since, but it was a photo of you and Fiona holding up champagne flutes, your earrings sparkling. The press could have found it themselves with a more thorough search. And Ridgeway certainly could have, too."

Could it really be this simple? That Ridgeway found the photo online? That I won't have to confess? That the real CA isn't after me and it's just Ridgeway fucking with me?

If so, then why is my chest tightening like it's in a car crusher? I've been moving closer and closer to the idea that I not only *need* to unburden my conscience, but that I almost *want* to, like it's this looming, unbearably steep ridgeline that I must climb.

If it's Ridgeway and not the CA, I could simply turn back now. My mind seesaws back and forth.

Not confessing at all no longer feels right. But fessing up hurts Jess. And lands me in jail.

I close my eyes, and when I open them, Alderson is watching me. "What?" he asks.

"Nothing." But it *is* something. The waffling subsides. A strong urge takes its place, hitting me square on, right in the middle of the county building in the interrogation room where I endured a follow-up inquiry about Coleman and Railes, where it all really began to go sour for me.

I need to come clean, even if I am only the target of a couple of idiotic copycats. I can't go on living a lie, despite the consequences.

The possibility of going to jail sends my heart right to my throat, but it's dawning on me that I might not have a choice in the matter if I'm to have any kind of a shot at a quality existence, or even a life at all if Ridgeway and Lasserio are not responsible for this and the CA is still after me. What would life be like for Jess and Sam without me around? Would it be better? Would it be worse for Sam if Jess falls deeper into depression with me no longer there to pick up the pieces?

It all breaks my heart in two, but it's my last day. I have to quit wavering and make a choice. I need to hold strong. I decide none of it should alter my plan to confess. I commit myself to following through no matter how much I'm tempted to weasel out of it . . .

Alderson tells me that they plan on having Greene stay the night at my house and upping the manpower to four deputies around my place instead of two, to be on the safe side. They tell me this is not a discussion, and I tell him that I'm more than happy for the extra security, still keenly aware of what happened to Deputy Zane.

Alderson looks at me with wide puppy eyes, wanting me to say something more, but he won't ask if I'm going to confess. I know he won't. He's too respectful of my situation. He and Greene both.

I drive south on Main Street to Vivian's address. When I find her apartment, I knock but she doesn't answer. Same response when I try to roust a neighbor. I leave my card under Vivian's door and write a note, asking her to call me.

On my way through town heading north, I pass the police station. I realize I never thanked Ewing for getting me through security earlier. I can hardly believe it, but a part of me feels bad. Is it possible I've been too hard on him? Maybe the backlash he helped deliver was reflexive loyalty to an old friend he'd worked with for years.

It doesn't make it right, but the fact is he demonstrated civility. I throw my blinker on, turn right, and park on the side street. If it proves to be another ill-fated impulsive decision, at least I'll be making it with good intentions. For a change.

Allison is at the reception desk. "Hey," she greets me. "How *are* you?"

"Hanging in there."

It's been three days since I showed up with Wallace to report this lunacy. In some ways, they have to be the longest days of my life; in others, they have to be the shortest, the days hurtling along to the killer's zero hour.

"Are you guys any closer to catching this guy?" she asks. "I heard a couple of agents have flown in from the Salt Lake City field office."

"They're working on it. The whole thing is so bizarre."

"I know. And the news—my God, hon, you are all over it. The latest, with your car. What was *that* about? I called you, but you didn't pick up."

"I know. I've just been so, well, crazed."

"Well, yeah." She gives me a concerned look.

"I'll explain when it's all over. We'll get lunch soon."

I want to add, *Because you look like you could use some food.* Allison was always trying a new diet, even though she didn't need one. Apparently, she's now succeeding at shedding the pounds, maybe a little too skeletal. A part of me worries that she has the same disease her sister had, Huntington's chorea, she had called it, and said she would test at some point to see if she had the gene for it. I'll need to ask her about it when the madness of this week has passed. *If* I'm still around to ask.

"Is Ewing in?"

"Ewing?" She blinks at that, as she well might. "In his office. Want me to ring him?"

"Sure. Tell him it'll only take a sec."

I hear her checking in with him, and soon Sergeant Ross escorts me back as he did a few days ago. Ewing stands as I enter.

"What's going on? You get him?"

"No, afraid not," I say. "He's the one that wrote on my car. And my sister's. I guess taking advantage of the circus to scare me off a case."

"So what can I do for you now?"

He's clearly aware he's done me one single favor. It doesn't begin to make up for everything else, but it probably does in his pea brain.

"I came by to thank you for getting me in. I appreciate it. Given the status of our relationship? You know? You didn't need to do that."

"You're welcome." He sighs loudly. He lays his hand flat on his desk as if he's thinking carefully about what he wants to say next. "Look, Mitchell, what happened with Hartley—it was confusing. He was my partner for years. I felt like I owed him. But what happened to you, if what you say is true—well, it's not like I condone that."

"You didn't just condone it. You went to bat for him. You encouraged everyone here"—I gesture around us—"to wear black armbands to protest against me before you even considered whether what I said was true."

"I was angry. I didn't believe you. I thought you were being overdramatic. As I said, he was my partner, my buddy. And, you know. The code."

"The code." I roll my eyes. The toxic code. *Always protect your fellow officer, at all costs. Loyalty is everything.* Corruption sprouts easily with that kind of fertilizer. "Can't say I miss that." The energy I find in saying this to his face has its own power, like the snap of a towel. It makes me realize that it's the real reason for coming, to voice my feelings and not only to thank him.

"I felt like it wasn't that big of a deal. Like, you know, so what? He'd had a few too many and got sloppy with you. I didn't think you needed to blow it out of proportion. He's older, and he grew up in a different culture than you. I felt like there needs to be some give-and-take in the gray areas of personal interactions or we're all going to go crazy."

"Trust me, that's what I told myself, too, even though I shouldn't have *had* to tell myself that. I did anyway, though, figured I'd live with it, right up until Lilly Wickes told me about what happened to her."

"I know. That's what I'm trying to tell you here. Now that I've had time to think it through, I get it. And now, well, now I realize I owe you an apology."

I stare in disbelief.

*Sorry?*

It's way overdue, but it's still sweet, *sweet* music to my ears. But does he get it?

"Ewing," I say. "Thank you. Your apology means a lot to me. But I do have to ask, if Lilly hadn't come forward and put me in that position, do you still think I should have shrugged it off and shoved it down? Chalked it up to Hartley having one too many and being a little slow at evolving with the times?"

He purses his lips, this time to consider my question, not to show pity. "No," he finally says. "I see your point, and no, I don't think you should have done that. I'm sorry. And I'm sorry the department has lost a good cop over this."

I know it will be a cuticle-butchering day. My mind whirls as I decide exactly how to confess—what to say and in what forum. How I'm going to put it all out there for *the world.*

Nonetheless, Ewing's words are a salve, an ounce of healing for the bruise.

I practically float down the hall. Something inside me has loosened, and I feel lighter.

I walk to the front with a smile on my face and stop at Allison's desk to say goodbye.

She looks at me curiously. "Why so happy?"

"He *apologized,*" I whisper to her.

"He did?" she whispers back. "For everything?"

"Time," I say. "Perspective."

She stands from her desk, leans over, and comes close to me, voice as soft as a baby's first words. "It's probably because someone else has come forward about Hartley."

"You're kidding. Someone internally?"

"In the community. Someone Ewing knows. You didn't hear this from me, but Ewing's daughter has a girlfriend who said she was over for a barbecue. Apparently, Hartley was giving her drinks that were way too strong and something happened."

"Oh my God," I say. "How old?"

"Well, if she's Ewing's daughter's friend, mid-twenties?"

"When did this happen?"

"A few months ago."

I sit with this for a moment. "That explains a lot."

"Like I said, you didn't hear it from me."

"That's not a problem," I say. "I've got plenty of other things to worry about."

I look to the exit, sinking inside at the prospect of what's waiting for me outside those doors. These are some seriously loaded doors, it occurs to me. Before I quit the force, I used to agonize over what waited for me on *this* side of them.

"I know you do." She looks at me with concern. She sits back down. "And don't worry about Jess. I'm going to her place tonight to keep them company."

"Thank you." I turn to go, but turn back.

Maybe because this is my last day to confess and I'm feeling sentimental, or perhaps because of Ewing's olive branch, the need to apologize overcomes me.

"Allison, I'm sorry for not being a very good friend since I left. I'm super glad and grateful that you've been good to my sister for the better part of this past year."

She gives me a comforting, motherly smile. "You don't need to apologize, Mitchell. I know you've had a lot to deal with, with Jess and what she's gone through and all. And getting your new business going. Don't give it another thought. You take care."

The worry in her eyes reminds me of what's waiting for me through those doors.

# Chapter 49

I stop at my office before driving home. I park in the lot out front, check that my gun is securely in my holster for the thousandth time, and go in, my senses on high alert. Reporters have stuck their business cards around the edges of my door sign.

Inside, once again, the first thing that hits me is the framed quote that Jess gave me:

**JUSTICE AND POWER MUST BE BROUGHT TOGETHER SO THAT WHATEVER IS JUST MAY BE POWERFUL, AND WHATEVER IS POWERFUL MAY BE JUST.**

So *lofty*. I shake my head. In principle, I've always agreed with it. It's why I opened my PI business. And yet, I've crossed all sorts of boundaries in my short time in law enforcement and my even shorter time as a PI, placing my own ideas of justice on a very shady continuum.

Usually, pride to know this little bastion is all mine swells in my chest when I enter. But this afternoon, I feel like it's a useless, cheap little space. Some tiny limp noodle I've picked out of boiling water to go up against a sharp blade of injustice. I try to shake it off and boot up my computer.

First, I call the hospital to check on Zane again. Still run into the HIPAA wall of silence, but I glean enough from the chat to know that he's stable. After I hang up, regardless of Aaron Lasserio stewing at the county building, I finish my report on him so that Graham Insurance can pay me and, please God, continue to use my services.

Then, even though wading back into the online muck is the last thing I want to do right now, I force myself to take the plunge. I tour my social media accounts for posts about the Confession Artist, to make sure nothing important is sitting right before my face.

It's a tornado of nastiness, as expected, its own forces snatching more and more foul comments. It's not all bad, though. Some people are worried about my well-being. As I'm deleting most of the foul stuff, my eye snags on a post I've already seen before.

*The truth will set you free.*

It's a common, trite thing to say. It doesn't surprise me to see it repeated, but I check to make sure it's not the same user posting it over and over. When I finally find it from two days prior, which takes tons of scrolling through a deluge of crap, I verify that it's not. It's from a different user. Long shot, I think.

When I get through the rest of the good, bad, and the ugly—and the neutral, all the folks reminding me that it's my last day to confess, as though it might've slipped my mind—Jess calls.

She says, "Crosbie, it's getting late. What's your plan?"

I'm happy to hear from her, but her voice is terse, like a nail gun firing. I still see the look of disappointment and disgust on her face, so I say what I say next tentatively. "I'm going to confess."

"You are?" I think I hear a small sigh of relief, but then she follows with zero sign of emotion. "What exactly are you going to confess?"

It hits me again, just like it did at the county building, that what I've been kicking around in my head is all-the-way, three-dimensional, in-the-moment, plain-as-day, heart-poundingly *real.* I am going to do it.

And there's something else circling around my head. If Ridgeway and Lasserio aren't the creators of the sketch of me out there, I want to catch who is. I want to draw them out so that I, the FBI, or even one of the deputies on duty can nab this killer. So my confession needs to come *after* the deadline, not before, even if it puts my life at stake.

As frightening as it is, I need to do this for me. If there's any chance that I am the target of the real CA and not just in Ridgeway's crosshairs, it will hopefully draw them out.

From here on, it's all about having alerts. I learned this on the force. Having a heads-up is everything when it comes to protecting yourself and others.

As long as I know someone's coming, I can take care of myself. My Ring system works surprisingly well, and I plan to always keep my gun on me and next to my bed when I sleep.

My old Kevlar vest from my time on the force is in my garage. Since they're formfitted you get to keep them, even when you leave. I haven't needed it as a PI, but I plan to dig it out as soon as I get home.

Yes, I need this to prevent future victims. Regardless of the fall-out for me.

And I know the price will be high.

And, in the long run, it might be just what Jess needs. For so long, I've wanted nothing but to protect and shield her. Clearly, that hasn't gotten me, or her, very far.

"Well," I say. "The whole Sophie situation and—"

"But do you really think it's that?"

"I wasn't finished," I say. "The whole Sophie situation *and* the whole Billy Railes and Leon thing, too. It's not a full confession otherwise. I have to explain my reasons, impulsive as they were. That's the thing that stings the most. What happened to Sophie and you, along with the harassment I endured. It was all motive for why I backed up Billy's lie. And I spoke to Tim Mooney, the guy who was targeted but wasn't murdered. He confessed partially at first and felt like he was *still* being stalked. He confessed more fully. Motive, rationalizations, and all. And he was spared. I won't use your name. I'll say *a woman I know*."

"It's a small town, Crosbie. Everyone will know it's me. Plus, my podcast and how I quit producing material. People will put two and two together." She's digging in her heels. "Don't be a fool."

Suddenly, something gives in me. "Jess, this is my *life* we're talking about here. I can't believe you'd make this all about *you* right now. If I'm willing to confess to the world that I was complicit in an officer-involved shooting, make that *killing*, and suffer the possible consequences, maybe it's time you buck up and deal with the reality of what happened. I'm facing serious jail time."

"Fuck you, Crosbie. There's a huge difference," she says, and hangs up.

Heat rushes to my face. I throw my phone on my desk and whirl around and grab the poster Jess gave me off the wall and bash it across one of my office chairs. The glass frame shatters. Shards fly across my office onto the floor, across my desk, onto the chairs. She's right. There is a huge difference. I was the perpetrator in my situation. She was the victim. There's no comparison. But now I'm a killer's target. Doesn't that make me a victim, too? Does she have no empathy for me?

My jaw is clenched so tightly, it's like I'm biting steel and it might crack. My chest rises and falls with each angry breath. I take deep ones through my nose to calm myself. I sink into my chair and shut my eyes to squeeze out my fear. To shut out my guilt. When I open them, I look down at my hands. They're quivering from too many things: my anger over the conversation with Jess, the fear of who's out there waiting to do me in, the deep resentment I feel over being targeted and exposed across the nation, over feeling like a victim, and the worst, the sense that I am what I've never wanted to believe about myself.

A coward and a hypocrite.

I check my gun, lock my office up, and leave.

The mess will wait.

Outside my office building's glass front door, a gang of reporters mills around the sidewalk. I curse the building for having only one exit. I think about going back up and staying for a little longer, but I can't hide in my office. Or delay the inevitable.

When I step out, I'm accosted. Their questions—all echoing Jess's—bombard me.

"What's your confession?"

"Today's your last day—what's your plan?"

"How scared are you?"

"What are you going to do to protect yourself?"

They follow me and fold in tight on either side as I slither into my SUV and shut the door. In my rearview, a woman in a tan trench coat and a man in a thick blue sweater with a camera stand behind my bumper. I put my car in reverse and begin to creep out, but not before someone swings open my passenger door and hops in as I'm inching out. I realize I've forgotten to relock my doors with all the chaos.

It's Jeremy.

"Jesus. It's you. Get out of my car. Now."

"Just drive."

"No, get out," I scream. I don't trust him. I don't trust anyone anymore. I want to draw the killer out, and if it's him, I want it on my terms. Not like this. Not an ambush in a parking lot.

My voice no longer sounds like mine. More like some shrill person I don't know. The reporters pound my window. *Bang, bang, bang.* Jeremy's too.

"Crosbie, just drive."

Calm. Sincere. Means it.

I push on the gas, and finally, they jump to either side of my rig. I sweep past them and rush out of the lot.

A light turns red at the intersection down the block, so I stop. In my rearview, I watch them scurry to their cars. One reporter has already gotten into his, has pulled out, and is close to catching me at the intersection. *Oh no you don't.* I run the red, drive two more blocks, ignore the stop signs, blow through those intersections, and swing a right. I pass several more blocks and take another right.

I follow the rules of the road again. I hit my blinker, pull over, and turn to Jeremy. "Get out of my car. I'm not saying *please*."

"Hear me out."

"No."

"Time is ticking and you told me you wanted to confess."

"I told you I'd get a hold of you."

"I need more than a minute if I'm going to write something thoughtful."

"How did you know I was here?"

"Same way all of them knew. Good guess. Your office location is not a secret. And as the day has crept on without hearing from you, I got worried. I went to your house. Some other patrolman is there. I heard the awful news about the shooting. And the new guy wouldn't tell me where you were, so I thought I'd check here."

"Okay, well, I'm fine, but I still need you to get out."

"But this is your last day. Things are bound to get more dangerous unless you confess something."

"Maybe I've changed my mind." I haven't, but I'm in no state to give him information about what's going on in my head.

He gives me a weighted stare. "Why would you do that?"

"Get out."

"You're not being wise about this."

*What's not wise is having you in my car,* I think.

He's examining me, and I stare back. I can barely breathe. My spine is a steel cable.

"Crosbie, what's going on?"

"*You* tell me. How did you know about the possible third sketch subject?"

"Tim Mooney? He confessed. I've been trying to get a hold of him to interview him as well, but frankly, you confessing right now is more important than getting an interview from him."

"He confessed along with a lot of others. Why did you zero in on him?"

"I'm good at my job."

"That's not an answer. And you know details on him that are beyond what you could dig around for. Specific things that were private."

"What are you talking about?"

"How do you know he got a fright? That that's the reason he gave a more thorough confession?"

He half smiles. "Is that what this is about?"

I don't answer.

"Ask your agent friend," he says.

"Alderson told you?"

"No," he says. "The other one. Guess she likes my smile."

I shake my head. Unbelievable. So Miss Perfect and Miss Precise and Miss Protocols is not so perfect after all. I can still hear Greene berating me in the observation room. Now I have a thing or two to say to her.

I stretch across Jeremy and open his door. "Please," I say. "Out. Now."

Finally, he steps onto the street.

I watch him watch my car through my rearview as I drive away.

On my way home, I refocus on Ewing's apology, to suckle on that feeling of vindication and satisfaction like it's a pacifier. But it can't compete with the desolation I'm feeling after the fight with Jess and the maddening talk with Jeremy and the throat-closing thought that I'm nearing the end of my last day. And to add to it all, I can't kick a niggling sensation that I'm missing something vital, something lurking at the edges of my mind, just beyond reach.

None of it matters, though. The plan stands: use myself as bait.

I call Greene. She doesn't deny that she *might* have let the information slip about Mooney, the third sketch near-victim.

A deep relief washes over me. He was being honest. But still, he was too conveniently, so coincidentally, in both Dallas and now here.

But with Greene's less-than-direct-yet-obvious admission that she's the source of the leak, I decide that even though I booted Jeremy out of my car, I will use him after all. If he's not the killer, he'll work anyway. If he is the CA, I'll be ready. I inform Greene that I intend to confess, but not until the seventh day.

"Why do it at all, then?" she asks.

"I have to," I say.

There's an awkward pause. Greene says nothing, like she's intuitively known all along I carry these ugly things.

"What do you think?" I break the silence. "Is it a copycat situation or not?"

"We can't say for sure, but I personally don't think it is. I don't think they could pull off the internet piece of this puzzle."

I take that in. My plan to confess a day late stands. I tell her that I'm using Jeremy. She doesn't object. No arguments. Just says, "If that's what you want, Alderson and I will be right over." I'm guessing they want to draw out and nail this killer as much as I do.

I slide to a stop and roll down my window to talk to my new watchman. He's been using a discarded bucket of Kentucky Fried Chicken to gather trash off the side of my drive. "Damn reporters," he says. "Who'd just dump your wrappers and crap and drive off? And they call themselves the watchdogs of democracy."

I park and step out, grab a few crushed soda containers. "Where are they all? Did they *all* go to my office?"

"The smart ones. Since you haven't been here much, some got bored and left. I take it you had a crowd at your office?"

I don't want conversation. If it were Zane, I'd fill him in on Lasserio. I think of Zane wounded, struggling to do something as basic as pulling in a breath. And behind that, I have a flash of Jess, her anger burning through the phone. And then another question: Have I been seeing her through a distorted lens all this time? Assuming I need to protect her because I didn't protect Sophie?

I thank the new guy for all the tedious time he's spent keeping guard and tell him that the agents and more deputies are on their way and that I might have a visitor soon who will need to be searched. I give him Jeremy's full name, go home, and call him. He'll be delighted to hear I want to use him after all.

# Chapter 50

There are too many things biting at me. Montana has fifty species of mosquitoes, and it feels like I know them all. There are too many things left undone, especially the Montana connection with the sister of the boy who was coached by Randal Askens. The girl who contacted Jess.

*Vivian.*

I hop back online and search Vivian and Ryan's mom and dad, Rick and Cindy Petronis. His dad doesn't use social media, but his mom is active. I scroll through her posts: shares of humorous cartoons, charity events in her community, book club reads. There's nothing unusual. Her page gets stale after her son's passing, which doesn't surprise me.

I'm about to click off when an old post stops me. It's from several months after Ryan died. It's a picture of a carbon-colored suitcase, packed and standing upright, and text below that reads:

> Packed and ready to head to northwest Montana.
> Pray for me that this will be a good thing.

I suspect she's referring to visiting Vivian in the valley since she goes to FVCC, but something about the heaviness of the comment makes me pause. I read all the comments from her friends below.

Good luck.

Praying for you.

Hope you find peace and healing.

The comments are out of whack for someone visiting their daughter. I wonder if she was coming this way to vacation alone after visiting Vivian, to perhaps deal with her grief. I'm about to dig deeper, to check for extended family in Montana, when Jeremy arrives.

I've already dug out my Kevlar from the garage and have put it on under my sweater. It's uncomfortable, but in a weird way, it feels good to be held in tight, as if it will keep me from dissolving into an amorphous pile of mush while I pour out all my secrets. That it will somehow keep me whole and upright.

Alderson and Greene have met Jeremy at the entrance to my drive for a thorough search of him and his car. When they're confident he's not hiding anything, they escort him to me, but I'm nervous enough to insist on doing my own.

"Not so fast," I say.

He stops and squints at me. "Huh? They already searched me."

"Then another won't hurt. I need to be sure, myself, or I won't feel comfortable enough to confess."

He looks at Alderson.

"I'd do what the lady asks," Alderson says.

"Fair enough." Jeremy shrugs.

"Slowly, and I mean slowly, put the backpack down, take off your jacket, and throw both at my feet."

"I'd rather not toss this." He holds up his pack. "With my laptop in it."

"Okay, put it on the ground."

He does so, carefully, just as he set the six-pack down the other night.

"Now take off your fleece."

He gingerly takes off his fleece and holds it out.

"Toss it over."

It lands at my feet. "Now, stay put. Don't move your hands. Even a millimeter." I pick up his fleece and shake it. It's too light to have a gun or a knife. I advance until I'm only four feet away. He's wearing a casual beige button-up made from thin cotton. It's clear there's no gun nudged into his waistline. At least, in front.

"Slowly turn around," I order.

His trousers are a sort of lightweight pant, almost flimsy—the kind you use to keep cool when hiking. No gun.

"Okay, you can face me now." Once he does, I gesture to his ankles. "Now slowly, and I mean it again, lift one pant leg at a time."

"Isn't this overkill?" But he bends down and lifts the left, exposing a wool sock partway up his tan, muscular calf. He raises the other. No gun. No knife. Alderson stands by, guarding.

I search the pack to find his laptop, several notebooks, pens, an extra long-sleeved shirt, and some jerky, energy bars, and trail mix in a separate front compartment.

"There's a deputy in front and out back. Both are right here if you need them," Alderson says. "We'll be working on you-know-what."

I know he's talking about Ridgeway and Lasserio and getting to the bottom of this copycat business. I thank Alderson and tell Jeremy to follow me.

I take Jeremy inside and he sets up at my kitchen table while I make coffee. When I sit down, he asks for my permission to use his phone recorder and sets it between us.

I start out slowly, my stomach in a knot, but once I get going, it takes me only minutes to get through what happened to Sophie. He listens quietly, without interjecting and rarely asking questions, but I suspect he's saving them up for when I'm done.

His fingers tap busily on his keyboard. It's nerve-racking at first, but I get into a flow. I start with Missoula, with meeting Sophie, and move on to our walk by the river when we first met Josh and the gang.

I describe the camping trip, the rape, the night in the woods, and the aftermath. "Sophie started using more and more as time went on," I say. "Eventually, she took a fatal dose of fentanyl."

Jeremy leans back and sighs. "Coping with rape through drugs," he says.

I realize how fast I've been talking and how shallow my breathing has been. "Yes, *coping*. Or not coping." My thoughts turn to Jess now.

"It must have been awful to watch your roommate go through that."

"It was. And you know the thing I can't get out of my head?"

Jeremy listens.

"She told me she was sorry. After the rape, after we made it out of the woods, at the clinic when she was getting checked over, she said she was sorry for flirting with Josh when she knew I liked him. She said it with such sorrow and sincerity, as if she thought she deserved what he did because she'd hurt me. I was speechless, it was so twisted. I mean, she felt guilty for taking him from me, but in an awful way, she'd done me a huge favor. I felt nauseous that I'd even had a crush on someone like him. I didn't know what to say. I told her that she shouldn't worry about that, but I'm the one who should have apologized to her. But I can't remember if I did. I can't remember if I told her I was so sorry for convincing her to go in the first place."

Saying these words out loud brings home just how bruised and shamed I've been for so many years. Tears press behind my eyes, but I hold them back.

Jeremy sets his hand on mine, a sweet, comforting gesture that makes me want to weep even more.

"It was particularly difficult to watch her personality change. And now." I shake my head, Jess's retorts echoing in my ears. "Now I'm going through it all over again."

"How so?"

"I'll tell you. It's part two, three, and four of this, but we should take a little break first. I need some air." I grab the empty coffee mugs off the table and set them in the sink. We throw our coats on and go out to my backyard. The new extra deputy stationed out back brings reassurance. I tell him we'll just be on the swing.

The air is brisk and the sky over the Whitefish Range is dramatic. Glowing white and deep charcoal–colored clouds layer above the ridges.

"Storm's brewing," he says.

"Grimly appropriate." The last moments of twilight cling around us. Herds of deer graze on grass in the surrounding fields.

"Sorry," he says. "But Montana has a way of mimicking our moods, doesn't it?"

"Montana is like a bad relationship," I say as we walk over to my old rickety swing.

"How so?"

"When it's bad, it's miserable, but when it's good—when the sun comes out and makes up with you and the lakes sparkle and mountaintops shine—there's nothing better and you feel like you can't live without it."

He chuckles.

We both sit on the swing's broad seat and rock back and forth.

"Speaking of relationships," he says. "You in one?"

The question surprises me. It could just be journalistic fishing, or it could be more. I decide to simply ask, "Is this a personal question or one for the piece?"

"Both."

Something like giddiness wells up, but I'm too frayed and spent to parse it, not to mention that my guard is as high as a mountain. I can't imagine it ever coming down. "No," I say. "Like I said, I dated Wallace for a while, but since we broke up, I haven't seen anyone."

"Which I guess should take us back to part two of this, don't you think?" He checks his watch.

"Yeah," I say. "In a minute."

Nerves creep up and my throat thickens when I think about telling him about part two. I brush it away and focus on Jeremy. His muscled thigh, taut against the fabric of his pants, presses against my leg. That brings on a whole other tension.

"What about you?" I ask.

"Me, relationship-wise? Well, given that you're not a journalist, I take it this *is* a personal question?"

"I guess it is."

"I've been seeing someone," he says, his voice low. "In New York."

I'm not sure how I feel about his answer. Partly, it pricks me, and I'm angry at myself for that.

I watch him keenly, trying to parse him. If he is the CA, I'm giving him what he wants, and I *should*, in theory, be safe. Also, if he is, I want to catch him and put an end to this thing. But all I can do right now is play along and see if he says or does anything odd. My senses stay on high alert.

"On and off," he adds. "But yeah, we're giving it another go."

I get up from the swing and clap my hands together once. "Time to finish this. The sooner we're done, the better."

"Wait," he says, grabbing my hand.

I jerk away, my hand seizing my gun.

"Whoa." He holds up his hands. "Whoa."

"Sorry." My chest rises and falls. "You can't grab me, Jeremy."

"I see that." The easy brown of his eyes is almost golden in the natural light, but there's real worry behind the ease. Is it for me? For himself? "I'm sorry," he adds. "Really."

"It's okay."

"I was just going to say, thank you for trusting me with your story." His hands are still up in surrender. "I know how unsure you were about me, about this. I want you to know that I don't take any of this lightly."

"I didn't do this on blind faith. I did it because you're right, that piece you did on Indigenous women . . . You were smart to give me that link. You showed me compassion. Well, *them.* You didn't exploit their pain. And you explored solutions and called for specific action."

"Well, I guess I'm a little sly, too."

"I guess you are." I smile.

He slowly lowers his hands.

I nod that it's okay. When my pulse settles a little, I say, "You need to be for your job. We all need to be. And you're welcome, but I have two requests."

"What are they?"

"I don't know how fast you work, but I don't want it to come out until tomorrow, until after my time to confess is up." I watch his reaction.

Confusion crosses his brow. "Why?"

The questions dart through my mind: *If you are the killer, what does this do to your sense of morality? Are you going to make a move to take me out because it's not on your timeline, or will you accept my full confession a day late?*

"I mean, it's going to be a crunch," he adds. "But yeah, I was absolutely planning to push this so it's posted well before midnight. Hitting that deadline's part of the point, isn't it?"

"No," I say. "I mean, yes. Originally, I thought I'd confess on the killer's timeline. But I realize I don't want that."

"But waiting, defying the killer. Won't that invite an attempt on your life?"

I don't answer. I stare into his eyes. I want to ask him, *Will it? You tell me.*

"And that's exactly what you want, isn't it?" His voice goes a notch higher, like he's nervous, too.

*Anxious and excited for himself to be near his prey? Or anxious for me?* I wonder again. But I say nothing. I watch him, try to see something, anything that will tell me the answer.

"That's a little crazy."

"If I don't find who's behind this, they'll move on to the next person. I can't have that. I know this will possibly bring about an attempt on my life, but if I can take down whoever this is, I'll be one fucking happy private investigator."

There's still so much to do to find out whether I'm only the target of some copycat or the real CA's hit, but Alderson and Greene are working on this central question.

Me? I still intend to track down Vivian and to investigate the towns where Mooney said there were suicides, especially the ones with addiction or grief clinics. I have a small hunch that a connection lies between one of these northwest Montana towns that Vivian's mom, Cindy Petronis, was visiting with her packed suitcase and the places Mooney said people died from the drugs he was pushing for Carssen. But everywhere I go from now on, I will have a bodyguard, and I'll wear my Kevlar, like I am now.

"But this isn't only about trying to lure the killer out."

"No?"

The mix of emotions whirling inside me makes me feel fluttery and conflicted, but underneath it all, I feel a release, a deep, nourishing sense of freedom to get this out. "It's about my story, one I've decided I want to share after all. One I've been keeping buried for too long. This isn't some flimsy confession in a social media post. Which leads me to my second request."

"You got my attention."

"What I'm about to tell you involves my sister. I do not want her name used. I will not give you the rest of this story unless you promise me that you will not disclose her identity."

"I promise," he says. "And if your sister isn't happy with it?"

"She definitely is not happy, but I'm past that. I want this out. So come on, let's do this before I change my mind."

# A CONFESSION

X: @ReginaSelway #CAConfession—Two years ago I took out a huge loan to buy my boss's veterinary clinic. Soon after, I hired an empl. who I later discovered was injecting lethal levels of ketamine into some of the pets and watching them die. I, of course, fired him but I never reported him. I don't know where he is now, but the whole thing was creepy. I should have reported him, but I didn't want my new business to suffer. I had just bought it, and I couldn't afford to have bad press! I feel so awful. I haven't had a decent night's sleep in 2 years.

# Chapter 51

***Zero Days***

Six a.m. My nerves are frayed. I didn't sleep a wink with questions pinging through my mind. How will the world take my confessions? How will Jess react? How will my friends and community take it?

I tried to block it out, but I kept swinging back and forth from too many people I've ever known, wondering what they'll think of me.

I pick up my phone and see more confessions getting some national attention. What? Someone keeping quiet? Not reporting someone else? Worried about the exposure and what it will do to their business? I shake my head. A little too on the nose, I think.

My phone dings with a text.

It's Jeremy. He's worked through the night.

> Check your email, see attached. You have final approval on every word. Four parts in all. 1) Sophie 2) Workplace harassment 3) Jess 4) Leon, Railes, Coleman, LIES.

I open the file.

He's written a thorough, sensitive piece. I only have a few edits regarding two inaccuracies on time frames, but I don't give him the go-ahead. Not just yet.

My cheeks are wet. I have no idea when I started crying. I try to parse the source. Is it because today could be the last day of my life? Is it because maybe, if I'm lucky, I'll be getting the killer off my back?

It's much deeper: I've been carrying this baggage for so long now. To finally release it is overwhelming, despite the consequences.

I could be charged with obstruction or, worse, conspiracy to commit murder. I could be charged with conspiracy to cover up the murder, impeding law enforcement's efforts to solve the crime. I would pay my dues in jail time. I would also lose my private investigator's license and never be able to reclaim it. No law enforcement agency would ever hire me again because I would lose my Peace Officer Standards and Training certification that allows me to be a cop anywhere.

Worse, the sheer shame of it all. Where could I hide? What foreign country could I move to? I couldn't even fathom leaving Jess and Sam anyway, so I swipe the thoughts away. Try not to think of life behind bars.

Jeremy texts:

All good? Do I have your go-ahead?

He has already informed me that after I give the thumbs-up, the piece will be published by midmorning on RollingStone.com, and a few days later in the magazine's *(Sub)Culture* section.

The persistent flutter in my gut spreads to my entire body like a giant bird inside me trying to take flight. Despite the relief to get things off my chest, there's a high-intensity tension saturating the air and coursing through me. Even though I haven't slept at all, I'm wired. What have I invited in by not confessing on the killer's timeline?

I take a deep breath like I'm about to dive into a cold lake. Then I give him the go-ahead.

But first and foremost, I need to tell Jess what's coming. My plan is to drive to her place before the sun fully rises over the eastern mountains and tell her in person, then prepare for whatever comes my way for the rest of the day.

Jess and Sam still have security stationed at her place. And as fearful as I am to draw the killer to her house, I need to tell her about the full confession in person. And if I don't survive the day, it will be the last time I see either one of them. I want to—*need* to—say goodbye.

I'm betting on it being early enough that the killer won't even have had time to eat breakfast yet.

I'm grateful for Greene's presence downstairs. Her company and her gun afford me enough reassurance to take a quick shower. I feel vulnerable and deeply alone, and it ends up being the fastest shower I've ever taken. I dress in a snap, don my vest, put on my holster, and go downstairs.

It's pitch black out still, but Greene is making coffee.

"Did you sleep at all?" I say.

"A little. In your easy chair." She scoops grounds into the filter. With her back to me, she adds, "Look, I'm sorry about the slipup with the reporter."

I don't have the energy to focus on Greene's failings. I have only two things on my mind: staying alive and informing my sister about Jeremy's article.

"I shouldn't have talked to him at all." She turns to me, holding a scoop in midair, and I see vulnerability in her for the first time. "I put you in a compromising position."

"It's hard to do everything perfectly in this business," I say, the understatement of the year, but soon enough, that will all be out. "Besides, Jeremy is quite charming. Maybe too charming."

She agrees with that, and we drop it.

"Any word on DNA on that Kleenex?"

"Not yet. You know the system. It always takes longer than we'd like, no matter how urgent, but we should have something by midday. Hopefully."

I tell her my plan to go to Jess's.

As I pick up my keys, she says, "I'm coming with. Just let me get us some travel mugs. It'll brew quickly."

"I'd like to speak to my sister alone, if that's okay with you. And I feel better with more eyes on this place after what happened to Deputy Zane."

"Not a chance." She turns to me, our eyes mirroring anticipation for the day to come. A charged alertness. "I'm coming, but I promise to give you some alone time with your sister."

"Okay then." I point to the cabinet to the left of the range where I keep some travel mugs.

◆ ◆ ◆

We take Greene's vehicle.

When I get in, it hits me that I haven't been in an official law enforcement vehicle with all its bells and whistles in over a year now. A deep sadness falls over me, but I brush it off. I have more important things to concentrate on.

I call Jess, waking her up. When I ask if everything is fine, she says it is, that Sam is asleep, and that Allison came over, true to her word, and ended up staying the night after watching a movie.

When we arrive, it's still dark. Jess's and Allison's cars are in the driveway. The same uniform from yesterday is out front watching the house in her dark sedan. Greene grabs a flashlight and says she's going to chat with the officer posted out on the street and make the rounds.

To my surprise, Jess is alert and already making coffee. She gives me a cursory hug in the open doorway.

"Come in." She stands aside to let me enter, still a bit cool over the sour telephone call. "Allison's asleep on the office futon."

Jess's hair falls across her face. She looks at me with puffy eyes. I scan her place. Everything is in order, except for a few of Sam's toys and one of Jess's bigger throws strewn across the end of her couch. I figure she's been waiting for me, curled up under it. In loose sweats, my little sister looks frail and painfully defenseless.

"What's this about?" Jess asks.

Surprise that she's not showing more relief to see me—isn't wrapping me in a bigger bear hug or offering a condolence or two—stalls me for a moment. "Some coffee would be nice," I finally say, even though I've already had a cup on the drive over.

We go to the kitchen, not speaking, and she pours me a cup. After Greene's done with her walk-around, she enters the back kitchen door and announces she'll be in her car making calls.

Jess turns to me. "So, what's going on?"

"I spilled my guts to a journalist. Every little scrap. The article is coming out soon this morning and I don't want it to take you by surprise. Your name isn't mentioned, as I promised. It just refers to *a woman*." I say it softly so Allison can't hear, but even if she does, she'll read about it soon enough.

She stares dully at me, but she doesn't erupt, which, in a way, frightens me because she might be moving beyond anger to total apathy. There's a deadness in her eyes that worries me. I press on. I'm here for more than apologies.

"I want to explain the article before you see it. There's a lot in it, everything from what happened with Sophie, what happened to you, *a woman*"—I use air quotes—"someone I care deeply for but no use of the word *sister*. And with Mark, then Leon. I told him about the shooting and my omission of the truth to the investigator."

*"Omission,"* she mimics. "Don't bother. I get it. You need to confess something. Your life depends on it."

"I didn't do it just to confess *something*. If that was the case, I would have had the article come out last night. I did it for other reasons."

"Like what?"

"For you, in large part. To confess to you and the world, to finally get all this out in the open so we can all move on. I don't want us to hide anymore, or cower, behind the secret of it all, what Mark did to you. And for me, the guilt. I figured, if *I* put it out there, in the tangle of all this Confession Artist commotion, most of the attention falls on me, not you. I know you think people will figure out that it's you, but they can only speculate, and even if they do, then if you get any negative media attention, whatever victim shaming or blaming or accusations of making it up for attention for your podcast can be dismissed because I'm the one who put it out there, not you."

I want her to say something, anything. I can't help it: I'm still shocked she hasn't expressed relief that I'm okay on the day after the deadline. And hurt, given how much I've always gone out of my way to protect her. Also, it feels a little like a slap in the face she thinks my confession is just to save myself, that she can't get out of her own headspace long enough to see how tortured I am by it all.

"Now that it's coming out," I continue, "you're free to do what you need to do to thoroughly deal with the rape. It's time. You need help. No more excuses. Your podcast is flailing anyway, you're not sleeping well, you jump when someone comes up behind you, you never smile or laugh anymore. Like you said yourself up on the stage in Dallas: Secrets are rarely better kept locked away."

She bites her lower lip. A storm is approaching, despite all her efforts to remain calm. "That's rich, Crosbie," she hisses at me. "Using my own words to justify you exposing *my* secrets to the world, stuff I could've exposed to a counselor or my own inner circle of support instead, on my own terms."

A part of me is glad to see her anger. She hasn't been to a counselor. The only friend she knows is Allison, and she's sworn her to secrecy. But the anger is better than detachment, which I know all too well is a defense mechanism.

In addition to the deep ache piercing my heart, I'm also furious at her, too. There's so much that hasn't been said.

"You can do this on your own terms," I say. "Like I said, your name's not even mentioned."

"Anyone who knew Mark Coleman in this small town knew he and I were hanging out at the Silvertip."

"That's conjecture, Jess. And for that, I'm sorry. But also, in a way, I'm not. This might be for the best." I know I sound a little callous, but quickly—very quickly—it's dawned on me that I can't shelter my sister anymore, even for Sam's sake. I clearly have done no good by doing so, and in fact, have made things worse. I brace for her reaction, but Allison comes into the kitchen before I get one.

"I smell coffee," she says. Sam is behind her, wide awake like he's already been playing in his room. Allison's in a pair of jeans and a rumpled T-shirt. "This little guy came and got me in the office wanting to play, can you believe it?"

Jess grabs Allison a cup, too.

"I thought I heard talking," she says. "You're here early. Jess reminded me that this is it. The day after." She has the same wide-eyed questioning look that Alderson had at the end of the day yesterday—a *what in the world are you going to do* look.

"Yeah, I had some things to tell Jess, but I'm leaving now." I can't tell if Jess has filled Allison in on what I told her the other night, and if she has, I wonder what she thinks of me and my actions with Railes, but I'm not going to hang around to find out. I still feel bad about letting our friendship slide, but mostly right now, I feel embarrassed and bruised. My heart aches in a way I've never felt before. But this is supposed to be a quick visit. I've accomplished my mission to fill Jess in, and now I need to get out of their hair and be on my own for a while to continue to investigate this, to pay very close attention to every single person who approaches me or comes to my house, and to coordinate all my actions with Alderson and Greene so that I have backup for wherever I go, like now. For simplicity, I plan to stay away from my office for the time being.

I hug Sam and snuggle him in close.

"What are you wearing?" Sam asks, wrinkling his nose.

"Oh, just a little armor," I say. "You know, in case one of your scary monsters comes for me."

He looks at me funny. My throat constricts. I am raw to my bones, not only from exposing the truth and from hurting Jess, but from knowing I may never see them again if I mess up today or the next. Or . . .

Even if I escape this mess and catch the killer, Jess may never forgive me. She may even withhold Sam from me. Sam squirms, and I force myself to let him go.

"Sorry if we woke you," I say to Allison. "But thanks for staying last night. I appreciate you keeping Jess company."

"I'm an early riser. Plus, I need to get going, too," she says, grabbing her purse from the counter. "Got to run home to clean up before I get to work this morning. I can do it again tonight, if you want."

"Yes," Sam says. "We had a sleepover." He smiles. "And Allison helped me with my space station. Will *you* help me today?" he asks me.

"Oh, that does sound so fun, but you have to go to school."

Sam groans. "After?"

"We can work on it next time, but right now, buddy, I need to get going, too." I give him one more hug, but he wriggles away.

"You stay safe." Allison grabs her keys out of her purse, then seems to realize she's sleepy enough she hasn't yet put on her jacket, a thin, shiny little black thing hanging over the back of one of Jess's stools. A tiny corner of white trails out of one of the pockets. *Tissue,* I think, and tell myself that every time I spot a tissue, for God's sake, I can't get weirded out.

But then she sets her keys down on the counter to put on her jacket. My eye catches on her key chain. Attached to a ring holding a flat plastic rectangle with a metal bottle opener on its end are her keys. And also attached to the ring is a colorful arrowhead made from agate.

I narrow my eyes and cock my head a little, trying to place where I've seen it. The plastic rectangle bottle opener faces down, so I can't see the picture on it, but the combination of a bottle opener and an arrowhead attached to a set of keys triggers my memory.

*Leon.*

*Leon had the same.*

Allison sees my glance and picks up the keys, closing her hand around the plastic.

"That," I say. "Your key chain. Where did you get it?"

She holds up her hand to show me the tip of the arrowhead. "*This?* These are so popular now. Got it in Polson at a gift shop there."

"Allison, did you know Leon Spencer?"

"Leon who?"

"The man involved with the guy Billy shot."

"Oh, that poor boy? No, why?"

"Your key chain. It's like his." I lift my chin, see her hand tightly palming the ring, barely showing the tip of the agate.

She gives me a quizzical look like, *What a strange thing to ask.*

"No," she says. "Like I said, they're popular."

There may be a gazillion just like it in gift shops around Montana.

Greene comes back into the kitchen. "Ready to go?"

I steal another quick hug from Sam, then give Jess a longer one.

"We're still sisters," she mumbles, gripping me tightly. When we finally part, she looks like she might cry. Was her indifference earlier simply an act, a way for her to stay strong for a change to get through this? My heart almost splits in two knowing that although she's fuming, she still aches and is terrified for me and the whole situation.

"Come on, Sam." Her voice cracks. "We need to get ready for school." She wipes her eyes and starts toward her bedroom.

"I'm going to wave goodbye." Sam darts to the front window and stations himself there in his green dinosaur pj's, which are now high-waters on him from his latest growth spurt.

"Okay if I grab a cup for the road?" Allison calls to Jess.

Jess points to a catchall cabinet above the fridge. I walk out with Greene. She begins telling me Alderson learned from the coroner that

Clarissa died from blunt force trauma to the head *before* water entered her lungs.

But I can barely track what she's saying. The fierce grip of Jess's hug, like she'll never hold me again, takes my breath away. At the same time, Sam is completing our ritual—waving to me from the front window until I'm officially out of sight.

I flash a big smile and wave back, trying to act carefree. I'm anything but.

Outside, dawn is beginning to rub away the night sky, but it's still dark enough to see through Jess's front windows, the lights inside spotlighting Sam at the window. I wave again, but as we get into Greene's black SUV, I'm picturing how tightly Allison gripped the key chain, her knuckles white. Wouldn't anyone have held it out if I asked about it? What was *that* all about? I'm not positive Allison has Leon's key chain, but I'm suspicious.

Of *what*?

Why on earth would she have that poor dead kid's key chain?

Have I gotten to the point in my life where I have nothing but enemies and can barely trust anyone in my orbit?

But I've heard a lot of lies during my time on both my jobs, and although I may not pick up on them all the time, when my senses wake up, there's usually a reason for it.

And they're tingling like hell.

"Mitchell, are you even listening to me?" Greene asks.

"What?"

"About Clarissa Hayes's lungs. She died from a blow, not drowning."

Greene puts her keys in the ignition and adds something about the DNA on the water bottle in Clarissa's pack. I watch Allison come up behind Sam, holding her to-go coffee. Sam is beaming. She is not.

Like a lens on autofocus bringing an object into sharp relief, I make out her expression more clearly. It's a complicated anxiety, like it's not just for my safety, but an examining of me and Greene all mixed. There's calculation in her hard stare.

Allison looks thin and gaunt, stressed in the same way Jess has been, like she's been through the wringer. Newly formed deep lines etch around her eyes.

Images flash through my head like a skipping film.

Allison doodling at her desk, sketching a lynx on notepaper and me complimenting her, telling her how good it was.

Allison mentioning once that, in Casper, her hometown in Wyoming, when her older brothers were angry at her, they'd bully her by tying her up to one of the pasture fences after dinner, forcing her to stay out till dark in the relentless wind, listening to the coyotes yipping out in the field until their mom yelled at them to go fetch her. She told me her brothers always said if she ratted on them, they'd exact revenge, use her for target practice instead of the old aluminum cans.

Allison complimenting my earrings at the banquet, moving in closer to get a better look.

Allison at the shooting range: *Try putting a picture of him on that bull's-eye*, she had said when we talked about Hartley, and I had laughed.

Allison raising her nephew after her sister deteriorated and passed on.

I never met the boy. By the time I joined the force, he was already in high school. I recalled how she sometimes left early for school events. How she talked about him with such warmth, bragged about him being smart and genuine.

"But her nephew?" I say this out loud. To myself. To see if I hear a *click*. "Could it have been?"

"Mitchell?" Greene starts the car. "What are you talking about?"

"You know Allison, the dispatcher? Her sister died from a neurodegenerative disease, Huntington's chorea, when her nephew, who she called . . . what did she call him? I've never even met him. She never brought him by the station or anything. When I asked her why, she said, *Would you bring a family member around these goons?*"

"So?" Greene asks.

"It was Tom, that's what she called him. She said she'd raised him since he was seven, just a year older than Sam is now. Okay, yes, it was Tom, not Leon."

I sigh loudly, feeling silly but relieved, but before I even fully exhale, more details flash through my mind. Leon's driver's license.

Thomas Leon Spencer.

But he went by Leon. I jolt straight up in my seat. Greene is pulling out onto the street. I refuse to take my eyes off Sam and Allison standing in Jess's window.

"Pull back in," I say, keeping my eyes glued on them. "Allison is Leon's aunt."

"Leon?" says Greene. "Who's Leon?"

# Chapter 52

Allison inches up close behind Sam standing at the window.

"Stop," I yell to Greene.

Allison taps Sam's shoulder and says something to him. Sam keeps waving at me to complete our ritual. "Oh my God." My voice rises. "It's her."

Greene puts on the brakes.

Allison sees us stop, puts her coffee down, and grabs Sam by the arm. *Grabs* him. Sam tries to twist away, but she yanks him to her and drags him away from the window.

Out of sight.

I leap out of the car as fast as I can. I pull my gun from its holster as I run back into the house, into the kitchen, but the back door is open.

"Sam," I yell. "Sam! Allison!"

Water is running in Jess's bathroom. She's showering, safe. I run into the backyard and scan. To my right, more backyards. To my left is a farmer's field. Beyond it, a wooded forest.

Where Allison yanks Sam, his legs resisting her efforts, into the woods.

I run.

Sam twists away from her grip. He breaks free and darts off to the right into the trees. Allison halts for a moment and yells for him, then continues running straight ahead.

Greene catches me as I enter the forest. I take a second to look around to see if I can spot Allison before I go in the direction I saw Sam dash. Allison is nowhere in sight. My fear for Sam skyrockets. I turn this way and that, scanning the woods. The forest is a sneaky cohort, every pine tree scheming to hide him from me, some areas thicker than others, the more open spaces profuse with prickly bushes grabbing at my ankles. I think of what they're doing to his little legs.

"What's going on?" Greene says, out of breath.

"Sam got away from her. I think he went that way." I point to the right. More pines. I look down for footprints, but the ground is too thick with brush. "I'll go after him there. You keep straight. Find her. And, Greene, if you see Sam before I do, do *not* let anything happen to that little boy."

I head to the right into a copse of dense lodgepole pines, looking for Sam's green dinosaur pajamas.

I don't want to call out loudly and broadcast my whereabouts to Allison, so I whisper his name. "Sam, Sam, where are you?"

I exit the dense trees and come into an opening. More bushes on my left, pines and cottonwoods in front of me and to my right. Pale light illuminates the forest. My pulse pounds like a hammer. Skinny and thick dark trunks mingle among the lighter papery ones of the cottonwoods.

If something happens to Sam? I can't let myself go there. I have to find him. "Sam," I call louder. Each step I take elicits a crunch from the dry fall underbrush.

I think I hear something off to my side in the tall bushes. I go toward the sound slowly, holding my gun up, my arm cocked when I hear the click of a gun's safety unlatching behind me.

"Move and you die," she says. "Lose the gun."

I freeze. My heartbeat is jacked.

"Allison," I say. "Allison, please."

"You're not a cop," she says. "Stop acting like one."

"Allison," I say more firmly. I want to scream, *What the hell?* But it's not a good time to piss her off. "What's going on?"

"Drop your gun."

The barrel of her weapon presses into my scalp. I do as she says, releasing it from my hands. It thuds to the ground. It's a terrible, naked feeling.

"Now put your hands behind your head and walk." She pushes me, forcing me deeper into the denser forest. "No games."

I think of the others she's killed: Loman brutally with a slit across her throat, Askens by gunshot. My head scurries to catch up with the realization. Allison? My friend? Jess's friend? She can't possibly be capable of so many terrible things.

But I can feel the cold metal of her gun against my own neck. I have my vest on, but it will do nothing if she shoots above my torso. I raise my arms and walk where she prods, stepping over fallen logs and dry shrubs, realizing she wants to get me away from Greene. I turn my head, trying to see her out of the corner of my eye. I pray Sam is safe with Greene.

"You raised Leon? Leon was Tom?"

"This is good enough," she says when we get into a thicker patch of pines and cottonwoods. "Turn around."

She's standing five feet away from me, her nine-millimeter pointing at my face. Her eyes are open so wide I can see the whites in the pale light. "He preferred Leon after he graduated."

It hurts so much to think of him. *Allison's nephew.* She raised him. I haven't raised Sam myself, but I've helped extensively. I'd do anything for him, like he was my own child.

Did Allison think of him as her son? How could she not if it was just the two of them? The air feels like it's less concentrated, like I can't draw enough oxygen from it. Jesus. I want to tell her how it pains me. At least try to apologize, but I'm trying to read the situation and what could make it better or possibly worse.

"You didn't back him." She winces at the memory. "I was out of town when it happened. He waited a whole two days—suffering—before he even called me and told me what happened. He told me how Railes lied about the knife and shot Mark in cold blood. He told me how the female officer didn't back him. And when I got back, you were on your fucking decompression leave. Jesus. As if *you* needed that. Then you quit. Ran, like a coward. Never even checked in with me."

Now it's becoming crystal clear. I did run and hide. Sneaked in one evening when I wouldn't have to see hardly anyone to clear my locker. I ignored all my friends, not just her. And then, not long after I left, she strengthened her friendship with Jess. I thought it was an innocent development, that they'd started hanging out because I'd been such a hermit. "But, Allison, why didn't you tell me?"

"I couldn't believe you were that officer, the one who wouldn't support him. I couldn't believe it. I was going to confront you when I got back into town. I rushed home to him, but by the time I got back, he had already hung himself. And you . . . you were fucking gone."

She pushes the anguish away and lifts her chin.

"You lied for the scumbag." Her tone hardens. "You hung Leon out to dry. His word against theirs. Why? I thought you had some decency, some guts."

"I know, Allison. I backed Railes. It hurts so much to think of Leon. Everything that happened. You're right about it all, but I didn't know he was your nephew."

"It shouldn't matter. You fucking *lied* for Billy Railes." Her voice is sharp in the woods. "What the fuck, Mitchell? How could you do that?"

"You know what Coleman did to Jess, right? She's told you?"

Allison doesn't answer. I have no idea if Jess has told her or not. It doesn't matter. "What he did to Leon, too," I say. "I didn't know Leon was, that he was . . ." I stop myself from saying *suicidal* or *unstable*. I need to watch my words. "You're right. It's no excuse," I say, my voice cracking, too.

None of it is justifiable. Mark Coleman was abusive. And a rapist. But none of it makes what I did okay. I feel the full density of it dead center, in my bones, not watching myself through glass. My culpability closes in on me like a colossal wave slamming me under. All the shame, all the anguish, all the guilt finally coming fully home to roost. My chest sears with pain. My knees begin to shake and nearly buckle. Tears sting my eyes. "Allison, I've regretted backing Railes every single minute, every single hour of every day since," I manage to get out.

"If you had such regrets, then why didn't you come clean after you quit?"

A second wave crashes over me. Again, I feel the same sense that something like sludge is filling my mouth. I could have. I had already quit. All my dreams to make detective had vanished. But Leon was already gone, and I needed to be there for Jess and Sam. I couldn't stomach the thought of being mired in it all over scumbag Mark Coleman when I needed to stay strong and unencumbered for her and Sam for something he caused. But here I stand—a total scumbag myself, causing endless pain and devastation.

"Thomas cared about him," she says about Coleman as if she's read my mind.

"I know he did but, Allison . . ." I drop my hands and open my palms to her like a sacrifice. "I'm so sorry."

But even I can hear how pathetic the apology sounds, a single drop of water out in the dry desert.

"Hands back up. Now." Her breathing grows more rapid.

I put them behind my head again. Allison is good with a gun. I'm not about to tempt her. A head shot would be easy for her. And here I stand with shaking knees right before her.

"The others." Her voice hisses, filled with wrath. "I haven't cared about seeing their faces, but yours, yours I want to see. I thought you had courage."

It's so spot-on my breath catches. This woman is going to shoot me. "I've already confessed," I blurt out.

"Don't outright *lie*, Crosbie, *again*."

"I did. There's an article that's going to drop in a few hours. I didn't want to just throw it out on social media. I wanted to be more respectful, thorough, like Tim Mooney. I wanted it to be complete—for you, for Jess, because I thought that's what you, the Confession Artist, wanted. Something complete."

I take a gulp of cold air but my lungs will barely let it in. Shame, fear, and even exhaustion crowd my chest. And deep, deep sorrow for this entire fucked-up mission Allison has embarked on—all of it born the day Railes shot Coleman and I didn't back Leon. I have no idea yet how Allison is connected to all the other victims, but I do understand that I could cry for a year straight, day and night, week after week, month after month, and it wouldn't be enough.

"It's my full apology to you," I say. "To Leon. The public was correct in naming you. You're the Confession Artist. It works."

I figure a little flattery might go over well.

"What you've accomplished is powerful," I say. "The people close to the victims can begin to heal."

Allison doesn't buy it. Or hasn't heard a word.

"Allison." I shake my head. "I feel so guilty for how I handled things with Railes, but you, sketching people? Really? Standing here now in the woods beside my sister's house, and *Sam*? Bringing *him* into this?"

Sam—*my nephew*. The irony isn't lost on me. I dip my head to the barrel. "Think of how this will affect Jess."

"I can't think about that," she says.

"But killing people?"

"Railes did it. And you helped him get away with it. Why should you care what other scumbags I've also taken care of?"

"I wish with every fiber of my being that I told the investigator Coleman didn't have a knife, especially after I found out what happened to Leon. I had no idea he'd take . . ."

Again, I can't say it out loud. The weight of what I did is too much for me to bear. A part of me feels this is what I deserve. That Allison, standing here with her bleach-blond hair luminescent in the dawn, is an angel sent to make me pay. There's almost something I crave in it, like drinking bitter lemon water. I feel as though I'm outside of myself, something bigger than me pushing my body right toward it all.

I wonder if this is what Randal Askens and Vonda Loman felt, too.

The woods press in around me. The trees, the air, the dirt under my feet, the sky above, the mountains rearing up rock solid in the distance—none of it cares about me. About Allison. About her state of mind. About my cowardice. The universe doesn't care whether we live or die. Whether I live or die.

So why do I?

*Jess. Sam.* It all swings back to them, the only family I have. They're my anchor.

I can't just lie down out here for her and let her kill me.

A new surge of adrenaline jolts through me. I don't want to die like Randal and Vonda. I want to fight for my life. I want to dart off through the woods. But she's a good shot, and she knows I'm wearing Kevlar from my interaction with Sam earlier. I force myself to stay still, my heart a mallet against my chest.

"Even Jess got me a card months later when she heard about my loss," she says.

At the mention of my sister's name, acid coats the back of my throat.

I had no idea Jess even knew that Allison lost the nephew she was raising. I was so preoccupied with what I had done, with Jess and the rape, with looking out for Sam. And later, no one, including Jess, ever mentioned that Allison lost Leon.

But yes, when I think back to it—to that nightmarish whirlwind of a week—I was mired in my own dishonesty and shame, my own shock at what went down with Railes. It barely registered that Allison was away the week Railes shot Coleman, but I vaguely remember she was on vacation, because I had wanted to talk to her—the one person who might provide some comfort even if I would never have come clean to her—but she wasn't there.

I was so preoccupied, I didn't bother to reach out to her when she returned because I had quit while she was away. From then on, I put my head down, kept to myself, let week after week, month after month, slip by without contacting any friends at all. I didn't reach out to her until much later.

But Jess . . . ? The information I found on Jess's desk about Ryan Petronis and his sister, Vivian . . . ?

And there's all the time Allison has spent with Jess for the past four to five months. Had Allison planned this since then? Just used Jess to get closer to both of us?

"Jess didn't know what you were doing?" I hate that there's even a question at all.

"No," she says firmly.

If I didn't have a gun pointed at me, the relief of it would drop me to my quaking knees. "The others? How did you know about Ryan Petronis?"

Allison glances around the woods. Where is Sam? Is he alone? Has Greene found him? I ache all over, inside and out. Pray that Greene has him or that he's somehow made it back to the house, to Jess. Or, at the very least, is safely hidden behind a tree somewhere.

"His mom. At the rehab facility in Arlee. Jesus, you didn't know I went there for rehab, did you? And Jess didn't think it was important enough to mention?"

I'm stunned. I guess not. I guess Jess was trying to keep me out of her personal business in a lot of ways over the past year. I stay quiet but keep connecting the dots.

Allison drunk at the fundraiser, one of the only times I saw her.

The packed, Teflon-colored suitcase Vivian and Ryan's mom posted on Facebook. She was headed to rehab.

"Poor Ryan," she says like she's read my mind. "My heart breaks for him and his family."

"And the woman in Santa Monica? Vonda Loman?"

"That bitch," Allison mumbles. "Poor Gus. Losing Somer like that. And Lauren losing her daughter." I don't know who she's talking about, but I'm sure they're somehow connected to people hurt by Loman and Mooney.

Her voice is distant and low. She doesn't sound like the Allison I know. The idea that she's separating from herself to shoot me out here is terrifying.

"Gus who? Lauren who?"

"Enough," Allison says. Her eyes flicker in all directions, looking for Greene or Sam. No twigs have snapped.

"It's everywhere, and it's getting worse. All the fucking *enabling*. All the delusions. It's a goddamn crisis." She practically spits it. "An epidemic of heartlessness. And you, you've followed right along. You were something in our department—a breath of fresh air—but I find you're as corrupt as all the assholes."

The ground I'm standing on is crumbling. Firm soil turns to mud. I'm falling away. I'm about to tumble down a deep, endless black pit. Without planning to, I lower my hands and take a tiny step closer, toward the barrel of her gun, like I'm asking for it, despite my terror. I want to pressure her a little, make her nervous enough to maybe make a mistake.

"You don't think I live with this every day of my life?"

"Stop!" she barks. Her voice pierces the quiet woods. "I mean it. Hands back up."

Her gun is far from steady. She's not cocksure of the plan.

The light between the pines is brightening. I get a better view of her face. It's puffy and her eyes have a frantic, electric glow. Her face flushes an angry red, and her hair is stringy and haywire. She looks on the brink. I've seen the look in people who've departed from reality before, who've entered some alternate sense of their own making. She doesn't remotely resemble the Allison I know.

There's no logic in this, no calculus explaining her need to hurt others the way she's been hurt by Leon's departure from her life because of what Railes did. What *I* did.

"Allison, listen," I say forcefully. "I know you're devastated. I know you're grieving, but there's help for—"

"Stop!" Her eyes burn. "There's *not*. It's all bullshit. All of it. He's *gone*. Everyone tells you so much crap. *He's in a better place.*"

She's slipped into a cloying, higher-pitched tone, her face twitching.

"*He's an angel looking over you. He's living on through your memories. God wanted him by his side because he was so special.* It's all bullshit! People need to *pay*. Don't you see? People need to wake up. They need to do the right thing. *You*, you needed to do the right thing." Her voice has now gone tinny and desperate. But also determined.

I'm losing her. I need to do something.

"And," I press. "Allison, listen to me, this is important, it explains how *after* Coleman was killed, it didn't help. I thought Jess's nightmares would go away, but they didn't. I thought I'd feel relieved he was gone, but I don't."

"No!"

Her voice slices the chilled air like a chain saw through an old cottonwood. I force myself to stand still. Be calm.

"You do *not* get to say these things to me after my boy is gone," she snarls. "Besides, you're wrong. It does feel good. Askens was the first. He was going to be the only one. But afterward"—a broad smile consumes her face in a frankly awful way—"I had a purpose. I found *purpose*. Isn't that what you wanted, Crosbie Mitchell? Why you became a cop? *Purpose?* And I got relief, too. There was such huge relief in it, so don't tell me it doesn't help. It took the pain away. I kept thinking about how good it must have felt for you to watch Coleman go down, and I wanted that, too."

Her chest rises and falls. Her eyes soften, as if remembering how firing two bullets into Askens's head after shooting him in the back was an injection of pure bliss. I'd imagined doing something exactly like it to Coleman many times myself before Billy Railes took my place. But now, the thought makes the acidic taste at the back of my throat bite harder.

"Allison," I say. I feel short on oxygen. My pulse beats faster in my throat. The trees and the clearing we're in spin like a merry-go-round being pushed and flung by an angry bully. "Allison, Allison, listen to me, what about you?" I try turning the lens on her, trying to throw her off guard.

"What about me?"

"This is about public reckonings, right?"

She lifts her chin, her nostrils flaring.

"And if it's about that, then don't you have something to say to the world? Shouldn't you confess what you've done to Askens, to Loman?"

Allison's face crinkles like a child about to cry, but she straightens out in the next second. "Enough of this," she says with a steely voice. She shakes her head like a dog repelling water. "You." She lifts her gun higher. "You need to get down on your knees."

My breath hitches high in my sternum. My knees go even weaker. "You shoot me out here," I point out, "and that agent will be here in a split second. You won't have time to get back to your car."

"You don't think I have something in mind?" she asks.

I shouldn't underestimate her. She has killed two people with cold-blooded proficiency, garnered national attention for it, all while remaining under the radar of the FBI.

But I don't believe her. She's full of rage, but there's also pain. She's not enjoying the killings. She's seeking justice, and some relief, and that's it. She doesn't care what happens to herself in the long run. She doesn't have a plan B.

"I happen to be a fast runner," she says, almost jokingly. "Now, keep your hands behind your head and get down on your knees."

"Allison, you know they'll catch you, and you'll go down for three murders instead of two."

"What's one more life sentence?" She makes herself laugh, but suddenly her face flashes hard again. "*Down.* Now."

I drop one leg at a time. My fingers thread tightly through my hair and press against my scalp. It's surreal, realizing this might be the last time

I touch my own head and feel my own hair beneath my fingertips. The damp, cold underbrush seeps through my jeans to my knees. I desperately search my surroundings for a solution but see nothing useful, not even a good rock or solid stick to pick up.

Allison angles her gun down at me. From my kneeling position, looking up at her, she looks like she could blow away with a strong wind.

And that's when a twig snaps off to my right. *Thank God,* I think. *Greene.*

But it's not Greene.

It's Sam. Slowly approaching.

*Sam.* A relief that he's safe washes over me, but then it's followed by a deep, stabbing fear. *Sam, not now.* "Sam, turn and go," I order.

"Please don't hurt my aunt," he says.

Allison looks at him through the corner of her eye. She's keeping her gun trained on me, which I'm grateful for.

"Sam," I command, feeling like a bomb has detonated in me and all my insides are crumbling. *You can't be here now, around this, around Allison with a gun.* "Sam," I say. "Go back. Just for a little while."

"Oh, honey," she says. "It's okay. You come here to me, and I won't shoot your aunt."

"No," I say firmly. "Stay right there."

He stares at us like a spooked animal, not moving.

"I mean it," Allison says. "Come here, or you'll give me no choice but to shoot her. You don't want that, do you?"

Sam starts slowly walking toward us.

Panic shoots through me. I try to gulp in air, like I'm going to have an anxiety attack.

The ground fully collapses from under me. I'm teetering on a thin wire with nothing beneath me. *Do something, Crosbie. Now. Do* something.

Sam witnessing his aunt getting shot and dealing with that nightmare, stealing his innocence in one fell swoop. Or worse, him getting hurt or shot himself flashes through my mind. My breath stops with fright. It's in this breathless moment that my plan arrives, fully formed. It's not a great one, but it's one I remember from my police training. When wearing Kevlar, try to get the perpetrator in a struggle with you and get the gun pressed into the Kevlar because if it goes off, it will most likely be into the vest and you'll be protected.

Sam draws closer to us and she glances his way.

"Get down, Sam!"

I scream it. I pitch myself and grab for her ankles. I only get one but use both hands and yank as hard as I can. She fires her gun, but I've thrown her off-balance, making her hand jerk upward. The shot rips above me.

*Oh God. Sam? What have I done?* I jerk my head around to look for him.

*Please let Sam be okay.* As I struggle with her squirming, trying to yank her in closer to my torso, I frantically search for him. She pulls her leg out of my grip and fires again. The bullet hits the ground, spraying dirt and debris into my face and mouth. My ears roar. I grab her leg before she starts to stand, jerk harder. She stumbles and trips, falling heavily onto her side.

I jump onto her and press the wrist of her gun hand down as hard as I can so she can't lift that hand. She squirms violently, trying to yank it free, but that's not happening. I straddle her for a second, but she manages to kick me and shove me to the side. My face hits something hard and sharp like a rock.

I have her wrist, can feel it wiggling under her jacket, and heave her toward me, her entire body flinging against mine. Her perfume and her underlying body odor, a pungent scent born of fear and insanity, fill my nose. She thrashes us into a new position and I'm able to ram an elbow into her hot, sweaty neck—once, and again, harder. She flies into a frenzy, jabbing and pounding me repeatedly with her free fist, while yanking her other arm free.

Greene's voice finally rings loud and clear through the woods. "Mitchell, where are you?"

"Over here," I yell.

I hear thrashing through the underbrush of the woods. Greene is yelling, "Freeze or I'll shoot."

I'm holding Allison's arm, shaking it so she'll release the gun, but she's twisting and turning.

My hands are sweaty. I'm losing my grip on the sleeve of her slick jacket. I hear Greene scuffle closer. And Sam? I get a glimpse of him. He's standing off to the side, stunned and exposed. Fear for him practically paralyzes me, but I keep holding her sleeve.

"Freeze, Allison. Get on your knees." I can't see Greene, but by the sound of her voice, she's close.

"Don't shoot," I scream. "Sam's here."

Sam's still standing off to our side. "Sam," I yell again. "Get down."

He doesn't budge. He is frozen. I'm struggling to hold on to Allison, but my hand keeps slipping. She's going to break free.

"Get down, Sam," I repeat. If he's down, she can't grab him and drag him with her again. And if she shoots again, he'll at least be on the ground.

Allison breaks free. She jumps to her feet.

"Sam," I scream. "Be the Teke Teke girl." It's all I can think of to break his spell of uncertainty. Something familiar. Something from his playful world.

It breaks through. He drops to the ground.

Allison bolts. I grab again for her ankles but get nothing but cold air and dry grass.

She takes off, disappears behind some pines, and fires her gun behind her without turning.

Greene shoots into the pines. Once, twice. Greene tosses me my gun, which she must have found back in the clearing where Allison sneaked up on me. She runs after Allison, jumping over deadfall and brush.

I reach Sam at the same time as the officer who was guarding Jess's house and who had joined the hunt. I place my hand on Sam's back and ask him if he's okay. When he nods, a relief as powerful as a tidal wave overcomes me and makes my knees go weak. I want to sit with him and never leave him, but I tell him to stay down, order the officer to stay with him and get him to safety when the coast is clear.

I bolt after Greene and Allison. I hear sirens coming from the direction of Jess's house.

It's not until I come to the other end of the forest that I see Allison up ahead of Greene. She's now in a neighboring field, close to another set of trees, and again, she fires erratically behind her as she flees, the bullet flying somewhere off to our right and pinging off rocks.

Greene has a clear shot now.

"Freeze," she roars. "Get down." She peppers Allison with more orders: "Now. Get down. On your knees. Now. You're surrounded!"

Allison is more than a third of the way across the field. I'm charging fast, tripping and flinging myself over gopher holes.

Allison fires another bullet.

Greene shoots, but misses again.

"Don't hurt her!" I yell. But even as my voice fades into the breeze, I know all that matters to Greene—all that should matter to me—is that Allison is armed and firing at us.

On Greene's fourth shot, Allison pitches forward, staggers a few paces, and almost makes it to another patch of woods on the other side of the field.

# Chapter 53

I walk Sam off the field, clutching him tightly to my side. The police officer who stayed with him in the clearing escorts us.

Jess runs out of the house toward us. Her hair looks strange, matted and tangled, and it takes me a second to remember that she was taking a shower when I ran after Allison and Sam. She must have realized something was wrong, maybe heard the sirens, before she even got to a comb.

Alderson and a police officer I don't recognize trail her. Jess frantically grabs Sam and pulls him in.

She's crying. But they're tears of sheer relief to have Sam safely in her arms. She strokes the back of his head, tightens her other arm around him.

When she looks up at me, she holds out an arm and pulls me in, too.

"Thank you," she says to me.

"For what?" I say. My mouth feels numb, like it's not moving. The smell of her flowery shampoo fills my nose.

Other sirens blare. Other emergency responders still arriving.

"For saving him," she says. "He told me"—she lifts her chin to Alderson—"he said Greene told him you kept Sam safe out there. I can't believe it was Allison. All this time, it was her? How did you know?" she asks. "Did you talk to Vivian about her brother? Come across something?"

I tell Jess about Leon's keys, such a small thing, but sometimes a little detail is the key to solving a crime. In this case, *literal* keys.

"Then how did she know about Vivian? Cros, I swear I didn't tell her."

I want to give her all the details, but my head feels thick, and I start to tremble. Jess's voice seems far away, but I hold tight. I keep inhaling the scent of her freshly shampooed hair like it's a lifeline. I don't want to let go of her or Sam. The three of us continue to stand in the dried and snarled grass of her field beside her house, wrapped in one another's arms.

My shakes grow more intense, uncontrollable.

Jess pulls away and looks at me. "Oh my God, you poor thing." She very gently nudges my chin to the side and studies the gash on my cheekbone from where I slammed it into the rock.

Before she can say anything else, Alderson places a hand on my shoulder.

When I turn to him, he points to the newly arrived paramedics.

Within short order, Jess's place and the woods and the fields swarm with law enforcement from the county sheriff's office and from all police departments in the valley, and emergency response units. Greene called it in as soon as she started running after Sam.

Sam and Jess are now inside the house with a paramedic.

A different EMT inspects my pupils out beside an ambulance and asks me questions to determine whether I've gone into shock before they'll let me go see Sam and Jess again.

"State your name for me, please. Do you know today's date? Do you know where you are?"

Other than the after-shakes still possessing my body, the cut on my face, some red welts that will end up as bruises, and very sore muscles from my tussle with Allison, I'm okay.

Greene looks exhausted, dumbfounded. It's status quo for Alderson: his usual sweet smile, though he's been very concerned for Greene and the tough decision she made.

I'm surprised at how comforting it is to have them by me. I slow-blink, and when I open my eyes, they're full of tears. When I swipe them away, I see Allison being carried out on a gurney. In a bag. The cold pit in my stomach grows larger.

Greene puts a hand on my shoulder and squeezes. "Are you all right?"

"Yes." I try to sound collected, but I can hear the strain in it through the thickening lump in my throat. I press my lips together to quell the deep unease. I look down at my hands and notice how, strangely, they're not quivering. I stare at them with interest and try to shove away the sense that this outcome is not right. That justice, once again, has not been served and that perhaps I should be the one crumpled in Jess's neighbor's field.

# Chapter 54

I spend hours giving my statement at the county building. They use the same room where Alderson showed me photos of Aaron Lasserio, Ridgeway's lackey.

Sam has been checked. Jess has taken him home. Alderson informs me Jess was torn about leaving but he told her that he'd make sure I got a ride over to her place when I was finished. He also tells me that they've lined Sam up for some more sessions with the trauma specialist who spoke with him at the station when we arrived.

Alderson has also contacted Vivian Petronis, the sister of the boy, Ryan, who died by suicide after being hazed by the football team, and Lauren Littlejohns, a mother from Arlee whose daughter overdosed on drugs prescribed by a doctor working with Tim Mooney. They're working on locating Gus Bauers. They believe he's the father of the girl, Somer, whom Allison mentioned to me.

Allison didn't give a surname, but they've searched on all of Vonda Loman's counseling files during the investigation and easily pinpointed a student named Somer Bauers who visited Vonda Loman for therapy. Somer died in a coma at a hospital. Two unidentified guys dropped her off and split, even though she was unresponsive. Her father, Gus, also went to the rehab facility in Arlee around the same time as Allison and Ryan Petronis's mother, Cindy.

So what they're gathering is that Allison met Ryan's mother, Cindy Petronis, at the rehab facility in Arlee. She met Somer's dad, Gus Bauers, and Nalia's mom, Lauren Littlejohns, at a grief group down the road from the rehab place in Arlee.

Alderson offers to drive me home, but when we get to the waiting area, Jeremy is there. Seeing him stand and approach us lifts something heavy off my chest. I smile. He gives me one of his lopsided grins. I'm surprised at how much I need these little offerings.

"Need a ride?" he asks.

"Sure. How did you . . . ?"

"When I couldn't get a hold of you, I went straight to your house. A reporter there said you'd already left early in the morning. I remembered you saying you needed to talk to Jess in person, so I went to her house, and when I got there, I ran into a wall of cops. When they brought you here, I followed."

Alderson gives Jeremy a sidelong glance and turns to me. "You sure? I don't mind taking you home."

"No," I say. "I'm good."

I give Alderson a hug, thank him, and tell him not to leave town without saying goodbye. As Jeremy and I turn to walk to his car, Wallace walks up.

I feel yet more strings in my heart ping. A compassion I'd forgotten I'd had for Wallace all along, an empathy that got lost in all this mess. Here he is, showing up for me as always.

"Crosbie." He throws his arms around me. "Are you all right?"

"I'm okay."

"I saw on the news they've caught the person. They haven't released a name yet, though. Who is it?"

I glance at Jeremy. "Can you give us a sec?"

Jeremy waits outside while Wallace and I stand in the corner of the reception room. "Wallace," I say, "the article. You've read it?"

"Yes."

"Then you know it recaps everything that happened with Sophie?"

"Yes."

"I'm sorry I didn't give you a heads-up this morning. I meant to after I spoke to Jess, but all this hap—"

"It's okay." He grabs both of my hands. "I'm glad you got it all out there. It's a good piece. Surprising, but sincere."

The fact that he isn't judging me makes me want to weep.

He tells me he's glad I'm safe and offers me a ride.

"I already have one." I point outside, to Jeremy.

"Oh," he says, trying to smile, but there's sadness there. But for a change, there's nothing pissy about it.

"You've been a good friend, Wallace. I'm sorry for the way I've treated you this week, and when—"

"When what?"

"When we got together and then I just ended it like someone in high school."

"I never held that against you."

"And that you were interrogated by the agents to boot."

"It's fine." He waves it away. "If they didn't interview me, I'd have thought they weren't doing their jobs. You know how much I care about you, right?"

I smile.

"But," he says. "You need more space than I've been giving you."

I nod.

"I get it. I think I've been hanging on a little too tightly because, in a way, you're all I have left of Sophie."

"I know the feeling." I catch the magnetic blue of his eyes. And for the first time in a long time, I recapture a glimpse of the calming sense of the friendship I had with Wallace before we began dating.

Already, however, that Crosbie feels foreign to me, a stranger you might spot across a crowded room. *That* Crosbie saw tranquility in Wallace and took it for dull and routine when we started dating, not strength and golden self-awareness. That Crosbie, in short, was searching for someone to push her, to test her. Not someone who was going to accept her for who she was. Because *that* Crosbie needed to hate herself for who she'd become.

# Chapter 55

"I meant what I said earlier," I say to Jess. Golden-hour evening light streams through the west-facing windows of her kitchen. Lines of yellow police tape flutter in the wind out back. Sam is conked out on the couch. Any sign of the trauma he's endured is buried behind a peaceful, angelic face.

For me, the shakes have subsided. I'm exhausted and want to go home and curl up and sleep for a week straight, but I want to talk to my sister and check on Sam. The car ride with Jeremy was quiet. He kept it light, sensing I was too spent and exhausted and focused on Jess and Sam to talk. I'm worried how this incident will affect my nephew, but I'm hopeful with some counseling that he'll be okay.

But Jess . . . I know I need to stop being her caretaker, but I want to see if she's willing to finally get some help after all this. Even though Allison confirmed Jess had nothing to do with the whole thing, I still wonder how much she understood about Allison's state of mind. After all, they've been hanging out on and off for months.

"So, now that it's out," I say, "I think you should get help. No more excuses."

She slow-blinks, as I always do. She's calm. She gives a shrug.

"Jess?" I rub my thumb against the smooth ceramic of the coffee cup. "I know you had nothing to do with this. But how much did you know about how off the rails she'd gone?"

"I figured you might wonder. Whether I somehow intuitively *knew* she was the Confession Artist?"

"No, of course not. But did you have any clues she'd snapped?"

The wind is picking up. Dying leaves rattle on her two maple trees out front. I wait. I'm afraid to hear the answer, that she suspected something but didn't share it with me, just like she didn't tell me Allison had lost her nephew.

"Okay. Yes. I know she's been super troubled. Like me. Like Ryan Petronis's sister, Vivian. I mean, Allison lost Tom—or Leon now. He was like her son, but I had no idea he was the one with Mark that night."

"Neither did I. Of course. Why didn't you mention that she'd lost her nephew to me?"

She gives me a look that says, *Come on, you haven't noticed the state I've been in for the past year?*

I don't say anything.

"She told me Tom, who was like a son to her, took his life. She told me he had been dating someone, but she never said who. But she said things didn't work out. But she didn't tell me it was Mark Coleman. I never connected the two. How did she know about Vivian and the others?"

"Remember the rehab place in Arlee she went to a few months ago? Well, Vivian's mom was there along with another guy, a man named Gus who lost his daughter." I fill her in on all the connections. I ask, "Did you know Allison went out of town when the others were shot?"

"God no. I mean, yeah, we've become friends, but I guess I was too wrapped up in my own stuff to notice what she was up to. Like you, I'd never even met Tom. You know, Leon. Don't take this the wrong way, Crosbie, but I didn't want to lean on you for everything. I don't want you to feel so much responsibility for me anymore. I guess I've been trying to insert some distance. I'm not a child. I've been trying to tell you. You're not, like, some superhero who's been assigned to watch over me. And you're not my mother. It's not your responsibility, so you need to just stop."

I swallow hard. This is on the money, and I know it. For so long, because our mom was out drinking so much, I'd taken on the role. And after she was gone, and Jess got so depressed, it was even more essential. Looking out for her is all I've ever known, but Jess is right. Somehow, in all the craziness of the past days, I've been recognizing it.

"Did you read the article?"

She nods. "When I read it, I didn't feel as angry as I thought I would. In a weird way, I got some kind of vicarious relief from it. But mainly, I'm scared for you—that it's all out there. What's going to happen?"

"I don't know," I say. "I'm scared." It's the truth, not sugarcoated for her ears, for a change. None of the usual *It's all going to be okay. I'll take care of it.* None of that. It feels like a veil has been lifted between us, like I can finally just be myself without worrying about her reaction. "But for now, I'm too tired to worry about any of it. I hope to sleep through most of the press the next few days." I give a weak smile. "But I can tell you one thing I know for sure. I'm glad to finally get it off my chest.

"I am responsible," I say. "In part, for Leon's suicide. For not exposing the truth of that night. But you're right: Initially, where I went wrong, before all my other sins, is that I thought I could control things, thought I could shield you somehow. I've been overprotective. I've been telling myself you and Sam need me this much, but really, I've needed it for me—and don't get mad at me for bringing this up again—but I've needed it because of Sophie."

Jess stares, surprise filling her eyes. "For Sophie?"

"You know, in a weird way, to atone for her. The way I've viewed you ever since Mom died, when you got depressed, has been through this distorted lens, blurred by my own guilt and shame about Sophie, and lately, exacerbated by Coleman and Leon. It's been overwhelming for you and Sam at times. I know that. I'm sorry for that. I need to knock it off. Is that why you've been so angry at me?"

"Maybe. I don't know. I'm struggling so much, still, after all these months." She turns away and looks out the window. "I guess I have my own anger."

The air in the room seems to have stilled, the whooshing of the trees fading into the distance. I have to admit, a part of me is still waiting for Jess to say she knew about Allison but didn't warn anyone. That she was vicariously finding satisfaction in the awful retribution Allison was doling out to random individuals.

It's not that I think my sister's a sociopath, capable of anything remotely like this, but I guess I'm realizing she's not only stronger than I think, but she might also be more resentful and vengeful than I realize. When she said to me after the rape, *Crosbie, it's fine. I was date-raped, taken advantage of, but I don't want to report this. Leave it alone. I'll be okay,* I didn't think she'd be okay, but she convinced me that she was bullheaded enough to keep on keeping on. But for these past days, I've watched the glint of anger in her eyes gleam a little too brightly.

I'm overly familiar with how hot the desire for revenge can burn, sear everything and make it hard to heal.

"I mean"—Jess turns back—"one day Allison asked me why I wasn't angrier at all the people on the side who don't care," she says as if she can read my thoughts. "That people will stop at stoplights and follow all sorts of little rules, but when it comes to the big stuff, to really caring, being decent and stopping bad things from happening, they turn away and allow others to do awful things, especially when there's money involved. She mentioned once that all the enablers deserved to be shot right along with the perpetrators. I got a strange feeling. But I figured she was venting like the rest of us."

"Venting is okay." I state the obvious. "Exacting revenge via murder? Not so good. I haven't murdered anyone, but what I did for Railes was all born from the same well. From anger. I guess I'm learning, Jess."

"Learning what?"

"That I can't do the healing for you. I've been trying so hard for so long to shield you from pain—the pain of losing Dad, then Mom, the devastation from the rape . . . It was foolish of me. All I can do is try to support you in whichever way you want."

The intensity of Jess's emotions crowds her eyes. She brings her knuckles to her mouth and presses them into her teeth. "It's okay," I tell her, pulling her in—like a sister, dammit, not a mother. "You can let it out."

# Chapter 56

***Two and a Half Months Later***

I pull my boots on and throw on my coat. I grab my bag. It's early November, and the air carries a raw humidity that promises snow. I pause outside and look to the mountains, which appear as massive, hovering humps in the gathering early light. Hunting season has arrived, and some wise elk have come down from the higher regions to the safety of areas closer to town. It's too dim to see them, but I can smell their strong, ungulate scent—hide mixed with dried hay. In the distance, I hear a reedy cry.

As I head to my car, my phone lights up. It's Jeremy, saying hello. He's on the East Coast, well into his work morning. I tell him I'm off to the office but was delayed admiring the elk. He writes back: poor you, halted by all that beauty! He tells me he misses the mountains. I tell him I miss finding that perfect Pad Thai for lunch.

The "on-and-off" nature of his relationship with the gal he was seeing in New York switched to permanently "off" when he returned. A month later, he called me. We took to spending long hours on the phone chatting about all my and Jess's losses growing up, about Mark Coleman and Leon, about Allison, about all my guilts.

We talked about his past, too, about how he grew up in the shadow of his older brother, who became a physician, about how his dad always thought his journalistic endeavors were never going to amount to much and how he found himself constantly wanting to prove him wrong.

We chatted and chatted until, somewhere along the line, we began touching base every day. We almost set in motion a plan that had him coming out to visit this month, but mutually stepped back from it with some relief, agreeing that I still have a lot to process after Allison, and he has some sorting out to do after his breakup. We're tentatively planning on something in the late spring or summer if we're still up for it—and I'm hoping we will be because, I have to admit, the thought of it kind of makes my heart sing.

When I get to the office, I'll be preparing for a deposition on the Robbie Ridgeway case. Since the Confession Artist insanity spent itself, I've been working hard with Greene and Alderson, who are trying to help the DA's office pin Clarissa's death on Aaron Lasserio and Robbie Ridgeway.

We may never be able to demonstrate Ridgeway hit her over the head before she went in the water, that she didn't hit it on a rock on the way down. But Lasserio has already sung and maintained that he was following Ridgeway's orders to stalk Clarissa and scare her off. Given the other facts—that Lasserio tried to get rid of her personal items and that Ridgeway also hired Lasserio to keep an eye on me because I was looking into her death—it was sufficient evidence to get the DA to open an investigation into Clarissa's death.

In addition to all the other evidence, that Clarissa died from a hit to the head before water entered her lungs and that Ridgeway's truck was in the same area as Clarissa the day she was out in the field taking samples before she was murdered, we have a statement from Palmer Edmonds, Jeremy's connection on the Blackfeet Reservation. Edmonds wouldn't talk to Paxton, but he did talk to me once Jeremy put in a good word, and it turns out he has a photo of the graffiti on Clarissa's car.

Clarissa had texted it to him along with a message that she was getting scared that Ridgeway or one of his men might harm her. The DA believes, at the very least, that a case can be built on circumstantial evidence because he had the most to lose from Clarissa's studies of the fen on his property.

Not only was one of his sketchpads from his ranch found in her backpack—proving she had some connection to his ranch—but Lasserio worked for Ridgeway, acted as his henchman, and Ridgeway owned, through inheritance, the storage shed where Lasserio kept her backpack after she died. Greene and Alderson are certain that the DA will assemble a good case against both Ridgeway and Lasserio.

When the elk are finished chatting and begin to move out of the field toward the ridges, where they'll go higher as the sun rises, I take one more gulp of cold mountain air and go back into my garage to hop in my car.

Jess has been making good progress in therapy, and already in the past two and a half months, I've watched her getting calmer and stronger. She's returned to being energized about her work at Rotical, and she's also back to her podcast, even doing several episodes on vigilantism.

She and I have come to an understanding that I will give her the space she needs to live her own life and she'll respect me enough to communicate honestly with me about how she feels. And Sam? He's in therapy, too. He tells me all about the sandbox with the dinosaurs that he gets to play with at his therapist's office. I'm beyond pleased he's remained just as talkative and inquisitive as ever.

Deputy Zane is finishing his rehab and will be back at work in the new year. I visited almost daily during his rehab and don't plan to quit bugging him, either. I tell him he's the baby brother I never had and that it's my right to spoil him.

Plus, Vivian, Gus, and Lauren—all strangely linked by Allison—have come together and frequently meet. Both Jess and I have spent time with them, too. All three have gotten their fair share of media attention since news of Allison's rationale for picking her victims went public. They've also decided to give Jeremy an interview on their own personal involvement with Allison, whether in group therapy or simply from seeing her in town in a restaurant, as Lauren used to.

As I drive south on the highway, the clouds above the Columbia Range to my left burn a fiery red. My phone buzzes.

It's Greene. "Mitchell," she says. "You busy?"

"Just driving to work."

"Oh, well, if you'd prefer to call me when you—"

"No, it's fine. Got you on Bluetooth."

"Okay, well, I hear you're one lucky lady," she says.

She's referring to the fact that the feds informed me late yesterday that they've decided not to go after me. It's called deferred prosecution. Because I confessed, cooperated, and helped to catch the killer, and because I'm willing to testify against Railes, who they plan to nail to the wall and put away for life for murder and hate crimes, I've earned lenience.

In exchange for a deferred prosecution, I've signed a contract for a six-year probationary period in which I must be a 100 percent law-abiding citizen; must cooperate fully with law enforcement whenever they need me to; must testify truthfully against Railes; must be available for interviews, depositions, and Railes's trial; must get individual counseling and attend anger management classes; and must volunteer community hours at my cause of choice. If I don't reoffend, I won't be arrested or have anything on my record.

In the meantime, I've had to give up my POST certification, which means my career in organized law enforcement is officially over. Thankfully, in Montana, a POST certification is not necessary to be a PI, so I get to keep my private investigator's license.

"Yes," I say. "I'm very lucky. Sometimes I think I deserve it. Sometimes I don't." All I know is the fact that I've evaded jail time takes my breath away when I know how many are not as lucky. "But I'm glad to be paying *some* dues. It feels right."

"I'm sure it does," she says. "And how's business?"

"Believe it or not, in some ways it's picked up because of the notoriety. There are people wanting to hire me because they think I'm scrappy. I have to break the news to them that I can't and won't do anything that's not by the book."

"That's a switch," she says.

"It's my newfound way, playing it straight. I have no choice in the matter since I'm on probation. But I have an inkling that even after my six years are complete, I'm going to keep it up. I guess I'll admit, it actually feels kind of good."

Somewhere along the line, I've figured out that the best way to respect myself is to walk the straight and narrow and be as honest as possible. Not doing so invites guilt. Invites shame and disgust. And trust me, trying to love and respect yourself while mired in all that toxicity isn't likely to happen. "Of course," I say, "some do walk, but some stay."

"I'm glad to hear that, Crosbie. And I have some good news about Ridgeway for you. We finally got Lasserio to come clean."

"What? You're kidding?"

"No, I'm not. His attorney convinced him it was better to cooperate and give up the goods on Ridgeway to reduce his own sentence."

"What happened?"

"He says it was an accident, that he was only supposed to rough her up on orders from Ridgeway. Ridgeway ordered him to scare her off from reporting on what she was discovering about the fen, but while he was talking to her, they began arguing and he tried to grab her. When she jerked away, she fell and hit her head on a boulder and was knocked unconscious. When Clarissa didn't come to, he went and got Ridgeway and the two of them disposed of her body in the river."

"Holy shit," I say. "He actually helped Lasserio do that?"

"That's what Lasserio says. And you were correct, he was tasked with getting rid of her belongings, but he took them to the shed first because he contemplated having the pack as a type of insurance against Ridgeway because he knew Ridgeway's fingerprints were on the pack and the sketchpad inside it because Ridgeway gave it to Clarissa when she first went to interview him. That was all before Ridgeway realized she was not all sweetness and smiles and was intending to expose that part of the land he was trying to sell was being polluted and should be protected. He's willing to testify against Ridgeway to lessen his sentence."

"Wow," I say. "What a game changer. It corroborates all the circumstantial evidence."

After we hang up, for the rest of the way into my office, I luxuriate in the thought of Ridgeway finally paying for what he and Lasserio did to Clarissa.

And what they *tried* to do to me. But I remember not to be such a hypocrite, that I've employed similar tactics in the past. Sure, not as egregious, but still, it's the reason I'm enrolled in anger management classes.

I park in my lot across from the old grain silos. A gust of biting wind blows my hair around and I put my hood up on my way in. If there's one thing I learned from Allison, it's that justice is complicated and difficult, and working in law enforcement, whether it's within a department or on my own, will always be a hell of a struggle. Violence often goes unanswered. But I know I won't stop working at it, one way or another. It's my life's work, God help me.

As I walk in, I see the poster Jess had framed for me lying torn on my desk, all the broken glass that used to be the frame swept into the bin and taken out months ago. But the torn poster remains on my side table. I spliced the two halves together with tape on the backside.

I read it for the thousandth time:

**JUSTICE AND POWER MUST BE BROUGHT TOGETHER SO THAT WHATEVER IS JUST MAY BE POWERFUL, AND WHATEVER IS POWERFUL MAY BE JUST.**

As unattainable as it sounds, Allison has delivered me to a turning point: I have to figure out how to try to bring justice and power together in the most ethical way possible, in whatever small ways I can manage.

As I stare at the words, it occurs to me that's what Allison's murderous crusade was all about. And—not that I'd ever say so aloud to anyone, except maybe Jess or Jeremy—as undeniably messed up as it was, she probably focused more attention nationally to some of these issues than I or Jess can ever hope to. In some ways, as twisted as it was, she lived up to her moniker: the Confession Artist.

For the immediate time being, though, I'm trying to focus less on Jess and more on myself. I've come to realize that I've employed my heightened protectiveness of my little sister as a type of shield, allowing me to attend to her and avoid doing some hard work on myself. In case you can't tell from the sound of that: I, too, have recently hired a therapist, even before signing a contract that I would, and have begun working through some of my own shit, notably the likely lifelong legacy of Sophie's tragedy, my failure as a cop and my complicity in the Coleman shooting, the trauma I faced at Allison's hands, and the harassment saga at the department.

I always figured that last one paled in comparison to what I'd witnessed on the job—all the domestic abuses and sexual assaults—and didn't warrant a paid counselor. But now I know that the smaller injustices—all the little cuts into the flesh—add up and leave their painful marks. Make your anger go from a simmer to a boil.

But like Jess said in her speech in Dallas, secrets are rarely better kept locked away—and knowledge and truth are powerful tools to begin the healing process.

The old saying, the one repeated to me so many times online when the Confession Artist was nipping at my heels, is holding true so far: The truth *is* finally starting to set me free. The smooth, unpicked skin on my thumbs, which I haven't slashed with my other nails in weeks now, is proof of that.

# Author's Note

Because this story takes place in the Flathead Valley, I've used the real names of the local law enforcement agencies to add a sense of authenticity. However, the events depicted in this book are entirely fictional. They are not intended to cast judgment on the vital work carried out by the Kalispell Police Department and the Flathead County Sheriff's Office, and nothing is based on, inspired by, or reflective of any misconduct I've heard of or learned about within these agencies. Additionally, all errors—whether intentional or by mistake—are wholly mine.

# Acknowledgments

An enormous thank-you to my readers—for waiting patiently for a fifth novel from me, and for encouraging me and showing me so much kindness.

To the many librarians, bookstore owners, book clubs, podcasters, bloggers, and so many others—for supporting authors' works in general and creating a magical nexus between readers and writers.

To Jessica Tribble-Wells, editor extraordinaire and amazing individual, for taking a chance on this story and for making it so much better with your expertise and creative feedback. And to the wonderful team at Thomas & Mercer—for all the diligence, skill, and hard work you've all brought to the publication of this book. A special shout-out to Tiffany Yates Martin for pushing me further in all the right places, to Liz Gluck for her managerial expertise, to Tara Whitaker, Kellie Osborne, and Heather Rodino, for your eagle eyes in copyedits, and to David Drummond for the lovely "edgy" cover art.

To my fabulous agent, Amy Moore-Benson—for your faith in my work and your energetic support, expertise, and wisdom. I had a feeling we might share a path when you delighted me over lunch in St. Petersburg years ago. And to the CookeMcDermid Agency—for all you do to help navigate the publishing world and provide wonderful opportunities.

To Mathew Martini—for inspiring me, plotting with me, reading, and taking long dog walks with me. This book and its inception would not have happened without you and your beautiful, creative mind.

To Mark Stevens—for your fantastic advice, endless patience, emotional support, and wise, diligent editorial input. Your help has made all the difference in this book's journey to publication!

To Paul Martini—for the fabulous sketches. They matched the characters I had drawn in my mind so perfectly.

To my dear friend Suzanne Siegel—for your friendship, patience, reading, advice, and bolstering.

To the wonderful women at EWW, Betty Kuffel, Kathy Dunnehoff, Phyllis Quatman, and Debbie Burke—for the loving support, resourceful feedback, and helping me push key chapters to their much stronger outcomes.

To David Downing—for your early, very valuable editorial input.

To Elise Hart Kipness, Danielle Girard, Lisa Mathews, Nadine Nettmann, Jay Shepherd, James Thane, Craig Thomas Naylor, and many other wonderful people in the crime-writing community—for the encouragement, general advice, beta reading, and simply checking in as I found my way back into the mix of the publishing world.

To Janet VanDermeer—for always being such a tremendous help.

And last, but not least, to my husband and my beautiful family, including our kids, my parents, my brothers and their amazing wives, and all my loving relatives many miles away—your endless love and support are essential to my entire process!

# About the Author

Christine Carbo is the author of *The Wild Inside*, *Mortal Fall*, *The Weight of Night*, and *A Sharp Solitude* in the Glacier Mystery series. She is a recipient of the Women's National Book Association Pinckley Prize, the Silver Falchion Award, and the High Plains Book Award and was a finalist for the Barry Award. Christine has an MA in English/linguistics from the University of Montana and taught college-level courses for over a decade. She currently lives in northwest Montana with her husband, loves the outdoors, and often finds inspiration from the wild beauty surrounding her. For more information, visit www.christinecarbo.com.